Copyright 2023 Mia Thorne

All rights reserved.

No parts of this book may be reproduced, distributed, or transmitted in any form or by any electronic or mechanical means, including information storage and retrieval systems, without written permission from the author, except for the use of brief quotations in a book review and certain other non commercial use permitted by copyright law.

THE RISING QUEEN

A LOST REIGN

MIA THORNE

To the lovely readers

TRIGGER WARNING

This book contains explicit content, mentions of blood, fighting, swearing, death and irregular (unhealthy) eating habits. Readers discretion advised!

THE FOUR KINGDOMS IN ADALON

Demeter

Origin of Upyr

Aerwyna

Polyxena

Origin of Custo

Oceanus

Origin of Tengeri

Descendants of Custo and Upyr

Magda — Blood Witches

Adalon

THE RISING QUEEN

Aerwyna

PROLOGUE

He turns the page revealing a picture of a dragon, painted in yellows, greens, and lilacs. The scales of the animal shine in the lamplight as if alive. The girl in his lap gasps her sapphire eyes big and round as she stares at the horrendous-looking creature.

"Do you know what happens next?" He asks the girl quietly, who looks up at him, drowning in the sapphire of his eyes.

"The prince is going to come and save the princess!"

A chuckle rattles out of his throat, gruff and unused. His hand gently pushes the long dark strands out of her face.

"Close," he turns the page and reveals a painting of the princess holding a sword in front of the dragon.

"The princess somehow conjures the sword of light of all belongings and slays the dragon herself. She saves the prince."

The girl's mouth falls open in surprise. Her small fingers carefully trace the painted princess. Armor clads her body, brass shoulder pieces sitting securely, like the silver blade in her hands. She looks up at the man, her eyes shining like the crystals themselves.

"When I'm big I want to be just like her!" She says excitedly, making him laugh again.

"Are you going to slay the dragon for your prince, Lánya?"

The girl crunches her face up in disgust.

"No. I don't like the prince. I'm going to slay it for fun!" She throws her fist in the air. The man chuckles again before shutting the book close.

"Alright, dragon slayer, it's time for you to go to bed." He tucks the girl under the comforter and presses a soft kiss against her temple.

"Thank you for the amazing story, Daddy." The girl says her eyes are already dropping close. A soft sigh leaves her lips as the pillow swallows her into one of her endless dreams.

The man smiles while he leaves the chamber, mumbling to himself.

"You haven't heard the end of it yet."

~ 1 ~

The image of emerald pine trees rushes past me at an alarming speed. I can feel little twigs and stones dig into the naked soles of my feet, blood trailing after me. I try not to focus on the foreign feeling that possesses me. I pump my legs harder, speed up the pounding of my legs but my heart rate stays steady and unbothered. Adrenaline rushes through my veins reassuring me that it is appropriate to be scared when you're running from death.
The wind howls my name, making my hair slap against my face as I weave around the trees of the Dark Forest.
My arms move elegantly as if they weigh nothing, the skin still defiled with Marianna's blood. The image of her soulless eyes and the stench wafting around her makes bile rise in my throat but I quickly swallow it down when I hear his steps racing behind me in the dark forest. My breath is barely labored at the speed I'm picking up and if it weren't for the blurry image of the passing trees I would not know that I am running at all.
It is weird to sprint in this new body I have. It is still my skin that I feel under my fingertips and the same face. My cheeks have the same sharp edge to them, and my hair is still in its long dark waves. And yet I smell better, I feel more, and hear everything. I hear the smallest twigs snapping under the impact of my steps, and the small trail of ants passing around the next stone. Things that no human ears could pick up on.
Not slowing down my run I raise my fingertips to graze the pointy tips of my ears. I shiver when I trace the edges, the feeling of wrongness amplifying dangerously.
Although I am fascinated that I can smell the Coast of the Lost advancing with every flying step I take and hear the crashing of the thunderous waves, colliding against the cliffs I am scared by the one sound that overpowers everything else.
It is a steady thundering, a beat so boisterous and heavy it makes my skin vibrate. It comes with an extraordinary scent, it feels

primal and instinctive for me to feel drawn to it but instead, my self-preservation tells me to flee.

I thought I would never hear the thundering beat of his heart, or smell the soft, cold fragrance of his skin again but there he is just a few feet behind me, faster than anything that I've ever come upon.

"Carina!" He calls my name, his voice echoing through the passing trees making the earth vibrate, and the little animals that are left in the forest scatter into safety.

The first time I heard him call my name I thought him a ghost, a phantom that was conjured by my guilt.

I cannot believe that I stabbed Cassian Moreau just minutes ago, the heir to the throne of the God of Death. As unbelievable as it feels it is overshadowed by the fact that the prince died and came back to life just a few moments later. The moment his eyes fluttered open and the intense green color struck me I was relieved. I was not responsible for another death.

But as sweet as the taste of relief was, it didn't last long, washed away by raw and utter fear.

I tried to kill an Upyr whatever creature that might be but I am sure once he gets to me – and he will – he will make sure I die a slow and painful death.

"Would you stop running?" He growls again. The sound vibrates through the forest.

"So you can kill me? Yeah, right." I mutter and throw a look over my shoulder, my eyes widening when I notice how near he is behind me. The look in his eyes triggers a rush of fear to run through me. The look is so murderous it halts my breath and my body for a moment. My foot catches on a stupid root and it is all over when my body soars through the air.

I break out onto the shore, the sharp edges of the rocks approximating alarmingly fast. I won't be able to cushion my fall.

I raise my arms in a last attempt to soften the impact, squeezing my eyes shut.

There is no way the hard and sharp stones will not slice my skin mercilessly, splitting my skull open. I ran for nothing, just to die at the hands of nature and my stupidity.

Instead of hitting the sharp objects from above something collides with my side and I groan. My body is yanked around by the impact, a gruff sound leaving my lips when it collides with a hard surface.

My body is still spinning, or is that my head? I can't tell.

A resonant sound pulls me out of my paralysis and I open my eyes just to stare at the dark sky. The stars are still glimmering, laughing at me and my weak attempt to escape the descendant of a god. I try to move but notice arms latch around me and when I realize that my bones are not broken and I'm not lying on the ground but attached to a body a soft breath escapes me.

"Are you all right?" Cassian's breath fans over my neck, making the hair stand and I swallow.

"Carina?" He questions again. His iron grip loosens on my wrist and I take that to my advantage. With rapid movement, I let my skull collide with his chin, noticing the soft clank of his teeth hitting each other. I roll out underneath him as he grunts, straddling his waist.

Like a viper, my hands shoot out and push against his trachea trying to cut off his airflow. "How are you alive?" I hiss, leaving enough pressure to let him choke on his first word.

"Carina—"

I tighten my grip on his neck. "Don't waste your breath, prince, tell me how you may still be alive. His eyes narrow and his hand sneaks around to my calf. I quickly adjust my position and trap both his arms between his body and my thighs.

"The blood oath." He finally chokes. I frown at him for a moment watching how his face slowly but surely turns red. "You can't. . .harm me. Neither can I, you." Realization dawns on me a moment later. My grip loosens for a moment making him inhale shakily.

The blood oath bound us to each other which means we're unable to harm the other. *What now?*

"As much as I like a determined woman, would you stop choking me?"

My eyes fly back to his. "So you can get the upper hand and do gods know what with me? How do I know you won't kill me the moment I let go?"

His eyes grow double their size. "Kill you?" I narrow my eyes at him and shoot him a curt nod. "I spend a third of my life thinking about protecting you and the other third *doing* it."

"Bullshit. You're the one who is responsible for all this mess. You've ruined my life!" Desperation claws at my throat and I can feel the treacherous angry sting pulling at my eyes.

"I never planned for it to go this way." His voice is desperate. I shake my head as I feel the rage returning inside me. I let go of him and slowly get up. My feet burn when the cold sand rubs into my open wounds but I keep my eyes on him.

Cassian doubles over, coughing a few times before his head raises to look at me. "I'm sorry, I am." I chuckle humorlessly at his words.

"For what exactly are you sorry, Cassian? Because I'm losing track of all the unforgivable things you've done."

The fangs disappear from his teeth, the green of his eyes back to their human color. I have to shiver when I think of the way those fangs ripped through Lord Romanov's throat so effortlessly. I don't even know how I'm keeping this composure with everything that happened tonight. My world tipped horrifically and even though I know there is no way leading back I try to ignore it. Suppress everything in hopes I don't turn crazy. It gets harder with every passing second as I realize that it is reality.

Whatever Edlyn did after she chased my father – or the man who called himself my father for my whole life – I know that now he must not be breathing anymore. The bloodthirsty look in her eyes was clear; she would not let him get away with anything.

"What I did might look wrong now but believe me you will understand if you give me the chance to explain."

"Well, why don't we start with the fact of what you did to me."

He takes a step forward but I raise my hand. His body freezes.

"You can explain it to me right from where you stand."

His jaw ticks, the ocean breeze messing up his hair. Despite his obvious disagreement, he complies.

"When your father—the king made me feed you my blood it triggered the magic inside your veins. That is why you changed."

My hand rises on its own accord just to feel the pointy tips of my ears again but I stop myself at the last moment.

"Why?"

"I can only assume it is what Adales wants. Soon they would've brought you to him, delivering you on a silver plate."

Horror spikes inside of me at the imagery. He takes another step forward and I quickly narrow my eyes. "I told you to not come closer." I rack my brain for the information I still desire.

"What does that make me now? Am I what you are? An Upyr?"

He quickly shakes his head. "You'd have to be a descendant of Demetrus to turn into an Upyr. You're the daughter of the Goddess Aerwyn and a powerful Faye warrior. It makes you damn special, Carina, and the only one of your species."

I try to wrap my head around his words. Acid burns in my throat and I feel the world start to spin. This is not a good time to lose my composure.

Somewhat trying to distract myself I decide to wash the crusted blood off of my body and walk over to the shore. The water must be cold and completely dark by now but when it washes over my feet it is lukewarm. My body reacts differently to every sensation and I sigh lightly as I make my way inside the waves.

Thanks to my heightened senses, I hear Cassian nearing the shore and I have to take a deep breath and squeeze my eyes shut to stop myself from screaming in frustration. Why isn't he fucking leaving? Lord Romanov is dead, the king presumably as well, I don't know what happened to Orkiathan – and I don't want to know – he might be miles away from the castle.

"There is no reason for you to stay."

"But there is. If you think I'm going to leave you're in for a big surprise, princess."

"Don't call me that." I hiss and whirl around to notice that his body is closer than I thought. My eyes throw literal bursts of fire at him, my hands clenching at my sides.

"You lost the privilege to call me that or any other name. If you think I will accompany you to your little kingdom you're delusional."

He tilts his head at my outburst, a foreign emotion swirling in the ends of his green eyes.

"You know that's not possible, we conducted the blood oath, Carina, and we are bound to each other in more than one way."

I shake my head at his words, turning my back to him before I start to rub at my skin, the water around me glimmering in red color.

The blood moon has already passed and hides somewhere behind the tall mountains in the distance.

"If I could turn back time I would, believe me. I tried to warn you the night we met. It was not a coincidence; I knew you would be in town because that son of a bitch, Romanov, hired Jamari to lure you out."

I freeze at his words but I don't turn around or give him any verbal answer.

"But fuck, you caught me off guard. I knew what my mission was, the second I turned sixteen, my mission was inked into my body. It was my first oath and yet when I took off that mask that night your presence hit me. I watched you from afar, for a long time; making sure you were safe. I knew you would completely flip if I offered you a world that only took place in nightmares." He sighs frustrated and I can visibly imagine him tugging at the dark curls of his hair.

What does he mean by mission? That it was inked into his skin? Even now when the only thing that can save this would be the truth, he is telling a story that doesn't make any sense.

"Carina, look at me." Even though I don't want to, I stop scrubbing my skin and turn around immediately regretting it. The little light of the stars above hits his beautifully carved face most intensely, making my heart squeeze at the spark of feeling that I hoped would die flare into something more but now I know it never will. It turns into a cold claw that feels like betrayal. It winds around my heart and crushes it, leaving nothing in its absence.

"It doesn't matter what you think of me or what you feel. I know this all doesn´t make sense and I am happy to explain but most importantly you have to come to Demeter with me. Aerwyna has no king anymore and it's not safe. Who knows where that little bastard went and worst case they told more people about your real heritage."

I take a few steps toward him, the water splashing against my body.

"I don't need anyone´s savings or protection. I can care for myself, I always have." I jab my finger into his chest angrily. "I have been perfectly fine until you decided to play the knight in shining armor. I don´t want you here, I don´t want your stupid protection and if I could I would not hesitate to kill you for what you put me through."

He flinches visibly at my words.

I need to get out of here. I need to get back to the castle pick up Henri and leave this kingdom. As much as it pains me to leave my subjects I´m much more a danger to them here. Someone else has to take the throne and Henri and I have to hide. Maybe we could go to Polyxena, Hector would be surely inclined to help us.

Cassian takes a daunting step forward the water parting around his ribs while it reaches almost my collar bones.

"Hate me all you want, scream at me, hit me, I won´t leave your side." He ducks his head even further making sure that he catches my gaze. "Because the only thing important is that you live." He swallows hard.

"We should get out of the water." He suddenly says his tone icy and I ignore it walking straight past him to get out of the water. I almost stumble over a stone when I see someone standing at the shore, hazel hair flying in the soft wind, a black cloak around her shoulders. I swallow and continue escaping the water, wrapping my arms around my body.

"Do you mind lending her your cloak, she's freezing," Cassian speaks up behind me and Edlyn already goes for the cloak sitting around her shoulders.

"I'm fine." I bite back but my friend ignores me and goes to wrap the cloak around me. I try not to stare at her but notice that the talons are gone and her eyes are back to their usual brown color. Everyone lied; no one even considered telling me the truth. They all continued their little play keeping me in the dark just so everything blows in my face. A shudder runs through my body but this time it's not because of the cold.

"I made sure the horses are ready, Eryx is waiting at the wall for us, we have to reside in the capital for a night before we can go, and your advisor is as tardy as usual."

"Stop calling him my advisor, Petri, you know he has a name." I'm perplexed by the casualty of their tone while she binds the tie around my neck her eyes placing themselves on me.

"I'm sorry you had to go through all of this; I wanted to ease you into things. How are you feeling?" She almost sounds worried and for a second I see my best friend in her, not the red-eyed monster that probably murdered the king.

"Like vomiting," I say truthfully causing pity to move on her face.

"I told him not to keep it a secret, it would've been a lot easier."

I restrain myself from answering. Now that they're two I'll be unable to leave, I have to wait until they're distracted enough for me to slip away.

"Yeah? I didn't see you telling her what you are, Petri." Cassian sounds impatient and I throw a small glance at him before I focus back on her.
"You two know each other," I state.
"Since his birth, he couldn't live without me."
"In your dreams."
"Oh believe me you're not taking part in my dreams, they're filled with hot-"
"No one needs to know that. We should go." He interrupts her and starts to stomp toward the dark forest he chased me through minutes ago.
 "I know it doesn't count as much but I am sorry, Carina, if I could I would've told you a long time ago but it was better this way. I promise you there were no times you were in danger." She says but cringes quickly before correcting herself.
"Besides tonight. I'm sorry that happened too, Cassian said you would be with him this night and make sure you were safe but that changed when you left."
I want to say something, anything that could somehow get rid of this feeling inside me. How can I trust any of them anymore? I pull the cloak tighter around me and refer to her spoken words.
"You said the horses were ready?"
She nods and throws a glance over her shoulder, Cassian is no longer in sight but he can't be far.
"We're staying at the green knight for tonight, an old friend of Cas' father is waiting for us to escort us to the capital before a small group joins us in the morning to travel to Demeter."
I inhale sharply at her words. She sounds so familiar and yet it seems like I can't recognize the woman standing in front of me. Whoever she played to be over the years wasn't the real her. Maid, friend, family. Now she is a stranger, a blood-lusting creature that I should fear. And yet I can't help but notice the warm bubbling in my heart telling me to trust her. "We need to get to Henri, I can't leave him here." I tell her as we slowly start to move, the crashing

of the waves becoming distant. Sudden exhaustion grabs ahold of my body, making me shiver lightly. Edlyn moves closer – subconsciously or not – and the body heat warms me up a bit.

"Henri is not coming with us; he is already on a ship leaving for Polyxena." My head swivels around to stare at her.

"What?"

"He can't leave with us, Carina, it would be too much of a risk for him. He left with Hector the moment after the ball. Hector will protect him." I have to gulp at her words grasping what she is saying. He is not safe with me because I am a threat; a literal god wants to see me dead. Not just a god but the god of all gods. Something plummets in my stomach, making me want to hurl up the contents of the banquet.

When I stop walking she follows my example and despite the revulsion, I grab her hands in mine. Her skin is soft, with no trace of the talons that grew out of them hours ago.

"You have to bring me to that ship, Edlyn. I can't leave him alone."

Her face contorts in empathy. "That is not possible. Even if I would bring you, the ship will already be sailing once we arrive at the harbor."

I tighten my hold on her hands. "We have to try. Edlyn if our friendship was anything but real you have to take me to my brother."

Her gaze softens, the hazel eyes melting. With great determination, she squeezes my hands. "Because our friendship is real I am not going to bring you to Henri. You have to think, Carina, your presence is a mere threat to his life."

I sigh knowing this is a fight I cannot win. My hands sink to my sides as I follow her. What now? Is it worth a try to escape when I have nowhere to go and no one to go with?

"I didn't say goodbye," I whisper as leaves crush under our feet, little rocks and twigs digging into the sole of my feet. I clench my fist shut, digging my nails into my palms, the fresh pain keeping me grounded.

"You will see him again but first we have to get you out of here and to King Ronan, where you're safe." At the mention of Cassian's father, I stiffen, my blood running cold.

"He is not as bad as you think he is, your memories are tainted. He reminds me a lot of Cas."

"Well, then my memories can't be tainted," I grumble, hugging myself to warm my body. I'm awfully cold. The wetness of my clothes only contributes to the shivers that rock my body. I was never as cold as this; it feels like it is creeping right out of my heart, making my limbs go stiff.

Edlyn grabs my arm lightly, stopping me from walking further as we break out of the forest and end up in the royal gardens. I look up into her face surprised. Her eyes flicker to my wrists as if she could feel the cold temperature of my body her brows creasing slightly.

"It might not seem like it now but everything Cas did was to ensure your safety."

"Seems like he didn't do a good job. I died." Gods, I died. I died and came back to life.

"And yet you're still here as healthy as ever. For now. You'll need to feed soon." My eyes almost fall out of their sockets at her last words.

"What do you mean feed?" My voice is breathless as a horrifying feeling spreads through me. It poisons my insides, spreading and rotting at lightning speed.

"Cas gave you his blood, to trigger the ancient magic in your veins, Demetrus and Aerwyna combined their gifts inside of you, to keep your identity hidden which ensured the magic stayed hidden. The second Cassian's blood was inside you the magic unleashed, practically humming with power, a wave rolled over the whole kingdom while you were passed out and I'm sure it carried onto other properties as well, which is why we need to keep you safe. Now that you're not human anymore you'll need to feed to complete the change, that is why your skin is so cold." She finishes and lets go of me starting to walk towards the royal barns as if what she just said isn't turning her world on its axis.

"I am not going to feed,"

I can't even stand the smell nor will I ever shed blood again in my life. So many people died because of me. So many wasted lives because of me. I will do anything in my power to redeem myself for it. The color of red blood will never taint my hands again.

"You won't need to after the change is complete. We. . .we don't know how things will work with your body. You are the first of your breed. And we can't ask a Faye because all of them are dead." Edlyn says.

The Faye are dead. My subjects and my family are dead. There is no one left but this fallen kingdom that is occupied by humans and not the real people that should be living in these lands.

"I won't feed," I repeat and she stays silent. I can feel her eyes studying me. Her arm brushes mine while we continue walking in silence. I don't care if I need to feed to complete the change. I'm not to anyone's value. Adales will find me sooner or later and I think I've brought enough pain over these lands. As if she could sense my thoughts Edlyn speaks up again.

"You're a child born with the magic of the Faye and a goddess, I don't know what that makes you but it makes you powerful, Carina. You have life in you, *you are life.* You are everything the people wish for and more. You are hope." My brows furrow at her words before she grabs my hand and leads me to a hidden side entrance to the barns. I try to ignore what she says and the fact that I have to feed – which I will not do, for the life of me.

We slip inside like two shadows and I notice what she said was the truth, two horses are already ready and bound for us to take. The view of Nighttail makes me exhale and rush over to her. I press my nose into her dark mane inhaling her beautiful scent. She turns her head and nudges my shoulder lightly making me smile up at her.

For the first time tonight, I can take a deep breath that reaches my lungs completely, expanding them fully.

"What if I don´t want to go? What if we just get out of Aerwyna alone, just you and me?" I can hear the hope in my voice as I turn to look at the woman I once called my friend.

She sighs and stops in her movements. "I wish we could but Demeter is the safest place for you right now, no one will dare to attack it. And I understand your hatred towards Cas—"

"Do you?" I interrupt her. She doesn´t hesitate a moment before nodding, "I do. But right now this is not about who you like or not. It is about your survival."

Edlyn moves up to us and takes the reins of the other horse. I feel unsatisfied with her answer. Her obvious loyalty to Cassian feels like a betrayal to me. She passes me hastily, a sad look in her eyes. "Cas will meet us at the wall."

~ 2 ~

Edlyn and I don't speak much as we lead the horses through the maze of the royal garden, without one single guard in sight. It must've been perfectly planned by them because once we reach the gate, attached to the enormous walls circling the grounds of the castle, it is already unlocked. A man standing at the trigger makes me stop, standing in front of Nighttail.

The man's black hair is partly hidden by his hood, his lips set in a grim line. His skin is as pale as the moon, and his statue overall looks almost frail the only thing vibrant are the green eyes shining ominously in the dark. The small lines in his skin are barely noticeable and yet I can tell he is old, maybe older than I can grasp. Various weapons are strapped around his hips making me wish for my trusty knives which the king probably threw down the Cliffs of the Lost, the second he got his hands on them.

"Eryx, where is Cas?"

Edlyn asks the man as she reaches him and he gives her a small smile, two sharp fangs glistening in the light of the torches. I stiffen slightly at the honed edges. Upyr. How many of them were in this kingdom and how come I never noticed such a strong detail? How is it possible that all of these kingdoms were bathed in magic and I didn't know? My father—the king did a good job of hiding the truth. Our lands were dead of magic, it was simmering underneath it all but it never met the surface. If what Edlyn says is true, if what these men say is true that means I have lived a thousand lives before without knowing. My magic stayed hidden in every life and so did the kingdom remain without any magical creatures residing.

"He'll be with us in a short moment. Is that her?" Eryx's eyes glide over me, an arrogant look on his face. I raise a brow in answer.

"Why don't you ask her yourself," I state, narrowing my eyes slightly. I move a bit closer.

"Well, seems like the prince has found himself a talkative wife." Rage flares up inside of me at the way he talks about me and I take a step forward, ready to show him how talkative I can get while slapping his face.

"Be careful Eryx, she's more dangerous than she looks. One moment of distraction and you find yourself with a dagger thrust in your heart." Cassian walks past me, his arm grazing mine in the process as I watch the man's brows raise perplexedly.

"Well if you're offering the manual to stab you," I whisper and Cassian turns his head slightly but doesn't comment on my words.

The prince hands Erxy a black pouch and I hope to the gods that it is not filled with someone's intestines.

When he turns his green eyes place themselves on my body, skimming from my naked feet up my torn suit and to my face. I swallow the tightening feeling in my throat and reciprocate his gaze steadily. I will not back down even if I have to go with him.

I have not stopped thinking while Edlyn and I left the stables.

I mentally plan to speak to the King of Demeter first thing we arrive and I will ask—beg even if it is necessary—that he undoes the engagement. It is probably the only possibility; he would be able to do this. Then I will finally have my freedom. Polyxena isn't that far from Demeter, I will travel to Hector the minute King Ronan breaks the bond and pick up Henri. From then on I will plan with him where we go next and what we do. I can't be a threat to his life if Adales doesn't find us.

"I brought you shoes." Cassian states with a hard swallow of his throat and he walks over to me, while I feel the eyes of Edlyn and Eryx on the both of us. My eyes fly down to the boots clutched in his hands and I hold out my hand to grab them but instead, the prince lowers himself to his knees, right in front of me.

"What are you doing?" I almost screech when his fingers wrap around one ankle and lift my foot making me tip over and grasp his shoulders to keep my balance.

"Making sure you don't freeze to death after I just saved you."

"You didn't save me," I say stubbornly. He slips one foot into a boot before he grabs my other ankle and I can't do anything else but stare at the pathway in front of us when Edlyn swings herself up onto the back of the horse, Erxy following. Once Cassian stands up I notice that we don't have enough horses and horror strikes me.

"Where is your horse?" I ask trying not to shiver at the warmth around my feet. The boots are lined with soft fur.

"You're holding it. You can go we will be right behind you." He tells the two and while Eryx turns with no word and starts to gallop through the gate, Edlyn shoots me a wary look.

"Go." Cassian orders with a dark voice, his eyes still on me. She gives me a small smile and pulls at the reins making her horse gallop away. I consider calling her back, to beg, plead for her to take me on her horse. Everything to spare me of this embarrassment. Of this torture.

"I'm not riding with you on the same horse."

"You are. I am not letting you out of my sight, Carina, you'll need to feed soon and until then you're vulnerable." He states with a steady voice and when I look up into his face I don't see an ounce of emotion in it. I shake my head again, hugging myself.

"Suck my dick." I spat and he raises a brow, light dancing in his eyes at my words.

"So dirty-mouthed, I forgot how much I love it." He says and before I can protest his hands grasp my hips and sit me down on Nighttail making me gasp when he swings himself behind me. With a swift movement, I jab my elbow right into his ribs. The prince groans and I move to hit him again but his hands get ahold of both my elbows.

"I swear to the gods, Cassian, if you don't get down I will–"

"What? Stab me? Been there, done that, princess."

"Don't call me princess." I huff out frustrated and move again.

"Would you at least give me some more space? You're taking up the whole godsdamn horse."

Instead of protesting, I feel his lower body distancing. For a moment I am surprised by the gesture but I don't let him fool me. With his body heat gone, I feel the looming presence I tried to push away over the past hours.

It feels like I'm not the only one in my body anymore; something rears his head since Cassian gave me his blood. It is looming in the dark but not ready to get out yet.

Soon we're far away from the walls of the castle, Edlyn and Eryx riding a few feet in front of us. A strong arm moves around my middle and I stiffen which he notices quickly.

"Relax. You're cold it'll make you a bit warmer."

"I could've ridden with Edlyn," I say ignoring his words even though I do feel warmer with his arm around me.

"No way and let her talk bad about me?" His tone is light and playful but there is a hard edge to his words as if he is trying his hardest to conceal his real emotions.

"She doesn't need to talk bad about you, you're managing that all by yourself," I say slightly and feel his arm tighten for a second. I wish he would make Nighttail go a bit quicker so we'd be within hearing distance of Edlyn. The wind is biting at my skin, the movement of the horse is making me slightly sick to the stomach and my sleep deprivation is making me cranky.

"I know you're not comfortable with me being close to you right now, I respect that but until we're in the safe walls of Demeter we both need to suck it up because the most important thing is to keep you safe."

"You already said that and I still don't understand. Why even bother? Who cares what happened over a billion years ago just let me die." I say carelessly. The silence that meets me in response is deafening. I feel him shift behind me and for a moment I swear I can hear—feel—the thrum of his heartbeat.

"Do you value your life so little?" His voice is a cold whisper when I shrug my shoulders.

"I have no one left; my brother was forced to leave because I am a threat to his life. My life is endangered by a literal god. I don't think I can outrun my death."

"You can and you will, but instead of outrunning it we'll defeat it."

"There is no we, Cassian," I say as I watch Edlyn's hair flutter behind her as she throws a look over her shoulder maybe to see if I have strangled him yet.

"Currently there is. I was born to protect you, Carina; it was written in the stars and told by the Fatum."

I freeze at his words.

"The Fatum are real?" I breathe out in surprise and turn my head inhaling sharply when my lips graze his cheek. He flushes when he moves his face to look at me properly.

"A lot of things are real that you believed to be a fairytale."

I bite my lip in wonder turning my head back away from him. The Fatum were told to be existent since the first god was made in Empyrean. They're older than Adales himself yet they seem to outlive every being. They're somewhat of an oracle, knowing of all the fates, even of the gods. It shouldn't surprise me after the recent events that they are a reality indeed.

My eyes catch onto a small bulb of light in the distance quickly joined by a thousand of them. The lights are arranged in a way that the capital glows like a halo surrounding the city.

My capital. The place where everyone should've felt safe but I was roaming the streets. Killing my subjects. Acrimony rises in my throat.

"You're telling me my fate is of so much importance the Fatum choose you to protect me?" I ask biting my lip, almost regretting that I asked. I'm not sure if I want to hear the answer to that question. I try to focus on the capital we're advancing with every step Nighttail takes.

"I wish you would stop talking yourself down like that. You are the only descendant of the Goddess of Health and Love and a very powerful Faye. Your blood is a mixture of her magic and the

Magic of Life that once flooded Faye's veins. If Adales succeeds in finding you, he will kill you off in a rage and ensure that every land on Adalon rots; every creature will be infected and life will not proceed as it usually does. Eventually, Adalon will cease to exist."

~ 3 ~

Eventually, Adalon will cease to exist.
Cassian's words ghost around the air the whole way into the capital. I don't dare speak one word scared that I might reveal things that could make this whole situation worse. As if that would be possible.
Me being the only thing left that can ensure life in this world?
I don't feel any of this life flowing in my veins, no spark of magic humming beneath the surface. The tips of my ears vanished a long time ago and even though my senses are still on overdrive there is nothing more. I ignore the gazes thrown on the four of us as we pass the villagers until our horses halt in front of the doors of the Green Knight.
Dawn must be a few hours away, the horizon slightly lit up by the sun making its way to the sky. The blood moon is over and the life I knew vanishes with it. I hop off the horse the second Cas halts not standing to be near his presence anymore.
"What are you doing?" He calls after me but I ignore him, including Edlyn before I sprint through the familiar doors. The inn is quiet with just a few customers left, sitting in the booths, their heads lulling with the amount of liquor they tortured their bodies with. My eyes scan the area searching for the dark hair and gentle smile. The moment Cassian steps into the inn a few heads turn curiously, wondering who dares to disrupt their peace this early. I don't know if it is due to my heightened abilities but the room fills with some kind of darkness when he steps in and my heart thrums at the beat of his steps.
"You can't just leave whenever you like, Carina. We are practically volatile and your life is on a god's hit-list." The rumble of his voice shakes the inn while his hand wraps around my wrist. I whirl around and glare at him, anger burning in my veins.
"Do not touch me again. Or I swear I will figure out a way to kill you even if it means ripping you apart limb by limb." I seethe and

his eyes glow. To my surprise he lets me go. We glower at each other for a moment before someone disturbs the silence.

"Carina?" I swivel around and a relieved sigh escapes my lips. Three steps. I take three steps before I'm in the arms of Gisella. The sweet scent of opium clings to her skin now more noticeable than ever. Still, I bury my face in her shoulder as she wraps her arms around me. It seems to be the last thing that breaks down my walls. Tears slip down my cheeks in a powerful stream, and pain lashes through me so persistent and haunting that it feels like my body is burning.

I barely hear Gisella speak up, telling the others she is going to take care of me. Her words are met with objections but she doesn't let anyone move before she leads me up the stairs my back to the others.

The water in the bathtub could be scalding hot, ice cold, or lukewarm. I'm sure I wouldn't even notice. My knees are tucked against my chest, and my whole body shakes as if I am freezing to death. I close my eyes when Gisella starts to soap my hair, her strokes soft and hard, slow and quick. I don't speak while I stare at the dirty wall of the bath chamber, my eyes not wavering from the small crack in the tapestry. The once-white color is now yellow-stained, displaying its age.

I don't speak up when Gisella adds a few bath salts to the water the cuts on my feet stinging before they close inhumanly fast. I don't speak up when she cleans my skin with a rose-scented soap. I can feel her eyes on me, the worry that shimmers in them. I can barely stand her wandering hands over my body. Over this body. It is not mine. It is not what I knew for almost eighteen years.

The skin is smoother almost glowing in the pale candlelight. There are no calluses inside the palm from holding a sword or a dagger. No bruises, no scratches not even a small thing out of order. It looks like a body from those weird dolls that were sold on the market when I was younger. A slight pressure on my shoulders tells me to get out of the water. I do as I´m told and step out of the tub before Gisella dries me. I don´t speak.
"I ordered for privacy. This is your room, Carina, no one will disturb you." Her words are dull as if I am underwater. I don´t know if I give her a nod or any kind of assurance that I heard her. I let her dry me, clothe me. I can´t stand the scent of rose clinging to my skin or the soft shirt and breeches she dresses me in.
"If you don´t need anything I´m going now. I will check on you in an hour." She speaks up again. I walk over to the bed, my hair dripping wet, and slide under the comforter. The bed smells foreign and it creaks under my weight. The pillow soaks the liquid from my hair and I stare out of the window to watch the light splatter of raindrops falling against it. They race down the glass repeatedly, trying to outrun each and every one. The sun has finally risen and I don´t think I can hear Gisella closing the door before I fall asleep.

I slip in and out of conscience for what feels like days. I don´t know if Gisella checks on me. I don´t know if it is the rumbling thunder that keeps waking me or the haunting eyes that follow me in my dreams. Eyes of Marianna, eyes of every innocent man I killed, eyes of Lord Romanov, and the worst, eyes of my brother.
My hands are dripping red, and my skin is stained with the souls of these people. I jerk awake when another rumble of thunder shakes

the inn, my breathing close to hyperventilation as I throw off the comforter. Instead of blaring red I meet the dull gray color of my breeches. I close my eyes for a moment exhaling. I flinch when another rumble of thunder moves through the capital. The soft rain changed into a downpour while I was asleep, lightning splitting the sky.

I try to clear my throat just to notice the raw scratching at my vocal cords. Swinging my cold feet over the bed I tiptoe into the bathing chamber. I chug a few swallows of water from the bucket, not knowing if it's ice cold or burning hot but it soothes the ache in my throat.

When I step back into the small room I hear a thrumming rhythm that alarms my senses. I turn towards the closed door knowing that someone will step through in a second. Bracing myself, my fists clench before the door opens. And reveals Edlyn. My muscles stay tense even though my brain tells me I am in no danger. Her steps falter when she notices me standing in the middle of the room.

"You're up." My eyes wander down to the tray in her hands, noticing a bowl of stew and a few pieces of bread beside it. She changed into tight black breeches and a fitted shirt. It is the first time I don't see her in a feminine gown. Still, the gold stitching that runs up her calves like tendrils makes her look elegant. The fabric glimmers with every movement of hers.

"I wanted to check on you. Are you hungry?" She asks while she walks over to the nightstand, discarding the tray. My eyes follow her tentatively, watching her mix some kind of herbs into the juice that she brought with her.

"It's still hot. Eat." She sits down on my bed and gestures toward the tray.

"I'm not hungry." My voice is hoarse and I cringe at the sound of it. How long have I been in here? Her hazel eyes scan my body slowly before she looks back into my face.

"You need the energy, Carina. You still haven't fed but . . . it seems like there is no need." Her words sound wondrous,

delighted. I don't answer. Instead, I eye the door that will lead me out of this room and into the hall of the inn.
I'm tempted to leave but I remember what Cassian said. The conviction in his voice when he talked about the Fatum. They have to be real.
I intend to do what Aerwyn told me. Go to Demeter and ask King Ronan to bring me to the Fatums, breaking the engagement would be a luxury on the side.
I hesitate, staying near the door.
"There is no way to go."
"Why? Because he won't let me?" I shoot back, narrowing my eyes at her. My walls are crumbling at the sorrow in her eyes. They lied. All of them lied. To protect you. They could've protected me differently. All of these lost lives could've been avoided. Marianna would be still alive. She was barely seventeen. Now her body was rotting in the dungeons of a castle that hasn't got a king.
"He would if it was safe."
Her voice is soft and soothing. I wonder if she is using some kind of power because my body eases slightly out of its defenses.
"You are not a prisoner, Carina. And he—*we* are not your enemies. Everything we did was to ensure your safety."
"You already said that."
My feet are getting cold from the ground and my hair is still a bit damp.
"Would you . . . listen, if I explain?" She offers and I think over her words. Will it change the way I think about what they did? Probably not. But maybe it would be less confusing. I nod tensely. Her eyes wander over to the steaming pot and my stomach growls lightly.
She gets up from the bed and walks over to the window giving me space.
I sit down and balance the tray on my legs. For a moment I hold my face over the steam just to feel nothing. I swallow the knot in

my throat and pick up the spoon. I can feel Edlyn watching me from the window, the storm unchanging behind her.

"What day is it?" I ask warily and take a bite of the stew. It tastes like ash in my mouth. Still, I chew and swallow.

"It's the day after the blood moon. You slept a few hours. Gisella checked on you a few times." She answers and I open my mouth but close it when I realize what I was about to ask. Instead, I swallow the question and concentrate on maintaining the food in my stomach.

"You wanted to explain. So explain." I edge her on and she nods. I focus my gaze back on the food because I can't stand to look into her face. Can't stand to see the guilt written in the hazel eyes, can't stand the fact that flashes of her red eyes and white hair, ghost through me. A blood witch.

"I think you know the tales of the blood witches." She starts to pace the room.

"Magda's have resided all over the continent for centuries. We were never accepted to be subjects in any kind of kingdom. It doesn't matter if we were created out of the fortunate event that an Upyr fell in love with a Custos. People look upon us and say we're an abomination, especially the Tengeri." I listen and scarf down the meal as if I haven't eaten in days.

"Most of the Magda ancestors were burned, and tortured, many wanted our magic. Their greed was insatiable. Numerous of us fled, everyone was on their own. I . . . traveled through various kingdoms, keeping hidden until I reached the borders of Demeter." She swallows and stops speaking for a moment. I finish eating and cross my legs on the bed, watching her. Something horrific shines in her eyes.

"Cassian's father was kind enough to let me through his borders. King Ronan understood, he cared. He offered me a place at his court, I was to spy on any of his enemies. Until after a few centuries Cas was born."

My breath halters at her words. Not at the name but at the timeline.

"Centuries?" She nods.

"King Ronan and Queen Aiyla couldn't create an heir for almost three hundred years."

I try not to choke on my next breath. I knew the blood witches could get old but I wasn't aware how old. I have to remember that King Ronan is not the human I thought him to be. An Upyr. A descendant of the god of death.

"When Zayne was born, the whole kingdom celebrated. I celebrated, we all knew what it meant. That another Moreau man was born." She looks at me, her eyes glowing.

"It meant you were on your way to rebirth." I exhale at her words and turn my eyes to the ground. How does one react when you get told that you've been living for centuries? Different lives that I can't even remember? If Edlyn senses my discomfort she doesn't mention it.

"We thought it was him to be your betrothed. For six years we waited. The whole kingdom held its breath for any news of a sapphire-eyed girl to be born. You were taking your sweet time. And after five years of waiting another wonder happened. Cassian was born." She walks a bit closer to me, leaning against the rusty bedpost.

"When I saw him, when I looked into his green, wise eyes I knew you would be not far away. King Ronan sent out for me to search for you. I should turn every stone; roam every kingdom until I found you. And I did. I did find you; I was close to giving up until I heard that laugh. You were in the capital, your chubby hand intertwined with your mother's. She was telling you something that made you laugh. Your eyes glimmered in the sun and the most beautiful sound escaped your lips. I knew it was you, the second I laid my eyes on you." She steps around the bed carefully. As if not to scare me.

I watch her sit down on the bed, the mattress dipping while I try to organize my thoughts.

"How . . . how did you manage to get into the Sebesyten court?" I ask warily. Her cheeks blossom with color as her eyes focus on the comforter, plugging at a loose thread.

"King Ronan permitted me to do everything in my power to ensure your safety. Cas was too young to oblige his task. A quite useful trick of our magic is that we can play with the minds of humans. I convinced your parents that I grew up in the palace and was an old friend's daughter, to be your maid. I shapeshifted along with you. I was with you your whole life."

"Did you do it with me as well?" I ask.

"What do you mean?"

"The mind-changing thing." Her eyes widen as her hands grab mine blindly.

"No! Never. I would never do something like that if it wasn't seriously necessary."

She leans a bit forward squeezing my hand, "I know how this must seem but despite keeping my real identity under the surface, everything I told you was the truth."

"Even though you know Cassian his whole life and that you were just at my court because I was a task." I slip my hand out of her hold. My head already throbs with all of this information. She must be well over 300 hundred years old if what she tells is the truth. I don't even know who I'm looking at anymore.

"I did it with honor. I would've gladly given my life to you then and now. It doesn't change who I am." I laugh bitterly at her words before I get up from the bed.

"Of course, it changes who you are, Edlyn. It changes everything. Nothing of it was real. You are all hell-bent on thinking that I . . . that I somehow have these magical powers because supposedly I'm Aerwyn's daughter. You protected me, and stayed with me because of my heritage, not because of the person that I am."

"I understand—"

"No, you don't understand." I whirl around and watch her eyes harden.

"You don't understand. All of you look at me like I am an object. I'm the solution to your problems. Whatever you think I can do about it, I can't." I tell her and she stands up from the bed walking towards me.

"You are not an object. You are my best friend. You are the first person that showed me how it feels like to live again. Maybe I was selfish—maybe I didn't want to tell you who I am because I was scared. I didn't want you to look at me in disgust and horror just because of the legends the lies that have been spread about the blood witches." Her eyes become blurry and something tugs at my heart. The tears almost make her look humane again. I take a deep breath but take a step back when she nears me.

"I am sorry. For everything that you had to endure because of your heritage. I am sorry you had to flee and I am sorry that you thought I was someone I am not. You can tell Prince Cassian that he doesn't need to worry. I'm going to Demeter without any objection. But I wish to be left alone." I hold my chin high and I almost take a step toward her when I see something crumble in her eyes. It is not the fact that she is a blood witch that repulses me, it is the lies. I am not expecting much from Cassian but I expected more from her.

She knew how I felt when my father kept secrets from me and yet she still decided to keep so many things a secret.

"I understand." She gives me a curt nod before she leaves the room. The second she is out the door I wish she would come back. I feel tempted to follow her but I don't. I get back into bed and flinch every time, footsteps near my door and retreat again. I recognize the footsteps and count them nearing five times and five times leaving.

No one enters my room again.

~ 4 ~

I wake after a few hours, watching the sun sink in the window. It is still raining but the thunder and lightning ceased. Someone dropped a new pair of clothes on the nightstand and I pray to the gods that it was Gisella. I grab them before I slip into the bathing chamber and take a bath. Again. I scrub my skin as hard as I can until it goes from pale to red until it feels raw and irritated. I woke up similarly with the feeling of blood on my hands, the image of Marianna on the ground still in the back of my mind.

The second the water stops feeling liquidy but rather thick and my vision turns red I get out of it. I dry my body as fast as I can before I slip into the new clothes. The smell of wind and musky soap hits me so unexpectedly that it makes me want to take them off again. I don't get the chance to when a heavy knock appears on the door. A few seconds after a tall boy steps through the threshold. I immediately retread and grab the nearest thing to me which is a—vase. It'll work. The boy raises a blond brow at me, a cocky smile on his lips and my body freezes.

"Nice vase. What do you intend to do with it?" His voice is soft like a sweet caress. I narrow my eyes at him while his grin turns almost feline.

"Smash your head in, your face, maybe use the shards to carve your heart out. There are options." I offer him.

His head tips back and my eyes widen when a roar of laughter escapes him. My hands turn sweaty and the vase slips slightly in my grip. While the stranger is too occupied with laughing I muster him. From the blond short hair that sits on his head, over the hard features of his face, the broad shoulders, and the narrow waist. He is rather lean but I bet there are muscles underneath.

"Now I understand why Cas likes you." He says still chuckling and my whole body freezes. He looks at me, his eyes sparkling. His green eyes.

"You're an Upyr."

The word sounds strange on my tongue. It's untrained and leaves a bitter aftertaste. The boy tilts his head slightly and grins. Even though his eyes have the same color as Cassian's they're not the same. His are more almond-shaped, narrow, eyes of a seducer. White lashes surround them. The green is playful and light instead of dark and demanding.

"I'm Kael. I'm the one who brings you your dinner." He holds up the tray that I now notice is in his hands. I narrow my eyes slightly. "Am I not capable of going downstairs on my own and getting myself dinner?" I ask, still clutching the vase to my chest. Kael puts the tray onto the nightstand as Edlyn did before.

"The inn is full of soldiers and guards from your palace." My eyes widen at that and I take a step closer.

"Who sent them?" He shrugs his shoulders while his eyes scan the room lazily as if he weren't interested in this topic.

"The palace is a mess. The king is missing as are the princess and prince. Maybe the soldiers acted on their own."

Why would they even search in the inn? I try to remember the queue of lords that would come next in line on the Sebestyen throne, their faces flashing—I stop and whirl my head back around to him.

"You said the king was missing."

"Yes, I recall."

He shoots me a grin and plops down on the bed, stretching his body like a big cat. The springs protest under his weight.

"Edlyn didn't . . ." I don't finish the sentence as horror spreads through my body. I assumed that once she followed him she killed him. But she didn't. My father—the man who pretended to be my father is still alive. The man who tried to kill me—no matter if it was to wake up the magic in my body—is still alive. And on the run. My knees buckle and the vase slips out of my hand crashing to the ground. Kael watches the porcelain crash before he looks back up at me.

"Why would he run? People believe he is the king."

"No, they don't. The second you got resurrected a wave of magic flooded the lands. The people know now that you are alive. You are the legitimate heir of Aerwyna." I exhale deeply at his words before I turn my back on him. I grab the roots of my hair closing my eyes. This is just fucking fantastic. Not am I just fleeing from a god but my pretend father is on the run too. And I know Daragon Sebestyen will not leave me be. We made a fool out of him, robbed him of his kingdom. He is out for blood now.

"Are you all right?" A hand places itself on my shoulder and I do the only thing I can think of. I turn and push the blond back, glaring at him. His eyes widen surprised as mine do when I accidentally use considerable power so that he flies through the small room and crashes against a wall.

"Fuck." I breathe out, eyes wide.

"I'm sorry, I'm sorry—" I take a step forward to look if he's hurt but he chuckles and stands up straight again with a groan.

"It was my fault. I shouldn't have touched you." He straightens his clothing and I try to swallow the knot forming in my throat. He stares at me for a moment and I think I see something like curiosity in his eyes. The look reminds me so much of Cassian that I have to divert my gaze.

"You don't need to be scared, Cas has everything under control."

"I'm not scared and I don't need his protection." I counter, my eyes staying on the shards of the vase. Gods, Gisella is going to kill me. I sigh and squat down to pick up the shards.

"He thought you would say that." My eyes dart to him when he says that. I watch him squat down and help me pick up the splinters. We work in silence for a few seconds and I try to bite my tongue but half the question slips out anyways.

"You're his . . .?"

"Friend? Companion? Lover?" I look up at him and he grins. I roll my eyes. Men are all the same.

"Cas and I are friends since we were in diapers—literally." He says now more seriously. We finish cleaning up the ground and gather the shards on the dresser beside the door.

"And you're here . . . because?"

"Well, you didn't think you'd go to Demeter all on your own. I came with Eryx last week; Flynn should be here in the morning." He grins when he sees the confusion written on my face.

"If you would let him talk to you, he would've explained." He says with a smug smile and I narrow my eyes. I try to look like I don't care and walk over to the window dismissing him. I don't want to talk to Cassian. I don't trust myself enough to handle all of this wisely.

Either I am going to crumble the second he apologizes or I'm going to get angry again. And I'm tired of being angry. I'm tired of hating him, despising him, and feeling like a dagger pierces my back. Talking to him would only lead to betrayal because that stupid little thing in my chest won't listen to my brain. I turn around to see Kael still standing in the room watching me.

"I know my words might not be of value because you don't know me. But Cas didn't mean any harm to you. Quite the opposite."

"Of course you would say that you are his friend," I tell him and cross my arms in front of me. I watch the playful look in his eyes disappear and be replaced with something else. Something older and wiser.

"It might not seem like it but Cassian is the most caring person you will ever encounter in your life. He makes sure that his . . . that people close to him are safe. Always."

"I died. I was not safe."

"But you are alive now." He says, arching a brow. He is right, I am alive. But I am this thing that has inhumanly powers, that grows fangs and pointy ears. I know it isn't his fault, it was something that always slumbered inside me. But he was the trigger—his blood was the catalyst that unleashed it.

"Am I?" He doesn't answer the question. Instead, he takes a step closer his brows narrowed.

"What you might think Cas did, is wrong. He is my friend and I hate that he's hurting. He's been hurting his whole life, taking every burden off us. I owe him my life and many others do as well. So I plead with you to give him a chance."

"I did give him a chance. And then I got stabbed in the back in the process." I tell him. He shakes his head the small blonde strands flying in his eyes.

"Did you? Because from what I've heard you believed a man without a doubt, who tried to kill you, when he said that Cas was a traitor."

"Because he was a traitor! He could've told me that I was about to marry him, that I didn't have a choice but to marry him. Instead, he teased me and riled me up. He did everything to get on my nerves and sabotage me." I say exasperated, my hands flailing around me. Why is he painting it like I am the villain? Who is he to judge me? Kael takes a step closer his eyes narrowing.

"What would you have done if he told you, you were to marry him, Carina? You despised him your whole life and didn't even give him a chance to show you he changed. He didn't tell you because he wanted you to have the choice. The choice and chance to get to know him and fall in love with him despite the deal."

"Well, I did," I say breathing harshly. My heartbeat thrums in my chest.

"I did fall in love with him but it brought me nothing but pain and death." I clench my hands into fists and fight against the tears. Kael's shoulders slacken. I can't believe that I am fighting with a mere stranger now. I watch the blond straighten his shoulders and nod.

"We are leaving Aerwyna tomorrow morning. If we stay any longer we might get captured." He says.

The playfulness completely vanished in his eyes and before I can do anything he leaves the room again. I breathe out frustrated before I fall face-first on the mattress. Either I lost any social skills to communicate or I'm enjoying fighting with everyone these days. I clutch the pillow in my hands letting out a frustrated scream.

Kael doesn't even know me. He doesn't know what happened at the castle. Yes, Cassian might have told him the events but they didn't know how much I fought. How I fought to trust Cassian to give him a chance. I gave him multiple chances. *Did you?* Yes, I fucking did.

I squeeze my eyes shut and let out another frustrated scream.

~ 5 ~

By the time my frustration dissolves, dinner is cold. I still scarf the meal down knowing that I will need the energy for our upcoming voyage. Leaving for Demeter in the morning. That means I have this night before I leave the kingdom. Gisella checks on me during my meal and stays for a while. She informs me that Lord Andréas is currently at the Sebestyen court handling the disarray. I barely remember the man; I just know he is a distant cousin of my father's. It calms me to know that I won't leave the kingdom without someone on the throne. Still, it feels bizarre. This is not my home anymore. Half of the people would deliver me to Adales out of fear; the other worships me as their queen.

Gisella leaves me after an hour and I take a bath. I scrub my skin until it's red; I use the rose-scented soap that makes my head nauseous for my hair and dress in new breeches and a shirt. These fit me better, they sit snugly on my body and I thank the gods that it doesn't smell like him. I watch the sinking sun through the small window. The rain stopped long ago and I open the window. The air smells crisp and damp and I lean on the windowsill closing my eyes. The view over the capital is endless and I can see it bordering on the forest.

The streets come to life, torches being lit up, men wandering the streets and the courtesans lingering in front of the doorsteps of the brothels. I watch them for a few minutes before I see a familiar figure gliding through the crowd.

He is dressed in dark breaches and a cloak that sits over a green linen shirt. The hood is not on his head, letting the people glimpse the hard lines of his face. He walks with ease and confidence. Somehow it looks like the shadows are clinging to his body, whispering in his ears.

A few women are eyeing him, the courtesans twirling their hair, pushing out their breasts. He doesn't glance at anyone. The closer he gets to the inn, the more I creep into the shadows of the room but my gaze remains on him.

Something silver glitters under his cloak and I lean slightly forward, to see better. He has multiple knives attached to his belt not bothering to hide them. I don't even know if he needs them. I saw the elongated canines of his teeth that could easily slice through human skin. The talons that grew out of his hands, could rip anyone that steps in his way apart.

His head moves slightly when he approaches the inn and I quickly crouch from the window so he doesn't see me spying on him. I hold my breath for a moment and count to ten. When I look back up I don't see him anymore. I close the window hastily my breathing uncontrolled. My heartbeat throbs.

I start to pace and concentrate, focusing my hearing on the bar downstairs. I hear glasses clink, the tables being cleaned, howling laughter, and steps. I block out the heavy stumbling and focus on the elegant steps. A steady rhythm differs them from the rest. They don't stumble, they don't stop at the bar. They operate precisely through the already drunken men and thud up the stairs. I walk over to my door grabbing the handle. The metal is cold under my skin, the brass shining in the daylight.

The steps walk down the hall and I hold my breath when they stop in front of the door. My hand clenches around the handle. I don't know if I'm trying to keep it closed or yank it open. A moment passes. A second. My muscles are taut and my breathing inclines. The door buzzes and I know he's standing behind it. A door is the only thing standing between us. I squeeze my eyes shut at the hum in my body, trying to persuade myself that this is not real. It's not real. I feel like this because the gods intended for him to watch me. The feet shuffle and my eyes fly open.

The body turns, and the footsteps disappear. I let out a shaky breath. I hear him retreating down the hall. I don't let myself think, just listening to the steady beat of my heart. I yank the door open and step out into the hall, my face flushed when I see his back retreating. The door shuts loudly behind me making him freeze. The muscles in his back harden but he doesn't turn. I clench my hands into fists trying to hear something over the erratic beating of my heart.

Go to him. Go to him, go to him.

I don't move. He doesn't either. Why isn't he turning around? Turn around and look at me. I scream at him, I glare at his back. His face moves to the side and I see the hard line on his cheek. His gaze is turned to the floor but I know he addresses me when he speaks up.

"Yes?" His deep voice travels through the whole hall and right beneath my skin. I block out the loud laughing, and howling that comes from beneath and stare at him. What did I want to say? I should've thought about this more. I open my mouth but no words escape. *Say something you idiot!*

He turns around, slowly. He leaves his gaze on the floor even though his body faces me. I just notice now that his shirt is drenched. I furrow my brows inspecting the shirt even though I swear it stopped raining. An acidic scent drifts over and my throat closes up. He is drenched in blood. Small splatters paint his neck and the side of his face.

"What happened?" I ask my voice quiet. His shoulders tense even more but he still doesn't look at me.

"Someone needed my help. The Protestants are now at the border. Everyone knows the king left." His words are clipped. There is no teasing tone, no familiarity. I intertwine my fingers nervously. Why is he stopping in front of my room every time but doesn't step in? Because you told Edlyn to be left alone.

"Oh." I breathe out, still observing him. I open my mouth again to say something but get interrupted when someone pushes past me.

"Excuse me." A gravely, feminine voice. I step to the side and watch a woman, barely dressed in anything, pass by. Her hair is fiery red, curved into seducing curls. Her features are elegant and they stretch into a feline smile when she passes the prince.

"Hey, handsome." She greets him with a small smile while he nods still looking at the ground. Even though he moves so she has enough space, her shoulder grazes him before she saunters off down the hall. I watch her retreating steps before I turn back to Cassian to see him looking at me. I take a step back in surprise at the intensity of his gaze. My heart flutters lightly and he clenches his jaw before he looks away. I bite my lip before I straighten my spine again.
"There are . . . a few things I still don´t understand," I say quietly. He takes a step forward and I swallow.
"Maybe you could enlighten me?" It´s an offer. To talk. I have not forgiven him and I don´t know if I can. But I am willing to listen to him, to offer me an invite into his mind. His eyes flicker up to mine before he nods stiffly.
"Of course. I will change first, the blood . . ." He trails off noticing my grimace. I nod, keeping my eyes from the red liquid on the fabric.
"Yes."
"I will come straight to your chambers afterward." He says and I nod. He nods as well. We continue to stare at each other no one moving. The three feet separating us feels like it´s not enough when he looks at me. I try to clear the haze in my brain and nod again before taking a step back.
"I´ll wait for you." I breathe out before I yank the door back open and step into my room. A breath escapes my lungs and I stare up at the yellow ceilings. I don´t hear anything in the hall for minutes. I count almost to one hundred before I hear his shuffling feet and his retreating steps.

~ 6 ~

"I was ten years old when my father told me about the bond. Which from my prospect now doesn't sound pretty bright. Imagine telling a ten-year-old boy that he was to sell his soul to a girl he barely knows. To swear that he protects her with his life because it is his lineage that always did."

I stare at Cassian, who's standing a few feet away from me, leaning against the dusty dresser. The paint is chipping off of a few drawers. I sit legs crossed on the bed, have been since he stepped into my room. I don't dare to move, speak, to even breathe. He knows since he's been ten. It is a rather weird concept to tell a ten-year-old boy he had to devote his life to a girl. A girl he clearly despised when he was younger. I remember every snide remark, every push, and every taunt. Not just from him but from his brother too. They did everything in their power to get a rise out of me when they visited the Sebestyen court. I wonder now if that was the reason I was never allowed to visit Demeter, in order to hide from me that the ancient magic does indeed still exist. Cassian grew up knowing of his full heritage, of magic, of creatures I believed to be just written in books about.

"It was pure coincidence that I had nothing to say against it. How could I? The moment you laid those fiery eyes on me I knew I was a lost cause. I knew I would go to any lengths to protect you. I was excited to have this immense task. I never expected it to be this hard." His eyes stay on my face, deciphering every emotion that I'm trying so hard to hide. He lifts his clean shirt and reveals the dark swirls tattooed on the side of his body.

I clutch the comforter in my hands while I let my eyes wander over the ancient words that are carved into his skin. The swirls dance over the side of his ribs and dip down his narrow waist.

"My mother was furious when she knew of the oath. She begged my father to let me be. I was barely sixteen when the High Priest tattooed the ink, mixed with my blood into my body. I was scared beyond everything but I knew it was the right thing to do." I shift slightly at the way he's looking at me. He lets the shirt fall back into place. I moisten my lips and take a breath before I speak up hesitantly.

"When you say bond. You mean . . ."

"I mean that we're bonded. We always were even before the blood oath." He takes a step forward and I tense. He hesitates to stay right where he is. I avert my eyes to the ground trying to grasp things.

"Demetrus created the bond with Aerwyn?"

"They did. To make sure your identity was hidden from Adales. Every time you rebirthed another Moreau man was born to ensure your safety." I cringe at the words. I can't help but feel like a book, a mere object that needs to be protected by a man. Cassian seems to think the same thing and goes to correct himself.

"It's not like you couldn't on your own. I know you can but in the past, the other lives you lived, you may have not been in a palace. You couldn't have known how to fight. Not every bonded Moreau heir interferes. My father didn't." My eyes fly up at his words. Does he mean to say that his father knew me in a different life? I shudder slightly.

"My father protected you from afar. He made sure you stayed safe. He watched you live and watched you die. My grandfather did die to ensure your safety—"

"Okay, I get it." I interrupt him. My hands start to itch and a nauseous feeling travels through my stomach, pulling at my navel. I don't need to know which strangers all knew me in their past lives. I don't want to know anything about a past life. I am living now and can't imagine, that I've been in this world for centuries, thousands of years without being able to remember. I run my hands through my hair, inhaling.

"Do you . . . want me to continue?" He speaks up after a beat of silence. I nod not daring to meet his eyes.

"I left Demeter the day I turned sixteen. I knew my father didn't need me in the castle he was perfectly fine on his own. My mother wasn't exactly enthusiastic when I told her I would leave. I had no intention of interfering. I thought I could stay away from you and I did. I did for three years and believe me when I say—"

"Stop, stop, stop." I interrupt his rambling and get up from the bed, my eyes narrowing. He looks at me brows raised.

"You mean to tell me that you've been residing in Aerwyna for three years because of me?" I ask and something swirls in his dark eyes. After a moment he nods. The room starts to tilt upside down and I grab at my roots trying to somehow stay sane.

"You were wandering these streets watching me—?"

"I wasn't watching you."

"Spying after me while I didn't know—?"

"I wasn't spying."

I whirl around to notice him glaring at me. He shuts his mouth and I clench my jaw, trying not to strut over and deck him in the face.

"Why didn't you tell me that night? Was I even intended to notice you?" I order and take a step forward. I watch his chest expand for a moment, drawing in a breath.

"I wanted you to see me. I thought if we talked first in privacy it would somehow soften the blow." I let out a bitter chuckle, shaking my head in disbelief.

"Soften the blow? You did it to your advantage. Don't tell me anything you did was for me."

"But it was! Everything I did, everything I do, is for you, Carina." He takes a step forward and I have to tilt my head back to look him in the face. I can't believe him. I want to, I desperately want to but there is still this small part of me. An insecure part that tells me to be cautious, to not trust him.

"What do you think you would've done when I just strut into the palace one day and declared that you'd be my wife? You already hated me enough." He takes another step closer and I clench my fists not backing down.

"Of course I hated you. Your behavior towards me wasn't what I would call loveable. And the hate was valid. You should've told me. You claim to do this for me but you left me in the dark and I'm not talking about just the marriage but all of this." I gesture wildly with my arms trying to grasp everything. To grasp this utterly confusing, magical world. I watch his chest rise as anger paints his cheeks red.

"Would you have believed me? That I was a descendant of the god of death? That I can snap a soul with one thought? Would you have believed that I was on your side and came to save you, from an imposter that lied to you your whole life, just to sacrifice you? You can't imagine what it feels like. Not being able to hold you, talk to you, tell you how much I—"He swallows, turning his face away before he continues. "I knew there would be nothing for me but hate from you. I knew you would never reciprocate my feelings. So I choose to protect you instead of risking losing you. Maybe that makes me selfish but at least you're alive."

I'm stunned into silence by his words. If it could, my heart would break again. His breathing is constrained and soft shadows swirl around him.

I take a step back and watch the black crawl in his veins and stain his fingertips as if he dipped them into paint. His body shudders and my skin grows cold. I fail to realize who is standing in front of me. My whole life I thought I was the most dangerous thing out there but I was wrong.

Cassian oozes power and I would be a fool to underestimate him.

I could beat him because he let me. My mind flashes to the time when the Protestants attacked the castle. Was he really hurt or was that pretend as well? Cassian notices my silence and the shadows disappear again, the black color vanishing from his skin.

"Maybe I wouldn't have believed you. Maybe I would. Now we will never know." I say and meet his gaze. Something finally crumbles in his eyes. I bite my tongue not to speak the words that want to escape me.

"I will come with you to Demeter. I want to talk to the king but what we did,"—I swallow drawing in a deep breath—"will not continue. I don't care what fate or the gods say I won't marry you. You owe me that. I know now about everything. I'm not stupid enough to stay safe." The words feel like ash on my tongue, acid down my throat. Cassian straightens his spine and nods.

He hesitates before he moves past me and I squeeze my eyes shut. His fresh scent wafts around me and I have to stop breathing not to turn around and grab him. To let his strong arms wrap themselves around me. To cry in his chest while he tells me that everything will be all right. That nothing has changed, that we are still the same. That he's still the stupid boy who hides behind a smug grin and mask of arrogance. But I don't. Because it is not real. Who knows if that boy ever existed? It is only he who can tell.

I hear the door open and his steps hesitate, a beat of silence passes but I don't turn around. The door shuts close. I listen to the retreating steps in the hall but instead of wandering toward his chamber, they thunder down the stairs. Across the inn and to the outside.

I open my eyes again and stare at the wall. Stare for hours until I sit down on the cold floor. He says there is a bond but why don't I feel it? I can't feel the magic that is supposed to thrum in my veins. For a moment I close my eyes, and try to listen inside. For what, I don't know. Maybe a spark or a glimmer, something that tells me I am not what I thought. That I am not human.

When nothing happens I snap my eyes open, staring at the godsdamned yellow wallpaper.

My knuckles turn pale as I dig the pointy tips of my nails into my skin.

The refreshing sting of pain makes me sigh. At least I can feel the familiar burn.

I choke on my next breath but rein myself in. I am done moping around. We will leave Aerwyna tomorrow morning. I will accompany him because where else do I go? Aerwyn made it clear that I have to talk to King Ronan. I will make sure he annuls the marriage. Annuls the bond. Annuls everything between me and Cassian. I will search for the Fatums and get my answer. And after that, I will kill Adales, even if it is the last kill I´m about to make.

~ 7 ~

I don't remember falling asleep. My dreams are plagued with creatures of the night, ruling over sky and land, chasing me. I don't try to run even though I scream at myself. Screaming to run, to move, to drag myself out of this world. The world starts to shake, debris flying my way, as the creatures dive into a fall to grab my flesh between their talons.

When my eyes snap open the room is dark. The earth is still shaking as something grabs my sweat-slicked skin. With panic in my veins, I clutch at the creature's wrist using my momentum to throw it under me on the mattress. My other hand moves for the broken chair leg under my pillow but before I can drive it through the creature's heart a panicked voice calls out. "Wait!"

I hesitate, my eyes getting used to the darkness and I look down at Kael's face.

"What the hell do you think you're doing?" I hiss, letting go of his collar. With one elegant move we're both standing and he dusts the fabric of his shirt off.

"Apparently, I am trying to get killed by you," he scoffs, "what do you think I'm doing? Soldiers from the palace have just entered the Green Knight looking for you. We need to go."

My arm sinks with the chair leg still gripped in my hand. "They're looking for me?"

I strain my ears and try to hear the commotion downstairs. The color of the sky doesn't indicate the time of the day.

"Of course they are, you're the most valuable person in this kingdom, now come on. The others are waiting."

He turns to go but stops when he notices I am not following.

"Carina, we need to go. Now."

I nod trying to shake sleep off of me. He opens the door to the hall which allows the shouting from downstairs to filter into the room. The blond looks both ways before waving me after him.

I throw a glance at the dark chamber before I follow him outside and into the hall.

"Is that a chair leg?" Kael asks incredulously while we tiptoe past the silenced rooms of the inn. "You know what? I don't want to know."

"If you keep on talking they might find us." I hiss at him as we reach the railing that overlooks the tables and bar downstairs. I freeze on the spot, realizing how many of them are here. A general is perched at the crown of the group of more than twenty men, the crest of Aerwyna stitched on their uniforms. Gisella is standing in front of the General talking in a soothing voice as she raises her hands. Kael gets ahold of my wrist and pulls me past and out of view.

"We need to help her! What if they find out she hid me from them?"

"They won't if we go now. We need to leave before they call the whole damned army."

Despite my anguish about Gisella, I let him pull me along. We take the back stairs down onto the first floor, passing a few doors that are propped ajar. The people have nothing better to do than listen to other people's business.

Kael halts at the base of the stairs that take us to the back exit.

The soldiers are moving towards the stairs, Gisella following them protesting. "There is no reason for you to roam this inn. I can assure you my guests will be dissatisfied if you disrupt their sleep." The soldier grunts as he keeps on walking, right to the stairs where Kael and I are standing.

"Back, back, back." He pushes me back up the stairs and along the hall, the soldier's steps following us. "I assure you ma'am your establishment is not the only one being searched right now. We're looking all over the capital for the King and his daughter."

Kael and I sprint down the hall, our steps echoing against the next set of stairs. My heart thrums with every step of the soldiers as we scurry back into the room I occupied.

Kael slams the door shut and without any complaint pushes the old dresser in front of it. He turns around to look at me with panic-filled eyes. "Walk to the window."
I turn to follow the instructions before I realize what he said. "What?"
"No time for questions, open the window."
"I'm not going to jump out of the window."
"Oh, you rather get captured by the soldiers while I get thrown into the dungeons?" He pushes past me and cracks open the window, letting in a cold breeze.
"Cas?" Kael whispers into the dark but there is no audible answer. Loud voices appear in the hall outside and a moment later the handle on the door starts to jiggle.
"Cas is standing right under the window, Carina, you have to jump."
I shake my head, I'd have to be mental to make that jump, we're on the second floor for the love of gods.
The door handle jiggles aggressively and a voice accompanies the movement.
"I order you to open this door now! This is a royal assignment."
I hesitate, fear creeping up my back and holding me in a vise grip.
"Carina, please," Kael begs, holding one of his hands out. "Cas will kill me if I leave without you."
"Cas can go to hell." I hiss, even though I approach him. "And I'll probably follow him when I jump out of this window and splatter against the ground."
Kael snorts as he heaves me up onto the window sill.
"I'll wait for the day he would let you fall to your death."
I glare at his smug face as I swing my legs out of the window. The booming against the door turns louder and the dresser groans under the repeated impact. With a look down I make sure that Cassian is standing in the dark. And surely he is, Edlyn is sitting on a horse beside him, a third unknown man with red hair woven into a long braid beside them.

"I'll catch you, I promise." Cas's voice carries upwards with the soft breeze. I hesitate, even though I know I have to take the leap. The dresser groans finally and the door bursts open. Before I can move Kael shoves me out of the window.

I try to scream but my breath gets lodged in my throat as I soar through the air.

This is it. The gods made me outlive assassins, opium dealers, vengeful creatures and now I'm going to die because I got shoved out of a window.

"Oof."

Air rushes out my lungs when my fall gets cushioned by someone's arms. I am not dead. I raise my eyes to look at Cassian who carefully puts me to my feet. "Are you all right?"

Before I get to answer his question a high wailing interrupts us when Kael jumps out of the window. He screams, even though he lands elegantly on his feet.

"I'm fine, thanks for asking." He throws the prince a smug smile who rolls his eyes.

Our horses are already mounted, Edlyn is on her horse not far away, her brows pinched in concentration. Eryx is not far from her, beside the red-headed man.

My eyes stay stuck on him for a moment, wandering over the broadness of his shoulders, the immensely tall figure. His hair is the deepest shade of red and if it was brushing against his shoulders I would've thought him for a moment to be Orkiathan. But he is much bulkier and while both of them have the same shade of turquoise eyes there is one difference. My blood freezes when I notice that one of his eyes is completely white. Stuck in its transformed form due to the deep, brutal-looking scar that runs from his brow, through the middle of his eye, and stops low on his high cheekbone. A warrior. He looks like a warrior who stepped out of an ancient war. Now that I know of the magic I know there is no denying what he is. Tengeri. A descendant of the god of the sea, Oceanus.

My ogling gets brutally disturbed when Kael shoves his arm against my shoulder. I stumble and narrow my eyes. He grins down at me.

"Flynn doesn't like it when you stare at him." He tells me and my eyes immediately fly back to the brooding man.

"Hey! Princess Katherina Sebestyen you will come with us back to the palace! Orders from Lord Andréas!" A guard leans out of the window screaming down at us.

I flip the man off before we usher towards the horses. Nighttail neighs as I swing myself onto her back. Kael whistles and a white mare walks over to him.

"Good girl, Honeycomb."

"Your horse is called Honeycomb?"

He turns his head to look at me, "Yours is called Nighttail."

"As interesting as your horse's names are, we better get out of here before the guards come storming out of the backdoor," Cassian says as he swings himself up on his horse. Edlyn comes up beside me, even though she avoids my gaze.

The backdoor to the inn flies open and I'm ready to run but instead, it is Gisella hurrying my way.

Her hair is in disarray, a slight look of panic etched into her angelic face.

"We need to go." Cassian's redheaded guard states but I don't make a move and grasp Gisella's hand in mine.

"I told them that a customer saw you leave for the southern lands in Polyxena." She tells him with a grim look. He grunts but doesn't say something audible.

"Are you all right, if we leave you here?" I ask her worried that she might be in trouble. She squeezes my hand and nods. "As long as you stay safe I'm perfectly well."

"Gisella, I don't know if I—," she interrupts me hastily as she draws nearer. I ignore the impatient sigh and crouch down so I can hear her whisper. "Aerwyna will always be your home, Carina, I want you to know that you can come back at any time."

She draws her hands around her neck to unclasp her necklace. "What are you doing?" I ask as she slips the necklace into my hands, the cool coin grazing my palm.

"A talisman for you to stay safe, it will protect you. You can give it back to me once I receive an invitation to your wedding." She glances at Cassian. Right, they all think we're still getting married.

"Carina," Cassian presses and I shoot him a look. "If we leave now we might have an advantage." I turn back to look at Gisella and nod at her.

"Stay safe," I tell her as I slip the necklace around my neck and turn Nighttail towards the others.

"You know I will."

Gisella and I don't say goodbye, she knows how I feel about it.

"Finally." The redhead grumbles and I shoot him a narrow glance.

"Ready?" Cassian asks me, his eyes sharp. I don't answer him as I push Nighttail into a slight jog. Edlyn is at my side in a second and no one says anything as we leave the inn behind, the shouts of the guards growing distant.

The six of us disappear into the morning dust of the forest, leaving the Green Knight behind, leaving the capital behind. Leaving Aerwyna behind.

Once we leave a gap between the capital and our group of six, we slow down our horses. Flynn and Eryx decide we should stay low and travel the land side of the kingdoms to avoid getting caught. Who knows what Lord Andréas will want from me once he's caught sight of me? I mostly stay quiet, observing the new group. Kael stays by my side and to my surprise he is the most helpful source of information I've ever come across. When Flynn rides forward and past me Edlyn scoffs and murmurs something at him.

Flynn's shoulders bunch but he ignores her completely before going back to stare at the trees passing.

"Edlyn and Flynn don't seem so fond of each other." I turn to Kael to see him watching me. He shrugs his shoulders carelessly.

"Well, they hate each other. For obvious reasons." I raise a brow at Kael and he elaborates.

"Tengeri and Magda are practical nemeses since they're born. But I think it goes beyond that for them, they can't stand each other since Flynn's at our court."

A Tengeri at their court? It's not a long way from Oceanus to Demeter but I wonder what motives brought him to leave his home.

"Don't say anything but secretly I think they should just fuck each other and get over all that tension."

I look back at Kael who shoots me a feline smile. My lips twitch for a moment because his look is so smug. Immediate guilt shoots through me when I think back to the way I spoke to him yesterday. I didn't even really know him and immediately assumed the worst. He's not that bad of company. I hide my smile and his lips stretch out even more, making his green eyes glow.

"Is that an actual smile I see? Progress."

"Shut up." I push him in his side and he lets out an airy groan, making my eyes widen.

"Oh shit, I'm sorry. I'm still getting used to—it didn't hurt, did it?"

I narrow my eyes suspiciously when he grins. I roll my eyes and look back at the other three. A small group to travel to Demeter. I meet the dark eyes of Eryx for a moment and a shiver runs down my spine. My stomach churns and something tells me that the cool outer experience of this man is just hiding what burns underneath it. I narrow my eyes for a moment staring at him before he finally turns and engages Flynn back into a talk on which routes to take.

And here I thought I was the only one with relationship problems. This is going to take longer than I have suspected.

~ 8 ~

One week. One week we travel through night and day, through rain and storms, through heat and sun. We travel through forests, through mud, through mountains. Staying clear of the cities we pass unless we need to refill on our resources. When Flynn said limited stops he meant limited stops. We barely stop at night and it seems like their energy is endless. Apparently, Tengeri, Upyr, and Magda's don't need sleep. Or food. Or water. One time I feel like I'm almost slipping off of Nighttail with the way that exhaustion hits me. Kael riding beside me, notices and proposes to the group to take a rest. Flynn answers with a brooding glare towards me but accepts. I understand Edlyn's disdain regarding him. He spares us three hours of rest. Three hours before I'm awoken from sleep by Kael and we continue our journey.

The further we travel south the warmer the weather gets. We pass more colorful-looking birds, and rivers that somehow have tree trunks that move on their own and if my eyes don't deceive me from the lack of sleep, I could swear I see footprints of a lone wolf on the way. The mood of the group doesn't get any better the closer we get to Demeter. Edlyn and Flynn keep ignoring each other, and when they talk it ends in discussion and bickering that takes Cassian to get them to quiet down. Kael shoots me a smug smile every time it happens. My communication stays between him and me and I ask him about Demeter. Ask him about the capital, Iason, the people, the palace, and the food.

He tells me that the people in Iason are generous and kind. That the capital is full of light and laughter. He tells me of the wine and the greasy bread sold on the market. He says the palace sits atop the mountains that oversee the kingdom in its all and when he talks of his kingdom it is as if it is alive, shining in his light eyes. He loves Demeter. It seems so weird, to have thought that King Ronan is cruel and his kingdom is drowned in darkness and horror.

Kael's words almost ease the tense feeling in my shoulders. About a week into our journey Cassian finally announces to take a rest without Kael needing to propose it. Flynn doesn't seem the slightest bit thrown off and dismounts his horse. We're currently stopping amid a clearing. The sun is already sinking, the reflections dancing on the green lake that lays in the circle of trees from the forest. I swear I've seen nothing but green and trees for this entire journey. I hop off of Nighttail and let her walk with the rest of the horses toward the water to drink their fill. She immediately seeks Honeycomb's side. I've suspiciously watched her closeness to the male and can't help but roll my eyes at her behavior.

"I don't think we should risk a fire, the nights are warm enough to handle without," Flynn says as he unlatches the satchel and gets out the scratchy brown blanket he has been using for the past week. Eryx says he'll scan the area through the forest while Cassian nods at Flynn.

I take out my thin blanket joining Kael in unpacking some things. My body thrills at the prospect of sleep for more than a few hours. Edlyn saunters off getting rid of her suit and walks straight into the lake with a soft undershirt and flimsy pants making my brows raise.

"She does that every time," Kael says beside me and I catch the slightly hooded look in his eyes.

"Stop staring you creep." I shove his shoulder and he laughs, looking at me. His eyes scan my body and I arch a brow.

"No need to be jealous, there is plenty enough of me." I roll my eyes ignoring his words and he chuckles before leaning forward.

"But I think there might be someone who has objections against it." He acts as if he's whispering but it is loud enough for Flynn and Cassian to hear. My eyes flicker to the latter to see his gaze on us, his jaw hardened while Flynn keeps talking to him. I decide to ignore him and turn back to Kael helping him smoothen the forest ground. My back isn't looking forward to laying on the ground all night.

"How long has Flynn been at your court?" I ask him while I pick up small rocks and sticks before we both flatten the earth.

"About four years."

My brows fly up at the words. I would've thought he'd be even longer with them. My gaze flickers to the prince and Flynn. Something in the way they communicate with their eyes, I expected them to know each other for longer.

"Feels like an eternity though," Kael says and I nod.

"You three seem inseparable." I focus on the mud that gets under my nails but don't stop flattening the earth to clean them.

He shrugs and nods at the same time.

"We've gone through a lot." His words are clipped, his brows narrowed as if in disdain from a distant memory. It's a touchy subject. It makes me all the more curious.

"How come that a Tengeri is at the court of Demeter?"

"Flynn found Cassian when he was about fifteen, King Ronan sent us out to Oceanus for political matters. We were young and dumb. We'd dared to swim in a lake racing for the other side when Cassian got pulled under by a Boszor. I tried to help him but we weren't in our element. Flynn found us and practically saved both of our asses." He shoots me a quick smile and I arch a brow. We throw both of the blankets on the flattened earth and I sit down cross-legged waiting for him to continue, even though I have no clue what a Boszor is. Kael lies down on his side propping up his face with his hand.

"He practically slayed those Boszor and afterward cursed us for being so stupid. He went on and on about why not to get into dark waters in Oceanus until Cassian told him who he was. Do you know what Flynn did then?"

I lean forward watching his lips twitch.

"What?" I ask curiously.

"He didn't give a single fuck." His lips stretch into a big smile and I break out into quiet laughter. I can imagine the look on the prince's face when he met the scary-looking warrior who didn't give one fuck if he was the crown prince of Demeter or not. That must've been humbling.

"And I still don't give one." My chuckle dies down when we both turn our heads to see the man looking at us. This is the first time he looks at me and I try my best not to linger on the horrendous scar on the left side of his face. It doesn't take away any of his beauty but his beauty is different from Cassian's. Cassian is littered with shadows and lingering darkness that makes him look alluring and seductive. Flynn has a hardness that the prince doesn't have. It's haunting and mysterious. His obvious handsomeness does nothing to my tummy as Cassian's once did.

"You two are lucky I turned up or you would've drowned in that lake."

Kael rolls his eyes and I turn toward the warrior.

"How did you end up joining them?" His turquoise and white eye turn back to me for a moment.

"I was on my way to Demeter anyway and Cas offered me to visit his court and show me his gratefulness for saving his life. I ended up staying." His answer is clipped before he turns and walks back to Cassian who has been listening quietly. I wonder why Flynn felt the need to leave his kingdom. I open my mouth to question Kael but a different question drops out.

"How old are you?" I ask Flynn even though his face is turned away from me.

"Too old to still be alive." A light voice drawls and we all turn to see Edlyn approaching us. I blink a few times, my eyes trailing over the sheer, soaked material of her shirt. She stops in front of us and starts wringing her long strands.

"Look who's speaking," Flynn says and my eyes fly over to him, noticing the way his shoulders are tense and his brows narrowed.

A feline smile builds on Kael's lips while Cassian rolls his eyes already fed up with them.

"I'll see if Eryx needs help." No one answers him or gives him the time of the day besides me. I watch his back retreat into the forest before Edlyn speaks up again.

"Well, besides others among us, I don't show my age. I think Kael can speak for me, can't you, honey?" Edlyn's voice sounds like molten glaze. The sound surprises me as I have never heard her talk like that before. Kael smiles smugly, his eyes dropping down to the two darker patches of her breasts.

"You don't look a day older than twenty, love."

Flynn huffs at his answer.

"His opinion doesn't count, he's barely a man."

"I can show you how manly I am and many other pleased females as well."

Flynn scoffs at Kael's words but I can see the faint amusement in his eyes.

"Some males live their whole life—how ancient it might be—without being a man." Edlyn taunts before she walks over to her puddle of clothing. When she bends over I see Flynn's jaw harden and Kael chuckles quietly beside me. Edlyn straightens up and shoots a narrow glance at Flynn.

"I'm going to change." She walks past him and his eyes flicker over her body, following her until she disappears into the forest.

Kael breaks out into barking laughter beside me and Flynn growls. The deep vibration in his throat travels through the ground. My lips twitch but I don't dare to laugh at the ballistic look on his face. Kael suddenly topples on his back and for a moment I think he's fallen on his own but after my eyes focus I see that Flynn threw his heavy satchel at his friend.

Kael still laughs when Flynn turns his back to us and I can't help my own lips from spreading into a small grin.

The forest is eerily silent once the sun kisses the horizon and the day turns into night. Everyone finally settled down while Flynn offered to keep watch on the forest. Cassian tells him multiple times to lie down and get some sleep in but the warrior doesn't accept. Instead, he keeps pacing the area of our small camp as if he expects an armada to march right through onto the clearing and shed our blood. I watch him for a few hours before I turn and settle my gaze onto the onyx lake. Kael is deep asleep beside me, his breathing soft and steady. I swear this man can sleep anywhere at any time. I know I won't be able to shut an eye. Now that I can I won't dare to. I know that if I fall asleep nightmares will haunt me again and I will wake up everyone with my screams. So I settle on watching the soft ripples the water of the lake makes and the way the stars and the moon shine on the surface. Now that we're closer to Demeter the sky seems clearer. I still haven't seen the sign of any clouds and the nights are filled with little stars. Kael said once we reach the borders of Demeter the sky will be littered with so many stars I won't be able to count them.

I turn on my back and watch the sky, the steady thuds of Flynn's footsteps echoing around us. I start to count the stars, count one, two, three. *Eighteen.*

When tears start to sting my eyes I look at Kael and the others to see that they're still asleep. I sit up and slip out under my blanket before I walk over to Flynn. He hears my steps before I even clear my throat but he doesn't turn his head until I speak up.

"Do you mind for some company?"

"Suit yourself" He nods and instead of standing like he is, I sit down leaning my back against a tree trunk, hugging my knees to my chest. We both stay silent for a moment. The trees rustle when a soft breeze passes us.

"I have nightmares."—I avert my eyes and watch my scruffy shoes as if they're the most exciting thing—"I don't know how to get rid of them. Every time I think they are gone I wake up again feeling like my hands are dripping with blood."

My voice ends in a whisper and the man stays quiet. His pacing has stopped and I don't dare to look up to find out if his eyes are on me.

"It's happening over and over again as if I don't see their eyes during the day as if I don't try to remember their death every time I wake up."

Another beat of silence. A tear slips over my cheek and I quickly brush it away before I clear my throat.

"I don't know how much you know—

"What you did—what happened won't go away. Be grateful to be reminded of the things you did. Use that reminder to redeem yourself. Use it and fuel your determination." He speaks up and I look up at him, feeling as if he knows what I am talking about.

"You can cry and whine and feel bad about what you did. Maybe it wasn't your fault, you were oblivious to the things around you. But you can also stand up, face the consequences and make those deaths count. Don't forget them, recite them, every day, to remember that it was what it was. That it won't happen again." His voice is steady and I don't dare to interrupt them.

"Is that what you do? Remind yourself every day?" I almost want to take the question back but I don't. He nods and his eyes wander over to the others, especially to a dark curly-haired head.

"I do. It took a fifteen-year-old boy to make me realize." My brows fly up at his confession.

"Cassian?"

He shoots me an arrogant look.

"You give him way too little credit." I scoff, nodding. He's not wrong. I gave Cassian too little credit and underestimated his whole scheming. He doesn't comment on my scoff and goes on.
"Despite what you think about him, his stupidity and arrogance are overshadowed by his intelligence and humbleness."
"That doesn't even make sense," I say as I arch a brow and watch the twitch in his lips.
"It does. Once he lets you see the side he was so adamant to hide." I don't know how to answer that so I stay quiet with my eyes on the small group of us. What a weird constellation it is. Half of the time I think they can't stand each other and the other half it feels like they would go to lengths for each other that I can't grasp. The way Kael protected Cassian, the way Flynn talks about him now. It sheds a different light on the prince, a light I've never considered before.
"It feels like everyone tries to convince me of his innocence." Flynn clicks his tongue at that.
"I wouldn't say the prince is innocent in any kind of way."
My cheeks flush at his words and I somehow worry that he can read my mind. Flashes dance in front of my eyes and I quickly squeeze them shut to will them away.
"What made you leave Oceanus?" I ask to divert the topic from the prince. Flynn's facial features harden in a fracture of a moment and I'm sure he won't answer my question. It stays silent for a long time until he speaks up again.
"You should try to get some sleep. We won't stop this long for another time." He says but I shake my head and lean it against the tree. I look up back to the sky and count the stars one, two, three. *Eighteen.*
"I prefer to stay awake tonight."

I somehow end up falling asleep anyway, drifting between a lucid and dazed state. I still hear the earth crunch under Flynn's pacing for a few hours before I hear another pair join him.

"Lay down, get some sleep. I'll watch her." The deep timbre of the voice is familiar but it feels like I barely grasp what it's saying.

"I would not have expected her to be like this."

I recognize Flynn's voice clearly, it's closer to me than the other voice. The fog clears lightly in my head and I feel the hard material of the trunk in my back.

"What do you mean?" The timbre asks again.

"I always expected you to end up with someone like Azzura, we all did. Not Someone this fiery in-obedient."

"You don't even know her." Shoes scruff against the forest ground.

"I don't need to know her. I know you." A beat of silence.

"Are you in love with her?" I hold my breath to wait for the deep voice that travels through my body and touches me in the deepest parts. I know it's him. Somehow I know by the way his presence feels around me.

"Since I met her. It's weird. It always felt like I fell in love with her more and more. But there was this one time. . ." Cassian trails off and my fingers twitch, anticipation building up in me. I slowly peek my eyes open and almost sigh, relieved, when I see both of them standing with their backs to me. Flynn has two twin swords strapped to his broad back while Cassian has his cloak over his shoulders. It is weird to see them beside each other so differently yet the air floats around them the same way. While Flynn is broad and strong like a bear, Cassian is tall and lean like a wolf.

"She told me how she hated me. How she wanted to choke me—"

"I don't need to know of your kinks, brother." Flynn interrupts him and Cassian shoves him a few feet away.

"That's not what I mean. She told me she hated me. Hated me so much that she couldn't live in a world where I wasn't in to hate. And it weirdly made me fall in love with her even more. The way she fights stands up for everything she's passionate about. She has a heart of fire with such a sweet soul. She's the most innocent person I've ever met. She's too good for me." Flynn stays silent for a moment and I can't believe what the prince is saying. Can't stop my heart from fluttering in my chest. My breath hitches and I pray that they don't hear it.

"She doesn't think that. She has nightmares."

"I know, I heard her every night in the inn." Something tugs at my heart at his words. The way his voice sounds so devastating.

"I want to help her but she doesn't let me."

"Give her time. It's supposed to heal all wounds." Flynn says and claps his hand on the prince's shoulder. I watch him leave and quickly close my eyes shut when I see Cassian turn.

"The wounds might heal but the scars stay." The prince mumbles before I feel him squat down close. I try to make my chest move evenly and keep my hands from twitching before he speaks up again.

"Happy birthday, princess."

I drift back to a dreamless sleep after.

~ 9 ~

I wake up the next morning without any back aches and no memory of any nightmares. I hear the soft steady breathing of Kael and sit up to see everyone still asleep. For a moment I blink disoriented, I could swear I didn't fall asleep here. I remember talking to Flynn sitting against the tree. Then I fell asleep. I look down to see two blankets draped over my body and slowly push them off of me before I get up. When I see the flash of Flynn's red hair my heart stops. He went to sleep after Cassian talked to him. Did he lay me down with the others? And gave me his blanket afterward? My blood runs cold before it turns sizzling hot.

My eyes fly over to the prince's spot to meet emptiness.

Happy birthday, princess.

I smash down the flutter in my chest, remembering what happened and stomp over to the lake. The water is now tinted in a soft blue color, specks of orange dancing across due to the rising sun. I shoot a look over my shoulder just to check that they're still all asleep. I slip out of my tunic and the breeches, standing in my silk shorts and under-blouse before I step into the water. I don't dare to soak myself completely but instead go into the water until I'm thigh deep in and clean the journey off my skin. I try to stay as clinical as possible and not to feel like I'm washing any red liquid off me. I don't think about the day and that it's my birthday. I don't think of the fact that Cassian remembered.

Instead, I watch the cool water trail over my skin and drop some of it over my head to soak my hair. The sun rises higher and higher yet I'm still the first one to be awake.

I'm so focused on the sensation of the water on my skin that I don't hear the splashing of the water behind me and almost have a heart attack when someone speaks up.

"Morning."

"Holy fuck—" I turn, clutching my chest to see Cassian standing in the water behind me. I almost choke on my next breath when I notice that he got rid of his shirt and breeches, standing in his undergarments in the water. Amusement flickers in his eyes but his face stays stoic.

"You scared the shit out of me."

I do not eye the gloriously naked chest presenting itself right in front of me. I do not notice how the lines of his body seem like carved stone, sharp and yet elegant.

"One might think with your heightened senses you could've heard me." He says and my eyes narrow.

"Well, I didn't." I turn my back to him again, my heart still beating too fast but not because he scared me. I start dipping my arms back into the water trailing it over my skin and hair while I hear the water splash behind me.

"Are you doing all right?" He asks me, his voice hard and cold. I should turn around, stop being so childish and face him. Ignore that his stupid skin is on display, so beautifully wicked. I should be able to control myself. I gather enough courage to turn around but instead of answering his question, I slip out my own.

"How did I end up back at the camp?" He stiffens visibly at my question and I almost want to take the question back. But I don't. I raise my chin and straighten my shoulders waiting for his answer.

"I carried you back. I switched shifts with Flynn. Thought you might be uncomfortable." He looks away, the water reflecting in his eyes. My first instinct is to complain. To tell him not to touch me or think about how I feel. Instead, I nod. It is uncharacteristically kind, even if it is uncalled for.

"How much longer until we reach Demeter?"

"If we keep up Flynn's tempo, half a week, maybe less." I nod and I cross my arms over my chest, suddenly feeling too exposed. How can someone stand this close and still seem so far?

The air is bending around him, trying to touch him, forming itself around his skin. I am jealous of the air which is able to touch him without any consequences. I clear my throat and focus on his face but the prince doesn't even look at me. His eyes are flying over the area cautiously as if he's scanning for enemies that aren't there.

"What's his story, anyway?" At that question, a small smile stretches on his lips before he looks at me.

"Curious as always. But sadly it is not my story to tell, princess. Maybe if you ask him nicely he'll tell you."

"Yeah, sure." I scoff because I don't think anything will convince Flynn to say more than he has to. Cassian opens his mouth again and I wait for him to say something but he gets interrupted before he can mutter one word.

"Stop playing around, we need to continue," Flynn calls over to us from the shore. We both turn our heads to see that everyone's been waking up and getting ready to leave again. I don't waste one second before I wade past Cassian to get out of the water and dress again. My arm grazes his and I curse the goosebumps that follow an insignificant touch as that.

Once everyone got ready and mounted their horses Flynn doesn't hesitate a second before riding through the forest. I find my usual place beside Kael who has a suspiciously smug smile on his face. I decide to ignore it and keep my gaze on the riders before us and my gaze lands on Cassian's back. He didn't try to talk to me again after I left the lake with him behind. My brain tells me that's a good thing, that I'm safe and should continue keeping my distance. It was a good decision to annul the wedding. No one knows yet and it was surprising enough that he accepted. But why should I question it? Why do I feel weird about it?

What do I do when it happens?

The question aches inside me, buries itself in my deepest parts, and feeds on my insecurities. If King Ronan does agree what do I do? If I can defeat Adales—which I highly doubt—what comes next? I could come back to Aerwyna and finally, do things my way. I could call Henri back and tell him to visit me in between his journeys. Maybe I could give Hector a second chance. We would have more time to get to know each other. Maybe those lukewarm feelings I have for him would blossom into more.

As if he could hear my thoughts, Cassian turns his head and catches my gaze. My cheeks flush in embarrassment and I scold myself internally.

He can't hear what you're thinking, you idiot.

I avoid his gaze, Kael distracting me when he rides closer on his horse. I turn my head and give him a small smile. He seems to act like some kind of buffer between Cassian and me. Well, not just between us but between Edlyn and Flynn as well. Both of them like him enough to keep it quiet every time he does say something to their bickering. Well, besides snarky remarks. But I can see what he means with the energy that travels between my friend and the warrior. They might hate each other but I of all can confirm that the lines become blurrier the more you hate someone.

"So, I've come across a birdie yesterday," I focus back on Kael who has a smug look on his face.

"And it told me that someone turned eighteen today." He raises a brow and I blink at him surprised.

My gaze flickers to the others riding in front of us and I know that they're able to hear our conversation but they choose to happily ignore it.

"A birdie?" I ask throwing a look at Cassian's back. Why would he tell Kael that it's my birthday? It's suspicious enough that he remembers the date because I can't even recall if I told him. But if his story is true it is no wonder that he memorized the date.

"Maybe it was a grumbling wolf. What's the difference?" Kael says lazily and I shake my head, hiding the grin that is about to split my lips.

"Some think it's a big difference." He waves me off before a small genuine smile moves on his lips. It makes his skin light up with an unknown glow.

"Well, what I'm trying to say is. That there is a tradition of gift giving on someone's birthday."

"I'm familiar with the concept, yes." I nod seriously, while I watch his smile brighten. I have no clue what he's going on about. The steady rhythm of the steps of the horses in front of us echoes in the back of my skull. It is weird how I'm able to hear and feel things so differently now.

"Great. So this will not make up any confusion." I watch Kael reach into his bag, attached to Honeycomb's flank. He digs through its various contents for a moment and I watch him carefully.

"It's nothing great, really, but I think eighteen is a special year in a young woman's life."

"Why would that be?" I furrow my brows and still watch him fumble for whatever he is searching in that bag.

"Oh, right. You don't know, it is the age, Upyr women settle. Their features settle and freeze, and their immortal life begins." He finally sits up again a small black velvet sack sitting in his hand.

"I'm not an Upyr though," I tell him and he rolls his eyes.

"Are you saying you're refusing my present?" My body freezes.

"You . . . got me a present?" His brows rise, surprised at my reaction. Affection warms my chest. I barely know him and yet he stayed by my side all of this journey even if it is because of Cassian's orders.

"Are you going to cry on me, princess?" His voice is panicked and the nickname gives me the rest. A tear slips from my eye and I quickly swipe it away. I chuckle when I see the alarmed look on his face. This small gesture overwhelms me so much that a few tears continue escaping my eyes until I pull myself together, reminding myself that the others are with us.

"When?" I ask him after I cleaned my face. His cheeks flush in a rosy color.

"When we stopped last week to stock up on supplies." He says quietly, holding out his hand as if to shove the small bag at me. I gratefully take it, smiling lightly. Kael meets my eyes and huffs out a small breath. He's completely overwhelmed by my tears.

"Thank you."

"Open it first before you thank me too early on." I nod even though I doubt that I wouldn't like it, whatever it is. The fact that he even got me something is enough. I'm glad he enjoys my company the way I enjoyed his over the two-week travel. I can see us becoming great friends in the future. *If you plan on staying in Demeter.* I ignore the stabbing thought and let go of Nighttail's reins for a moment to open the velvet sack.

"Edlyn helped me pick it out so it's not just my present. But I thought something familiar would be good, mixed with something new. The woven gold strands are something we do in Demeter." He tells me while a dainty braided bracelet drops in the palm of my hand. A small breath escapes me when I see it for the first time. It is made of really fine leather bands, braided in an unfamiliar pattern I can't recall. Golden strands are woven in between, glittering in the rising sun and I could swear sparks are flying from the material. How can gold be braided? I blink as I turn the bracelet in my hand and my heart stutters when I see the stone attached to the middle of the bracelet. It is circled with golden strands coiled around it as if to protect its precious power. Purple, dark blue swirls dance inside the stone and I release another small breath. Bloodstone.

"It's beautiful, Kael, thank you." My voice is barely a whisper when I look up at him. A broad smile stretches his lips and I watch him puff out his chest, straightening his spine. I have to chuckle at the proud look on his face.

"Really, this is probably one of the nicest things someone has done for me." He shoots me a quizzical look.

"You have not known many nice people then. Come on, I'll tie it around your wrist." My eyes widen when he leans over without falling off Honeycomb's back. He gently pries the braided bracelet out of my hand and ties it around my wrist.

"It is a present to keep you safe, now that you don't have your usual . . . protection." As if on instinct my thumb glides over the empty space on my ring finger. I remember my father—Daragon saying that the stone could be a weapon or savior. Protection against dark magic just as it is a weapon against Upyr. The fact that Kael trusts me to have this, and wants me to have this makes my heart warm again.

"Thank you."

"I'll take your thanks in coins." He says with a grin once he's finished tying the bracelet. I roll my eyes and push his shoulder so he sits back straight on his horse. Even though he could hold the position it's giving me too much anxiety to watch him like that. He shrugs his shoulder as if to play it down.

"Remember it's not just me who picked it." He nods over to Edlyn riding in the front making a knot form in my throat.

"I'm being an utter asshole, aren't I?" I ask, not taking my eyes off her red cloak.

"Not necessarily an asshole. You acted in ways that you think were right. It's not like you're forever stuck with the consequences. Do something about it." I turn my head to look at the blond and he gives me an encouraging nod. As if it is that easy to overcome your own pride and admit that you were wrong. I still stand for what I said, she didn't have to lie to me but I understand her side of the point. And besides the fact that she lied—maybe to protect me or not—she is still my best friend. I know I'm not able to live a life where she isn't a part of it. But it's just so hard to tell her that.

"I can actually hear the wires turning in your brain—oh look there's smoke coming from your head."

"Shut up." I tell Kael who snickers.

"I was wondering when you started to insult us all again." I turn my head surprised.

"Cassian wasn't exactly secretive about the things you did."

"I didn't do anything."

"You literally stabbed him." I roll my eyes.

"I didn't stab him, he fell onto my dagger." A cough interrupts us and we both turn our heads to the front to see the prince look at me, brow raised.

"You have something to say, Your Highness?" I say tilting my head to the side.

"Well, yes, I might have. I think I remember you stabbing me, there was no falling involved, whatsoever." I narrow my eyes slightly at his words.

"I remember you correcting me on my technical way to kill you. I just used your advice." I tell him with a sweet smile. He shakes his head, his curls flying around. They've gotten longer over the journey making me want to—no, no.

"I told you how to kill an Upyr, princess, not to kill me." I bite my lip in mock distress.

"What a bummer, it seems like we've got some kind of miscommunication going on there."

"Seems to happen a lot." He grumbles and I glare at him.

"What was that?" I hiss and ignore Kael's snicker beside me. My eyes flicker toward Edlyn who watches us with a small smile on her lips.

"Nothing." Cassian answers and I nod.

"I thought so," I say and he finally turns his head back to the front. The anger that simmers in my body guts me right then. My face hardens when I realize how everyone found their amusement in our bickering. This is not good. Well, besides Flynn, who rolls his eyes and grumbles incoherently.

"You two are awful." That is what I think he says.

~ 10 ~

We ride on for another few hours, the sun gradually rising in the sky. For once there are no clouds in sight and I can't help my gaze from flickering to the bracelet around my wrist which shimmers in the morning light. Kael switched places with Flynn in between, resulting in me making most conversation with the redhead and him occasionally grumbling an answer. It is not until hours pass that Flynn speaks up but not to me.

"Hey, Cas, I think we're awfully close to the borders of the next city. I would advise to outride it on the left." When Cassian doesn't answer I furrow my brows. I look at Flynn whose brows are drawn in, confusion written all over his face.

"Prince?" He asks again and I watch Cassian turn his head slightly to the side.

"We are on the right path, Flynn. I want to make a final stop before we reach Demeter."

The moment the rage oozes from Flynn's body beside me is clear. He looks at Cassian as if he's gone mad.

"Are you mad? We're on Protestant land, if someone recognizes you—"

"I'm aware of the threat, thank you." Cassian's response is sharp as his dark eyes meet Flynn's. A shudder runs over my spine at the look of him and for a moment, the shadows around him flicker. My heart stops at the look in his eyes. I thought he looked angry whenever his eyes were placed on me but I was wrong. This is what Cassian looks like when he's angry. I shiver again at the air that buzzes and forms his will around him. His eyes flicker toward me and the shadows disappear. I inhale what seems to be too loud before he turns his face back to the front.

"I'm the only one who is in danger to be recognized. Everyone got an hour to kill before we meet up again." He says. No one questions him again. We strut forwards as an eerie silence moves around the forest. I can feel Flynn's anger radiating off of him and can't help but feel threatened. If someone like Flynn thinks it is a risk to make a stop at the city why would Cassian risk being recognized? A tight band winds itself around my heart and squeezes mercifully. I watch the prince's stiff back for a few moments wondering what his plans are. Our reserves are not quite full but there are enough to travel toward the borders of Demeter within a few days. I look at Flynn to see his eyes trained on the prince's back as well.

"Is he stupid for doing this?" I ask quietly and his eyes flicker toward me. I try not to linger on the scar and white eye on his left side. He watches me for a moment before he shakes his head.

"Not stupid. Absolutely, life-threatening stupid." I narrow my gaze at his words. Anxiety starts to bubble in my chest and I harden my grip on the reins of Nighttail. With a light shove in her flank, she gallops up beside Honeycomb and I shoot Kael a small smile.

"Mind trading partners? Flynn seems not to be the conversational type." Kael snorts at that.

"Understatement of the century. Go ahead, princess." He falls behind to ride beside Flynn and I take his place beside Cassian. His face stays focused on the front as if he doesn't even notice the change in his partner. Still, I don't speak up as I let my eyes wander over the black stallion riding beside me, the strong thighs that grip the sides of the horse, and the hips that move balanced on top. Once I believed the most arousing picture was that of a naked body but I can confirm now that I changed my mind. Cassian riding a horse is probably one of the most attractive things I've seen in my life. Focus.

I open my lips intending to question him but he interrupts me without even looking at me.

"I'm glad you're getting along with my friends." I hesitate, ponding over his words for a moment.

"What do you mean?" I watch his eyes flicker down to the bracelet around my wrist and I blink surprised. His jaw clenches for a moment, his knuckles turning white as he grips the reins of his horse.

"It is a birthday present," I state, not knowing what to say.

"Looks great." His answer is short and stiff. I sigh. I can't believe this man is being jealous over his friends. I don't feel like I'm in a very generous mood so I egg him on.

"Kael is great, I can understand why you keep him close."

"Well, he is known for his charm and special skills." I blink in surprise at his words and suddenly the anger washes off his face. Regret of his words or something else takes place now.

"What do you mean by that?"

"Nothing."

"Nothing?"

"Yes. Nothing." I sigh aggravated by his short answers. We continue riding beside each other in silence for a few minutes before he speaks up again. This time in a much gentler tone.

"I wouldn't have expected you to wear it." I turn my head back to him to see his eyes trained on the bracelet.

"Why?"

"The golden strands, it's something we do at home. The gold is liquefied and formed into strands by the few witches that reside in the kingdom. They do it a lot in their hair, and on their face; it is a great gift and honor to be able to wear it. It presents the blood witches and Demeter in some kind of way." His eyes flicker up to my face. The meaning behind the gold in the bracelet goes deeper than I thought. I knew it was not normal to be shaped like this, it is as if I could feel the magic used on it.

"Do you expect me to hate everything that is linked to your kingdom?"

"Not my kingdom, my father's but—yes, I do. You made it clear what you think of me." I would think the stabbing would be a hint enough as well but still.

I shrug one shoulder and look at the bracelet.

"I don't detest the people in Demeter or their traditions. You're not representing every individual just like I am not representing the people who live in Aerwnya."

"Is that not what we are? Representatives?"

"Would be depressing if we were," I mumble. I do not think that just one person can represent a whole kingdom. There are so many little things, so many details that form the kingdom that it is impossible everything resides in their leader. Their leader might be a symbol of the subjects and the heart of the kingdom but it is the people that breathe life into the lands.

"What would we be without our subjects? We'd have no purpose whatsoever. Our subjects are still alive without us, they would still exist, live their lives and breathe into our lands. A kingdom is nothing without its followers. The Protestants don't seem to have a leader and they're doing fine."

I meet his gaze for a moment but quickly avert my eyes when I feel myself being sucked in by the green intensity. Dangerous thoughts swirl in my head and I barely manage to lock them down and away in the back of my mind.

"Don't you think it's kind of unwise to invade their lands?" I ask him and he looks back to the front shaking his head.

"They'll barely notice it and there is something I need to do."

"And what is that?" His head turns and he shoots me a boyish grin.

"Highly confidential but you'll find out. Soon enough." My shoulders fall slightly at the lack of an answer.

"If you're going to tell me anyway, why keep it a secret now?" I ask and his grin widens, exposing soft dimples. The thing trapped in my chest flutters.

"Where's the fun in that?" He tilts his head to the side mustering me. I'm too cowardly to answer or respond to his words. Instead, I turn my head to the front and ignore the deep rumble of his chuckle. For the first time, something close to peace settles in my chest. Before it crumbles again. Destroyed by the thoughts of betrayal that fight through me.

We proceed to ride beside each other. I feel the air becoming hotter and my heightened senses hear a jumbled murmur. The trees become fewer and fewer, the soil gets drier, and our horses more restless. The murmuring settles into voices. A thousand of them. I hear carriages, pots clattering, and people shouting, laughing, and cursing. The city is coming nearer. The others feel the shift in the air as well and it is as if I can sense Flynn's disarray. He still thinks this is a bad idea. We halt when Cassian tells us to and jumps off his stallion.

"We meet exactly here after two hours, I want everyone to go in two pairs. Whoever doesn't make it back in two hours gets left behind, I don't bother to haul your asses back here, understood?"

Everyone nods, besides me. I narrow my eyes at him as I get off my horse.

"Problem, princess?" Cassian asks me as if he can feel my irritation.

"No," I grumble while I feed Nighttail an apple and bind her around a bark. Kael binds Honeycomb beside her making both the horses neigh lightly.

Of course I have a problem. How can he just leave anyone behind if they're late? What if someone gets in danger or needs help? Is he just going to abandon them?

"No need to worry that rule doesn't include you," Kael speaks up and I look up at him surprised. I forget every time how tall he is when he stands instead of sitting on his horse.

"What do you mean?"

"I mean he would gladly haul your ass out of the city if you're late."

Well, that's comforting to know. I shoot a look at Cassian who obviously listens to our words. My eyes flicker to Eryx beside him, who's been awfully quiet during the last few days. His dark eyes are trained on me yet again before they flicker away.

I choose to ignore his strange behavior and walk over to Cassian whose face is tense in anticipation. Instead of halting in front of him I pass him and stop in front of Edlyn. Her hazel eyes flicker over my face unsure.

"You want to buddy up?" I ask her with a sheepish smile. She watches me for a moment before a grin splits her lips as if she knows what I am doing.

"It would be my honor."

We both turn and I catch Cassian´s raised brows, an arrogant look on his face.

"Well, what are we waiting for, wasn´t it you who initiated this stop."

Cassian sighs before he nods at Flynn who teams up with him.

"Let´s go." He grumbles making Kael chuckle as he teams up with Eryx.

~ 11 ~

I always thought that people like the Protestants were loud, vulgar creatures. Humans who lost their sense of reality and could see nothing through the fire of their rage and anger. They possess so many lands around the kingdoms that I can't count and they were going at it wanting more and more since I can remember. I don't know what I expected, maybe tents and small camps huddled on the dirty ground. Torches lit up over walkways and campfires glisten in the middle. What I didn't expect are proper buildings. Or a fully developed city, working resourcefully. Buildings are scattered across the land highly functional and beautiful with rugs hanging out the windows in various colors. Red, green, and blue materials flattering in the soft wind, curled ornaments stitched onto them.

I don't know if Cassian did it on purpose but the opening that borders the city leads right into a gigantic market. Stands are built up on both sides and filled with bowls that carry a thousand spices. Jugs filled with wine, sparkling juices, and a red liquid that seems to be rather popular among the customers. Lemons are swimming in the red drink and an old-looking woman lures me in and ushers me on to taste some of the drink. It takes Edlyn to tug on my sleeve before we saunter off and past jewelry stands, and tables filled with cotton and silk. The people eye us as we walk past but there is no recognition glistening in their gaze. They just see some unknown little girls that they can lure in to buy some of their goods.

I would never believe it if I didn't see it with my own eyes. This city is alive with happy people. Real people, mothers, fathers, daughters, and sons. The children are screaming in joy as they outrun their scolding mothers, bumping into our legs in the process. When a small boy looks up at me his eyes widen and he quickly runs past me. I turn and watch him run down the path while turning his head a few times.

I can't help the smile that spreads on my lips. This city is alive. I knew deep down, there had to be more. These soldiers that fight against us aren't any different than our armies. They are protecting their children and their wives. Maybe a few of them are evil-spirited like the one I fought against at the palace but there is also evil among the royals. Lord Romanov is a perfect example of that. If the king would've listened to me I'm sure these people would've agreed to a treaty. We have so much land in the kingdom how could we not spare them some? How could we fight against them, knowing they're doing it for their families?

Edlyn and I wander between the crowd that builds up and I'm distracted by an old woman that sells beautiful wind chimes. Small amethyst dangle from the rings. The crystals clink against each other when a soft breeze moves past and ruffles up my hair.

"Take a look dear, these are some special stones." The old woman speaks up in a scratchy voice. My eyes lift from the wind chime and travel over her small, hunched-over figure. She is dressed in a jewel-toned gown, light and practical for the warmer weather in the southwest. A transparent scarf is wrapped around her head, her skin a deep color, painted with lines.

"Special stones? How do you mean?" I ask her as I step a bit closer eyeing the other wind chimes. There is one small enough that it fits on your hand, with small amethysts dangling from the ring above. A wire is wrapped around the ring and bend into the same swirls I saw on the rugs that are hanging out of most windows.

"The stones are rumored to be enchanted, a good luck charm for a young woman like you." Something in her voice makes me shudder slightly when I feel Edlyn step up beside me.

"Enchanted? By who?" She asks the woman skeptically. I watch her raise a brow and cross her arms.

in front of her chest, her demeanor cold. Her dark skin glows in the afternoon sun, making her look like an angel of wrath sent down to our world.

The woman arches a brow as she lets her dark eyes wander over my friend. I can't make out the color of them because the schal throws a dark shadow over her face.

"Who knows? Maybe the Fatums, an enchantress, or maybe it was one of you, Magda?" Edlyn's body locks up in a matter of seconds.

"You know the Fatum?" I question and lean forward, the wind chimes long forgotten. The old woman grins at me dubiously before she gestures with a hand to her products. She doesn't need to speak up. I know what she wants. Buy a wind chime and ask questions.

"Let's go," Edlyn whispers beside me and I shoot her a wary look. Her brows shoot up surprised that I would even want information from an old hag.

"What's the harm?"

"She's clearly after your money." The old woman snickers and Edlyn shoots her a glare.

"A bit condescending, aren't you?" She asks her and Edlyn narrows her eyes.

"Well, why wouldn't you answer her question without wanting her to buy something?"

"Because you're holding up the line and I think the princess can afford to buy a little wind chime from an old hag like me." My head swivels around to the woman. How does she know I'm a princess? Or the princess? Edlyn laughs coldly.

"What in hell are you talking about?"

"You know what I'm talking about." The woman looks at me again and a shiver runs down my spine.

"Let's go." Edlyn tugs at my arm again but I shake my head. I turn back around to the woman knowing that I'm playing with the devil right now. Still, I point my finger at the smallest wind chime.

"I'll take that one, please."

"Wise choice." She nods and I can see at the corner of my eye that Edlyn is rolling her eyes. We watch the woman pick up the wind chime and wrap it in lilac paper before carefully slipping it into a small sack.

I fish out a few gold coins and pass them to her while she passes me the sack. She eyes the coins for a second and I roll my eyes.

"If you know my title you know these are real."

"I'm not one to be fooled because of arrogance." The woman says and bites the coin.

Both Edlyn and I grimace when she reveals her rotten yellow teeth. Well, good luck with the one she's trading those gold coins for.

"Well?" I ask, my foot tapping nervously as she slips the coins somewhere inside her gown.

"The Fatums are the ones traveling between the realms. The realms of gods and humans, of nothing and everything. They decide how life will proceed, they decide what steps into your path. Fate is molded by their hands." Edlyn scoffs beside me and my reaction isn't any different.

"We already knew that. Everyone knows that." I tell her, narrowing my eyes. The woman shrugs her bony shoulders.

"You didn't specify what you wanted to know, girl."

"If I were out to meet them, where would I go?" I press and take a step forward. Something flickers in her eyes as a small smirk settles on her wrinkly lips. She knows more than she wants to reveal.

"One does not meet the Fatum. The Fatum meet you if they want to." I furrow my brows at her cryptic answer.

"But how do they know that I want to meet them?"

"They know."

"How?"

"They know."

Edlyn scoffs again and turns around, clearly exasperated by this woman.

"Let's go this is not worth it. Before she calls the soldiers onto us." She tells me but I'm not ready to leave yet. If I follow Aerwyn's advice I need to find the Fatums however difficult it might be.

"If I wanted to, I'd already yelled down the market that a blood witch is wandering our lands." The woman says and they both glare at each other for a moment. I step in front of Edlyn and look at the woman raising my chin and locking my shoulders.

"I know you know more. I bought your wind chime, you owe me a real answer." She musters me for a moment, her cold eyes wandering over my face. I don't cower and stare right back at her. I need to know how to find them. It's the only thing that's holding me together these past weeks. They know everything, and they will be able to tell me what to do. That all of this was worth it. How I'm connected to everything and why everyone thinks I'm the one who molds life. Besides my changing form, I have no ounce of magic in me. The amount of faith these people have in me is admirable but it is uncalled for. There has to be some accident or mix-up because I think I could tell if I was able to create life.

The woman takes her sweet time before answering. She unwraps a golden sweet and chews it in her mouth, making Edlyn fake gag behind her hand.

When the woman is finished chewing that awful sweet she finally answers.

"The path you are on right now is the one that will lead you to them. Demeter is a kingdom with many opportunities. Sometimes things are not what they seem."

"This is foolery, we're leaving." Edlyn grabs my wrist and drags me away with her strength. I don't protest, confused by the hag's words but I turn my head while being dragged away when the woman speaks up again.

"Carina! Good luck to you and your companions, you will surely need it." An ominous look forms on her face but Edlyn is dragging me away from the stand and through the crowd.

"Why the hell would you ask her that, Carina? This woman is a liar and a Protestant!" Edlyn scolds me, her grip on my wrist becoming painful.

"Would you stop dragging me for a moment?" I hiss and tug at her grip. To my surprise, it slips right out of her hold and she staggers back with such force that I fear she will soar through the crowd. My eyes widen and I quickly shoot my arms out grabbing hers so she doesn't fall backward.

"Fuck, sorry, sorry. I forgot the whole strength thing." I look her over to see if she's all right, the panic subsiding when I see that I didn't hurt her. When a chuckle disrupts her and her body starts to shake I look up surprised to see a grin splitting her soft lips. Her chuckle turns into a hearty laugh and for a moment I fear she's going mad. She tries to contain her laughter while I continue staring at her until she gasps out the words.

"You . . . almost threw me over the whole damn crowd." A chuckle bubbles out of me and I don't know if it is caused by the surreal situation or if her laugh is just too contagious. She grabs my wrist just as I grab hers so we don't fall, our laughter ringing in the crowd. I barely notice the curious glances around us, the people that stop for a short moment until our laughter finally dies down.

Tears escape my eyes which I quickly wipe off my cheeks as I look at my best friend. Her cheeks flushed and the intensity in her eyes is what makes me grab her shoulders and pull her in for a hug. It feels like I'm almost crushing her bones but her grip is just the same as we cling to each other. The people weave around us, some smile and some nod their heads. I can't acknowledge them enough because, for the first time in the past weeks, it feels like everything is going to be fine.

"I am sorry." I halt mid-sip and turn my head to look at Edlyn whose gaze is turned down to the piece of stale bread in her hands. After half an hour of wandering, we decided to settle down in a secluded alley, the bread and the jug of red wine our only companions. The bustle of the market is a constant ring in my ears and I'm sure I wouldn't be able to hear it if I still had my human form.

"What are you sorry for?" She turns to look at me with a rueful smile on her lips.

"For not telling you all of this." She gestures with her arms and I don't know if she just means the fact that she is a blood witch or everything else as well. The magic of the kingdoms.

"Please don't apologize."

"But I think I need to." I shake my head holding the wine out for her. She grabs the jug and takes a swig. Her lips tint red from the liquid.

"You don't. You actually don't have to explain yourself at all. Now that I've heard what this world is made of. Now that I've seen this city, the things on the journey. I don't know what I would've done if I was in your place." I tell her honestly. I mean how would she have started to explain all of this? It would've seemed completely out of the blue and if I'm being honest with myself I know I wouldn't have believed her.

"I should've tried. But I was scared. I have seen—felt—what my heritage does to people." A dark shadow moves over her face and my heart squeezes in pain. I quickly grab her hand so she looks at me.

"Just to make one thing clear, Edlyn. I am not and I never was angry or disgusted because you are a Magda. That was never the point and it will never be the point. People are disgusting for holding you guilty for the things your ancestors did. You are not them."

"But they did kill a lot of people. I killed a lot of people." She looks at me and I know she isn't lying. The weight of death is painted in her irises, swirling, and haunting her every day.

"But do you still do it?"

She shakes her head.

"People make mistakes, Edlyn. It is our choice if we forgive them if we let them redeem themselves, or if we charge them guilty for past mistakes. But mostly it is our choice to forgive ourselves. If you can't forgive yourself no one else can." She stays quiet for a moment. I watch the shadows disappear as her jaw clenches. She takes a deep breath before she looks at me again. My eyes fly over her face searching for the delicate soft girl that was my best friend for my whole life. I can still see her in the softness of those hazel eyes but now I realize there is more. Strength, power, and centuries' worth of wise essence.

"I was scared. I thought you would never talk to me again."

I thought so too. I thought that I might not be able to recover from the betrayal but I was wrong. I was foolish to believe the feelings that came with the shock. They disappeared after a while of thinking, they dissolved when I saw the way Cassian treated his friends and they vanished when remembering what Edlyn means to me.

"I watched you grow up over the years. You were so delicate, so easily breakable. A human girl that is supposed to be our leader. But I never doubted you once. The fire inside you is untamable and I knew one day you would lead us to the life we dreamed of for centuries. You were a job at first but then you became my friend. You saw me for who I am not for what I did. You didn't see the blood, the pain, the horror that I've dealt with. And you became my sister. My soul sister."

I don't know what to say. I still don't know her full story, the things she's seen. I thought it wouldn't be possible to be like her after the things she has outlived. To still be this lively and warm and kind.

"You were the first person to show me what love felt like. Gave me the feeling that I deserved it."

Something tugs at my heartstrings and I put my cheek on her shoulder breathing her calming scent.

"Thank you," I murmur when she puts her cheek atop my head.

"For what?"

"For being my friend. For never leaving my side and listening to me whine about such little and irritable things. For this." I hold up my wrist with the bracelet on it.

"It's nothing." I look up at her and raise a brow. "It's not nothing. It's everything, Edlyn. If there was a chance to choose your family in life I would pick you over everyone else. Always."

"Is that a tear I see, Lynn? How touching."

We both look up surprised to see Cassian leaning against a wall opposite of us. I flinch in surprise before my eyes narrow.

"What are you doing here?"

"Picking you up." He tells me with a grin and I shoot Edlyn a look whose face is lined with guilt.

"Is this some kind of plan you two came up with?"

"Not me! He compelled me." My friend protests and I raise my brows.

"As if you would let me compel you," Cassian says with an eye roll before he pushes himself off the wall. I watch him stagger towards us and take the bottle out of Edlyn's hands, taking a sniff at the liquor.

"Are you trying to make her drunk before my surprise?"

"I thought I'd make your presence more bearable." Edlyn bites back, shrugging one shoulder. What surprise?

"Are we late? I thought we still had an hour." I say and finally stand up dusting off my breaches. I hoped we could spend more time in the city and I could forget about the fact that we will reach Demeter in the next few days. The prospect of meeting King Ronan after all this time again is nothing I'm looking forward to. And especially meeting his other son again as well.

"We still have time. But something is waiting for you." Cassian says while he glances at Edlyn for a moment. I can't help but feel like something is up.

"For me?"

"For you."

I turn to look at my friend who nods at me as if to usher me on.

"I'm meeting Kael for something anyway." She says as she gets up and I blink at her. Are they teaming up? Against me?

"I can join you, I think Cassian can keep his company to himself," I say and look at the prince who grants me a disapproving look.

"It's one hour, princess."

"Even five minutes are not worth my time," I tell him and he huffs out a laugh. I don't want to go with him to wherever he planned. But I can't stop the curiosity from bubbling up in my body wondering what he came up with. I should be smarter than this. We should be smarter than this. It would be safer if we all go back to the horses and leave the city before someone recognizes us like the old lady at the stand.

"What do you want?" Cassian asks now, stepping closer.

"You have nothing you can give me that I already have," I say and cross my arms in front of my body.

"I beg to differ."

"You're a fool then." I take a step closer and he narrows his eyes.

"A fool for you, if that is what you mean." I roll my eyes at his words.

"What do you want?" He asks.

Nothing. I don't want anything but I love the way he's getting aggravated just because I'm not following his plan. I shrug lazily. "Come up with something." I hear Edlyn stifling a chuckle.

"Okay. I owe you. Would you come with me then?" I smile sweetly.

"Lead the way, Your Highness."

~ 12 ~

We part ways with Edlyn to follow the path of the secluded alley. I don't speak when I follow the prince, watching how his back muscles shift as he walks in front of me. We walk deeper and deeper into the heart of the city and after a long time, I feel like I have lost count of the times we turn around a corner. Either the prince is leading us toward a ridiculously far place or he's just walking in circles to wear me out and get on my nerves. I stay quiet behind him not uttering a word as I process what could be happening. He doesn't speak either, doesn't tell me where we're going, or why he feels the need to keep it a secret. I wonder if he knows this city. He has to, the way he slips around the alleys like a shadow as if he has a memorized map inside his mind.
I don't know how I expected my birthday to go but I didn't expect to be walked to death. The heat is excruciating, burning through my dark suit without any effort.
"Are we close?" I speak up, frustrated with all this walking. The prince doesn't stop but he looks over his shoulder nodding.
"Just a few more minutes."
 "Listen, if this is some kind of master plan to keep me fit I assure you it's doing nothing." Cassian chuckles at that before he stops walking. We're standing in front of an archway covered with a colorful rug. He swipes it to the side and gestures for me to walk up the steps that are hidden behind.
"No master plan here, princess, just showing the guest of honor the best view."
"Guest of honor? I would say I feel flattered but who knows how you treat your guests." I walk past him and up the stairs. I ignore the fresh smell of pines and wind. I can feel him climb the stairs behind me and the light dims down with the small windows that are etched into the sides of the walls. It looks like some kind of dungeon but the fact that we walk up defeats the purpose.

"Just so you know, if you brought me here to kill me it's kind of useless."

"I wouldn't dare insult you with an ambush." He says and my muscles lock up for a second.

"Didn't work the first time," I mumble and I know he hears it because he remains silent. We continue to climb the stairs until another rug appears and he swipes it to the side for me to reveal some kind of closed balcony. My heartbeat is already pounding against my ribs from the damn steps but when I enter the room it seems to triple. The room is in some sort of hexagonal form and every edge has a big opening etched into it. Windows without glass make the light pour into the room like it's bathed in it. The floor is filled with lush cushions and rugs and oriental lanterns are littered on the floor. The canopy spans over the place is out of a midnight blue material, sheer enough to see the clouds travel along the sky and I wish I could lay here in the night to see the stars glitter against it. I make my way over to one window, my fingers traveling over the grainy texture of the wall while I lean out. A small breath passes my lips.

Blue, red, green, yellow. A sea of colors and emotions, smells and feelings. You can see the whole city from this point. You can watch every little colorful house built beside each other, every person wandering the streets. Children are skipping town and if I squint my eyes I can make out the market Edlyn and I wandered through an hour ago. This is the heart of the city.

I turn around the swirling emotions dancing in my body when I look at the prince. He's still standing at the entrance, his hip perched against the archway, his strong arms crossed over his chest. His eyes are glowing intently as he watches my reaction.

"Why did you bring me here?" I question him, not moving from the window. I'm not trusting my body enough to not do something stupid if I move. He finally starts to move and pushes off the archway to walk a few steps over.

"This is the first time you're in a different city. I thought a good view would be essential."

"Huh." I exhale not knowing what to say to that. He steps even closer, the air rustling against the lanterns around us.

"Your first birthday away from Aerwyna. I can imagine it being difficult." My eyes fly up to his in surprise. I didn't expect him to actively address the fact that it's my birthday today.

"It's not," I say, and before I know it his hand grabs ahold of my wrist and we both look down. His long fingers wrapped around my wrist like a bracelet, chaining me in. His skin got tanner over our journey because we are exposed to the sun all the time. The more we travel south the deeper it gets but mine doesn't have the affinity to get any darker. The only thing that changed are my freckles which are more prominent now. I watch his thumb graze over the bracelet and the stone embedded into it.

"My father never actually celebrated my birthday after my mother's death," I say quietly as I watch his thumb draw circles on my skin. My throat closes up but I still feel the need to continue, to bathe in this small moment of peace.

"He would allow me to have celebrations but I never cared much for it. I preferred to spend the day with Edlyn and my brother. So this is nothing new." I'm hesitant to meet his eyes, still not grasping his intentions. His eyes are cast down, a small frown etched into his face.

"You would've deserved anything you wanted, princess. You deserve anything you want." I pull my wrists out of his hold and take a step back clearing my throat awkwardly. I don't like the shift in the air that surrounds us every time we get close.

"It's no big deal."

"How can you say that?" He turns suddenly, devastated, his hands running through his dark hair. I watch him for a moment, surprised by his sudden desperation.

"How can you not see yourself? Your whole life got turned upside down, your beliefs, your viewings and you're just coping,"

I wouldn't say I'm coping because the first few days I was indeed crumbling.

"You're taking it as if it's normal for you. And I guess it is normal for you, to accommodate situations, to people, no matter how they treat you. Daragon was a bastard, Carina." I flinch when he speaks my father's name. Cassian turns back around to look at me.

"I'm not taking shit from anyone, Cassian. But I hate to break it to you, I'm not the great heroine you all think I am. I don't know who I am, all right? Maybe I am Aerwyn's long-lost daughter but I don't have any memory of it. I don't have any magic I can wield and create life! I just know what I have learned in this life. I just have the memory of *this life*. And if you think I am so shallow that I care about my birthday, when I'm in a situation like this, you don't know me at all."

I shake my head, suddenly angered.

Why is he the one angry over my situation?

Yes, Daragon was an awful father but he was the only one I had. I don't know this Kaycen they're talking about and I don't have the energy to grieve for a father I don't know and who is already dead. I'm not forcing myself into a messed up situation like that.

"Who said you need to be Aerwyn's daughter?" He asks now, his eyes fiery hot. I shake my head and laugh frustrated.

"You! You and everyone else! Since I turned—changed—whatever you might call it everyone's been looking at me. Waiting, lurking. I can see it in Edlyn's eyes, feel it in Flynn's tense shoulders. I can see it in the way your hands clench or Kael's smile turns too bright. You're looking at me like I'm some kind of Saint sent from the heavens to save you all. Well, great fucking news I'm not. I killed my own subjects, tricked by a man to believe that they were guilty. And maybe they were. It doesn't change the fact that I have their blood on my hands. So stop waiting, stop looking at me like that! *I can't bear it, I hate the feel of it. I'm not good. I never was and I accepted that. I don't want to be.*" I have to inhale deeply, my chest rising and falling rapidly. Cassian crosses the small balcony with two steps before he's standing in front of me. He ducks his head down so I can't escape his gaze.

"You are far from bad, Carina, you are the epitome of good. The essence of everything I am not. Do you think I care about the fact that you're Aerwyn's daughter? Do you think I would care if you weren't magical at all? It wouldn't change a thing for me if you were human and it doesn't change a thing for me that you don't have any magic. You are enough. Because you're the only thing I need to survive. Every kingdom is blessed to have you living under them and they should treat you as such. I will make sure that everyone will kneel in front of you and will feel honored that you're walking among them." His voice drops low and I can't remember how we ended up here.

Our noses bump slightly against each other, my heart beating in a strong rhythm. Something is different.

Was it always this intense?

My blood sings and my fingers curl. I clench the fabric of my tunic trying to hold myself back. Trying to ignore the intense burning that seems to ooze off his skin.

My bottom lip grazes his for a moment and I squeeze my eyes shut, not able to move, think, or feel. The thoughts in my head are pure chaos, whirling spewing words at me. You hate him. He's a traitor. You hate him. Do you hate him?

Just when I think that I can't hold myself back anymore the prince sighs. His forehead drops against mine for a moment sending a thrum from the skin-to-skin contact through my whole body. I open my eyes when he retreats and watch him fish out a roll of parchment. My cheeks are burning in embarrassment and I try to scold myself. How did I let this escalate so easily? I may have done him wrong and I judged too quickly. I give him that but I'm done with this. I'm done with him and I and whatever was between us. I left it behind in Aerwyna.

"This is for you. I planned to give it to you when we arrived in Demeter but it's your birthday and . . . whatever." He pulls his hand back but I'm quicker and slip the roll out of his hands. I raise a brow and try to overcome my embarrassment from the moment before. But to my surprise, I see a light red hue linger on his high cheekbones. Is he embarrassed?

I start to unroll the parchment and Cassian turns his back to me, presumedly staring out of the window. I ignore him and grant my rapidly beating heart a break when I try to make sense of the words and sentences of the scroll. It's a lot of semantics, and fake politeness but when I read further my mouth drops open silently.

When I finish reading the scroll my eyes fly back up and read it again. And again. Talks of armies, support, disregarding laws, traditions, and administration of the system. I look back up to find Cassian's back still turned on me. His shoulders are tense, his muscles taught.

"What is this?"

"Didn't I already say? Your birthday present."

He turns back around and I blink at him. He doesn't move. I don't move.

"You're giving me freedom?"

"If you want to call it that." He shrugs and I swallow. This scroll entails the details of my reign. The fact that Daragon fled the kingdom and Lord Andréas isn't the next in line because I am. But if one would go after the right rules I would have to marry Cassian to take over Aerwyna. But I refused to marry him. And he somehow convinced the kingdoms to let me reign . . . without a consort?

"How did you even do this? When did you do this?" I can only guess how much convincing and work this took. He would have to address the King of Oceanus, his father, and Hector. The advisors of every king and their high priests.

"When I took my oath I did everything I could to convince the kings. To let you have your kingdom." He says it as if it is no big deal. Barely an effort but I know that is not true.

"You mean to tell me you pleaded with the kings and their advisors to let me have my kingdom and rule without a husband, three years ago?"

"What else was I supposed to do, so you could back out of marrying me?"

"Uhm I don't know maybe anything else!" I hiss and his brows narrow.

"Are you angry . . . at me?"

"Yes!"

No. Of course not.

How could I be angry at him? How long did he have the approval of the kings and their advisors? Is he giving me this now because I'm refusing to marry him? Or would he have given it to me anyway? My hand sinks while I look at him. I don't know what to feel. He's done everything so I could be free and I feel like I'm supposed to be angry but how can I be?

"You said you didn't want to marry me." He speaks up bitterly and I look up at him, swallowing. His face is tinted in darkness, the green in his eyes lost its intensity.

"I did."

"So then why are you angry? This certificate allows you to go back after we cancel the marriage. There are no strings attached, I swear." But how am I supposed to go back with Adales wanting me dead? Wherever he might be we all know he will strike sooner or later. Maybe if I go to the Fatums and they somehow tell me how to defeat him I can go back afterward. But maybe I don't need to defeat him. His worries are unconfirmed, I'm no threat to him and his powers. But the things he did, the people he slaughtered in his anger were supposed to be my people. Half of my blood is of the Faye. The people who were slaughtered. It's a lost reign, I have nothing to rule over besides the humans residing in Aerwyna.

"I don't blame you for being angry at me,"

Ripped out of my thoughts by Cassian's voice I look back up to see him pacing, a grimace on his face.

"What I did behind your back was wrong but it was for your safety. Be angry at me for that but this isn't fair. I am willing to let you go if that's what you want. What else do I need to do for you to forgive me?"

His steps halter and I open my lips not knowing what to say. But before I can even utter a word a cold blade is pressed against my throat, another pressed to my stomach. My breath hitches when I feel a body pressing itself at my back, an unbearable stench clogging my nose. The prince's eyes widen and six masked men jump through the windows out of nowhere armed to the teeth.

"What do we have here? It's a long way from your kingdom, Princess Katarina."

~ 13 ~

"I swear, if you just touch one hair on her head you will regret it." Cassian's voice thunders through the small space as the six men corner around him but he doesn't look the slightest bit threatened. His eyes are stuck on me and I don't dare to move. If he would just have the blade against my throat it would be easy to use my hips and legs. But one wrong move and he will slice open my stomach with no mercy. So I try to stay as still as possible as a dirty laugh escapes—what I think is the leader—the throat behind me.

"You are on Protestant land, Princeling. We can do whatever we want."

"I would love to see you try." An arrogant smirk moves on the prince's lips as he straightens his shoulders. His eyes glow such an intense green that the men around him shuffle their feet. Their faces are covered by fluttering fabric, the eyes a striking lilac color. My brows furrow because somehow I'm sure I've seen that color before. One of the men's eyes flickers towards me for a moment before they focus back on Cassian, who sighs.

"You really picked the wrong day to piss me off." He says and suddenly black shadows start to trace along his hands and body. I gasp quietly when I see the inky color stain his hands, talons growing out of his nails. My heart stutters when I see the canines grow and the beautiful green in his eyes disappear. The sky grows darker and the men start to look around panicked but the hold on the blades around me doesn't falter.

"You make one wrong move and your love will be dead in seconds." The blade presses tighter against my throat and I feel a trickle of blood trail down my skin.

"What do you want?" I hiss at the man behind me while Cassian freezes and growls. He growls. A shiver runs down my spine at the murderous look on his face.

"We want revenge!" One of the men calls and they all howl in response. How vile.

I raise my brows and look at them, trying to look down at them while a blade is pressed against my throat.

"Revenge for what?"

"You know for what, princess. Our people died and you and the prince were involved in fighting against them."

"Yeah, because they were attacking us, you idiot." I snap back and Cassian snickers at my comment. I relax a bit, knowing that if we were cast in real danger he'd act differently. The shadows are still swirling around him but there's a flicker of amusement in his gaze. He's letting me play. The man behind me growls and winds a hand around my throat squeezing. Cassian's amusement disappears in a flash and he steps forward.

"Touch her again and your fingers are going to rot and fall off. For every bruise, I will cut off one limb, stack you all on a pile before I burn your souls, and send you to Gehenna where you relive your death over and over for burning eternity." The grip of the man softens and I can't help but grin.

"He has some small anger issues," I mutter, making Cassian's eyes narrow at the snide remark. Apparently, the men have enough of our little play and the temperature drops visibly. They attack with a roar and my eyes widen. Cassian might be strong but can he take out six men at once, however untrained they are.

"Now you can watch your lover die in front of your eyes." The man murmurs in my ear and disgust shivers through me. I stomp on his boots making him yelp and yank me around. I ignore the yells from the men and use my momentum to knock my forehead against his. Hard. The man lets out a curse as he stumbles back and I unsheathe the dagger at my boot in one movement. I slightly bend my knees and get into a defensive stance. The man pounces at me again swinging his two Talwar at me. I duck down and land a kick against his knee that makes him stumble.

Gods, why did I choose to come without a sword?

A dagger against two Talwar, it's practically impossible. I continue to duck down and swipe my dagger but I only slice

through lots of fabric. My eyes flicker through the window they sneaked in and a small plan forms in my mind while the adrenaline floods through my veins, pumping the blood at a fast pace. Instead of ducking further, I take steps forward. The Protestant is so concentrated on fighting me and keeping his stance that he doesn't notice that I'm cornering him. A few steps further and I can kick him out that window.
A burning sensation runs through my arm when one blade pierces my skin and I hiss.
"You bastard."
The Protestant grins but his joy doesn't last when he suddenly freezes. My gaze narrows as I watch his arms pressed to his sides, the blades dropping from his hands. The only thing he can move is his eyes that flit behind me. I whirl around to see Cassian standing behind me. A low gasp escapes my lips when I see that all six Protestants are lying on the ground. They look fairly normal, with no cuts or bruises, and no slices in the skin. It is their faces—oh gods.
Their faces are all drained of blood, their eyes wide open. The lilac color vanished and made a place for pitch black. But the most horrific look is the blood that runs out of their noses, their mouth, and their eyes. My gaze flickers back to the prince who approaches me, shadows dancing at his hands.
"What did you do?" I whisper horrified. Yes, I wanted to throw the Protestant out of the window but I hoped he would survive and I wouldn't need to kill him.
"They got what they deserved." He says and steps up beside me, his eyes placed on the last man alive. My blood freezes when I turn around and realize that Cassian is using his powers to paralyze the Protestant. The man's face looks drained, his skin turning ashen, his eyes flickering around in fear.
"Not so tough looking now, are you?" Cassian taunts beside me and saunters toward the unmoving man. He doesn't respond as

tears trail down his cheek and I have to avert my eyes when he wets his pants. An awful stench wafts around us.

"Speak." The prince says in a frosty manner and the Protestant regains the ability to move his mouth.

"I am sorry—sorry, please." Cassian sighs dramatically.

"It's always the same. All talk and no action. They all resort to begging in the end. Look where it got them." He stops behind the man and gestures to his companions. I don't dare to turn around, the stale scent of iron is enough to make me nauseous. The Protestant escapes a sob.

"Please-p-please what can I do?" The man sobs out and I can't move. I can't breathe. I can just stare at Cassian who's standing behind the man with no trace of gentleness in his features. His intense gaze is placed on me as I stand frozen.

"You threatened my—princess, that was a wrong fucking move and usually I would crush you into nothingness because that's what you are. But I grant you a chance to redeem yourself." The Protestant escapes a shuddering breath of relief. But I don't move, I see what's glimmering in Cassian's eyes and it is nothing good.

He finally steps away from the man and nears me.

"Neal."

He tells the man while he watches me. The force that has a grip on the man compels him to his knees. He's kneeling in his urine and I can't stand the picture. I look at Cassian and shake my head.

"Let him go." He cocks his head to the side when he reaches me,

"But I haven't even had my fun with him yet."

I grit my teeth at his taunt, it feels like I'm looking at a stranger. No. It feels like I'm talking to the Cassian that I knew before he came to the castle.

"You've humiliated him enough. Let's just get out of this damn city." I hiss while his eyes fly over my face.

"As you wish, princess." He bows before he turns back to the man. My gut tells me that even though he agrees he's still not finished with the man.

"I always wondered how it would feel like if my insides turn to acid. Why don't you tell us?"

A piercing scream explodes around us in such a horrific way that I have to slap my hands over my ears. My eyes widen when I see the man writhing on the ground, screaming his lungs out. There is no visible injury and Cassian is looking at his nails as if he has nothing to do with this. My eyes tear up as I watch the man wither and scream until his voice is hoarse from the excruciating pain that travels through his body.

My lungs tear apart with every breath I try to force into them. Infuriating anger ripples through me and I stalk over to the prince and shove his chest. He doesn't move one bit as I glare up into his face.

"Are you mad? I told you to let him go!" I yell over the screaming man. I clench my hands, my nails digging into my palms and the pain distracts me from the horrific wailing of the man. Cassian's blazing eyes meet mine as he drops his lazy stance.

"He threatened you. If he thought he could get away with his little attack unharmed he is a fool."

"Yes, he threatened me and I had the situation under control. Let him go, Cassian!"

I shove his chest again so hard that he grabs my wrists in a bruising grip. I try to wriggle out of it but he doesn't budge.

"Under control my ass! *YOU* wanted to shove him out of the window. That lucky bastard would've survived." He shakes his head as if he's disappointed and I narrow my eyes.

"Because I wanted him to survive. We are in their city, Cas, and of course, they feel threatened by us. Did we let them leave when they were in Aerwyna?"

"They attacked the palace, it was their fault. If they would get you alone they wouldn't grant you any mercy." His voice drops low as he dips his face down. I don't waver in my decision.

"So because they want to kill us we should do it too?"

"That's how it works, princess."

"Don't call me that and let go." I wriggle again to get away from him and to my surprise he lets me go. The man is still screaming and instead of shouting at the price I look at him pleadingly.

"Please. Stop whatever you're doing to him. If we kill them all we are not better than them."

He looks at me, his gaze flickering as he hesitates.

"Let's get out of here and continue our journey, he has suffered enough."

"If we let him live they could think we are weak, vulnerable."

"Or they think that we carry compassion that we are not out for blood." I take two steps closer to him again and wrap my fingers around his wrists, gently. His eyes drop down to watch my hands.

"Please, Cas, let him go. I want to leave."

I stare into his eyes and block out the sobs of the man. His screaming eases but I know it is not due to lesser pain but because his voice has given out. Cassian turns blurry in front of me before he sighs.

"Fine." I quickly wipe a tear away that escaped and turn to the Protestant. He's lying on the ground in a fetal position, silent sobs escaping his lips. Blood is running out his nose but to my relief, there is no blood coming out of his eyes or his mouth. I exhale for a moment before my eyes flicker to the prince. His green eyes meet mine without an ounce of guilt. He would've killed this man if I hadn't stopped him. He wouldn't even bat an eye if he kills him, with no mercy nor forgiveness. Whatever his motives are it's not acceptable. Killing someone in self-defense is something different.

But purposely dragging out someone's death, and making them suffer like a lunatic is something someone does without a soul.

"Don't look at me all condescending. If this man had the chance he would kill you without a second thought."

I don't answer him. I don't look at him when I walk past. We need to get to Demeter as fast as possible and finally cancel this engagement.

Demeter

~ 14 ~

I don't talk to Cassian when we leave the balcony, rush down the steps, and dive back into the chaos of the city. He stays uncharacteristically quiet while he leads us through the labyrinth of the alleys until we meet the others in the forest.

I don't talk to him during the journey again and I don't even spare him a glance. I know the others know. Edlyn tries to find out what happened but after a look of mine, she remains silent.

Over the next five days, we travel without many breaks, and when we do we rest for only two to three hours. Edlyn and Kael take turns in riding beside me and I enjoy their company. Kael tries to lighten the mood with bad jokes and innuendos that make Flynn grumble but the packed air around us doesn't shift. I feel bad that the others have to suffer through it. Cassian is as rigid and cold as an ice block. He is angry and I don't know why. I am the one who is supposed to be angry. He is torturing people on my behalf, even though I never asked him for it.

How would he feel if I killed people in his name? He would probably bathe in happiness that madman.

Even though I feel guilty for the way Cassian snaps at the others in his bad mood I don't make an effort to apologize. I wasn't wrong and if he wants to ignore the fact that he tortured these people it's his responsibility. We could've scared them off with no effort but he had to make a show out of it.

So we all endure five days of silence and the occasional jest until we cross the borders of Demeter. Giddiness wipes away the small bit of anger that resides in my body. The air is so fresh that I wonder if the magic that floods the lands has some kind of effect on it. Instead of traveling right through the cities as I hoped, Flynn leads us through another forest. Pine trees litter the lands around us as the mood visibly lightens. They feel like they're back home. A certain buzz travels around the group and I watch Kael's hands tighten on the reins of Honeycomb as we ride through another pine forest.

"I fear you have a slight obsession with pine," I state and he flashes me a charming smile.

"We like to think that it complements our eyes." He blinks repeatedly and I grin. He is right though, the color of the trees does remind me of the eyes of an Upyr. Flynn picks up his pace and we all join him. With the buzzing happiness, even I find myself excited.

After all this traveling and sleeping on the cold ground, my body is in desperate need of a bath. And a bed. If I ever have any time for luxury like that, my priorities lie in canceling the engagement, asking King Ronan about the Fatum, and finding them. Preferably in that order but I´ll work with what I get.

My eyes flicker to the satchel attached to Nighttail´s flank where the small wind chime is stuffed in. Beside lays, the crumbled scroll Cassian gifted me for my birthday. My brain can´t grasp how a person can do something like obtain me my freedom and then turn and enjoy torturing someone. I spiral in my thoughts so much that I don´t notice when the others stop their horses. Kael reaches for my reins and stops Nighttail gently. My head flies up examining the spot. We have broken out of the woods and an enormous mountain extends before our eyes.

I inhale a gasp and hope that no one hears it when my heart gallops into a swift rhythm.

It´s breathtaking.

The mountain is so high its tip dips into the soft clouds that soar in the sky. Pine trees are littered everywhere as if they were soldiers protecting a sacred treasure. The air sizzles around me, whispers and sings. The mountain has almost a hypnotic effect on me, drawing me in, and telling me that every problem will evaporate the second I´m under its protection.

But while the mountain is beautiful as ever it is the castle that takes my breath away. The Sebestyen castle is surrounded by an ugly dark wall that is supposed to ward the dim castle from intruders but the coldness of it makes it look like a prison and not like a royal palace. The opaque bricks were always suffocating, the garden was the only soft thing about my home. But the Moreau castle is the complete opposite.

"Holy Fuck." I whisper and feel Kael lean close to me but I can't drag my eyes from the palace.

"Welcome to the Moreau Court, princess." He says teasingly as I muster the white castle. Yes, white. There is no wall, anything that protects the beautiful architecture. The walls of the castle are ridiculously tall and are made out of some kind of material that looks like white marble. But it can't be, can it? Thousands of windows are carved and with my enhanced vision, I can see the swirls that are painted on the prismatic glass that shines magically when the sun graces it with its rays. The castle itself is sturdy yet elegant but it's not just its beauty that makes it so mystical. It's the fact that the castle is joined by the mountain. It looks like it got chiseled out of the stone of the mountain and they made some kind of tunnel or connection. The castle *is* the mountain.

"You said the castle was up on the mountain," I say my throat dry as I finally pry my eyes from the view and look at Kael. The group stays quiet but I can feel them listening to our conversation as we pick up our pace again and travel up the mountain. Kael shrugs.

"Technically it is up on the mountain."

"Kael, it *is* the mountain. I've never seen something like it." I blink, curiosity swirling in my body.

"Can you go into the mountain?"

"Of course you can."

"Fuck, that's awesome." The words slip out before I can stop them and a small snicker makes us both look forward. I see Cassian's shoulder shake but he doesn't turn around. Edlyn shoots me a grin beside him.

"You're right it is pretty awesome." She agrees and I feel my cheeks flush. Right, they all already know the basics of the castle.

"How deep or high can you go?"

"As deep or high as you want," Kael says and looks at me before he continues.

"The banquet hall, throne room, and various guest rooms are in the main part of the castle which you can see," He points to the part that is not inside the mountain. Walls that have high arches as windows, make the light pour into the chambers.

"Some creatures don't like to be inside the mountain. Some don't like it deep or high so we let them rest in the main part. If we have someone from Polyxena over they usually reside high up in the mountain so they can easily go for a fly." Right, they can fly. Hector is one of them. Gods, I feel like I'm surpassing these kinds of information all the time. I look at him tilting my head.

"Where's your room?" He grins.

"Why, you want to visit me?" I roll my eyes and shove his shoulder. "Shut up."

"It's up high. I like the fresh air." He answers finally and I nod. My eyes flutter over to Edlyn and she grins.

"I don't like any heights I'm down with Cas." My eyes flicker to the latter who rides beside Flynn, his face turned away from us. Eryx ignores us like always so I don't even bother to ask him.

"What about you, Flynn?" I ask and the warrior grumbles.

"We don't speak grumbles, Nayaran, speak up." Edlyn taunts the man who quickly glares at her. Why did she call him Nayaran? I lean towards Kael who grins when my friend and the warrior start to bicker.

"Why did she call him Nayaran?" I whisper, to not grasp their attention.

"It's his birth name. Nayaran Charrier." I blink surprised for a moment. I know the Charrier line they're far royals—wait Flynn is royalty?

"That means . . ."

"Yeah, grumpy over there is of royal blood and one of his cousins will be next in line, now that Marrus is dead." My eyes fly over to the Tengeri whose gaze is narrowed.
I shrink when I realize he heard our conversation. Instead of satisfying my curiosity and asking why he would let his cousin take the throne rather than himself, I remain silent. Better not to wake the sleeping dragon.
"Why do they call you Flynn then?" His face darkens even more at my question and I grimace but to my surprise, he answers curtly.
"Because Nayaran is what my father called me." I don't dare to make him elaborate on that and I know he wouldn't even bother to. We continue in silence for another moment as the horses climb the cliffs.
"You didn't answer my first question." Flynn looks back at me, raising a brow. For a moment I watch the scar deepening on the left side of his face.
"Where you reside." I elaborate.
"I don't think it's any of your business."
"Right. I'm still curious." I insist but he doesn't tell me and turns his head back to the front. Kael snickers and I narrow my eyes.
"Maybe you should call him grumpy instead of Flynn," I say loud enough for him to hear. Edlyn and Kael both chuckle. My friend looks at me and grins shrugging one shoulder.
"Just do it like me, I like to switch. There is a variety between asshole, bastard, and arrogant ass. Cocky—"
"Shut your mouth. You're not entitled to call me anything." Flynn grumbles and Edlyn's grin widens.
"But my favorite is still Nayaran. Sounds like an entitled, cocky bastard."
I don't know how it happens. One second my friend is grinning with mischief and the next she's suddenly on the ground pinned by her wrists, Flynn's body hovering over hers. I inhale sharply when I realize that he pounced at her and threw her off the horse. I try to

get off Nighttail when Edlyn snarls and fights back but Kael stops me.

"Let them play."

"Play?" I ask when I visually watch my friend transform. Her warm hazel eyes transform to blood red, her hair shimmers in white strands, and black talons grow out of her nails. The color travels like ink across her knuckles just like it does when Cassian changes. I flinch when her talons dig into Flynn's forearms. She kicks him right in the stomach with her knee and overpowers him. Flynn growls when she throws a punch in his face and they both roll and roll, no one keeping the upper hand. I arch one brow not really sure if someone should prevent them from killing each other.

"This is so fun." Kale is glowing beside me and I look at him as if he's grown mad.

"Get your dirty hands off me you, Magda—"

"Make me, Asshole." Edlyn hisses back and gets a good scratch across his chest. My eyes widen when I see blood gushing around them not knowing if they're both hurt or not. My eyes flicker over when I hear a sigh. Cassian watches the two exasperated as he drops off his horse in one motion.

"Do you know that you two are the worst part of my day?" He questions them but both don't listen. Edlyn has the upper hand as she locks her thighs around Flynn's ribs. She grins down at the warrior who looks up at her, his cheeks flushed, his chest rising and falling quickly. Her hands wrap around the warrior's throat and my mouth drops open. My cheeks flush at their position and Kael snickers beside me.

"Now you understand what I mean?"

I nod with flushed cheeks, while Cassian stalks over to them. Before my friend can choke the red-haired man to death, the prince grabs a fistful of Edlyn's cloak and lifts her off of Flynn with one arm. My mouth drops open again when he puts Edlyn back on her feet. Flynn gets up in a flash and stalks back to Edlyn but Cassian blocks him and holds him back as he places a hand on his friend's chest.

"Don't you have any honor, brother? Attacking a woman?" Kael hollers at Cassian's question and I hit his arm.

"Stop laughing this isn't funny." I hiss at him.

"She's not a fucking woman she's a Magda!" Flynn growls and Edlyn raises her brows. Her red eyes glow.

"Last time I checked I still have tits and—"

"Enough, Edlyn." Cassian shuts her up.

"Now, can you two behave like fucking adults or do I need to tape your mouths and bodies shut?" He asks the two. Flynn and Edlyn don't answer him and glare at each other. They're actually crazy, I thought Cassian and I couldn't stand each other. These two loathe each other. When Edlyn doesn't back down Flynn sighs.

"If she behaves, I will too." Cassian looks at Edlyn who crosses her arms over her chest.

"If he doesn't pounce at me, I won't need to defend myself."

"Good, so that's settled. Now get your asses back on your horses before I turn you two into ashes." He growls at them and they strut back to their horses like two children who got scolded by their parent.

"No worries, Flynn, I'll keep your ashes in a pretty urn, if he changes his mind."

"Shut up." The warrior hisses at Kael beside me. My gaze dashes back to Cassian who's pinching his nose between his fingers and takes a deep breath in. When his eyes open and his hand drops he looks at me. I hold eye contact for a moment before I focus my eyes on the reins in my hands. They all get back on their horses and we continue our ride.

"If anyone speaks another word, I will crack their spine." Cassian threatens.

"Does that rule count for Carina as well?" Kael asks with a grin making the prince turn his head and glare. Kael clamps his mouth shut and acts like he locks it up and throws the key down the mountain. I bite my lips to refrain from laughing when Cassian catches my gaze. His eyes flicker down to my lips and his twitch before he turns back around.

It takes us almost half an hour to climb the mountain with our horses. The castle grows more beautiful the closer we get and when we cross through the iron gates where the guards greet the prince with warm smiles and deep bows, anxiety races through me. I'm just a few feet away from the King of Demeter.
The doors to the castle burst open so violently that everyone in the yard turns their heads. A girl not older than me stands behind them, her eyes scanning our small group until they settle on the prince.
"Cas!"
Her voice, raspy yet soft, exclaims before she bundles the fabrics of her gown and dashes forward. I watch her fly over the few steps leading to the courtyard before she swings herself into his arms, her long black hair creating a curtain around her.
He mumbles something so quiet and fast that even I can't comprehend it as he winds his arms around her.
Who is that?

~ 15 ~

Her skin is brown—different than Edlyn's—with more of a wheatish undertone. Her bare arms shine in the sunlight, so luminous I wonder if she massaged oil onto her skin. Both her wrists are bedazzled with golden bracelets the same color as the multiple rings that adorn her slender fingers. Her nails look like they've been dipped into a turmeric color. The same color that gathers on her high cheekbones. Her lips are pointed just like her nose, which is pierced with a small golden ring through the left nostril.

When she retreats out of the hug, her thick eyebrows, the same midnight color as her hair, relax. Her hair ends right at her hips swinging with every movement of her body. She is dressed in a long rosy skirt that wraps around her body, the same color as the matching blouse that adorns her upper body.

"I was so worried about you. Night and day I thought of nothing else."

My throat feels dry as she speaks up again.

"We had a bit of a delay due to certain people needing breaks." Flynn is the first one to speak up as he hands the reins of his horses to a young boy. Cassian presumes staring at the girl, who doesn't even glance our way.

"I see how worried you are about all of us, sweetheart," Kael speaks up, and finally, finally, she looks our way. Her green eyes pierce my skull as she settles her gaze on me, lashes so long and full I find myself yearning to count every single one. Her features harden nonetheless, letting Kael pull her into a hug. Edlyn passes us but doesn't greet the beautiful girl and I wish I could go with her.

Once Kael retreats I watch his cheeks flush an adorable red.

"And you are?" The girl looks at me a bit bored and underwhelmed.

In a second Cassian is at my side, his hand burning against my back.

"Azzura this is Princess Katherina Sebestyen, Carina, meet Azzura. Her family is one of the oldest friends of my family." The prince introduces us and I inhale deeply. I reach out my hand for her and after a moment she grabs it. Her skin is cold but nothing can compete with the frost in her gaze.

"Pleasure." She arches a black brow. In a matter of seconds, she turns her head to the prince again, her gaze softening. "You probably have a lot to do until dinner. I'm sure we meet up as always?"

"Of course." The prince answers her and it is in such a casual way that it reflects the history in their eyes. His hand remains on my back but it feels like it is scorching my skin.

Azzura turns and walks back to the entrance of the castle, Kael staring after her wistfully.

Cassian clears his throat and the blond shakes his head before reaching for Nighttail's reigns with a soft smile.

"I'm going to make sure Honeycomb and her share a stall." He says with a grin and I roll my eyes. He seems to like playing matchmaker with anyone.

"I'll take the rest of the horses, Your Highness. I am sure your father is already waiting." Eryx tells Cassian who hops off his stallion elegantly.

"Thank you, Eryx." The man bows and grabs the reins of the three horses left.

The courtyard empties and I take a deliberate step away from the prince. I can breathe again once I don't feel his hand on me.

I stare up at the grand castle not knowing how to feel. I should let the spark of hope ignite, after all, this is what I wanted. I can finally talk to the king and request the help I need.

"Are you ready?" I turn my head to look at Cassian. My eyes widen when I realize what he means.

"We're going to meet your father now?" He furrows his brows.

"No, usually I wait a week or two before I greet him. It's not as if I haven't seen him last three years ago." I blink, confused by his sarcasm.

"You mean to tell me you weren't in Demeter for three years?" He chuckles but somehow it sounds bitter, almost acid-like.

"I told you that I took the oath and went to Aerwyna for your safety."

"Yes, but I didn't think that you never left the kingdom in between." My voice sounds airy and panicky. I can't help my hands from getting clammy at the realization. He didn't get to be home for three years because of me. Because he felt like I needed protection. Which is completely ridiculous and should make me angry because I'm perfectly fine with protecting myself. Still, the thought closes up my throat and it is an effort to swallow.

"I can't meet the king now. Not looking like this and after I haven't had a proper bath for weeks." I change the topic instead and the prince rolls his eyes.

"My father is already waiting for us and believe me when I say he doesn't care about your appearance after you almost got killed and I *did* get killed." He arches a brow and I narrow my eyes.

"I didn't kill you, you're perfectly fine."

"For now."

I huff out a breath and nod, seeing no sense in stalling the meeting. The quicker I get this over with the better. I can get a bath afterward and then get ready to leave, wherever I need to go. Satisfaction settles in his features before he leads me up the marble stairs and through the double doors that lead into the palace. The first thing that hits me is the air. A strange thing but the fresh scent is so prominent that it feels like I'm taking a proper breath after weeks of choking. The ground beneath us is made out of the same marble-looking material, polished to no end. If I stare long enough I think I can see myself looking back at me.

Cassian doesn't speak a word as we pass various maids in the halls and I stay quiet, too stunned to speak. While I'm completely mesmerized by the golden ornaments painted by hand on the walls, the marble columns in between, and the dangling chandeliers I notice the ceiling rather late. When I do, I stumble over my own feet and have to hover for a moment. All the breath is knocked out of my lungs when I look up and my eyes meet midnight blue. The whole ceiling is painted in color, glowing like the night sky and it looks like actual stars glittering on the surface.

I raise my arm for a moment foolish enough that I could even reach such a high ceiling. But something about the glimmer calls to me and makes me want to graze the tips of my fingers over it just to feel if it is as smooth as it looks.

"Carina?" The bubble around me bursts and my arm falls back to my side when I look at the prince. He's already gotten a few steps in front of me, his head tilted to the side as he watches me.

"Sorry," I mumble, somehow embarrassed with the way I got engrossed by a ceiling. I scurry over to him but he doesn't start moving again. When I crane my neck to look up at him I see green flashing over my face as if his eyes are searching for something. I stay still, not saying a word. He starts to move again.

Suddenly I feel really out of place as we continue our way to the throne room. Well, at least I think that is where the king will meet us. Our clothes are dirty and dusty, dull against the rest of the stunning palace.

"Maybe Kael can give you a tour later." The prince suddenly says, as we round a corner.

"Maybe," I mumble in response. I don't know if I want to see the beauty of the rest of it. Especially not the part that's actually inside the mountain. I don't fear that I won't like it, I fear that I will. Somehow this castle seems so much more likely than my home. The distant humming that I hear, the clicking of shoes against marble, and the sound of pans that reaches us probably from the kitchens. It may be my new hearing and still, this feels like a home. For a moment I do the forbidden thing.

I try to see myself living here, spending the rest of my life in this magical place. I see myself walking in the halls in the morning, barefoot as I sneak my way outside onto the lands. I see myself dressed in beautiful gowns being chased down the halls by Cassian, our laughter echoing in the palace. I see myself reading in the gardens, dozing off on the lands, breathing, and living here.

Completely wrapped up in my nostalgic thoughts I don't notice Cassian halt and walk right into his back. I stumble back for a moment and he looks down at me.

"Are you all right?"

"Yes," I say clipped as I rub my temple.

My heartbeat accelerates when I notice that we stopped in front of golden double doors. I quickly brush my fingers through my hair, trying to comb out some knots and rub at the skin on my face to get rid of any dirt that might be stuck on it. Cassian's fingers wrap around my wrists and stop my fumbling, driving me to glance at him.

"Stop that and take a deep breath." For the first time since I know him I listen. I inhale deeply, my skin prickling where his fingers are still wrapped around my wrist.

"There is nothing to be afraid of."

"I'm not afraid. I just look like I got chewed up by a dragon and spit out again," A rumbling laugh erupts from his lips and I narrow my eyes before I slip my wrist out of his grip and push his chest. He stops laughing but still smiles as he looks at me. That stupid fucking dimple. His eyes shine as he watches me, amused before his gaze turns hooded.

"You look beautiful in any way, so don't worry."

Easier said than done. To talk to a king you've always thought was cruel and destructive. I watch Cassian's hands curl around the handles but before he opens the doors he looks back at me a last time.

"The throne room is a bit different than what you will expect. Give it a chance before you judge."

My brows furrow and I open my mouth to ask what he exactly means by that but he already pushes the doors open wide and reveals something I have never seen before.

~ 16 ~

I was never a person who was afraid of the dark. I was fond of the lack of light, the shadows you could hide under. It provides you with some kind of security, it overshadows your vulnerabilities. But the dark can be threatening, it can be intimidating if you're not sure what's hiding in the shadows with you. If you're not the most dangerous thing lurking in the dark you should feel scared and I am. I am fucking terrified when Cassian and I step into the throne room. And into complete darkness.

For a moment I fear I've passed out but then I'm aware of the scent of pines and wind. I can feel Cassian beside me and suddenly his hand is around mine, his fingers intertwining with mine. I inhale a shuddering breath and want to pull my hand back, not wanting to feel the surge of energy running through me at his touch. I stop when suddenly the shadows disperse and scatter off into the edges of the giant room. Blackness meets my eyes, so raw and beautiful I have never seen it before.

My eyes wander over the black shining floor, the black walls, and the black ceilings, and get stuck on the throne. Black. The throne is made out of the same black stone, polished and shiny with a soft glimmer set around it. It looks like the whole room is made out of onyx but it can't be, I have never seen something like this. It looks so disturbing and frightening, how the walls seem to close in on you, how the ceiling looks like it might suffocate you.

I take a step forward, feeling the smooth stone under my boots. Once I take a closer look I see golden swirls surrounding the throne like shadows, the paint is moving. It is moving like smoke is trapped inside the black stone. My heart flutters curiously at the sight, it feels like this room pulses with a heartbeat as if it is completely alive.

"The throne room is probably the most powerful in the castle. Many powerful men sat on that throne, it carries all their magic inside once they die." I turn to look at Cassian who hasn't moved since we stepped inside the room. His eyes are watchfully gauging my reaction.

"The shadows are there to keep intruders outside; just members of the royal family can make it scatter." I nod, somehow fascinated. I let my eyes travel over the small details in the room. A small black table sits on the side books scattered on top, ink splashes on papers. A goblet filled with red liquor stands beside it indicating that someone was reading and writing moments ago.

"It's—"

"Odd, I know. You get used to it." Cassian says and shrugs his shoulders. I furrow my brows and shake my head.

"It's beautiful. It feels like it is alive."

"I know—you think it's beautiful?" A surprised breath leaves his lips and I look at him confused. I mean why would I not? The clear elegance of the room is mind-blowing; the throne looks intimidating but not less stunning. It is the kind of beauty that the dark captures, dangerous and frightening. It reminds me of Cassian. I look back at the astonished look on his face and go to tell him but get interrupted.

"You've arrived early, brother."

Both our heads whip around to the far end of the throne room. It seems like there is a second back door to the room where a tall man steps out. I'm surprised that his tall figure passes through the door without any effort because holy shit. His stance is proud and arrogant as he approaches the prince. His hair is a dark brown, almost black and it curls in the same way Cassian's does, though it is shorter. My eyes travel over bronze skin that is revealed by the airy shirt that covers his broad shoulders and narrow waist. I follow the path up over cunning lips that tilt slightly to the side, a narrow nose with a pointy tip, high cheekbones, and—green. Not the same green as Cassian's this is more haunted, cruel. A green I never am excited to see.

He approaches Cassian with ease and when they reach each other they end up in a bone-crushing hug. They look like exact copies of each other.

"I missed you, Zayne." Cassian's voice is so rich with emotion that it touches something deep inside me. Now that both of them are so close I see the difference. Cassion has more defined muscles and his features are stronger whereas Zayne's are rather sharp, almost bony.

A weird feeling crawls up my spine now that I realize that this is Cassian's brother. The other Moreau brother found a liking in torturing me and getting on my nerves when I was a child. He especially had a liking in manipulating his brother to behead my favorite porcelain dolls.

He was always the one who kindled the fire and watched from afar as he destroyed any happiness I had when they were around. Zayne's eyes flicker toward me as he lets go of his brother.

"Gods, you reek like hell." He tells him, making Cassian chuckle. I know that look in his eyes, it's worship and pride. He always loved his older brother. The brother who was supposed to marry me. A disgusted shiver rakes through me.

"You try traveling through the whole kingdom incognito, with a boy who takes nothing seriously while Edlyn and Flynn try to rip each other's throat out. Not much time for a bath."

"Yes, I can tell."

Zayne's eyes still haven't left my physique but I don't dare to cower. I meet his gaze, lifting my chin lightly. A dark brow arches unimpressed. Cassian finally turns to me and stretches out his hand for me to take. A new glimmer flickers in his eyes and a soft smile sits on his face. A strong wave hits me with his beauty, it's so overwhelming that I take his hand and let him pull me close to his side.

"I imagine you still remember Carina." He looks at me so intensely that I choose to stare at Zayne before I flush red.

"Of course I do." The sleazy look on his face disgusts me and, even worse, he takes my hand and presses a kiss against my knuckles while his eyes stay on me. I smile tightly, even though I want to do nothing but rip my hand out of his grasp.

"It is a pleasure to finally have you at the Moreau court. It was long overdue."

"Was it?" I ask when he straightens up again. The challenge glimmers in his eyes evoking the desire in me to strike him in his arrogant face. While I always know when Cassian is teasing, I know that the sarcastic tone of Zayne's words is always meant to taunt, to get some kind of reaction so he can pounce. A snake disguised in human form.

"I couldn't believe it when Cas wrote that you were on your way. Should I congratulate the love birds?" He completely runs over my question and grins at us. I decide to do the same because Cassian doesn't feel the need to take part in this conversation.

"We came to meet King Ronan."

"I must apologize, he's running late. The queen asked for his company. He will be with us in a short time." I furrow my brows while Cassian decides to speak up beside me.

"How is mother?"

"The usual." The answer is clipped and for the first time, I see genuine sorrow inside Zayne's eyes. A look passes between the brothers.

"You can go see her after this meeting." Cassian nods at that.

"Well, while we wait, why don't you both sit down, you look like you're hungry. You can update me on what happened."

I would rather starve than spend any more time in his presence but he already calls for the maid while Cas settles by the stone table.

"Is your father actually going to speak to us?" I whisper, making his brows furrow.

"Of course. If Zayne says he will be with us then he will be." I doubt that. What would be so important that he would be late to our arrival?

"Is your mother ill?" I ask while he sits down on the black chair. I go for the other chair but suddenly I'm pulled back and with a small shriek I land in his lap.
"What the fuck do you think you're doing?"
"Sitting down as my brother instructed." His voice is cold and his eyes won't meet my gaze. I try to wriggle off his thigh but he pulls my back flush against his back, his arms around me.
"I believe that chair is occupied by my brother so it's either my lap because I don't want you to sit on his." His breath hits my neck with his words and I throw a glare over my shoulder.
"I can gladly sit on the floor." I protest and wriggle again but his arms tighten and I freeze.
"No chance. You can't get up now." My eyes widen when I feel exactly why I can't get up.
"You should've stopped the wriggling, princess." He whispers and my heart speeds up. I don't dare to move again when Zayne sits down on the chair opposite us, his eyes flying over our position with a raised brow. A few maids scatter into the room and place various biscuits, sweets, and some herbal tea on the table. I'm too nervous to even think about eating right now.
"So how did this happen?" Zayne asks with an unsure hand gesture and I narrow my eyes slightly at the obvious amusement in his eyes.
"I stabbed him," I tell him and his eyes widen for a moment.
"Turns out it was the wrong blade. So I stabbed him again." I say.
"You let yourself be stabbed by a woman?" Zayne asks his brother and my hands tighten into fists.
"What do you mean 'let'? He didn't stand a chance."
"I doubt that." I push my nails into my palm, anger rushing through me at his foolish words.
"Because I'm a woman?"
"For one, yes." He says, nodding. I wait for him to elaborate but Cassian doesn't let him.

"Just before you go into a verbal sparring I should warn you, brother, she is more dangerous than you think."

"I doubt that." He repeats and I almost throw my hands and slip off of Cassian's lap but he intercepts me.

"Come on now, princess, he is just joking."

"I don't care if he's joking or not. He's being a misogynistic bastard." Cassian chuckles at my answer while Zayne's eyes narrow.

"I could rip you into parts before you can blink. Your arrogance is disgusting." A smirk moves on his lips.

"You rather chose a fiery one, brother."

"He didn't choose anything, I am not his." I seethe and immediately feel Cassian's hold on me loosen slightly. What does he expect? That I just sit here and act like everything is fine, letting his brother insult me?

I finally slip off his lap and stalk toward Zayne's chair. In one movement I've my dagger in my hands and hold it against his throat, my other hand gripping the back of his chair.

"Sadly it's not bloodstone but I swear I will rip you apart limb by limb and stack you onto a pile, your heart on top. Then I will find a bloodstone dagger and slice it right through it." I hiss and the arrogant smile drops from his lips. I mean every word.

"Carina—" I whirl my head around and glare at Cassian.

"Shut up. I swear you say one word Cassian and I'm out of here. Don't think just because you did one good thing I have forgotten everything else. If all you're not better than him. I've had enough of you Moreau's."

I watch his jaw harden as he gets up from his chair and suddenly I'm pushed back. Zayne stood up as well and in a blur, he slams me against a black wall. I swear I hear it cracking underneath the impact. I groan when I see canines grow out of his teeth, his eyes turning black.

"You stupid bitch think you can threaten an Upyr and get away with it?" Zayne hisses and I barely stand up, my head throbbing as he stalks toward me. Talons grow out of his nails but there are no shadows around him.

"You should gravel in front of me on your knees!"

"Enough."

A steady wall moves in front of me as I finally get onto my feet again. A dull throbbing settles at the back of my neck as I watch Cassian stand in front of me.

"Do you have a fucking death wish? Throw her like that again and it will be the last thing you do in this world." A shiver runs over my spine at his threatening words.

"You are picking her over me? Did you not hear what this bitch said?"

One moment Zayne is all growling and dark and the next he is cowering in front of Cassian a panicked look on his face. Cassian hasn't moved from in front of me as he stares down at his brother.

"I would pick her over you any day. I would pick her over the fucking world. So you touch my girl again, I will forget that we are brothers."

My eyes widen surprised as shock thunders through me. I swallow as I watch Zayne grit his teeth, kneeling in front of his brother. The latter turns his head at me and looks at me with black eyes. The hard lines move from his face the moment he glances at me.

"Are you hurt?"

"No, I'm fine." It's a lie. My head throbs but I fear if I tell him he will kill his brother. His jaw tightens and the shadows dancing at his fingers expand.

"You're lying." I shake my head no.

"I'm fine."

"Come here." His voice is gentle and I step forward. His fingers graze my arms for a moment when I stop in front of him. Green moves back in those eyes for a second before he nods over ordering me to look at Zayne. His gaze is dark and I swear if he could move he would choke me.

"Apologize," Cassian says, his order not leaving room to argue. Zayne's eyes widen.
"What?"
"Are you deaf? Apologize. Now."
Zayne grits his teeth when Cassian makes him kneel even further.
"Fuck, no."
"Apologize," Cassian repeats while his fingers dance over my skin. Zayne is kneeling right in front of me and a strange surge of power runs from me. For a moment I get lost in the energy surrounding me, knowing it is Cassian's magic. I push my nails into my skin when Zayne moves upwards for a moment, his eyes placed on me. I narrow my gaze at him when he spits out the words.
"I'm sorry I attacked you."
"And?" Cassian asks. Zayne's jaw clenches.
"It will not happen again." He hisses. His whole body collapses forward when Cassian's magic lets go of him. I watch him lean down and speak lowly.
"You touch her again, if I don't kill you, she will." A surge of satisfaction runs through me even though I'm still shocked. I thought nothing could stand between him and Zayne. And he just threatened him with his life just because he acted on my provocation. I don't dare to look at him because I fear those feelings swirling inside me evolve too much when I see the look on his face. Luckily he doesn't get the chance to speak up again when a thunderous voice booms through the room.
"What in the world is going on here?"

"Well, I'm waiting. Will any of you two explain?"

The room is silent and empty. Yet it is filled with power to the brim, risking to spill over and make the walls burst. I barely remember King Ronan from his visits; he was always just a dark shadow, with stern black brows and an evil grin.

The brows are in the same stark line, and the dark eyes tightened. He still has that aura of authority surrounding him, clinging to his skin in shadows. But what surprises me is that I've never actually recognized the magnificence of the man. The bronze sun-kissed skin, the thickness of his forearms, and the wideness of his shoulders. The high cheekbones that I know Cassian inherited from him. The prince looks exactly like his father and then again he doesn't.

For a moment I think Demetrus is eyeing us three suspiciously but I see the difference. In all three of them. Demetrus was good-natured, and witty while Cassian is cocky and youthful. King Ronan still doesn't look older than his late twenties but it is the eyes that tell you differently. Eyes that have traveled the world and seen things I can only dream of.

Zayne gets off the ground with a grunt while I watch King Ronan stroll over, fascinated. Something stirs in me and it makes me queasy. A weird kind of recognition flutters in my mind.

"Cas was being an ass."

"Sure, I was the ass." Cassian glares at his brother as he shifts beside me but I ignore them. I still stare at the king whose eyes are now placed on me.

"Did I not teach you better than to cause such ridiculous ants in front of guests?" The king asks his sons and I finally force my eyes away to catch Zayne's angry gaze. I glare right back while I feel Cassian's knuckles graze mine. My attention draws to him and I meet his gaze.

"I expect that Cassian has already apologized for your horrible behavior."

"Why do you think I—" Zayne stops protesting and leaves the room with a dark grumble. I can't help but feel like this isn't the last bad encounter I will have with him.

"It is so good to finally have you at our court, Carina. I am very sorry that you didn't earn a proper welcome. My boys can be animals sometimes." King Ronan has a gentle smile on his face as he approaches me. I am surprised when he grabs my arms and pulls me in for a hug.

It is over so quickly that I don't get the time to even reciprocate it, making my arms dangle awkwardly at my sides.

"It's fine." My eyes flicker between his as I notice the soft scent of jasmine and honey.

"I hope your journey was rather uneventful?" He asks me and Cassian and guides us back over to the small table.

"Mostly. We needed to stop in Protestants lands for a day and got into a predicament but I handled it." Cassian answers for us both. I sit down on the chair opposite the king while the prince keeps on standing beside me. His hand places itself on my shoulder and I slacken.

"Any witnesses? I don't want word around that you were not in Demeter."

"As I said, I handled it." I stiffen at his words and think about the Protestant we've left behind. Is he going to tell people we were in their city? My heart rate spikes and Cassian squeezes my shoulder to reassure me. King Ronan eyes the motion for a moment. If the Protestant keeps his mouth shut there is still the risk of that peculiar woman spilling word. I think I'm going to be sick.

"I can't say how sorry I am for the way that everything happened, Carina. I hope you will feel at home as long as you want to be here. My son has already informed me of your wish to annul the wedding?"

My body freezes just like Cassian's does. He already told him?

"I—yes." I can't meet the king's eyes when Cassian's hand slips off my shoulder.

"I respect your decision and hope that Demeter will still stay at your side if you allow us. We are still allies." I nod at his words as a cold claw wraps around my heart.

"Thank you, King Ronan. I appreciate your consideration and I am thankful for your help."

"Of course. Please call me Ronan, dear, it feels weird to be so formal." I nod, even though I have no intention of calling him Ronan. That would be odd.

"Well, I suppose you are very tired from your journey. You might rest in the guest wing if you would like to?"

Panic floods me when he gets up and I jump off my chair with wide eyes.

"Wait! I mean—I. . ." I take a deep breath. What the hell is wrong with me? Why am I so nervous and why does this feel so wrong? The king halts and looks at me curiously. Cassian remains silent beside me.

"I have another favor I would like to ask you." I straighten my shoulders and try to look as confident as ever as he motions for me to go on. I eye Cassian wishing that he would just leave but his expression is stoic. He won't move from my side.

"Is there any chance that I could have an audience with the Fatum?" King Ronan's eyes blink confusedly.

"An audience?"

"I—yes. I know it sounds absurd but there are serious matters to discuss and I think I would require their help. I just thought you of all might know if there was a way of reaching them?" I wring my hands while I feel Cassian's eyes on me. He's just as surprised as his father by my request.

"I certainly have never heard that someone could just conjure them." The king's eyes glaze over slightly as he thinks. I can practically feel his curiosity but I am thankful that he doesn't pry. I misjudged his whole persona.

"I might need to consult my advisor and visit the library but I promise you to look into it. Maybe you could hold a seance at one of the temples in Iason."

He looks back at me and it feels like all the weight lifts from my shoulders.

"Thank you. It means the world to me—thank you." His lips stretch into a small grin and he nods. The resemblance of Cassian in that smile is undeniable.

"Well, now it is time for you to rest. My son will direct you to your chambers and we will further discuss your other . . . complications."

He means the fact that a god wants to see me dead. I nod, the exhaustion finally crawling into my body. He leaves the room with a soft clap on the prince's shoulder. A look passes between them and it feels like they're having a whole conversation through it. I'm too tired to analyze it further.

Once we're alone Cassian finally speaks up.

"Why do you want to see the Fatums?"

"I feel like I'm going to pass out any second. Can we not do this now?" I ask and to my astonishment, he nods stiffly and leads me out of the calamitous room.

~ 17 ~

The guest wing is located on the normal side of the palace which is connected to the mountain. It is only a few halls away which gives me less time than I thought. Cassian and I don't speak and I don't know if I prefer it that way or not. I thought that things would turn out differently. More difficult. The fact that Cassian's father immediately agreed to annul the marriage and help me with the Fatums seems strange. What do he and his kingdom get out of an alliance with a princess that is supposed to hold magic but can't use it? I have nothing to give him. Technically I can't even decide if Aerwyna and Demeter will continue being allies because I didn't claim the throne. Lord Andréas might be a distant cousin but I don't know this man. I can't stop but feel like there's a catch to it. When I turn around and feel safe, someone is going to stab me in the back. Well, been there done that already.

I try to stay cautious even though it feels like King Ronan is being genuine with his help. Cassian doesn't say anything as he leads me into the room and I don't bother to as well. I don't bother to look around either or notice the gigantic balcony before I fall face-first into the pillows of the queen-sized bed. If I weren't so exhausted I would marble over the way the blue canopy looks like the deepest parts of the sea or the floor glitters like it is carved out of onyx.

I don't notice that the doors to the outside are wide open, the curtains fluttering in the wind when my eyes fall shut and sleep invades my body.

Shadows. Shadows, dark like the night sky, travel around my naked feet, mixing with the red of the blood that is sticking to my skin. I'm running. I'm standing still. The shadows don't leave, they cling to me like a promise pushing me to the edge. It's cold and I know I'm going to die. My teeth start to chatter, the sound echoing in the darkness around me. My limbs feel strange, a foreign heaviness to them, though they are light as feathers. The stale scent of death invades my nostrils and I know I can't do anything about it. I am going to die.

When I wake up I sit up straight, ignoring the sweat that clings to my skin as I try to rein in my breathing. My heart thrums against my ribs as if it is trying to escape the cage my body built around it. I sit in the dark for minutes, my chest falling and rising steadily by the end. I wipe the strands clutched to my forehead away and my eyes fly over to a small table perched in the corner. For a moment I let my eyes wander around the guest chamber taking it in in the dark. The queen-sized bed is taking up half of the space, a small nightstand perched beside it. A few bottles with liquids I don't recognize are scattered on the surface.
There's a door on the left of the bed which I assume leads to the bathing chamber.
I'm surprised when I find a few bookshelves filled to the brim in the right corner with the small table beside it. I notice a small satchel placed on the table. Folded clothes lie at the edge of the bed, which my legs don't reach. Someone must've dropped new clothes for me. I swing my legs over the bed and get rid of my clothing. I tear off the breeches, the shirt, even the undergarments

wanting nothing that reeks of the journey stuck to my skin. I shiver lightly when I slip into new undergarments and a light nightgown. The fabric falls to my ankles, the sleeves cover my arms. Whimsical stitching runs along the color and for a moment I find myself in awe of the beautiful work. Swirls and curves create a stitching pattern like smoke whirling around my arms.

I turn and just notice that the left side of the room is almost completely made out of windows, grounded with big window sills and two doors leading outside on a balcony caged by a white balustrade. The sky is still tinted in deep blue, and the mountains that you can see from the window are looming in the dark. I remain quiet for a moment and listen for any sound occurring in the castle. Once I'm sure that everyone is asleep I step past the doors leading to the outside. For a moment it steals the breath from my lungs. The picture in front of me looks like it was painted by an artist. The mountains are so high you can't see the tip as they disappear into the clouds. The bottom is glazed with pine trees that look black now but I know that they will glow in a beautiful green once the sun greets the sky. A soft breeze settles over my skin accompanied by the soft scent of pine.

I tip-toe over to the stone railing and let my hands wander over the smooth surface for a moment, listening for something in the dark. It is strange how eerie silent the lands are. No animals are surrounding the castle. It is creepy yet somehow peaceful.

"It's beautiful isn't it?" My heart stutters and I whirl around clutching my chest.

"Holy fuck. You almost gave me a heart attack." I hiss when I see Kael stepping out of the shadows. He raises a blond brow and for a moment my eyes dip down and notice that he is shirtless, just a pair of dark breeches hanging low on his hips. The defined v that slips into the fabric looks like it might be carved by a stone mason. "This is an interconnected balcony, princess, you're the one looming around." At his words, I furrow my brows and look past him for a minute. He's right. The balcony doesn't end with the doors to my chamber. It seems to travel around the whole castle connected to every chamber so anyone could step out here.

"I'm sorry, you just scared me." I turn back around leaning against the railing. I hear his steps as he leans on it beside me, his arm grazing mine. His body warmth is welcoming in the cooler night air.

"Had a nightmare?" He asks and I turn my head to see him mustering me. I don't need to answer that question.

"I hate nightmares."

"No way, you do? I adore them." I say sarcastically, making him nudge me with his shoulder. I grin for a moment before I stare back at the mountains. The view somehow steadies me.

"I can't get them out of my head. It's like their ghosts are haunting me. Blaming me for their death." It's a whispered confession. Usually, I wouldn't tell anyone this but I know Kael won't judge me.

"It's not them that are haunting you, Carina. It's yourself. You need to let it go, and forgive yourself so you can move on."

"Easier said than done." I turn my back to the view and slide down the railing to lean my back against it. Kael follows my actions. Our knees knock together as the air settles around us.

"I know it's no use to keep on thinking about it. They're dead, nothing is going to change that. But if I remind myself I have the hope that it will not happen again."

"It won't happen again. Not if you don't let it." I turn to look at him and sigh. It's time to change the topic or I will bathe in self-pity for the next hours.

"Why are you wandering the balcony in the middle of the night."

"I can't sleep." His voice is filled with something raw and it makes me lay my head on his shoulder. "Why?" He shrugs his shoulders.

"I can't stop thinking about the fact that these Protestants could track you and Cas down in the city. Doesn't it seem convenient?" At his tone, I look up surprised. "You're still thinking about that?"

"Of course. How would they know where you are? Or know that you're even in the city. It just feels off."

"Maybe someone saw Cassian wandering the streets and they followed him."

"Seems unlikely. Cas is pretty good at staying undercover."

I raise a brow at Kael.

"I detected him in the capital when he was lurking around." Kaels lips split into an arrogant smile and my mouth drops open at the realization.

"He wanted me to notice him."

"I'm surprised you didn't already catch up on that."

"With all the catching up I have to do it's normal I miss some things." My voice sounds bitter and I hate it. Sympathy flickers in his jade eyes.

"Can I be honest with you? Without you getting angry at me?"

"Depends." I narrow my eyes lightly at him to find out where this is leading to.

"You need to promise me not to murder me."

"I won't murder you, Kael," I tell him with an eye roll. He suddenly holds up his pinky and I blink in confusion

"Pinky promise." He insists and I tilt my head slightly.

"How old are you again?"

"Age doesn't matter, baby, everyone should hold up to a pinky promise." He says it so seriously it makes me almost burst out laughing. I hold myself back and wrap my pinky around his. He shakes our hands for a moment before he crosses his legs to look at me seriously.

"I feel like this is an intervention," I say confused as I stare into his green eyes.

"You're too hard on him."

"I—what? On who?"

"Cas. I know you're angry at him. And gods be angry at him but why are you annulling the marriage?"

Why am I annulling the marriage? Because he betrayed me because his feelings weren't real. It's just some stupid oath he feels obligated to hold. Because he went behind my back and pretended to be interested in me.

I know that he tried to protect me when he acted as if he was on Daragon's side.

And he did convince a crowd of people that I could reign on my own. This could be seen as astounding because all these old men clung to thousands of years old traditions.

But it does not mean I owe him forgiveness. Nonetheless, my cheeks flush in shame.

"I know of my heritage now. I am willing to defeat Adales or talk to him or whatever Cassian wants me to do. But it just seems unnecessary to marry him."

"But I thought you loved him?" My gaze snaps up at his words, surprised.

"I—no. Yes—I guess I did." His gaze is persistent on his next question.

"And do you still love him?"

"I feel like I fell in love with a stranger. An act he put up to pursue me. It was not real." Kael chuckles at that. I narrow my eyes at his laughter.

"Why are you laughing? You can't tell me he isn't glad we're not getting married. He's not putting up against it."

"Because he wants you to be happy, Carina. Are you that blind?" I furrow my brows at his question.

"He's in love with you. He always was. It was fucking exhausting hearing him talk about you all the time. I would dread the few days when I visited him in Aerwyna because I knew he would rant about how your hair shines in the sun and how your eyes glitter when you glare at him. Of course he doesn't want to annul the wedding. But it doesn't matter because it's what you want. Everything he ever did was always for you."

My heart squeezes at his words and I suddenly feel awful. I escape his watchful eyes knowing that he will be able to read every emotion that's displaced on my face.

"You're awful," I complain and he smiles lightly.

"I'm not trying to make you feel bad, Carina, I just want you to stop conjuring this false image of him. Cas is good, " Something flickers in his eyes a distant memory that haunts him, "He is one of the best people I know and he doesn't deserve to be perceived as the villain. His opinion of himself is bad enough." I wonder what he means by that. I go to ask him but he interrupts me again.

"I'm a half-breed." My eyes flutter back to his face to see his cheeks flushing. He avoids my gaze and stares at the floor in front of us, toying with a loose thread on his breeches.

"My father was an Upyr of the higher ranks and it was a scandal when a human girl stood on the doorsteps of the palace with a round belly."

"Your mother's human?" I ask surprised.

"She was. Yes." My heart bursts at his words. Sorrow tints my vision and I grab his hand in both of mine squeezing lightly.

"I am sorry."

"It's all right. I never got to meet her anyway. My dad wanted to take her in, he was not in love with her but he was an honorable man—or that is what King Ronan told me— but it was uncalled for. People don't like to see humans and magical creatures . . . mix."

I grimace. "That's awful."

"It is. That is why they killed them." I exhale sharply even though I knew it was coming. I draw soft circles on his hand and he shoots me a genuine smile. Under all this bubbly light personality there lies someone greatly older and special than I thought."King Ronan was kind-hearted enough to let me live in the castle when I was just a newborn. I was raised by maids, I dined with the Royal family and I earned my place beside Cas. But you know how it is...people talk. At first, they were whispering but gradually they

stopped hiding their words and opinions. Let me tell you it's not great to hear everyone call you a half-breed bastard. I didn't let it get to me. Then they started to just outright call me a whore. Created rumors of my changing partners. I owe it to Cas that it stopped. Just one word and he would make that person regret it."
He stops talking and it's like I can feel his pain travel through me. His shoulders sack with the next breath that escapes past his lips.
"I'm so sorry." I feel like I am repeating myself but there is no greater way to put it. My heart aches at his story, wishing that people were more tolerant and interested enough to look past a label or prejudice.
"It's alright. I got over it."
"It's nothing someone even should get over," I tell him seriously. I look at him and he finally meets my eyes.
"You are one of the kindest people I know. You forgave me so quickly after I was rude to you. You gave me a birthday present, even though I am a bitch and I'm shitty to your best friend." I say and my thumb slides over the bracelet on my wrist. He grins at me all bubbly again.
"What can I say, I'm pretty amazing."
"You are. And I swear if I hear anyone saying anything they will get stabbed." He arches a brow at me and grins.
"I'm being honest."
"I know." He grins and something urges me forward. His eyes widen in surprise when I press a light kiss against his cheek. When I lean back a soft grin spreads on his lips and his cheeks flush. I have to laugh at his embarrassment and roll my eyes when he wiggles his brows.
"I think you missed." He puckers his lips and I lightly shove his face away. We both chuckle in the dark before a deep rumble of a voice slices through the air.
"I hope I'm not interrupting?"
I'm on my feet in a matter of seconds as I watch the tall figure step out of the shadows lazily, hands pushed into the pockets of the

breeches, dark hair a tousled mess of curls. My heartbeat speeds up at the seducing picture of the man in front of me. And he looks nothing but angry and annoyed as the stars light up his features.

"Not really. Carina and I are having a slumber party, wanna join?" Kael pipes up behind me as he gets up, a slight grin on his face. His eyes sparkle mischievously as he stops partially behind me pushing his flexed stomach against my arm.

Cassian's eyes turn into two slits as he eyes the motion and his shoulders tighten visibly. I catch the spark of shadows dancing at his back and feel the tension sizzle around us dangerously.

"I couldn't sleep. Kael kept me company." I say quickly because I don't want him to misinterpret.

"That's nice of him." Cassian's voice is ice cold and he doesn't even look at me. I frown lightly and step forward, even though I don't know what I'm about to do.

"You know me, I'm nice. But I'm pretty tired now so I'm gonna hit the sack. I wish you both a good night." I turn around confused but Kael already speed walks down the balcony but not without shooting me a feline smile. I narrow my eyes at him before I turn around to see Cassian already staring at me.

For a moment I just stand there, meeting his gaze as the wind bristles through my hair. The prince relaxes slightly but the cold look stays in his eyes. His mouth opens but I'm quicker.

"I think I should go to sleep as well."

His jaw hardens before he gives me a sharp nod. I exhale and quickly walk past him ignoring his familiar scent. Ignoring the pull at my heart.

~ 18 ~

"He will attack when we least expect it."

"Do you think he will come with an army?"

"Maybe he isn't even coming and is letting someone else do it."

The jumble of voices fades into one giant buzzing noise as I stare down at my untouched plate. The greasy bread looks crispy and fresh when the maid puts it down, the berries arranged in a beautiful spiral. I don't try to look around the banquet table and listen to Kael and Flynn discuss Adales and his plans. I couldn't sleep a lot last night, too disturbed by my loud thoughts. I understand their worries but what difference does it make if he comes with an army or without? If he decides to do it or hire someone else?

The fact is that it won't matter because I can't squish an ounce of magic out of my fingertips.

Something nudges my shin and I look up at Edlyn who eyes me worriedly. She's the one who slipped into my chambers this morning and got me ready. It almost felt like we were back home when she scrubbed me in the rose-scented bath and pinned my waves up with small little citrines. The dress she brought is light and flows beautifully. It is in pale jade and I was relieved when I saw that no corset was required to put it on. I felt different when I looked into the mirror today, I got used to the breeches and practical clothing we wore on the journey and complained to my friend who told me to 'suck it up'.

To my dismay, the topic swiveled over when she found the script roll and I let her read what Cassian did for me.

"Are you all right?" Edlyn whispers beside me and I nod stiffly. My eyes wander over the head of the table, the chair empty. Cassian didn't join our first meal today and I keep glancing at the chair as if he will appear out of thin air. My eyes flicker to the chair beside it, occupied by none other than Azzura. Her sleek hair is pulled into a complicated braid, her dark skin glowing in the morning light. She dressed again in a jewel-toned skirt, a matching blouse and a long schal that connects the two pieces. Edlyn told me it is called a saree which is considered traditional clothing from the place Azzura was born in.

"I'm fine."

The voices untangle from their chaos and I look up at something Kael says.

"Maybe there is some kind of trigger. When was the last time you changed, Carina?" His pale green eyes place themselves on me and I blink. I refuse my body from blushing in embarrassment because I didn't listen.

"Sorry?"

"When did you change again to your true form, after the first time of course."

I look around the table confused, three pairs of eyes placed on me. Azzura is picking at her breakfast lazily, uninterested in the topic.

"I didn't change again." I watch Flynn narrow his eyes. "Then how did you feed to fulfill the change."

"I didn't?" This conversation is making my head spin.

"She's telling the truth, she didn't need to feed. I was wondering about that too. Maybe it has something to do with the fact that Aerwyn didn't need to feed." Flynn scoffs at Edlyn's answer.

"Aerwyn was a goddess and Carina is still half Faye."

"You don't need to sound so condescending about it." I snap at him but he doesn't even give me the time of the day as he glares at my friend.

"What are you implying? Why would we lie about the fact that she hasn't fed again? She looks fine to me!" Edlyn says and I hear Kael snicker. Here we go again.

"I'm not implying anything. I just find it highly suspicious that she doesn't need to feed even to fulfill the change. And now she can't even wield her magic?"

"She is a literal half-goddess, Nayaran, if it is one thing it is impressive that she didn't need blood to fulfill the change and is not suspicious." The conversation halts at the new voice and I turn my head to watch Zayne approach the table. His walk is lazy, his orange shirt half unbuttoned as he chooses to sit down in the chair beside Kael. The one in front of me. Flynn stays quiet and I eye him for a moment to see his jaw clenching, his eyes trained on his plate. Azzura straightens in her seat and throws a slow glance at the prince.

"Excuse me?" I speak up so Zayne can repeat his words. He stares at me with hard features, not letting me see any kind of emotion that swirls inside him.

"Well, you must've made the connection, mustn't you? Cassian might be the next ruler of Gehenna, King Hector the protector of the skies and whoever might take Marrus's place will rule the ocean but none of them are gods. Our blood is all washed down over centuries. We are merely regents. But you are the direct daughter of a goddess. Which makes you a half-god." Zayne has a smug smile on his lips when nausea hits me. I think I'm going to be sick.

"You all right there, darling? You look a bit pale." Zayne pops a cherry into his mouth grinning, satisfied with the chaos he unyielded on me. I can't be a half-god. I can't even conjure magic nor can I change, how would I be a god? I would definitely be a lousy one.

"Holy shit, he's right." Kael looks at me expectantly and I shake my head. "I'm not a half-god."

"The facts speak the truth, princess, you kind of are a half-god. Goddess." Now I'm really glad that I haven't touched my plate yet. My heartbeat strums at the realization that dawns on me. No matter how much I remember from my past lives it doesn't change the facts. Even if I hate to say it, Zayne is right. I grab the nearest goblet and fill it with the wine, splashing some of the liquid onto the table before I get in a few gulps.

"Look at what you've done. You've made her an alcoholic, Zayne!" Edlyn tries to grab the goblet out of my hand but I maneuver around her until I've finished the drink. Kael snickers and Azzura rolls her eyes.

"I would love to see drunk Carina."

"Of course, you would," Flynn grumbles before he gets up from the table. Azzura follows suit, not sparing us a goodbye as she leaves. Her hand travels over Zayne's shoulder and she whispers something in his ear before she disappears. I barely register them leaving the room as I put the goblet back onto the table. The liquor already makes my head swim and I need to grab the sides of the table to steady myself.

"Fuck." I whisper as I try to get a hold of everything.

"What a pathetic excuse of a human am I?"

"Correction. Pathetic excuse of a goddess." Kael holds one finger up and I shoot him a glare. He grins lightly but his eyes are cast on the door where Azzura disappeared behind.

"You seem to be handling this information so very well," Zayne speaks up again and I can see in the way his eyes glitter that he's going to drop another bomb. I try to braze myself and tighten my hands around the table while I feel Edlyn's energy beside me.

"The fact that my brother isn't here just proves what he thinks of your usefulness—"

"Stop being an ass, Zayne. You know that's not why he's missing." Kael suddenly interrupts the prince and my brows fly up surprised. Zayne turns his head sharply but Kael doesn't cower under his gaze. He doesn't feel the slightest bit threatened by him. A spark of proudness ignites in my heart at the way he's defending Cassian.

"Yes? Then why is he missing the table? Is it not because Carina has been treating him like a mere convenience? Is it not because she stabbed him and killed him?"

"Technically I didn't kill him—"

"You should not be talking right now!" Zayne's voice booms through the hall as he slams his hands on the table making it crack under the impact. I don't dare to flinch as I meet his glare. He's gotten up from his seat and his whole being is seething—burning with anger. Why is he so angry at me? What was it that I've done to receive such hatred since we were children?

"Do you think I would listen to you and let you forbid me to talk?" I stand up as well staring at him over the table. The whole room seems to vibrate with power.

"You have no right to speak. You are not entitled to be spared with pity. He has done EVERYTHING for you! He has left his home, his family, and his sick mother to ensure that you stay alive. He has annulled the wedding because you wanted it to! I watched my little brother leave the kingdom at the age of sixteen because of some stupid girl that can't protect herself—"

"I am perfectly able to protect myself you asshole! If your brother—" In a flash, Zayne has rounded the table and now towers with his enormous form in front of me. I inhale a sharp breath but don't take a step back.

"If it weren't for my brother you would be dead by now. He brought you here to safety, even though it endangers this kingdom. His kingdom. He brought you here because you are the one to defeat Adales so this continent can live in peace again for the first time after centuries. But look at you. You can't even perform any magic."

"That's enough!" Edlyn growls and steps in front of me just as Kael does. My body freezes, rigid with his words. He just confirmed what I knew all along. Cassian is endangering this kingdom, and the people here just because he thinks I can defeat a god. It is me who Adales wants. He won't attack the kingdoms once I'm dead, will he? He will rule over Adalon again in peace and lazily sit on his ass. He will have his revenge on Aerwyn and will let everyone else live in harmony.

Zayne's bitter laugh makes me look up again.

"Look how you're all protecting her. Do you think she is your savior? She is nothing but death spreading over all of our lives." Something cracks inside me. I tell myself that I shouldn't listen to a word Zayne says. He is cruel, he always was, so his words shouldn't count. Still, it does because it confirms all my suspicions. What did he mean when he said, sick mother? Is the queen curing an illness? Can an Upyr even get ill?

I stare at Zayne, clenching my hands to stop my burning eyes from tearing up. Kael and Edlyn both don't move from in front of me and I hate that they feel the need to protect me. The room suddenly drops its temperature by a few degrees and as if on instinct, as if it was calling to me, I turn my head to look towards the doors.

"I send you to go fetch the princess and you pick a fight. You are capable of nothing aren't you?"

Cassian leans against the gigantic door frame dressed in all-black clothing. Soft gilded vines litter the bottom of his breeches and I catch a few glints of gold rings that wrap around his fingers. The color complements his now bronze skin. His curls are tamed but still, a bit in longer strands, curling at the nape of his neck. He looks majestic. It's the first time he looks like a king rather than a lazy prince. His features are hard and cold but something glints in his eyes as he stares at his brother.

"Do you have anything to say in your defense?" He arches a dark brow and I just hear Zayne scoff, my eyes not willing to move from the prince. I take a step forward as if someone got a hold of me and lurched me forward.

His eyes flicker to me barely for a second before he focuses back on the others with me. Something inside me deflates.

"I'm thankful for your consideration of protecting Carina but I can assure you she can do that herself. You are excused." I blink surprised at his formality but Kael and Edlyn both bow down and start to leave the room. I watch them and Edlyn throws an apologetic smile at me. He is their prince after all.

"You too, Zayne," Cassian says, his voice now aggravated. My eyes fly to the older brother who clenches his jaw angrily.

"You can't really tell me that your affection for her hasn't fizzled out long ago. She's the epitome of all your problems and all your worries!" Rage bubbles up inside me at his words again. Would he stop being a fucking asshole?

"You. Are. Dismissed." The words are barely audible and still, they crawl over my skin like a dozen spiders. And whatever it is that he uses to crackle the air around us it makes Zayne clench his jaw and storm out of the chamber. I watch him leave angrily and stare at the door even after he is gone. I don't dare move my eyes to Cassian. I don't know what to think, what to do with all the things that Zayne revealed.

"My father has requested our audience in the throne room." My eyes flicker toward Cassian who watches the wall behind me intently.

"All right." I can't remember why I was angry at him. Can't remember why I was so judgmental and condescending. I don't move from my place and stare at him until he finally places his eyes on me. I have to think back to last night and the way I fled the scene. Him catching Kael and I on the balcony must have him thinking all kinds of things. Tension builds in the air and for a moment I think he's going to say something. To do something. I urge him in my mind to do so. To make all this confusion disappear and tell me himself that it doesn't have to be complicated if it is real. So I can finally feel alive again and shed this miserable cover that makes me pretend. Half the time it feels like I'm in pieces, cradling them all together with my arms but how long will I be able to hold them if new pieces fall off every day?

His lips part and I almost try to lean closer, even though I'm feet away from him.

"My father doesn't like to wait." He turns and disappears from the room.

I haven't memorized the way to the throne room so I quickly hike up my skirt and travel after him into the hall. To my surprise, he waits outside for me, and once I'm in view he starts to walk again. I don't have the time to wonder about what the king wants to talk about or if he found something about the Fatum. I'm too busy keeping up with Cassian's big strides.

One step of his equals three of mine.

If I don't know better I would think he's trying to flee from me. But I don't give up until I strut beside him with much effort. He doesn't spare me a glance as he leads us through halls filled with servants running around, passing wild-looking paintings, and various gilded doors that are closed to any prying eyes.

The closer we get to the throne room the more restless I get. Something buzzes inside me and it feels like the sound is growing more and more telling me to turn around and run. Maybe it is my nerves or my anxiety telling me that I don't want to get back into that dark room. It did fascinate me but somehow the mood Cassian is in concerns me.

"Do you know why your father wants to speak to us?"

"Maybe he wants us to sign the annulment papers." He says shrugging his shoulders lazily. I watch him beside me for a moment. "Zayne said something and I wonder if it is true."

"Zayne usually likes to twist the truth." I am aware of that. Still, I speak up again my curiosity and maybe an ounce of guilt urging me forward. "He said that the queen . . . your mother is ill?"

He suddenly stops walking, making me stumble and almost kiss the floor. His arm shoots out and gets a grip on my elbow. I look up, surprised to see his features completely frozen.

"He told you that she is ill?" Something weird rings in his voice. His touch on my arm sears through the thin material of my dress, making me blink unsure.

"He did. But it was out of rage I don't think he would've said anything if—"

"That damn bastard can't keep his mouth shut." Cas suddenly lets go of my arm and continues his walk. I quickly jog after him, not ready to let the topic go.

"Is an Upyr able to get ill?"

"No."

"But she is?"

"Obviously."

"Why didn't you tell me?" He stops abruptly at the question and I notice that we've reached the throne room.

"Why didn't I tell you? What would you have done, Carina, tell me? She is ill, I had to leave her in her illness to protect you. She begged me not to go and I still did. End of story."

"Why?" I ask quietly and he takes a step forward. I stumble and try to retreat but feel the cold material of the doors dig into my back.

"Why?" The question sounds almost agonizing to him.

"Is it still not clear what I feel for you? What do I have to do so you understand I would go to the end of the world for you?" He takes a step closer, our bodies almost touching. My breath hitches and my brain seems to shut off completely.

"Tell me." He whispers and I close my eyes when the tips of his fingers trail over my collarbones and up my neck. My heart thrums in my chest and I fear that it might break a rib.

"Tell me what I have to do so I'm yours and I will. No exceptions, no holding back." His fingers travel along my jaw and over my cheekbone. I open my eyes again to stare into a dark forest.

"If you want me to leave you alone, fine, I will." His lips travel over my jaw and my skin buzzes, my body singing in anticipation. I barely notice that I'm grabbing his shirt, pulling him even closer to me.

"But then you have to stop looking at me like that or else I might crumble." His nose bumps mine and I manage to get out a whisper. "Look at you like what?"

"Like I'm the only one capable of saving you. Like you wouldn't want anyone else than me." I shudder at his words and can already taste the sweetness of his mouth as it inches closer and I don't dare to speak up. I don't move. I squeeze my eyes shut as if to ignore the truth and fist his shirt, waiting for him to kiss me. But instead, I'm falling.

I'm falling backward as the door gives away behind me and my eyes widen in shock to see Cassian just as surprised as I am, as he wraps an arm around my waist in order to keep me upright.

I turn in his hold to see the doors have opened to the throne room, the black stone glimmering ominously as I stare into familiar eyes. Eyes I didn't think I would ever see again.

~ 19 ~

"I know you." My face goes numb when I speak the words. I don't dare to move as my eyes travel over the tall figure of the boy. His hazel hair sits in the same fluffy chaos on his head, his features are the same soft lines as the last time I saw them. And his eyes. His eyes shine in the identical lilac color they did when I talked to him in the Sebestyen castle.

A boyish grin spreads onto the Protestant's lips. "Glad I stayed in your memory, Your Highness." He bows and I just now notice King Ronan standing a bit behind the boy. "This boy claims to owe a favor from the both of you because he has saved your lives?" The king questions us as Cassian lightly steps in front of me. I furrow my brows at his stance.

"It was a very wrong idea to come here, boy." He says darkly but the Protestant doesn't seem the slightest bit threatened by him. He's strapped in dark brown leather gear, a belt securing small knives to his waist and a bow tied to his back.

"Pleased to see you back on your feet. A thank you would be gladly accepted by me." He's still grinning and Cassian takes an aggressive step forward, making me clutch his forearm.

"What are you doing?" He hisses and I glare up at him, wanting to hear what the boy has to say.

"What are you doing?"

"I was about to snap the neck of a Protestant."

"Gods, you are ridiculous." I sigh before I push him behind me and look back at the boy. He's grinning as he watches the interaction between me and the prince. "What are you doing here?" I ask the boy who now struts a bit closer. I eye the sword at his side, colliding with his thigh with every step he takes. Strangely the sight of all his weapons doesn't feel threatening. Cas thinks otherwise as he puffs out his chest behind me and I'm tempted to slap him across the room.

"I came here because my queen is here. There are things you must know, Your Majesty, and I am willing to contribute that information." He suddenly kneels before me and I blink.

"I'm not a queen."

"Yes, you are. The Queen of the Faye and all living life." I can't help myself and burst out into a small chuckle. The boy looks up at me confused. Now that he's closer I see that his eyes aren't completely lilac but have some green swirls in the deep ends. I kneel as well the dress giving me enough space to do so and put my hands on his arms.

"The Faye are dead and I don't even know your name. I am no queen."

"My name is Kian. And the Faye aren't dead." I sit down on my calves confused. I don't care if it is called improper for me but the cold ground beneath me gives me some sense of control. The cold spreads through my body like a virus winding around my mind.

"What do you mean by that?" Cassian asks behind me and I turn to see his eyes narrowed in suspicion.

"I believed you to be smarter, prince. I mean by that that the Faye are alive, many of them and I am one of them." My heart plummets until it dies down for a second completely.

"But . . . Adales killed them—where are they?" I question Kian who looks at me with a small smile.

"They were always right in front of your nose." It takes me a moment to register. But I make the connection quicker than Cas and his father do.

"The Protestants." The way the city buzzed in colors and light, the way those people ogled me on the market, some of them knew. I knew. Deep down I did. The way I trusted Kian the first time we met him was not purely coincidental. It feels like the ground beneath me opens up and swallows me whole.

"That's impossible." Cassian kneels down as well, his arm brushing against mine.

"But why did they attack Aerwyna? Why do they attack the castle?"

Kian grimaces lightly at my question. "Many have forgotten. Others are burning in rage, thinking that you are the one that is responsible for all those deaths. I don't. I never did. It is Adales who deserves punishment. It is he who killed families, children, and parents. You never did. But some Faye won't listen and they were the ones who attacked the castle. We try to keep them at bay and most of the time it works. Most of the time it doesn't."

I can't believe what he is saying. The Faye are alive. The people who would be my subjects.

"But why would they think that I am responsible for all these deaths?" I question, trying to wrap my mind around what he is telling us. Kian's eyes divert to the onyx floor, a soft flush spreading on his cheeks.

"The order to kill any Protestants came from the Sebestyen court, I guess they just figured it was you. Even though I know, " He looks back up at me, devotion shining in the depths of his eyes. "I know it would never be in your heart to damn all these people."

My heart is in my throat, stuck without moving up or down. I look at my hands in shame, hands that despite Kian's beliefs were able to kill people. After a beat of silence, he carries on.

"The second word came around that you finally arrived in Demeter. We made our way over. There are many on your side, my queen, we are willing to fight. For freedom and your reign." Kian sounds prideful and it makes guilt bloom in my chest. They certainly deserve someone better. Someone who can do something about this situation. I can barely grasp, rather understand everything.

"When you say we. Who do you mean?" Cassian utters beside me and I don't know why but my body grows so cold that I search for his hand. Once our fingers bump he intertwines them and squeezes assuringly.

"Right, I have brought a guest you might still remember." Kian looks towards the king whose eyes fly over to me. He doesn't say anything and the second door in the throne room opens and I braze myself. I braze myself for an Armada of Faye. Warriors, fighters, scarred faces, and hands. I expect Protestants that claim to be Faye, claim they want to live under my reign. But what we get is one person.

A woman. Dressed in a skin-tight suit, black long hair that is braided delicately and falls down her back. Her features are hard, her body is tense with muscles. A soft mouth adorns her face, her skin shimmery almost translucent. Karambit knives are strapped to her belt. It is not the armed weapons that make me hold my breath, nor the lilac eyes that glow when they place themselves on us, kneeling on the floor.

My lips part in a soft breath. "Holy, Fuck." I flinch but realize that the words are spoken by Cas as he stares at the woman. Her lips spread into a gentle smile as she looks at me.

"Hello, sweetheart."

The first thing I do is not burst out in tears. I thankfully don't faint, I don't scream either. I'm not disappointed, not even shocked. The only thing that escapes me is a chuckle. It is not filled with humor. I lift my hands in shock and cover my mouth but the laugh doesn't stop. Cassian eyes me warily and I can't blame him. I must seem like a crazy person. To my surprise, it is King Ronan who speaks up first.

"This all has been very much. Maybe you want to go to your chambers and rest, Carina?"

"No it's fine—I'm fine," I say and finally control my laughter.

"Well, I will leave you to it then. Cassian, will you join me?" He looks at his son whose eyes flit toward me. I don't want him to go, gods, I don't even know how to handle this. Shailaigh Sebestyen is standing a few feet away, alive and unharmed.

"Please, stay." The words slip out before I can stop them. Cas doesn't waver as he nods at me. "I will join you afterward, Father."

"Very well." The king leaves his throne room to spare us some privacy. The prince helps me up to my feet and Kian follows our example.

"I don't think anything can surprise me these days anymore," I mumble as I straighten my skirt before I look back at my dead mother. My once-dead now-alive adoptive mother. Her features soften at my words and she takes a step forward so she stands beside Kian.

"I wish we could've done this differently."

"Believe me, I thought we would never do this. Because you know, you're actually dead." I can't help the sarcasm from escaping. A knot forms in my throat when I let my gaze wander over her. She doesn't look a day older than the last time I saw her.

"Baby . . ." She takes a step forward her eyes vulnerable but I take a step back right into Cassian's chest. He doesn't move nor does he take a step back.

"You are here now. However that might be possible, so explain yourself." The hope in her eyes deflates and instead of speaking up Kian is the one to do it.

"It was purely coincidental that Shailagh was the one to find you on the day of your rebirth." I shake my head instantly. I don't want to hear any stories anymore. I've had enough. Kian hesitates and I look at my mother. What I thought was my mother.

"You left. You left and knew that you would leave me with someone who is an imposter? And now you're back, conveniently, at the time when we get rid of Daragon and I have rumored magical powers."

"I know how it seems but it's not the truth."

"Then what is the truth, mother? Tell me that you didn't leave me and Henri behind. That you didn't flee the scene the moment you found out—what exactly?" She takes a step forward but freezes when she looks at Cassian behind me. Whatever he looks like it makes her freeze in her spot.

"I did leave, yes. And believe me when I say that it was one of the things I regret most in my life. But it was my only choice. When I found out that he knew who you are and that he wanted to sacrifice you I knew the deal with King Ronan wasn't enough. But Daragon found out that I mistrusted him and he tried to kill me."

"So you simulated your own death," I state and watch her lilac eyes turn to the ground. Her shoulders are tense, her skin so pale it makes me believe the blood flow underneath has stopped for a moment.

"I did. But I came back for you so many times. Why do you think the activity of the Protestants was so high in Aerwyna? I tried to get you and Henri back into safety—"

"Safety?" I laugh humorlessly, taking a few steps forward. I wait until she meets my gaze. Her eyes once told me stories and whispered with me to the stars. They filled me with warmth and security but now I only see a stranger in them, a liar. A person I mourned for over years, that I willed to come back to me. Now that she is, I don't know if I want her back.

"Your people. The Protestants tried to kill me! Tried to kill the man I—" I gesture towards Cassian whose eyes burn when they look at me and I hesitate. "—the man that was to keep me safe."

"And I'm sorry about that, *gods*, Carina, I'm sorry. We didn't know that many of the Faye kept their vengeance. How many of them were clinging to revenge."

"Apologizing won't change a thing, mother." I want to hurt her. Hurt her the way that I hurt when I thought she was dead. She should've tried harder. Not just for my sake but for Henri's too. She should at least care enough for her legitimate son.

"Maybe we should all take a deep breath and think about what we say next." Kian suddenly speaks up and I look at him for a moment hesitating. My whole world has been flipped over yet again and he expects me to be calm? Still, I inhale deeply for a moment.

"Why did you come back?" I ask no one in particular. I can't stand the look of my mother so I glance at Cassian who's still standing near me. I can see his fingers twitch at his sides when he meets my gaze.

"We came back because we know you need our help. The way Faye operate with their magic is unique and hard to learn. We can help you study your powers and control them so you can defeat Adales." I turn back around to look at Kian. His lilac eyes are gentle as he watches me, so much knowledge lies underneath that color, even though his face glows in youth. "It's a pity to disappoint you but there are no powers to study."

"Yet." He says and I furrow my brows. "You can't tell me you can't feel it?" Shailagh suddenly speaks up and my eyes fly over to her. New determination settles in her stance, confidence etched into her luminous face. It just occurs to me now how a soft glow surrounds them both. The air bends to their will with the light, so similar to Cassian when he lets his shadows traverse. I don't know what to tell her. Admitting that I don't feel anything different in my body.

"You must feel it at least when you're close to him." She suddenly goes on and nods her head at the prince who freezes. I don't dare to look at him as my eyes stay on my supposed mother.

"The way the magic slumbers in your veins shudders when you get close. It calls to you." Something in my face seems to encourage her to keep going. "It recognizes his power as much as it recognizes yours. There are ways to make you work with it so you can use it to your advantage. Cassian is your counterpart. Both your magic stems from the same power so it's likely you're drawn to each other."

An uncomfortable silence settles over the room, creeps into the edges, and cracks on the surfaces. Soft buzzing forms at the back of my head and I know it will soon travel to the surface and end in a pounding headache. I've heard enough.

"I appreciate your willingness to help and I am sorry for all the Protestants who got hurt who had no ill intent towards Aerwyna. But I will not train with any of you. There is no magic. There never was." I can practically see something crumble in Kian's eyes but I don't bother to stay to see the ruins. I turn and start to leave the suffocating room. I don't hear the voices calling my name back as I storm out into the light hall. The walls seem to close in on me and there's just one thing on my mind, escape.

"Your Highness—" a guard tries to address me, his voice muted like I'm underwater. I barrel past him and the ten more that I meet on the way, my breathing turns faster, faster. My steps are quicker, something sizzles underneath me. Oh, gods, I need to get outside, now.

My sight turns blurry, the thundering of my heart a steady rhythm as I almost fly out of the entrance. The fresh air doesn't reach my lungs and the rays of sunlight don't reach my skin. I storm even farther, a tight knot forming around my heart as I burst through the iron gates and right into the pine forest. I can feel the earth vibrate underneath my feet, and the air reeks of acid as I sprint deeper into the forest. The trees disappear in a blur of green and brown until I finally reach the edge of the mountain.

Only then I stop, resting my hands against the solid material, trying to catch my breath.

The thundering of my heart gets overpowered by a new sound. A sound of a second beating heart. I don't turn, knowing it's him. Of course, I do.

"I'm fine you can go." I breathe out harshly as I squeeze my eyes shut. My sides are hurting and I feel sick to my stomach.

"Clearly not." His voice is a soft timber and it travels right over my skin.

"I'm fine, Cassian, if not I'm gonna be." I snap and am greeted by humorless laughter. "Is this what you're going to do every time something doesn't go your way? You're just going to run away?"

I whirl around angrily not understanding why he won't let me be. He stares at me with a green blazing fire in his eyes.

"Running away? I came with you to this godforsaken kingdom, didn't I? I'm sorry that I'm freaking out because my once-dead mother isn't as dead as I thought?"

"And what does it change? Does it make you upset that she's back?"

"It makes me upset that nothing seems like it is! It makes me upset that everyone does what they want and expects me to be fine with it! But I should be because everything everyone has done was for me to be safe, like I'm some kind of object that is going to get rid of all your problems!" Rage slams through me and we both inch closer to each other. He doesn't back down; he is as angry as I am.

"Do you think I wanted to leave my family for three years? Do you think Edlyn wanted to run away, to risk her life, and ask my father for shelter? Do you think the Faye wanted to stay in hiding and try to somehow save their queen by making so many great losses? This is so much bigger than we are, Carina, it would be selfish of us to run away. To cower and whine about people that pretended to be dead, people that lied so you could be safe."

I stare at him, angry tears stinging my eyes. Yes, I've been whining about useless things, things I can't change and? Do I not have the right to it? Cassian keeps on going and urges forward and my instincts flare up. He looks ballistic. I take a few steps back just to feel the rough exterior of the mountain dig into my back.

"You've lost your parents and I mourn with you, every day. Your best friend had to lie to you, I had to lie to you and I break every time you hold it against me." His voice is so raw with anger that it makes my skin tingle and my heart rate speeds up for a different reason. He places both his hands at the sides of my face, caging me in.

"But you were never alone. You had your brother, Gisella, Edlyn would burn the world for you, even my own friends latch you into their hearts. I would pick apart the world, stone by stone to ensure your happiness. You have people willing to sacrifice everything for you not because you are Aerwyn's daughter or have her magic. But because you're you." The fire seizes in his eyes and his breath fans over my lips.

My eyes flicker down to them just for a moment and I can see in the light in his eyes that he saw it.

"Are you telling me I'm being a whiny child?" My words come out in a breath. The anger still flares around us and sizzles in the air but it is a different kind of anger now. A yearning to unleash the energy.

He huffs out a rough laugh.

"I'm saying you've gone through so much. And that I see your emotions and that your feelings are valid. But the Carina I know wouldn't cower under the pressure. She would get up, grab her weapons, and let no one survive under her wrath." He leans even closer and my eyes fall shut when his lips graze my bottom one. My mouth opens inviting him, my body tensing in sweet anticipation but I can't. I can't do it. Just when I feel like I taste his lips I turn my head and they graze along my jaw.

A soft breath leaves his lips as he slackens. He takes a step back, his chest heaving as if he ran for miles. His jaw clenches and I shake my head slowly.

"If you kiss me now, I won't be able to stop," I whisper. "Would that be so bad? Do you hate me that much for what I did?" His tone changes to one that feels like it's crawling under my skin and pulling at my body.

"That's the problem. I do not. I don't hate you at all." I shake my head repeatedly, my body burning with every second it doesn't touch his.

His whole body tightens his lips open in a breath.

"And why is that a problem?"

"It's a problem because it makes me forgive you for anything you do no matter how wrong I think it is. It's a problem because it gives you so much power over me that you could tear the world apart and I would stand at your side and help you. I'd let you do it."

~ 20 ~

I stay leaning against the mountain as I sort my thoughts. Cassian fled the scene when Flynn appeared and told him that Oceanus got news regarding the death of Prince Marrus. I let him go gladly, not bearing to look into his face knowing what I confessed so carelessly moments ago. We need to focus on the tasks ahead, which include finding the Fatum and discovering how to defeat Adales.

Suddenly, an almost inaudible crack travels through the forest, forcing my eyes to scrutinize the trees. My heart plummets as my eyes wander over the earth littered with branches and twigs but I don't see anything. The sun rays don't reach this part of the forest and now that I'm alone, the anger vanished. It feels gloomy to be out here. I inhale deeply trying to relax before I hear it again.

I grab the soft skirt of my dress and make my way through the trees abruptly, feeling like I'm being observed. Which is impossible. I'm on the safe grounds of the castle. Still, my heart beats a rhythm too fast to be normal and my breathing is too quick for my liking. Somehow the cracks grow louder and the air grows colder as if someone is breathing right in my neck. I break out into a run.

I try to stay focused and light-footed as I practically sprint and weave around the trees, not knowing what I'm running from. It feels like someone is bolting behind me, arms stretched out and just grasping the tips of my hair, ready to yank me back. A relieved sigh plummets past my lips when I break out and the empire's iron gate greets me.

The guards at the gate look at me alarmed when I bolt through without a word, my steps hurried as I climb the stairs, leading towards the entrance. I stop at the top and finally turn around. You can almost oversee the whole forest that stretches around the castle on one side. Shadows lurk around the trees but none of them seem unnatural. From this position, the forest doesn't look threatening at all, it looks warm and friendly like it would welcome you like an old lover. The rising and falling of my chest finally slows down. Something winds around my heart as I stare at the pine trees, an eerie feeling that I still am unable to shake off.

I close my eyes for a moment. I´m starting to see things that are not there.

I turn and make my way through the archway, greeted with a soft Jasmine scent when I step into the halls of the castle. The scent instantly calms me and that something that slumbers inside me settles. Maybe it was just a scared animal or a branch that fell off a tree. I continue down the hall not looking where I'm going.

What have I become? I'm frightened by shadows and little sounds now. Maybe it's the fact that now I know what's really hiding in the shadows, waiting for some ignorant little girl like me to fall into their trap. Now that I know of the magic in the world I don't feel superior. Once I was the one people were scared of, and people ran from me. Now I'm the one doing the running. The hiding. If there is one thing I hate most in the world it is hiding.

I feel merely like a fugitive in this big castle, staying on the kindness of a king who hopes I'm the savior. I wonder why Adales hasn't made a move yet? This waiting, wondering is excruciating. Maybe they're wrong, mistaken by legends. Maybe Adales doesn't hold a grudge over millennials, he is a god, and he can probably feel that I don't have any powers. Besides from pointy ears and canines—which I can't even grow on command—, I can't create life. He probably feels it and maybe lets me be. Foolish thoughts that I wish would be true.

I have had my fair share of power-hungry men. If there is even the slightest chance that someone could steal your power, you eliminate them. No questions asked. Lost in my thoughts I stagger for a moment before my eyes refocus on the world in front of me. It takes me a moment to realize that I've not ended up in the wing with the guest chambers. I wandered so deep that the daylight can't reach this hall and the colder temperature tells me that this must be the pathway that leads into the mountain.

I hesitate and look around. I'm alone and no one told me I wasn't allowed here. So instead of listening to my brain to get back to my chambers and clean myself up, I take a small step forward. Another and another until I'm walking again. The jasmine scent somehow becomes stronger in this part of the castle and a weird thrumming in my chest—which is not my heart—arises. The furniture and hall look completely identical to the rest of the castle, white and elegant, and gilded ornaments are drawn onto small tables and vases, paintings, and ceilings.

The hall splits into two paths one that has stairs, leading upwards and the other that directs downwards. I follow the jasmine scent down the stairs. I know I must be in the mountain now, even though the exterior doesn't indicate it. I could've been walking along a dark hall in the castle. My fingers start to tickle lightly as I trail them along the light wallpapers and the thrumming becomes louder, harder.

My fingers catch on the next doorway that pulses with power. The door is somehow reinforced with gold thread and it feels like it's made to keep intruders out. I know I should go back the way I came from and work on the important things. I should write a letter to Henri, should talk to Edlyn about what happened this morning, talk to King Ronan and see what his process is with the Fatum, and maybe ask him to join his research. But instead, I let my hands travel over the golden ornaments and towards the handle.

If they would want to keep intruders out this door would be locked. I'm going to push gently and if it's locked I'm going to turn around and get the things done I mentioned.

My heart already deflates at the thought.

I push gently until I hear the mechanism of the lock click and the door swings open. I look around me to check if I'm still alone and when I notice I am, I slip into the small space and close the door behind me. A soft breath escapes me when I'm met with complete darkness.

My eyes take their sweet time adjusting to the sudden darkness of the room. I stay alert, hypersensitive to my surroundings and don't move when my ears focus on a second heartbeat. I can barely make out the room but it's almost empty, clean in every corner.

A soft pulsing glow emits from the only furniture in the room. A queen-sized bed, the origin of the heartbeat that I feel. Oh no. I shouldn't be here. Someone is lying in that bed and I can feel that the person is not conscious. Not asleep but not awake either. I try to turn and get the hell out of here but instead, I take three steps forward. The glow flares up with every step I take, illuminating the room in a blue glow. It's as if I can hear it flicker quietly, drawing me in, calling out my name. I squint my eyes at the intensity when I step close and once my knees hit the frame of the bed it feels like the light wraps around me, offering me the view of the person tucked under the comforter.

A soft breath escapes me once the angelic face is revealed.

A woman is tucked safely under the bed, her facial features drawn in as if she's in pain. Her long black lashes flutter against the bronze skin of her face, her soft mouth pinched uncomfortably. Long black hair lays behind her head like a curtain, the color faded, somehow pale. She is young, maybe a few years older than me but something inside me tells me that she is much older than she looks. Never judge a book by its cover.

Now that I'm closer I can hear the soft thud of her heart, it's weak and slow. Her body seems paralyzed, yet it feels like she is thrashing around, screaming in pain. Pure agony travels through me so hot and fast that I don't even realize tears have been running down my face. This is Cas' mother. I know it in the way her dark eyebrows have a small lift at the end, in the way the lines form around her mouth, in the way her lashes flutter against her cheekbones.

She's in excruciating pain. Why is she all alone in this room? They said she is ill but not that it is contagious. Whatever they thought they were doing, they thought wrong. She's withering in loneliness. I can feel it so deeply as if it were my own feelings. I can feel that something is poisoning her mind, crawling in the depths but its form is changing so fast that I can't make out what it is.

The fact that I can feel her agonizing pain is the trigger that does it for me. The pulling and thrumming and screaming inside me urges me forward and I drop gently into the space beside her and grab her cold hand in mine.

The moment our skin meets the light explodes around the room. I gasp at the electricity that thrums between our skin and I have to close my eyes shut at the pulling sensation in my body. Pictures flicker in front of my eyes, voices, emotions, and pain. So much pain.

Pain that now flows between our bodies and moves into mine as she pulls and pulls and pulls the energy out of my body. Another emotion flickers and I hear a voice I know. A voice I trust.

Please don't go, baby, please don't leave me.

You know I have to, mother. She needs me.

The timber of a voice echoes inside me and for a moment I forget where I am and what I'm doing. My head grows dizzy and I try to remember what I came here for. But there are strong arms pulling me back, pulling me into the sweet scent of pines and fresh wind. Cassian. I try to move forward to run into his arms but someone pulls me back.

Don't. You need to let go now.

I don't want to let go. I want to get to him. To see those emerald eyes sparkle in mischief, those sinful lips turn into a crooked grin.
Leave now, Carina.
Ice cold spreads over my body and I rip my hands away. I blink, one, two, three times. My eyes adjust to the dim lighting of the room. I somehow ended up on the ground, my body freezing cold, trembling. I feel like I've been sucked out like a pint of beer. An annoying sound travels through the silence and it takes me a moment to realize that it's my own teeth chattering from the cold. How the hell did it get so cold in here?
I slowly get off the floor, my vision clouded with spots as I hug myself to keep up some warmth.
"What did you do?"
I whirl around in surprise and almost fall flat on my ass again when I see Cassian's mother sitting up in bed. Her eyes are zeroed in on me, narrowed so much that I can barely see the green slumber behind it. Her canines are showing and her muscles are taught. Gone is the painful expression on her face as she glares at me. My mouth drops open in surprise as I let my eyes wander over her. Her black hair is rich and shiny, her skin glimmering in the blue light. What the hell happened?
Because I still have some sense of manners in my mind I bow lightly.
"Queen Aiyla I don't know if you recognize me—"
"Of course I recognize you. I am not stupid." Her words are fiery as she spits them at me like a cobra rearing its head. No one would believe me if I told them this woman was withering in pain just moments ago.
"What did you do to me?"
"I didn't do anything!" I protest as I watch her get out of bed elegantly. She's dressed in a long sleeved nightgown that pools around her feet and slips off her shoulders. I swallow the gasp that builds up in my throat when I see her frail figure. Her fingers are long and slender, the knuckles so prominent that it looks like they

could pierce through her skin. Her collarbones are so prominent it looks hurtful and her shoulders are as bony as the rest of her body. She looks like she should be dead.

For a moment the queen hesitates as she is surprised herself that she could stand up. Once the surprise fades from her eyes she focuses back on me. And whatever happened, whatever I have done, I know I'm in big trouble. My body feels so weak that it screams at me, yearning for a moment to rest. But Queen Aiyla doesn't allow me to.

"You are the reason my son had to ruin his life. You are the reason he's crying at the side of my bed, the reason he hasn't fed for months! Do you know what that does to someone like us?" A cold laugh escapes her when she advances on me. My eyes flicker to her canines as they graze her red lips.

"Of course you don't. You only ever cared about yourself while he risked his life. You're not good for him."

How did we end up here? I don't know but the murderous look in her eyes tells me I should get out of here. She's still stalking me and with every step she takes I take one back, hoping I will end up at the doors that lead me into this alternate hell.

"And now you look at me with those innocent eyes, those innocent hands, and soul, pretending as if you are not incarnate of the greatest evil himself. If I ever get my hands on you I will rip your flesh apart—"

She doesn't get any farther than gritting the last of her words. And that is because I kick her straight in the stomach. My eyes widen as I watch her body fly to the ground with so much force that she slithers back. She growls in pain but I don't give her the time to stand up again as I fumble for the goddamn handle and sprint out of the room.

A scream roars and shakes the walls around me as I hastily skitter across the hall, losing a fucking shoe on the way as I run for my life. My heartbeat explodes in my aching body as I run and run and run.

Whatever this crazy lady has planned for me I am not going to stay a second longer in this mountain. My sides ache and my throat hurts, my skin feels raw as if it's been scraped against rocks and granite. My eyes burn and something inside me stirs, nausea hits me but I won't stop running. I don't stop running when bile rises up my throat and I don't stop running when spots appear in front of my vision.

I only stop when I burst through my chambers and into the bathing chamber where I hurl up my breakfast.

~ 21 ~

"Rise and Shine, beautiful."

An obnoxious voice breaks through the heavy fog of my sleep and I quickly push my face into my pillow.

"Hey, I said get up." Someone tugs at the end of my duvet exposing my feet to the cold morning air.

"Go away." I blindly kick with my feet at whoever is disrupting my beauty sleep.

For a moment silence settles and I feel myself drifting back into the deep ends of sleep before I'm bathed in freezing cold.

"Hey!" The comforter is yanked off my body in one motion and I prop myself up to glare at a blurred form of Kael.

"What do you think you're doing? And what in the gods' names are you doing here?" I blink at him, trying to convey my distaste for his antics. He casually ignores the daggers I throw with my eyes as he plops onto the mattress beside me. I bounce with his added weight as he grins at me bopping my nose with his index finger.

"You and I have a date today." I stare at him blankly.

He rolls his eyes before rolling on his back and stretching like a feline. "One night and you've already forgotten the dooming of your fate, a god wanting to kill you."

Like the force of a Taifun, it breaks over me. "Right, The Fatum Temple." I rub my face trying to get rid of the sleepiness.

"If you're too tired to leave we can stay in and wait for Adales to destroy us all."

"Don't be ridiculous. And get off my bed." I try to shove him off but he doesn't budge. He puts his arms behind his head, letting out a soft yawn.

"I'll get in another nap until you're ready to go. Make sure to wear something honorable, we don't want the Fatum to feel provoked by your usual attire."

I freeze in mid-movement to get off the bed. "What is wrong with my usual attire?" I arch a brow and throw a glance at him over my shoulder. His eyes open and I can see the mischievous glance in them. His lips stretch into a lazy smile.

"You're unbelievable." I grab the first thing I can find, which is the silken pillow I slept on, and throw it at his face.

His muffled "Excuse you!" Is ignored by me as I slip into the bathing chamber to get ready for the day.

Fully clothed, our bellies filled with nutrition, Kael and I ride on Honeycomb and Nighttail toward Iason. Most of the people were still asleep in the castle except for a few servants bustling around, readying breakfast. I can barely stomach the butter bread and honey, my body in tight knots at the prospect of our day. Kael says that before we visit the temple and ask for answers we should be as prepared as possible. It would be a great mistake to come without any bearings and gifts for the ancient beings and demand answers. We have enough on our hands with the wrath of a single god and we rather not burden ourselves with the dismay of the Fatum.

Our first stop is a small wooden shop which is squeezed between two tall houses, windows drawn shut, rust gathering at the once green shutters.

The shop reveals over a thousand little figures whittled out of oak wood. An old man, barely reaching Kael's sternum, greets us with a toothless smile and raves about the figurines. He is delighted when Kael asks for a whole set of them, enhanced with small little rubies as eyes. I find them highly disturbing but hold my tongue as I watch Kael converse with the man. If charm could be personified I bet my left arm that Kael would be it. The way he charms the old white-haired man is so fascinating that I watch closely as we step out into the midday air. People notice Kael, they whisper behind held-up hands and a particular group of young girls giggle and flush as they pass us.

"Amazing," I mutter, making Kael beside me look down at me. "What?"

"You don't even notice it."

He blinks at me. "You only have to walk around the city and everyone is enchanted by you."

He follows my gaze to the group of girls that passed us. His cheeks flush as he notices them still looking. He ducks his head, even though that doesn't make him the slightest bit less noticeable.

"Come on, there is one stop we still have to make." He grabs my wrist and pulls me along the crowd of people. The market is still rather empty due the early hours of dawn but the further we pass jewelry stands, fruit tables, and honey pots the more people we pass.

"Did I say something wrong?" I ask the blond, who is still dragging me, now staring intently at the ground beneath us as if it is the most interesting view in the world.

"Huh? No, of course not."

"Kael." I wait until he looks at me. His steps slow as he lowers his voice so it's just me who can hear him. "I rather not talk about how people perceive me. Because you might see it as a compliment but it is only a curse."

"How can you say that?" A sick suspicion forms and I rather hope that I'm wrong. He shrinks further into himself. "My charms…is never something that I have been proud of. It is what people hated about me…punished me for."

"They punished you for being naturally charming?" His hold slips from my wrist but I quickly grab his hand in mine sensing that he does not want to talk about it.

"No matter what anyone says, Kael, I can say that I regret a lot of things but I could never regret meeting you. Your soul is beautiful and if I could capture it and show it to every single person in this world so they could see how special you are, I would. I must say I hesitate."

He flushes. "Why?"

I pull him closer, smiling lightly. "I'm far too selfish. I'd rather keep your unique soul hidden from the world before it gets spoiled by anyone and—" I huff out surprised when he pulls me into a hug.

His body trembles slightly with emotion and I quickly wind my arms around his torso. His peppermint scent fills me and a familiar feeling of care spreads in my chest. "Thank you." He mumbles into my hair and I tighten my arms around him. "Anytime."

We part and he clears his throat before a smile spreads on his lips. "Now let's get this fish before it is sold out."

"Fish?" I question confused before we dive through the market again.

I realize Kael wasn't joking when he stops in front of a stand smelling starkly of sea creatures. Fish are hung up on a line, their scales glittering in the morning light. I stare at him as if he is mad as he bids the seller for it.

I almost protest as I watch him hand over a sack of golden coins. A whole sack. For three stinking fishes. "I see, my boy, charming the lady." The dark-haired seller smiles as he bags the fish for us. Kael winds an arm around me, pulling me into his side. "My sister isn't so fond of fish but it always helps her with her complexion, isn't that right sweetheart?" Kael winks at me and I roll my eyes.

"Oh yes, my wife uses the fish oils for her skin and it helps formidably, especially the smell." The seller raves on and I furrow my brows. Is he able to smell?

Kael and I eye each other quizzically before taking the bag. "Have a wonderful day, sir." We quickly say our goodbyes while the seller goes on about the soft, oily skin of his wife.

"I'm rather confused if he is in love with his wife or the fish." Kael chuckles as he puts the bag into the satchel attached to

Honeycomb's side. "I rather not know," I say before I mount Nighttail.

"Now that we have your stinking fish and whittle figurines, where to?" I ask as he swings himself onto Honeycomb.

"The temple."

The temple is located not far from the farmer's market. We pass a few houses, with people bustling about, throwing their duvets out of their windows, watering the rose bushes in front of their houses. Screeching children fill our ride along the cobblestoned streets, occasionally filled with scolding parents telling them to stay away from the pathway of the carriages and riders.

The capital of the Kingdom of Death is more lively than I had anticipated. But that is not the first thing I was wrong about. I try to promise myself to see things as they are and not believe what everyone has told me my whole life. At the time we reach the temple, the air has grown so hot and stuffy I fear rain clouds will replace the sun in a few hours.

When I voice my concerns to Kael he shakes his head. "This weather is normal for Demeter. The sky is blue like forget me nots, not a cloud in sight, it will not rain."

I trust his expertise, knowing that he has lived in the kingdom since he was born.

Once we break from the busy streets and travel over a landscape filled with nothing but plants the air grows even hotter.

Behind a row of oak trees, it stands. The building is not tall, shaped like a rectangle, with open arches on every wall. High steps lead up to the temple made out of stone that looks so ancient I fear it might fall apart. A high *távcső* is located on the top, the symbol of the star of the Fatum at the top, marking this as nothing other than an honor to them.

"That is not what I pictured."

I turn to see Kael watching me. "What did you envision?"

"Well, first I thought it would be bigger. And maybe more color but this," I get off of Nighttail to stalk further to the building not taller than a small house. You can see the marble flooring inside the temple, the walls etched with the constellations of our world, "I just thought it would feel something when I see it."

"You mean sparks of magic or rainbows full of power?" I shoot him an incredulous look.

"Come on, let's get this over with." He grabs his fish and the whittled figurines. We climb up the steps and I still try to feel something. Maybe some kind of electricity or shock, something that tells me that power resides in the ancient walls of the temple. Nothing.

"There is never a residue of their power when the Fatum visit. We don't even know if this is going to work but this is our only choice right now." Kael says beside me. We enter the temple and at least it is much cooler than the air outside. I turn around and look at the etched symbols in the stones trying to decipher if anything looks familiar to me.

"Usually people come here if one of their relatives has fallen ill. It is more of a symbolic gesture to pray upon the Fatum." I turn to see that Kael has spread the Fish and Figurines on a small wooden plate.

"And we pay our respects with fish and wood?"

Kael gets up and nods, cleaning the fish out of his fingers with a cloth. "One of the sisters is rumored to love little figurines especially if their eyes are replaced by rubies and the fish is rather a sacrifice."

I grimace and he arches a blond brow. "Would you rather we sacrifice a human?"

"Don't be ridiculous. Now, what do we do? Do we wait or sit or lie down?"

He nods me over to the plate. I just notice now the three statues standing at the end of the temple. Kael and I stop in front of them. "They look strange." I find myself whispering as I eye the creatures. They do not look human, one cannot decipher if it is female or male, an animal, or what else it could be. The curves on the stature are precise and every stroke is carefully planned.

"Well, how would you imagine creatures as ancient as time to look like?"

"Not like this," I tell him. He chuckles before motioning for both of us to get to our knees.

I glance at him to watch him place his hands, palm up, on his thighs.

After a moment of silence, a language unknown to me slips past his lips.

"A segítségeteket kérjük, ó ti hatalmasok."

My body tenses at them, something strange flaring deep inside me.

"A mi alázatunk a te jogod, a mi fájdalmunk a te akaratod." He squints one eye open but nothing happens. A breath rushes past my lips as disappointment floods me. The plate is residing where Kael placed it not even a breeze makes its way through the arched open endings.

"It's not working," I whisper and Kael glances at me still on his knees.

"I'm aware, thank you," he breathes in before trying again.

"Tanácsot kérünk, ó, hatalmasok."

Nothing happens. I stare at the blood trickling along the fish's neck like a tear. I sigh and sit down on my calves.

"I'm sorry Carina, I hoped this would work." Kael sits down as well, worry lines running along his forehead. "It's all right, no one said it would work."

"What language was that?" I ask him as we hover.

"The Old Tongue, it is rarely used in Demeter anymore, I know it because Cas learned it and we used to talk in it when we didn't want the common people to understand us."

Black ink flashes in my memory. "His inked oath is it also the Old Tongue?"

Kael nods before getting up. "Makes him seem noble doesn't it?" He grins as he holds a hand out. I get up with his help and roll my eyes.

"You can't deny it, the ink turns you on,"

"Shut up, Kael." I know what he's trying to do. We leave the plate where it is and exit the temple as he teases me about the ink until my lips spread into a grin. "All right. It's not bad looking."

Kaels grin spreads further. "I knew it," he mumbles and goes on but is interrupted by a loud crash. We turn surprised as the sky is suddenly lit up with lightning. Thunder crashes a moment later.

"Didn't you say it wouldn't—" Before I finish my sentence, rain pours down on us so hard we're soaked in seconds. I turn glaring at Kael who already has an apologetic smile on his face. "Oops."

~ 22 ~

Cassian steps out of the shadows, his arms crossed in front of him. He looks furious, shadows dancing at his back for whatever reason. Crinkles riddle his white shirt, hastily tucked into his breeches and his hair looks disheveled as if he has been running his hands through the dark strands, multiple times. We all remain quiet as the constant dripping of Kael and I′s wet clothing sets an echo across the hall. Kael and I both share a glance while Cassian raises a brow at us.

"I think I better go and change," Kael says, completely abandoning me. When he passes Cassian he nods a quiet, 'brother'. The only thing he leaves behind is the muddy traces of his shoes, mixed with droplets of rain. Not standing the silence I remain where I am though I speak up.

"How did things go with Oceanus?"

He takes a step forward now and into the light of the open entrance.

"Oceanus is going to decide who will take the throne in the next few weeks. Word has traveled of the imposter who pretended to be Marrus." I shiver at the thought of Orkiathan.

"Flynn left Demeter this morning to travel to the sea."

"Because he is royalty and considered next in line?" I ask and the prince's lips twitch for a moment before he moves his back to me. He seems to be in a peculiar mood and I cannot help but fear that maybe somehow he knows that I traveled to his mother's chambers last night. No one seemed to know of what I like to call the incident and the queen hasn′t been walking the halls so I presume she remains in her bed.

"Flynn is a bastard. He may be royal but many cousins would come before him. He's going because his cousin Aalton asked him to. It is rumored he will be the next in line." His words linger in the vast space. Flynn is a bastard? Could that be the reason for his distaste of his birth name? I don't get the chance to ask because

Cassian speaks up again his back to me. "I assume you and Kael have not made any progress." It's not a question but I answer anyway.

"No sign of the Fatum yet. Maybe our sacrifice wasn't big enough."

"Or maybe they are a myth after all." He turns to look at me, his eyes wandering over my shivering shoulders. The cold of the rain starts to creep under my skin and pierce my bones. "I better change as well."

He nods, his hands on his back as he observes me. "Will you be joining us for dinner?"

"I'd rather not, I feel tired from the trip to Iason." I watch him nod but he doesn't look at me. Something is up, it's like it crackles in the air around us. When he doesn't speak up again, I start walking past him. My wet boots squeak awkwardly on the ground.

"It has nothing to do with the fact that my mother suddenly joined us at breakfast after free months of lying in her bed, has it?"

"I—what?" I swallow surprised and turn back around. My heart seems to slide up in my throat, beating viciously.

"She mentioned you were the one who healed her . . . That you sneaked into her room. Is that true?" I adjust my stance as he walks over to me. His body heat travels over me as he stops a hairbreadth away. "I don't—"

"The truth, Carina. Have we not promised ourselves to continue in honesty?" He asks.

"She is not healed. I just . . . I don't know what happened, all right? Whatever I did, she's not fine yet."

He releases a shuddering breath, his head lolling forward. A surprised breath escapes me when he pulls me flush against his chest, his arms around me, his face in the crook of my shoulder. He doesn't care that I'm soaked to the bone, his clothing is now soaked as well. I shiver when I feel the warmth of his body.

"Thank you."

It's barely a breath when he whispers the words against my skin and they travel along my spine and down my body. I don't think I've ever heard him sound this relieved.

A moment after he lets go of me again, his eyes shine brightly.

"Whatever you did, however you did it, I will forever owe you for it."

I shake my head quickly, still a bit dizzy from all that has happened. "You do not owe me. I don´t even know if I helped her."

"You did. This is the first time in a while that she has been able to walk, to be this conscious again." He presses and my cheeks flush. He catches me in surprise when he presses his lips against my cheek. The contact sends a zing through my body, my stupid heart fluttering like the traitor it is.

I feel like I do not deserve credit for whatever has happened. He bows his head for a moment, his curls bouncing with the movement. "Maybe later we can talk about the temple. You should rest now."

I look into those deep eyes, the plea laying in them. I nod suddenly breathless at the intensity of his gaze.

He walks past me briskly, his hand grazing mine in the process. Though he is not fast enough for me not to see the relief glistening in his eyes.

~ 23 ~

After I have changed into dry clothes and managed to gather the soaked strands of my hair into a knot, Kael and Edlyn join me in my chambers for dinner. The latter informs me that he has had the grace to tell King Ronan about our failed mission. He promised he would look further into the Fatum, not stopping until we get to them. After a few minutes of silence, we find ourselves talking about the queen.

"She is not healed just so you know. Whatever it is that happened to her, it's still inside her. I don't know how but I think I somehow just gave her some of my energy. It was a strange siphoning feeling when I touched her."

Edlyn has a thoughtful look on her face. Kael speaks up around a mouthful of stew.

"She didn't leave her bed for the last three years, Carina. So whatever you did, it was damn powerful." He shovels the next full spoon into his mouth while my best friend remains quiet.

"I don't know what it means. I didn't do it on purpose I don't want Cassian to think—"

"He doesn't expect anything of you. The fact that you already did it is more than enough. We're going to figure out how your powers work eventually."

But do we have enough time for that? I fear we have not. I look at him but he's already eyeing the leftover stew from Edlyn.

"Have at it," she says, waving lazily with her hand. Kael doesn't hesitate before taking it.

"Have you seen her? Was she alright?" I ask Edlyn. Despite her ill-treatment, I don't want her to come to any harm, after all, she is the prince's mother.

"The king burst out in tears when he saw her. She was always kind of lucid, they made sure to visit her and talk to her. Our healers give her strong pain-relieving potions which make her sleep a lot.

No one could ever say what it was she had. She says she hears everything when people talk to her."

"And she has been in this state for months?" I ask and she nods.

"The healers made sure to infuse blood now and then and practically she was alive but not really. It started just a little before Cassian took the oath and from then on it only got worse. Soft migraines turned into a hammering at her skull. She wouldn't come out of her chambers for weeks. She stopped eating and said it made her sick and nauseous, she's really sensitive to light and says it makes her bones hurt and her skin ache. She needed to stay in the sterile room without any source of daylight for years."

No wonder she reacted so aggressively toward me.

"This is the first time she came out and she ate, Carina. She is fine, no matter how long it's going to last. She is fine right now. It's phenomenal, everyone lost their hope over time, even though no one dared to say it."

The weight of her words settles on my shoulders. Kael finished eating and before I can offer him my plate I realize he has already snatched it.

I lean with my elbows on the table dropping my face in my hands to somehow shield my body from the thoughts in my head. Sometimes it feels like I'm drowning alive, losing myself in everything that develops inside my mind.

A soft knock against my chamber doors interrupts our companionable silence.

"Yes?" I ask and a moment later Cassian resides in the doorway. His eyes flit over our small group settled at the round table.

"I wanted to check in on you, I think we settled on a talk a while ago."

Right.

Edlyn and Kael quickly get up, the latter throwing a wink at me. I shake my head watching them go, Edlyn taking our devoured dinner plates with her.

When the door falls shut the sound echoes in my chamber.

"How are you feeling?" The prince asks from his place at the door. "Better now that I am in dry clothing." I get up and trudge over to my bed, my limbs feeling heavy with exhaustion. Maybe that is why I pat the space on the mattress beside me. I watch him saunter over, his hips moving lazily before he sits down beside me, our thighs brushing. There is a new healthy flush residing high on his cheeks and I wonder if the newfound health of his mother is responsible for this.

A heavy sigh leaves my lungs as I let my eyes rove over his face. I have been thinking a lot since the temple this afternoon and came to the conclusion that if I want to succeed in any of my plans I need the prince's help. Because alone I will not be able to do it.

"What is it?" He asks. If I want us to work together, for this to work we have to be transparent.

"I'm telling you this even though I know it will hurt you but you need to promise me something first." His gaze turns wary but his words are rushed.

"Anything you want." He says it in a heartbeat. My gaze flickers to our hands beside each other, our pinkies almost touching.

"I know how much you love your mother and I was very happy to be able to heal her,"

I pause thinking how I can say this in the most sensible way.

"I don't know if I'll be able to do it again. It . . . somehow drained me. I was really nauseous afterward and it felt like she was taking my life if that makes any sense."

I look up at him worried. I hate that my suspicions get confirmed when I see the troubled look on his face. I know he would not make me risk healing his mother when it means hurting me. But now that he found something that really helps her, how could he deny her the help? He moves his pinky to touch mine, a graze barely existent.

"I would never—never—make you do something that would hurt you."

"Good. Because I wouldn't let you." I tell him and watch his lips twitch.

"We'll figure something out. There is so little we know about these powers and maybe we could ask—"

"Hell no." I protest knowing which name he's going to say. He arches a dark brow at me and I pull my hand back.

"I'm not going to talk to her again. Over my dead body." I shake my head vigorously and he starts to laugh.

"What? What's so funny?" I say, narrowing my gaze at him.

"You're cute when you're stubborn." He says with a grin and I narrow my eyes even more. "I'm not stubborn."

"You are."

"I'm not."

"You are but no worries. I'm totally into it." He drops his hands behind him to sit in a more relaxed stance.

"I'm not stubborn, Cas."

He sighs and lets himself fall back, staring at the midnight canopy above us.

"The fact that you keep on insisting that you're not stubborn is stubborn, princess." He mumbles and I stay quiet. All right, maybe I am a little stubborn.

"Well, it doesn't change the fact, I don't want to talk to her."

"You don't have to. But how about you talk to Kian? He is a Faye too and he could maybe help you get a grasp on whatever it is you can do?" He looks at me.

"I guess I could ask him," I say hesitantly. It's not the time to be proud and not ask for help. "Good." He suddenly tugs at the ends of my drying hair. I can't help the shiver that runs down my back.

"Is that all you wanted to talk about?" He wraps one strand around his finger.

"About what I said the other day, in the forest. About us." His eyes flicker up at that and he unwraps the strand from his finger.

"So there is a possibility of us?" He asks, almost hopeful. Light flares on his face and I can see soft wisps of shadow trail along his shoulders.

"Everything we did at the Sebestyen court was so fast and intense. I don't know if I am able to trust you yet. I want to have my space and my own choice. And even more important I need the truth. In everything. No more lies about anything." He stares at me, his hands grabbing mine.

"Even if you wouldn't have said it, I would never lie to you again, Carina. I swear we do everything how you want it at your pace." I exhale softly.

"Good. Because there is something else I need to tell you." I can see him brace himself, his eyes placed intently on my face.

"When I was . . . dead something happened." I slip my hands out of his hold because I need to get up and pace for a moment. Maybe it will be easier to talk about this if I'm focused on something else.

"I fear I'm not going to like this." His voice is hard and somewhat suspicious. Before he can make too much out of it I just burst with the information. I tell him how I was in Purgatorium and was able to talk to Aerwyn and Demetrus. I try to pick up everything they said, everything they have ordered me to do. The expression on his face turns darker with every sentence I add and in between, he gets up from the bed and starts pacing. Once I finish I watch his tall form stride in front of the balcony doors. The moonlight lights half of his face up, the other side resting in darkness.

"That's fucking bizarre."

I almost have to laugh at the first words that escape him. My lips twitch when he looks at me. "She told you to come here? That Demeter was the place to look for the Fatum?" I nod and he starts pacing again. It is amazing how easily he can slip into the role of a prince in a matter of seconds. Something itches at the back of my mind, something Aerwyn said as well but I can barely remember what was said in so much haste.

"Did she say what the Fatum would tell you? How would they help?" I shake my head and he scoffs.

"Well. That's fucking helpful." He shakes his head in disbelief and I walk over to stop his pacing. I turned her words over for weeks, day after day trying to solve this puzzle. I wondered if her words had a different kind of meaning, that she may be hiding a message in between the verses. But I came up with nothing and Cassian will come up with nothing also.

"That's why I came here in the first place. Your father is the only connection to the Fatum that seems not grasped out of thin air." I tell him and he nods, his eyes focused in the distance, his body here, his mind calculating every possible outcome.

"But the temple was a failure and he still hasn't come out with anything else, there is not a word from Adales or Aerwyn and Demetrus. I never saw them again after that."

"How could you? From what you describe, it seems like they're traveling through realms to stay hidden from him. I just don't understand why they wouldn't tell you everything they know." I halter at his words searching his green eyes confused. "You think they withheld information?"

"You don't?" I never actually thought about it. I trusted the gods because . . . hell because they're gods and apparently my mother and uncle.

"What motivation would they have to keep information from me? If all they aspire to is for me to kill Adales?" He shrugs his shoulders nonchalantly but I can see the shadows dancing in the back of his eyes. He thinks they're lying.

"They obviously know the Fatum have information that are prerequisites to kill Adales, it is likely they also know how. Maybe they're using the effect of power, they think you would trust the Fatum more?"

"Trust them more than my actual birth mother?" I question and he puffs out some air. I shake my head, my mind swirling with thoughts. "Like I said it's just a waste of time trying to understand, we just have to trust I guess."

"I hate that." I have to laugh at his expression. For a moment his eyes flare up, and the seriousness on his face washes away. The mockery I wanted to make out of his trust issues gets stuck in my throat when I stare at him. My fingers twitch lightly before I break the eye contact.

"Is there more?" Cassian asks while I try to focus on the forest outside the castle. "More what?"

"More information I should know?"

My mind flashes to the creepy woman at the market, and how she knew what Edlyn was and I can't shake the feeling that she knew more about the Fatum. But it's just a guess so I shake my head.

"Okay, I will make sure to help my father with his research, if it is what Aerwyn said then we shall find the Fatum." He thinks for a moment before continuing, "I respect you not wanting to talk to your mother so ask Kian. We somehow have to start somewhere until I let you help my mother again." I furrow my brows at him.

"That is not your decision to make."

"Hell yes, it is, if it means you feel horrible afterward you're not going to heal her." Anger surges through me, who is he to decide if I risk feeling awful or not? I want to snap at him but his eyes start to glow intensely when he speaks up.

"Please don't make me decide to sacrifice the health of the two most important women in my life."

That gets me to shut up quickly. My body warms ridiculously quick at his words. I can't stand the look in his eyes and rather focus on the sinking sun visible through the windows.

"It's not your decision to make."

"It is not yours either. My mother won't agree if you'll get hurt in the process." I doubt that. I think she would be delighted if she knew she took my energy for her health. I don't voice my thoughts to him. I sigh because I know he's right, even though I still think it is not his decision to make.

"I'll talk to Kian, just because I want to," I state.

"Good. We'll tackle this together, princess. I know you always feel the need to do everything straight on your own. But we're a team now . . . if you want us to be?" I nod, one time, two times before speaking up.

"All right, then we'll start with the most important thing we conquer as a team." He nods, waiting. "How the hell are we going to beat an ancient god?"

~ 24 ~

One week. One week of waking up, sitting through three meals a day, walking along the castle, avoiding Zayne, avoiding Queen Aiyla, and especially avoiding Shailagh Sebestyen. Zayne's hate grows even worse against me when he finds out I am the one who is responsible for the fact that his mother can walk the halls of the castle again. Expectantly he's very vocal about his protests, his disdain, and his lack of liking for me.

Queen Aiyla manages to ignore me completely, too enraptured in seeing her sons and her husband. She is still doing fine after a week but I can see it, feel it even, how the energy floods out of her body, and dismisses it. It is as if her body refuses to heal itself, refuses to use its own magic to get rid of whatever is infecting her mind. I don't try to make conversation with her, hell, I'm happy if no one addresses me at all in her presence. This is not the case, contrary to his wife and son, King Ronan is delighted with my stay. He can't seem to thank me enough which his wife and Zayne accompany with silent glares.

Shailagh is the toughest to avoid. Not only does it feel like she turns up at every place I try to find my peace but Kian and Shailagh are also invited to every fucking meal that takes place. So it is one big theater where we all sit at the table and watch ourselves pretend. Watch Kian pretend as if he isn't the buffer between Shailagh and me, watch Edlyn pretend as if she isn't throwing suspicious and worried glances between Cassian and me, watch me avoid every try of my mother to find forgiveness, watch Zayne pretend like he doesn't want to lunge at me over the table and watch Kael pretend to not notice the thick tension around the room. He's trying to ease the bad mood with jokes. Keyword *trying*.

I find myself almost missing Flynn's and Edlyn's banter. It was harmless in contrast to this purgatory. The only light at the end of the tunnel is Henri. I've been writing him this whole week and he told me he is fine. That Polyxena is fine. He knows about everything but most importantly that he is not fully human. Hector told him about Shailagh's heritage which makes him out to be half Faye. He says he doesn't feel any of it but Hector is teaching him how to channel magic. Even though I've barely thought about Hector this whole time, I am glad he is with my brother, it is one less worry that plagues me at night.

I watch everyone's mood turn worse over the week and I especially notice the change in Cassian. His skin is even deeper now with being so much in the sun but somehow his cheeks turn hollow and his under eyes lilac. Queen Aiyla's accusatory tone echoes in the back of my mind every time I notice it. He needs to feed or else he is losing his strength. Weakness is one thing we do not need at the moment. So one afternoon I try to ease one of his worries as I slip out of the castle while I avoid looking at the ghostly forest. I didn't step into it again and I don't plan to anytime soon.

I've noticed Kian slip off after every meal and this time I follow him around the castle towards the back just to end up at the shore of the lake, residing beside the castle. I gape at the rippling water in front of me, stretching out until the horizon. Its deep green shines back at me, reflecting the color of the pines.

"The first time I came out here I wondered if it was the ocean," Kian speaks up suddenly, even though his back is to me. He must've heard me follow him. I take a few steps to stand beside him on the small strip of sand that runs along the water. "Demeter doesn't border on the ocean," I tell him and he nods.

"I know. Turns out it's just a giant lake." He turns his face and gives me a half smile. Somehow the look on his face reminds me of Henri just like it did when I met him for the first time in Aerwyna. I relax my shoulders lightly, whatever it is that clings to him it makes me calm.

"Why do you come out here so often?" A soft shrug of his shoulder. "It grounds me. The peace and quiet. No one interrupts

me here until now." He grins again and this time my lips twitch too. I sit down on the cold sand and draw my knees against my chest, closing my arms around my legs. He follows suit but stretches his long legs beside me.
"Guessing you didn´t come out here to talk about Shailagh, I can´t help and wonder why?"
"Can you tell me something about them? The Faye." I ask and watch his lilac eyes turn on me. "What do you want to know?" I ponder his question for a moment. There are many things I want to know, it feels like there´s so much to learn but not enough time for it.
"Is it true that you can create life?"
"Depends on what you understand about creating life. We cannot bring the dead back to life or necessarily create new life. Our powers define themselves in their healing abilities. Healing the ill. The people and nature." I nod and urge him to go on. "At the age of eleven, the first signs mostly show, sometimes flowers grow at the path a child walks, or trees grow in the middle of winter. But it is not always that pleasurable. When I turned twelve I accidentally let an oak tree grow right in the center of our living room. Shailagh was livid, our roof was destroyed and squirrels started to flood our house." He chuckles lightly, his eyes distant, swimming in the memory.
"You live with her?" I ask, surprised. Kian cringes lightly before he nods.
"Shailagh took me under because I was an orphan; she is my friend as much as she is my teacher." Something dark swirls underneath the purple but I´m cautious to act on it. Everyone has their past and I am not one to pry. He turns his head back to me. "We Faye age differently. While our minds can grasp things quickly and mature at the age of sixteen our bodies are different. Many Faye struggle, even some that are already living for fifty years. The key point is to find your balance."

"Balance?" I ask and he nods. "You can't create life without taking. You can't have the day without the night. Everything has some kind of sacrifice that's how the circle of life goes." He doesn't specify what some sacrifices are.

"But it is much to grasp if you don't actively practice it. When a Faye child shows symptoms of their magic we go to school, train, and try to control and grasp the concept but not only with our mind. We train our bodies as well, even though I have to say I'm not very good at close combat." I don't know why but the sheepish look on his face makes me laugh. He looks at me surprised before his lips stretch into a grin.

"I think you would get along with my little brother very much," I tell him and he smiles. "I'm sure I get the time to meet him and you do too. You will reunite." My heart warms at his words. I tighten my hands around my legs before an idea sparks in my mind. "What if I would train with you? I'm pretty good at close combat." He arches a brow.

"Wasn't it you who I had to save?" I roll my eyes. "Cassian got hurt not me. Don't tell him I said that or his ego will be crushed." He smiles and I grin mischievously. "I swear I'm good and in return, you can teach me how to conjure and use my magic."

"So you did have an ulterior motive." He scolds me but the gentle smile on his face remains. He doesn't ponder long and when he speaks up he bows his head lightly. "It would be my pleasure to be trained by you, My Queen."

~ 25 ~

"Channel your magic. Try to not see it as something strange living in you. You are the magic, Your Majesty, and the magic is you." Kian repeats as he grants me an encouraging nod as if we haven't been doing this for hours. Every day we come out here to this cursed lake and I try to go easy on him with the close combat. By now he must be picking up some sort of skills but he hasn't . He's clumsy, stubborn, and not concentrated enough to listen to me. He was right, he is bad at close combat. But probably not as bad at it as I am with magic.

"I tried. It is not like there's anything within me, I can't feel it."

I'm hungry, tired, and sweaty. I would give everything for a hot bath and some bread and cheese. I focus my gaze back on the boy who has a stern look on his face. Even though he is oddly polite and sees me as his rightful queen, he is very strict with the training process.

"Close your eyes." I follow suit and take a deep breath.

"Try to listen to the sounds around you, try to listen to the draft rustling the trees, the soft rippling of the water every time the surface breaks, try to listen to the song the earth sings, the dance the sky carries out." I try.

And it's not like I cannot hear what he tells me, even though I can't change my form I still have the effects of good vision and hearing. But the way he says it sounds magical, like they're living, breathing things.

"Nature has a kind of fingerprint, it's the biggest fuel for the Faye. It gifts us with its power and we gift it with ours, it's—"

"The cycle of life, I know." I sigh and open my eyes again. This is not going to work.

"It doesn't work, the only thing I feel is the itchy sole of my boots, the dagger sheath digging into my hip, and the breeze carrying the scent of our sweat." He arches a brow at me.

"Did you try hard enough?" I huff out an offended breath.

"I did," I say through clenched teeth before I let myself fall onto the cold ground, my spine not able to hold me any longer.

I watch Kian's face turn thoughtful as he ponders something. "You healed the queen, right? How did you do that?" He puts his hands on his hips waiting for my response.

"It wasn't something I actively did. It just called to me, I had no control."

"That's your problem." He says and I furrow my brows. "What is?"

"The magic doesn't act on its own, it listens to your commands. Maybe it felt like it was calling to you but it was you who conjured it. It was your mind that wanted to help the prince's mother." He squats beside the water, his hyacinthe-colored eyes tracing my features.

"Maybe we have to work differently. You obviously have some kind of blockage, maybe we need to fix that first before you try to conjure the magic." As if I was able to. I'm trying not to lose hope but it seems like healing the queen was some kind of accident or slip-up rather than a conscious decision.

"Can you show me?" I ask him and he looks at me surprised. "Show you what?"

"How you conjure it and do a magic trick or something." He rolls his eyes and grins. "There are no magic tricks."

"You know what I mean. Maybe if I see you do it, I can somehow grasp the process." That and I receive a small break from this madness. My head feels like it's exploding and the sun is already setting. Kian gets up on his feet again and stalks over to the water, he stops until he's ankle-deep inside. His eyes close for a moment and I push my hands into the sand to feel the magic flooding the land, to feel it pulsing or singing for me.

Nothing.

When Kian opens his eyes again they glow in their lilac color, flecks of green disturb the irises but it doesn't make it less impressive. His hands rise slightly from his side, up and up and up.

For a moment I think he's doing it for effect but then I realize what he's doing. The water is rising with his motion. It follows his hands, chasing for contact but never quite reaching.

"Your Majesty, would you do me the favor and unsheathe your dagger." He asks, half his body enveloped in some kind of whirling surface of the water. I'm too entranced to object and get up, unsheathing the dagger at my hip.

"Once the case is closed you throw it at me."

"I beg your pardon?" I ask him and look at him as if he's mad. The water rises and hides the grin on his lips. "Throw the dagger at me." His voice sounds as if he is under the surface of the water once the shell closes. The water swirls like a whirlpool and even though I am unsure I get in a stance. Tense my muscles and focus my eyes on where I saw Kian standing last. The dagger leaves my hand in a skilled throw and I feel tempted to squeeze my eyes shut and avoid the damage but I demand them to say open.

I gasp when the knife slices through the water like predicted, already sprinting towards the boy. I told him it was stupid, how could he—my foot kicks something at the shore as I'm halfway to Kian and I look down. The dagger is laying on the beach, the water pushing it forward as if it got flushed to the bay.

The sound of crashing waves erupts and I look up to see the cover dropping around Kian.

"What. . . ." I try to form some coherent words and he grins.

"That was amazing!"

His grin widens even more. I can't believe it worked. He somehow connected the shell with the lake water, making the knife slice the water and end up in the lake again. I didn't even know that was possible.

"That was fucking impressive. Can you do that as well, princess?" Kian and I whirl around at the voice, just to see Kael approach us with a big grin on his lips.

He's mocking me. He knows how little progress I've made over the days. I look at him grimly, pick up the dagger from the ground and in a whirl throw it at him.

Kian gasps but Kael stays calm as he catches the blade in his hands before it can slice through his face.

"So impulsively violent." He murmurs and shakes his head.

"Cassian warned me not to provoke you."

"Then why are you doing it?" I grumble as Kian and I make our way over to him.

"Because every time you get angry your cheeks flush adorably and there's this vein in your neck that looks delicious—"

"I swear I'm going to stab you if you finish that sentence." He chuckles delightedly and I feel tempted to deck him in the face. But his face turns serious very quickly. One thing I learned about Kael is that he is never serious, so I speak my next words alarmed. "What is it?"

"Flynn has come to unexpected delays, he's probably going to stay another week in Oceanus."

"I thought they decided who would take the throne by now? Was it, not his cousin, Aalton?" I question, feeling Kian grow restless beside me. Kael's eyes wander to the Faye and his spine locks up again. "Yes, Aalton will take the throne but you should know it, princess, it doesn't take a day to turn someone into a queen."

I can tell from his tone that the topic is over now. I furrow my brows but I can understand that the Upyr might be wary of Kian's presence. "Is she any good yet?" He now asks the Faye as we start to walk the path up to the castle. "She's as good as she can be." I have to laugh at his answer. "I'm a failure, just admit. There is no use in lying anyway."

"It is not easy for someone to grasp the concept of magic, who never even believed in it, their whole life." Kian shoots me an encouraging look but it does nothing to drown my doubts.

"So what is your magic even made of?"

"Well, mostly we can heal, defend. It is more that we give than take." Kael lets out a small huff. "Sounds boring."
"Everything is boring to you where no teeth or blood is involved," I say arching a brow. The blond grins at me. "Damn, right. Especially teeth, teeth are alluring." He winks and I roll my eyes before I notice something and my steps halter.
"Do you have your shirt on wrong?" My eyes widen when I realize it indeed is wrong. Kael blushes—*blushes*—while he scratches the back of his neck.
"I came here in a hurry after a very important business I had to endure." I cross my arms in front of my chest and raise a brow.
"Important business. Ah."
Kian looks like he wants to flee the scene which he does with a murmured ′later′.
I watch the boy scurry off and realize that we reached the entrance to the castle. "Don´t you talk to me in that condescending tone." I raise my hands defensively.
"I´m not condescending, maybe I should feel honored that you stopped—whatever you stopped—to fetch me. For what exactly, again?" I grin lightly because it looks lovely when he blushes. The fact that he is such a charming and playful man and still blushes when caught is adorable.
"I wanted to ask if you´d like to have dinner with me. Kian didn´t look like he was going to let you go." He shoves his hands into the pockets of his breeches and stares at the ground.
"I would be delighted. Lead the way, sir." I grin and he offers me his arm, his eyes lighting up. I hook my arm around his and we ascend to the castle.

Kael lets me take a bath and get rid of the smell of fighting and sweat before he joins me in my private chambers with dinner. Edlyn is visiting Iason, the capital of Demeter to receive traces on the Fatum and Cassian is occupied with his research and his father. Kael says Zayne has been in a foul mood all morning and wants to get out of his hair before the prince implodes.

Dinner with Kael is always fun and relaxing. He's the perfect distraction from everything that's going on and I enjoy his presence very much. I notice quietly how often our conversation strikes Azzura's name and find myself curious about her person. I try to pry some information out of the Upyr but I don't figure out more than that she has been residing here for a long time and her parents are friends of the royal family for a long time. They reside in the southern lands of Polyxena and I wonder why they have sent her daughter here, all on her own.

After a pleasant dinner, Kael leaves for the night just before a knock interrupts us.

Kael freezes in his stand, looking at me for confirmation that I have a planned meet up.

"Come in." I call, wanting to know who has come to my chambers this late. The door opens revealing a fit physique, dressed in dark breeches, the upper body clad in a shirt the color of pines. Cassian looks at us surprised as the air immediately electrifies with his presence.

"Am I interrupting something?"

Kael grins as he advances on the prince. "I was just about to leave, brother."

He squeezes his shoulder before the blond slips out of my chambers, not without throwing a wink in my direction.

I quickly get up, flattening the linen of my gown.

"Has something happened?" I question Cassian who is still hovering in the room, his eyes on the table Kael and I sat at minutes ago.

"No," he swallows before taking a few steps forward, "I was wondering if you wanted to spend the evening with me?"

My body instantly tenses as he conjures a folded box out of shadows. My mouth drops open. "Did you just. . .conjure a chess board out of nothing?"

His lips twitch amusingly as he looks at the chessboard. "Not out of nothing. Just out of my sleeping chamber."

He arches a brow as I marvel over his powers.

"What do you say? Are you in the mood to lose against me?"

I know he is goading me because this is not a good idea. Every time Cassian and I are in close proximity to each other my heart betrays me. I should say no and listen to the rational part of my brain.

"I hope you deal with disappointment."

Fuck.

He grins, the dimple appearing in his left cheek. "Only if it is as bittersweet as you winning."

"You can't move it that way, princess."

A soft chuckle leaves Cassian's lips. I look up from the chess board to look at him all sprawled out on my bed. His head is propped up on his hand as he watches my hands. I am too tired to sit at the table which led us to, me sitting on my bed, my still wet hair a cooling sensation on my back from all the thoughts that have been swirling in my head since he lied down.
The green dress shirt rides up every time he moves a piece, revealing a sliver of bronze skin.
"Why?" I ask, surprised, my hand hovering in the air. His lips spread into a slow grin as he looks at me through those long, black lashes. "Because the rook can't move diagonally." I furrow my brows.
"But I want him to." I insist and kick one of his horse figures off the board, placing my rook onto the small quadrangle.
"If we would play this according to your rules you would always win."
"That's the point," I say with an arched brow and his booming laughter is the answer. I watch him for a moment, struck by the sudden moment. I can't help but be enchanted by his beauty. The way his curls flop in his eyes, his hair still a bit too long, the dimple in his left cheek making him look a year younger than he is. The dance of the candlelights highlights his cheekbones and makes his lashes create shadows on them.
He seems to notice me staring in silence as he quiets down and stares at me. His lips open in a soft breath and my hands start to tingle at the fire in his green eyes. For a moment time is frozen as electricity floods my veins, boils my blood, and makes my mind spin. "It's your turn." I breathe out and look quickly at the chessboard. Cassian's behaving uncharacteristically sweet this week. He is considerate and his suggestiveness still shines through but there has been nothing more than lingering looks, grazing knuckles, nothing more.
He looks at me with half-lidded eyes. "How am I supposed to play if you're not following the rules?"

I try to adjust in my crossed leg position and his eyes flicker down to my skin covered in goosebumps.

"Are you cold?" He suddenly sits up and pushes the board onto the floor. I swallow as I watch the pieces tumble around and move backward on my bed. Cassian sprawls forward, his eyes turning darker. My heart thuds in my chest, my middle squeezing in anticipation as I watch him. "I'm not—I'm not cold." My voice is a whisper and I flinch when my back bumps against the headboard of the bed. I'm cornered, there is no way to escape. But do I want to escape? He half hovers over me now his eyes intently on my face.

"You're shivering." He states and lets one finger wander over my arm. I almost sigh at the soft touch but clamp my mouth shut, and bite my tongue until I taste blood. "What are you doing?" I ask breathlessly, my chest rising and falling like I've been running for miles.

"I don't know." He murmurs his hand traveling up my arm and stopping at the juncture of my neck. He stills as he feels my racing pulse underneath the skin and suddenly I'm struck with it.

"Are you . . . hungry?" He stills at my question and finally looks up at my face.

I hold my breath when his mouth opens and one word escapes. "Starving."

Instead of moving closer he suddenly moves back and I quickly follow him, brows furrowed. "What are you doing?"

"This is a bad idea." He swallows and turns his head and I blush when I catch him adjusting his breeches. For a moment I hesitate, he is right it is a bad idea. I wanted to take things slow, maybe become friends first so I can trust him again.

The words of his mother flash in the back of my mind. He hasn't fed for a long time and even though it might be bearable it's not comfortable for him. "Do you want to?" I ask hesitantly and his eyes flicker back to me.

"Do I want to what?"

"Feed? You—Daragon, said you wouldn't feed off anyone else than me." I breathe out, trying to steady my shaking hands. I crawl closer to him and he shakes his head and seems to hold his breath when I sit down on my calves in front of him. Our knees touch. "You can if you want to. I don't have a problem with it." I place my hand on his thigh and he shakes his head again, looking almost agitated.

"I won't. I won't." A harsh breath escapes him as I move closer. My heart is a steady pound in my chest when I grab his hand in mine. I place it back on the juncture of my neck making him swallow hard. We push the straps of my nightgown to the side, his eyes following the movement.

"You said to move things slowly." He choked out and I shrug softly.

"What good does it do us if you're distracted by being hungry?"

I slip off the mattress and take the dagger from the nightstand. A ruby is embedded into the metal grip, shining softly in the candlelight.

"I don't want you to do this because you feel like you have to. I'm willing to do things differently."

I stop before him and he looks up at me through his lashes.

"We're doing things differently. I am *deciding* to give you my blood."

He still looks not convinced.

"I, unfortunately, need you Cas, which means you have to be at your full strength."

I move the dagger to the side of my throat but his hand shoots out and his fingers wrap around my wrist.

"Please," he says quietly, "just please not there."

I look at him surprised.

"Why not?"

He manages a small smile, "trust me, you don't want me too."

I am beyond unsatisfied by his answer but I listen and let the dagger glide over the skin on my wrist. Holding my arm out to him, still seated on the mattress, I watch the canines grow past his lips. The green in his eyes vanishes as he takes hold of my wrist, so delicately like I am made out of porcelain. It seems like he is trying to restrain himself but the moment my blood runs over his thumb he lashes forward. I bite my lip when his teeth pierce my skin, tugging at my veins like a starving man. He pulls me forward as he drinks, my thighs bumping against his knees in the process. Something tingles inside me, a sort of recognition and I feel myself growing slightly dizzy.

Cassian rips himself from me and backs a few feet away on the bed, before meeting my gaze. Green creeps slowly back into his irises as he watches me out of his half-lidded gaze.

"That's enough."

"It better be," I say a bit winded. I sit down on the mattress and watch him for a moment.

"Thank you."

After a moment he moves closer again, the canines gone. A flush runs over his cheekbones as he takes my hand and presses a soft kiss against my knuckles.

"Do you feel dizzy? Headache?"

"I'm all right." I pull my hand out of his hold.

"Can I ask something?"

"Anything."

"What does it taste like?" His eyes flit back up to me. "You want to know what blood tastes like?"

"Does it differ with every person?" He pushes a few strands of my hair over my shoulder, watching it closely. "Everyone has their taste." He murmurs. I decide to pry even more. "What do I taste like?"

His green eyes meet mine softly, the hunger inside them swirling deep down. "You, princess, taste like life."

I stay silent, an emotion so deep and powerful floods my body. I'm scared to say something.

"Will you stay for a little bit?" I ask.

His gaze flares. "I'll stay as long as you want me to."

~ 26 ~

I let my eyes travel over the dark blue canopy, counting every stitched star like the number is the answer to everything. Cassian is still beside me.

"How is your mother?" I dare to ask in silence. I turn my head to look at him and decipher the fleeting emotion on his face.

"Don't lie for my sake," I tell him quickly and turn to my side. He releases a heavy sigh, the tips of his fingers driving through my strands.

"Like you predicted, it is getting worse again, her energy is leaving her. Don't feel obligated to do anything you aren't ready to do, princess."

I don't feel obligated to do anything when I think of her lack of gratefulness after I healed her. Still, the deep lines on the prince's forehead tug at my heart. "You said it started around the time you decided to accomplish the oath and got your tattoo?" I ask and he nods in confirmation.

"In the beginning, we thought it was stress. That she was worrying herself and getting ill."

"But it's not," I say and his green eyes flicker to mine. "I saw something. It was like some kind of virus feeding from her. I can't describe it but it was not the origin of her, it's like an essence, a trace from something foreign." I try to grasp the cold feeling of claws that were embedded into her mind but it's hard to recall. I don't know if I even want to.

Cassian turns on his side to look at me, the dark curls spilling over his forehead.

"The healers checked for any kind of poison. No traces." I'm not surprised. It doesn't feel like poison, it clings to the surface mostly. This . . . thing—whatever it is—has clawed itself into the deepest parts of the queen. I don't dare to tell the prince, too much pain is showing on his face already.

"I hoped with your training you would be able . . .—but it doesn't matter." He shakes his head quickly but I put my fingers under his chin to make him look at me.

"I'm really bad at this whole magic thing but I promise I will try to help her as best as I can. For you."

He closes his eyes and it looks like the last two words make his whole body shake. I hesitate before I lean forward. His breath hitches when I press a kiss against his cheek. He sighs and I shriek when he suddenly rolls back over me with a soft groan burying his face into the crook of my neck. His whole weight is now on my body and I wheeze out a small laugh. "Cas, you're choking me." I wind my arms around his neck and he gets some of his weight off me as he plants a soft kiss against my neck. I shiver in response.

"Did you know that's the most beautiful sound in the world?" He props himself up to look at me and I have to smile at the intense glow of his eyes.

"What is?"

"Your laugh. I wish I could bottle it up and take it anywhere I go. If life would have a sound it would be your laugh."

I blush like a damn tomato and sit up as well, our fingers brushing.

"If life had a taste it would taste as sweet as you." He mumbles, staring at our hands. My heartbeat accelerates when he slowly drives his fingers between mine. "And if life had a smell, it would smell like you."

"What do I smell like?" I mumble trying to concentrate on his words and not on the electrifying feeling when our fingers touch.

"You smell like wickedness and the night, like rain after a drought and those damn roses."

I need to remind myself to thank Edlyn for the continuous rose baths.

"You were driving me insane every time you walked past me and I got a hint of your rose scent. I would wander in the royal gardens at night and stay by the roses just to be reminded of you, like a fucking puppy." His eyes fly away from my face when I let out a surprised breath. His tan cheeks blush and it is the most beautiful look I've ever seen.

"Duck!" I quickly bend my knees to escape the thrown dagger at me, panting. I glare at Kian who tilts his head at me, brows raised.

"Your task is not to duck, Carina," Edlyn says, lounging like a queen on the sand with a smug smile on her lips. She's dressed in a skin-tight blood red suit because she came back from Iason this morning and wanted to join today's training lesson. Word has made its way through the castle about my miserable magic tricks and now everyone wants tickets to the front row. As if I don't know how bad I am. I still can't conjure a simple shield like Kian can.

He says that it takes time to grasp the work of my powers but I can see it in his face. I'm taking too long to figure it out and for my circumstances—meaning that I am the daughter of a goddess—I should be able to wield shields fantastically now. Cassian says not to make a big deal out of it but I can see in the furrow of his brow that he is pressed. There is no news from Flynn and Oceanus, I'm still hiding like a fugitive in Demeter and it feels like the whole continent has gone still.

We're all waiting for a blow from any side but nothing happens.
"It isn't as easy as it looks," I growl at my best friend who grins at me. At least one of us has fun.
"Was the trip to Iason at least successful?" I ask her and she grimaces.

"I'm sorry to say that most of these witches are insane. Talking about rituals and demons, most of them flipped after I asked them about the Fatum."

I sigh disappointed, King Ronan isn't getting any closer to the answer either. It feels like we're all stuck in the same fucking cycle. Edlyn carefully inspects her nails as she keeps on talking. "I grew up with some of the oldest witches and never realized how crazy most of them were. Their blood rituals are mostly hogwash and just for dramatization. I shouldn't be surprised that they believe in curses as well. But it doesn't work like that, sadly."

Edlyn told me that the oldest witches believe in sacrifices and blood rituals to thank the gods that they're still wandering the worlds. That some clans sacrifice their own daughters which sounds rather unpleasant.

"Stop concentrating on her. Focus on me." Kian pulls my attention back to him and I straighten my shoulders. He has the dagger back again in his hands. I try to focus on the soft breeze around us and listen to the sounds the water in the lake makes and the rhythm of my breath.

Kian stands in position and throws the dagger with lightning speed, I tense, daring not to move and call to nature, pulling at the roots in the ground underneath me but I fail. My heartbeat pounds in my chest because I witness it's too late, the blade flies closer with alarming speed. I should've ducked earlier because now the blade will pierce right through me— I look down at my chest when I notice that the dagger went right through me without me feeling something.

The image of the dagger rippled into nothing and I look up to see Kian disappears into nothingness as well. It was just an illusion. I try to release a relieved breath but my instincts scream at me to turn around.

I do so quickly just to see Kian throwing the dagger again. I raise my arm on instinct to catch the blade in my hand, preparing for the feeling of the blade sliding through my skin but nothing happens. I realize I squeezed my eyes shut and when Edlyn curses out loud I open my eyes.

"Holy fuck." My voice is shaky as I stare at the dagger that hovers right in the air in front of my hand. The air ripples around the blade, manipulated by my magic! Edlyn jumps up cheering and I join her while the dagger crashes onto the sand again but I don't care.

"That was fucking amazing!" Edlyn exclaims as she presses a kiss to my cheek and I chuckle before my eyes fly to Kian who has a smug smile on his lips. He walks over lazily and I narrow my eyes.

"You did it on purpose!"

He created an illusion to throw the dagger at me so I was surprised by his second attack.

"Well, I thought about what you told me when you healed the queen. That it was instinct to heal and I thought if I somehow trigger your instincts we could get through this blockage you have." I nod because his words do make sense. "We kept going from the wrong angle. We wanted you to actively do magic but that's not how it works." Edlyn nods agreeing. "It's the same with witch magic, no thinking just doing. It's like an extension from yourself, not a part you have to ask for allowance."

I nod again, somehow her words make me think. They keep telling me that magic is not a separate part from oneself. That the magic is listening to one's command because it is a part of you . . . an elongation. I turn to look at my best friend when something clicks in my mind. Her hazel eyes widen alarmed when she sees the look on my face.

"If someone gets poisoned healers can immediately detect it in someone's blood right?" I ask both of them and they share a confused look.

"Right?" They say in unison. I start to pace on the soaked sand. The cold claws, the feel of something different in her essence.

"When you say magic is an extension, does that mean it has a different essence? Even if the Faye's magic is the same as the witches, every single individual has a personal kind of style?"

"You're acting strange, Carina," Edlyn says warily and I shake my head. "Everyone has a different essence, right?" It is Kian who answers. "Technically yes."

"And you can feel it, characterize my magic?" He nods again and I pull at my roots because it's been so clear. "That means if someone is cursed by someone else's magic I would feel it. Would feel the difference. Healers wouldn't realize someone is cursed because they're searching for the poisons that are on the surface."

I look at Kian whose face tells me he is understanding. "What the hell are you talking about?" Edlyn says and Kian goes to enlighten her.

"The queen is not ill, neither was she poisoned." Edlyn's mouth drops open. "She was cursed."

~ 27 ~

Our steps thunder through the walls of the castle as we run in hurry. Edlyn's hair is flying behind her like a great cape while I try not to stumble over the hem of my gown. I feel my feet become lighter, faster until it feels like I'm soaring and my hands start to tingle. Instead of feeling put off, I embrace the sensation and my magic floods me in a soft haze, I feel my ears elongate and end in tips, the sharp edge of canines growing in my teeth. My vision becomes even clearer as we pass servants who look after us but we ignore them as we travel deeper into the mountain, leaving every light behind us. The air becomes thinner the deeper we run but I don't let it slow my steps until I feel Edlyn's steps decelerate until we come to a stop.

Not the slightest bit breathless, we share a short glance.

We stop in front of big double doors that look like they've been carved out of stone. When I told Edlyn that we needed to find Cassian and his father she mentioned they were in the palace's library which seems to be located behind those doors. Without hesitation she opens them, the hinges groaning slightly at her strength. I don't know what I exactly thought to find behind those doors but the look of it surprises me nonetheless.

The library is nothing different from the palace library in Aerwyna with dark wooden shelves winding a labyrinth around the gigantic room, small candles, and a big chandelier lighting up the space. There is not a single shelf which is not stocked to the brim with literature, some even scattered on the small tables that have been put up in some aisles. The shelves are so high they require ladders, which are leaning against them, waiting to be used. Nothing seems out of the ordinary; it is a normal library. The strange thing is the two men perched on the ground, their backs leaning against shelves, legs stretched out with various books in their laps. A few books are staggered around them carelessly, some with their pages open, others discarded completely in a corner.

It is one of a painting to see the King of Demeter sitting on the ground like a servant but it is the other man who holds my attention. The way his curls fall into his face, his rolled-up sleeves that reveal his tan complexion, and the way the candlelight flickers across his skin. The light encases him like a halo so different from his otherwise dark characteristics. He looks like a god of wrath.

At our arrival, both of the men look up, surprised and whatever Cassian sees in my face makes him drop the books on the floor and appear right in front of me. I'm caught off guard when his hands clasp around my shoulders and his green eyes search my face.

"What happened? What's wrong?"

I'm so stunned by his obvious worry that I can't get a word out as he shakes me lightly. "Are you hurt? Carina?"

"No, I'm fine," I say quickly and watch his shoulders slacken. King Ronan approaches us his black brows drawn in concern. "I need to see your mother, now." Both Moreau men share a confused look.

"Why?" I straighten my shoulders, ignoring the thundering of my heart. "Because I can help her."

"Are you sure?" Cassian, Edlyn, and I rush through the halls of the castle as he shoots me an incredulous look. King Ronan immediately went to lock down the castle because whoever poisoned the queen is still inside and won't get an option to flee.

"It's the only thing that makes sense," I grasp my skirt as we rush around the corner. "The way she felt, it was so cold and unstable. I thought it was because her mind was exhausted but it wasn't that. It was some kind of feeling."

"What feeling, Carina?" Cassian asks as we come to a stop in front of the familiar archway that leads to the chambers of the queen. I share a look with Edlyn who shoots me an encouraging look.

"It felt like something was clinging to her. No, not something but someone, like a shadow. Someone was inside her mind."

I can visibly see the prince shuddering.

The hope that sparked in his eyes when I told him about my theory is brighter than ever. He nods before we burst through the door without a knock, instantly bathed in darkness. I squeeze my eyes shut for a moment trying to adjust to the lack of light when a soft groan meets my ears.

The queen is perched under the covers of the bed and it looks like she tries to blink in our direction but her powers leave her.

"Mother?" Cassian whispers carefully as he takes a step towards her, his hands trembling. His whole body is taught, his voice like one of a little boy.

"Cas?" His mother's gentle accent calls back and the prince exhales relieved. All three of us advance on her bed.

"It is so hot, please, honey, turn down the fire a bit." There is no fireplace in the room. Cassian looks at me over his shoulder, pure panic written on his features.

"Why don't you wet a towel in the bathing chamber for her?" I ask and squeeze his shoulder before he disappears into the attached chamber.

I swallow rolling up my sleeves as I look at my friend.

"I have no clue if this is going to work or if it is going to fight against me. Are you able to hold her down?" She shoots me a curt nod.

"I'm right by your side, Your Majesty." She gives me a crooked smile when her eyes turn red and her hair bleeds into the color of snow.

I advance on the queen with a trembling breath and watch her eyes flutter back and forth. She's not awake but not asleep either.

"Your Majesty? It is me, Carina. I know you're in incredible pain, will you let me help you?" I watch her brows furrow, her forehead damp with sweat, and some of her dark strands stick to her skin.
"She's delirious she can't hear you," Edlyn states and I nod.
"Okay, grasp her shoulders."
Edlyn follows my orders just when Cassian appears to assess the situation. He's as pale as parchment and I slowly grab his hand and urge him to come closer.
"Talk to her I think your voice is soothing her."
His eyes flicker from the queen towards me. "Are you sure?"
"I am. Come on." I tug at his hand and he sinks to his knees beside the bed, placing the cold towel on her forehead. I sit down on the mattress beside the dainty figure of the woman before I share a look with the prince and Edlyn.
"Everyone ready?"
In answer, Edlyn's grip on the queen's shoulders tightens and Cassian's hand wraps around his mother's. I slip one hand under the neck of the queen and the other at the side of her face and pray.
"Please, let this work." I inhale deeply, the air floating through my nose down my cervix, and into my lungs.
Everyone tenses and waits. The queen keeps on mumbling words while Cassian tries to calm her. I concentrate on the soft curve of her mouth, the once-tan skin, and the fluttering eyelids riddled with veins.
"Why is nothing happening?" Cassian says agitated.
"Give me some time," I whisper and wait for it.
The tug, the pull. And there it is. Darkness greets me and smiles at me like an old friend and this time I don't swallow it down. I welcome it with a tug of my magic and the world explodes in lilac. Light bursts from every corner of the room when the queen cries out and arches her back.
"Edlyn!" I cry out and grit my teeth as I try to contain my grip on her. Edlyn pushes the queen deeper into the mattress when the temperature drops to a burning cold.

I shudder when I feel it, let my magic pull me in and the next thing I know is that I'm not in the chamber anymore. The heartbeats escape my hearing and I land in the deep pits of darkness. A soft laugh lingers, evil and malicious. I shudder while I try to grasp the feeling, trying to find out where I am.

It feels like I'm wading through mud, every step hard and slow. I can't move further, the black shadows clinging to my skin, my heart, and my soul. I grit my teeth and try to remember Kian's words. Magic is an extension of me, magic is me. I invite it inside let it flow through me and wrap around me like a protective shield. I feel the darkness rear its head suspiciously creeping into nothingness but it is too late.

"Let her go!" I don't know if I'm speaking the words or rather thinking them in my mind. The darkness winds tighter around me, choking my magic down like a viper. I don't back down. I try to fill it with everything I have gone through these last months. The good and the bad. Pain is never terminal, it comes and goes and it is only important to not let it get a hold of you. Let it come like a wave, duck you under the water, drown you. And then come up again.

The darkness freezes and I smirk.

So many shards I've stepped on in my life and now I'm going to use them to help me. They raise higher and higher until there is no escaping and it floods the nothingness. Light swallows the dark and burns it down like a virus. A wildfire that spreads with the help of liquor.

A wave rolls through me and pushes me back when my eyes snap open. I'm panting, my skin sticky with sweat as I stare down at the queen who's stopped struggling against my invasion in her mind. My skin prickles with the darkness still lingering around me, the cold covering my body in a thin layer.

The room is still dark and when I meet Cassian and Edlyn's horrified faces I freeze.

The queen lifts in the air her body held up by an unknown source. Her eyes have rolled back in her head, her mouth gaping open.

"What is happening?" Edlyn cries as shadows gather around Cassian. He has transformed ready to fight whatever caught ahold of his mother.

"I wouldn't do that little prince." A dark voice vibrates out of the lips of the queen. It is not her who is speaking. Cold sweat clings to my back as we stare up at her ill form. The prince hesitates, his shadows subsiding.

The queen turns towards me.

"I've seen you have found your way to your powers, Katarina Sebestyen," I shudder at the way she speaks my name.

"It is unfortunate how you're hiding behind the borders of the Kingdom," The queen lets out a choking sound, and as if on instinct I step forward to help her. I feel the hot pulsing of my magic at my hands, a soft glow emitting from them.

"I will give you thirty days to come back to Aerwyna and meet your fate or the queen won't be the last to endure pain because of you," a satisfied laugh escapes the voice as the queen's lips spread into a horrifying grin. "Until then."

As if it was never there the body of the queen drops, shadows leaving her body and the room.

"No!" Cassian exclaims and dives forward, catching the body of his mother in his arms. Still frozen I watch him gently lay her down on the mattress again. Something cold grasps my heart in a vice but this time I know it is not a foreign force but my own guilt that is trapping me.

"Are you all right?" I flinch surprised as I look at Edlyn.

"If it has worked I am." They both stare at me as if they've never seen me before.   "What?" I furrow my brows.

"Do you remember anything that happened?" My friend asks and I look around unsure.

"You were glowing, Carina. We had to close our eyes not to turn blind and a whole fucking wave rumbled through the castle."

"Really?" I ask confused as I look around the room. It is still tinted in darkness but the cold finally makes its way out of the room and before I can grasp what my friend is saying a soft groan erupts around us. Our heads flip around to watch the queen's eyes flutter open. I hold my breath as I watch the color return to her skin and her lips. "Mother?" Cassian is back at her side, pushing the black strands from her forehead that stick to her sweat. Her jade eyes flicker around the room, for a moment she seems to be confused still. I try to blend in the shadows, still trying to process what has happened.

"You." Cassian turns his head to look at me for a moment. Moisture is glistening in those emerald eyes before he looks back at his mother.

"How do you feel?" I ask her unsure and she exhales like it is the first time she does so.

"It is gone. The darkness is gone." She murmurs and I exhale relieved. My shoulders sag for a moment, I was so scared this wouldn't work.

"Help me up, honey." She tells Cassian who eyes her worriedly.

"Are you sure?"

"Yes, please." With a soft groan, the prince helps her to sit up against the headboard when I feel something wet trail down my nose. I quickly raise my hand and swipe underneath, my eyes widening when my skin is tinted red. I quickly clean my face, catching a glimpse at Edlyn who's watching me.

"I want to talk to you." The queen says and Edlyn and I nod.

"Of course, we'll leave you to privacy."

"No. You." She nods her head at me and I freeze.

"Me?" She arches a dark brow. "Am I squinting?"

"She was the one who helped you, mother—"

"I am aware of that, Cassian. Why don't you get Ronan in here." She pats his hand and I'm still astonished at how well she is doing. Minutes ago she was delirious barely in our world and now she is sitting with sweat-slick skin more elegant than I ever could be.

Edlyn curtseys before leaving the room not without shooting me a look. We will discuss what happened later but we all know whose voice it was that spoke through the body of the queen.

"Fine." Cassian presses a kiss against her temple before he leaves but not without shooting me a look out of his eyes that travels right through my skin. I swallow, confused, and straighten my spine when the door closes shut. I brace myself to meet the cruel eyes and turn to face the woman.

~ 28 ~

The chamber lays in eerie silence as the unearthly woman stares at me. I don't dare speak up and disturb the quiet before the storm. My eyes flicker around the room hoping, and wishing that someone saves me from this but when her voice disturbs the silence it is fairly normal. No evil hint to it.
"Sit down, child, and fix yourself." I look at her confused as she pats the end of the bed and gestures around the skin under her nose. I plop down and quickly scramble to clean the newly escaped blood from my nose.
Her eyes are narrow as she watches me quietly.
"I suppose there are thanks in order."
"What? No, of course not. I did what I had to, honestly, I don't even know what I did or if it worked."
"It worked. I can feel it and I'm sure you could too." She tilts her head and studies me.
"The question is at what risk did it work? There are always consequences when it comes to magic."
"I'm fine," I tell her weakly. I feel a little shaky and cold but it just feels like I had too much wine to drink. The queen shifts in her position.
"Usually I don't like to owe things to someone."
"You don't owe me anything, Your Majesty."
"Stop being so modest and accept my thanks." I tense up and nod.
"I do."
"Then stop looking at me with those judgmental eyes of yours." I inhale sharply.
"No need to deny it, honey. You can't stand me and the feeling is very mutual."
I frown confused, fiddling with the material of my dress.
"It is not that I can't stand you, Your Majesty. It is just that I don't understand you." She laughs coldly and I look back up at her.

"Of course, you don't. You don't even know half of your story, but I do." She nods as if confirming her words.

"I have watched many lives be destroyed because of you." Her words stab at the wall built around my heart. "It was not my intention."

"It doesn't matter if it was your intention or not. The lives are gone, the people dead." I nod agreeing and straighten my shoulders.

"You are right. Nothing excuses the pain people had to go through because of me. I am sorry, I can understand why you wouldn't want me to be friends with your son." She scoffs and a shiver runs down my spine.

"As if I could hinder him from loving you. It is not that easy." My treacherous heart flutters at her words and her gaze sharpens.

"Cassian does what he wants since he was born. But it doesn't mean I won't talk some sense into him. You saved my life and I see it as repayment of your debts."

It's my turn to scoff and I get up.

"I know you can't stand me, for whatever reason, but I don't remember any debts." An evil smile adorns her lips. "Innocent Katarina Sebestyen. The Moreau lineage has sacrificed themselves for you for centuries and you don't even remember them. How do you think Cassian's grandfather died?" I take a step back. The Queen isn't finished with me, rage glimmering in her eyes. "My love almost sacrificed himself for your life. All these men are doing is saving your life and for what? Just so you can come again and now you will take my son?" She shakes visibly, her eyes glimmering with unshed tears. "I won't let you take him. Ronan never interfered with your life because of what happened with his father but Cas is different. He is smitten with you, he always was. I won't let you take him from me." She shakes her head as deep sorrow spreads in my chest.

I sit back down on the bed, the mattress dipping under my weight.

"I am sorry. I really am, I never wanted anyone to get hurt." She shakes her head and cleans the tears from her cheeks. "Then why are you here?"

I fall silent at her words. Why am I here? I'm here because I want to find the Fatum, they're my last hope. Maybe they can tell me how to defeat a god. I'm here because, for one damn time, I want to do things right after everything that I've done. Everything these people sacrificed for me shouldn't be in vain.

"I don't remember my past lives. I am not responsible for the things I did then. And I am sorry so many people had to die for me. That you feel like you're losing your son to me, which you are not. Cassian is devoted to you and adores you. You're the most important thing to him." She shakes her head, her features hard as stone.

"You still don't understand. I begged him on my knees not to go, to stay in safety and do it as his father did it. We always planned for him not to interfere actively. But he wouldn't listen. There are no ways my son wouldn't go for you, Katarina. And he would walk through Gehenna with a smile on his face if it meant you would be safe," She smiles sadly, "and nothing that I would say could stop him."

"Maybe. But that is his choice. I can't make him." Her hand suddenly clasps mine in hers, mine cold and clammy, hers alive and warm.

"But you can. You are the only one he would listen to."

I worry my bottom lip as I stare at her. Her skin is rough as she stares at me, a glimmer of hope in her eyes.

"I don't know who I was in my past lives. But I know who I am now and that is someone who will do things right. I can't force Cassian to stay away from me if he wants to help. Because this is bigger than us." She deflates visibly and my hand slips out of hers.

"But what I can promise is that I will make it right this time."

Just as the queen looks up a soft knock interrupts our interlocked stare.

A second later a maid comes rushing in and behind her the king. His features look desperate, his breath frantic when he meets the eyes of the queen.

"Aiyla." Her name is a short breath but filled with so much emotion that I quickly slip off the bed and make space for the man. He drops to his knees as his hands envelop her dainty face.

"My light of life, how are you feeling?" The queen shudders at the skin contact as she eyes him lovingly. "I am well."

Her eyes meet mine when he hugs her close to him and something close to a white flag shines in her eyes. She thanks me that I saved her life, I tell her that she doesn't owe me. I slip with a last look at the reunited couple out of the chamber. Light floods me as I step out into the hallway and lean against the door.

My eyes study the embezzlement on the ceiling as a shudder erupts from my skin. The words of the queen float in my mind and I do understand her concern. Especially after Adales has possessed her body to tell me to leave Demeter, it seems the safest option. I don't want anyone else to get hurt on my account but I wonder if that seems to be inevitable. Something scuffs against the floor of the hall making my body lock up.

My eyes fly towards a dark corner to see a man watching me. I straighten instantly when Zayne steps out of the shadows, his eyes intently on me.

"Just the person I wanted to see."

The shadows in the hall draw sharp edges on Zayne's face as we both circle each other, our eyes never wavering. One moment I have the safety of the chamber doors behind my back, the next I'm standing right under the archway with nothing but air left behind me.

I try to hide the slight tremble in my hands and pray that my nose won't start bleeding again as the older prince hovers, and waits—for what exactly? I clear my throat, and straighten my shoulders, even though my spine protests, yelling at me to lie down and rest.

"Are you here to see your mother?" I break the silence because it doesn't seem like Zayne plans to.

His lips tilt into a smile. "Why else would I be here?"

"You tell me."

"Well, I've heard that the generous Katarina found out how to heal my mother and came straight here." I narrow my eyes at his mocking tone.

"I was shocked, honestly, when it was said that she was poisoned."

"Shocking indeed." I agree as I watch him inch closer, the gold embroidery on his dress shirt glints in the light of the chandelier, shifting a sparkle into those green eyes. "How lucky that we have you here at our court."

"I try to help where I can." I clench my hands, the fresh pain of my nails digging into my skin, the only thing that keeps me steady. The prince stops right in front of me, the scent of ash wafting around me. It clings to my body like a second skin, making me feel dirty.

"Is that all?" I ask when he tilts his head to the side. He raises his hand and I flinch when his fingers travel through my hair.

"Allow me." He pulls a white feather out of the strands. I exhale unsteadily as his hand retreats.

"I think there are thanks to speak."

I shake my head and take a step back. "There is no need. I did it because I wanted to. I just hope that whoever is responsible gets caught fast."

"Indeed. Well, the gates to the palace are closed so whoever did this is trapped here inside with us." He shifts his weight and pushes his hand into the pocket of his pants. He doesn't look concerned, considering the fact that his mother was poisoned by someone's magic over and over again. Whoever did this, accomplices with Adales which no one knows besides Cassian, Edlyn, and me.

"Do you have a guess?"

"Pardon?" I raise both eyebrows when he smiles secretly.

"Can you guess who did this?"

"You sound like it's all a game. Some kind of riddle to solve and not reality." He shrugs his shoulders nonchalantly, a few black strands falling around the sharp edges of his face. If it weren't for his cruel character one might find him handsome. Suspicion arises inside me like bile wanting to fight its way out.

"This is your mother's life we are talking about."

"It is the queen's life we're talking about. A mother's life, not mine's." I furrow my brows confused. "What do you mean by that?"

"I mean that she was no more mother to me than yours was to you." The glint in his eyes makes me understand. For a moment it looks like the shadows on his face deepen into sorrow.

"Oh. Don't look at me like that, Carina."

"How am I looking?"

"Like you're pitying me." I control my facial expression, crossing my arms in front of me.

"I don't deserve your pity, you hate me, remember?" His eyes fly between mine and I dare say he is waiting anxiously for my answer.

"I don't hate you, Zayne. For the sake of your brother, I don't. Just because you're a cruel person it doesn't mean you don't have feelings."

He laughs coldly, triggering a shiver to run down my spine. His eyes glint crazily as he looks at me.

"No human is born being evil, it is always the circumstances that make them villains. And yes, I believe that even you deserve pity." He shifts his weight.
"You're a fool if you think that."
I shrug carelessly. "Call me a fool then."
"Seems like the princess has accommodated to our ways. You're defending my mother, pitying me, what comes next?" His lips tilt to one side, a playful glint in his eyes. But I know what this is, I've spent half my life hiding my feelings behind a mask. But it is no use. To hide. Sooner or later the wall is going to collapse and take everything with it.
I don't know what relationship Zayne has with his parents and, to be frank, I don't care. I take a step closer and tilt my head to the side.
"Who knows? I feel like I'm in a generous mood."
A soft laugh escapes him and his eyes wander over my face for a moment.
"I know you, Carina, you're the most stubborn person in existence. If you start to hold a grudge against someone you don't let it go easily."
I shake my head. "I do. If someone proves me differently. Your brother proved me different and maybe I will give you the chance to prove that you're not pure evil, Zayne."
"What if I don't want a chance? How can you believe that I even care to be in your good graces?" He arches a brow and I smile lightly. "Because, Zayne, I know you as well. And I know that you love your brother and that even the darkest monster craves human contact and love, no matter how hard you deny it." I pat his chest lightly as his gaze narrows.
"You love Cassian. And maybe that is the only reason why I'm still talking to you." I turn to retreat in the hall when he calls after me.
"If you think there is some good in me, why don't you ask me?" I freeze, my back still turned to the prince.

"Ask you what?" I turn my head to see him hovering in my peripheral.

"What's been cursing your mind since you stepped out of that chamber."

I turn my head slightly to see his form still frozen under the archway. The light of the chandelier reflects in his black hair, his skin dark against the white dress shirt.

"Was it you who poisoned the queen?" I hold my breath, my muscles taught as I await his answer.

I turn to fully look at him, to watch the cruel smile grow on his lips and reveal glinting white canines. His eyes glow as his face turns lethal. "No, Carina, it wasn't me who poisoned my mother."

~ 29 ~

Blood oozes out of the meat as my knife cuts through it like butter. I watch the blood form a trail on my plate, mingling with the garlic potatoes and soaking into the white flesh of the bread. A steady sound accompanies the silence at my right and I turn my head to shoot Kael a glare. He doesn't even notice my glare and keeps on happily smacking his lips, oil shining on them as he tears into the burned piece of meat. "Seriously, Kael." Edlyn snaps sitting beside me, her piece of meat and potatoes on her plate untouched. The blond freezes and looks at both of us confused.

"If you keep on smacking your lips like that I will seriously consider ripping out your throat." My friend grumbles and I raise both brows confused by her mood. Kael swallows his bite and his lips turn into a small smile.

"I already heard Flynn is back for Speaking Death, is that what got your panties into such a twist?"

Edlyn glowers at him.

"Nayaran does not affect my panties, I just hate it when you eat without your mouth open, you pig." My confusion buries further.

"Flynn is back?"

Kael nods before shoving another piece of meat into his mouth.

"Came straight back when Cassian heard about the traitor and Adales. If someone can find out who it is, it is him."

"But Oceanus is a day's travel away from us."

"On foot," Edlyn grumbles as she eyes her sharp fingernails, acting like she doesn't care at all about Flynn's whereabouts. She looks up as if she senses my confusion.   "Nayaran is a Tengeri, you think he goes to foot everywhere?"

"You mean to tell me that he *swam* back to Demeter?" My fork clutters against the plate when I let go of it. Kael nods his head and grunts in agreement.

"But we do not connect to the ocean." Kael shrugs his shoulders, "There are enough rivers connecting us to Oceanus."

Edlyn scoffs.

"Don't look that impressed when you see him again. He's probably already paying his price for the fast journey and sucking on an innocent life's throat."

I shudder at the thought while Kael rolls his eyes.

He points his fork at me as he goes on, "If he doesn't find the culprit until dawn, the king has to cancel the festivities."

Edlyn protests, "Don't be ridiculous, as if he could cancel Speaking Death. He has no chance but to celebrate, even if Nayaran finds the traitor which I doubt, might I add."

Kael opens his mouth to answer but I hold my hands up confused.

"I feel like you're speaking in a different language. What do you mean celebrating?" They both turn their heads, confusion adorning their faces.

"You don't know of Speaking Death?" Edlyn asks and I raise a brow.

"It's probably the most important celebration in Demeter." She goes on.

"Right, even I know that," Kael says, going for the potatoes on his plate.

"No one told me about it." I shrug my shoulders. I haven't seen Cassian again after I healed his mother this morning. Edlyn blinks a few times before crossing her legs and turning towards me. "You still gonna eat that?" Kael points at my plate and I shake my head. "Go for it."

I turn to look at Edlyn who rolls her eyes.

"Speaking Death is one of the most sacred celebrations in Demeter because of Demetrus' heritage. It is a way to celebrate and remember the weight that has been put on every Moreau man carrying the task to watch over the souls. To consider who travels the world of Gehenna and who doesn't." I nod understanding her point and she keeps on going with a glimmer of excitement in her warm gaze.

"No one knows if it is just leftover of Demetrus's ghost that lives inside the lands or this palace but every night on this day everyone gets the gift of sight."

"What does that mean?"

"It means that at midnight, you can see thousands of colors rising in the air, floating with the stars." I watch Kael shove more potatoes in his mouth while I think about her words. "What you mean is that we can see the souls in the sky?"

Edlyn nods with a smile, nostalgia shining in her eyes.

"It's pretty awesome." Kael pipes in and we both turn our heads to watch him gulp down some wine.

"And you wonder why Azzura doesn't spare you a second glance," Edlyn tells him, making the boy sputter, his cheeks turning red. I kick Edlyn's shin scolding her and she rolls her eyes lazily.

"We're all going to dress up in beautiful gowns and celebrate tomorrow."

"That is why you'll need to find the traitor till sundown." I wonder and they both nod their heads. "But what if they don't? I mean it could be anyone, there are no current suspects."

Kael shrugs, leaning back in his seat. "Then we'll have to celebrate with the knowledge that a traitor is under us."

I exhale, my appetite gone. I would feel much better if I could talk to Cassian and maybe tell him about the characteristics of the magic. Perhaps it has some kind of fingerprint, he knows the people residing in the castle more than I do. "Uh-oh, I know that face." I look up at Edlyn, her lips spreading into a small smile.

"It's the scheming face." I worry my bottom lip, tapping the rest of my stool before getting up.

"What are you doing?" Kael echoes when I get over to my dresser, opening various drawers until I find some ink and parchment. I scramble back over to them and shove the plates out of the way.

"I lived with a traitor once in my castle. I don´t feel like repeating history. Adales didn't do the dirty work, he had someone hired to poison her."

I unroll the fresh parchment, the scent of it filling my nostrils. Kael stacks the plates on top of each other to make some more space. I start to scribble on the paper the ink splattering in chaos on my skin. "If I know one thing, it is that it is always the one you suspect the least," I murmur and Edlyn agrees.

"Who would´ve known Marrus—Orkiathan—would kill innocent people."

"Exactly." I nod at her and look at Kael whose brows are drawn in.

"You said her symptoms started showing when Cassian left the castle for his—mission."

"Yes." He nods, his curls flopping on his head. "Which means you´re the only person who could know them because Edlyn was at the Sebestyen court. Who would want to hurt the queen, who would have a motive?" Kael exhales, raising his brows.

"That could be anyone, Carina. Someone who would want to weaken the king or a past lover who holds a grudge. The question is why did Adales do it? How could he foresee that you would heal the queen?"

Edlyn shakes her head, "King Ronan has no past lovers he was always faithful. And whatever Adales' reason might be, maybe it is not the same one as the one of the perpetrator."

This is harder than I thought, with barely any information on the suspect. Kael leans forward suddenly, something glinting in his eyes. "But why would someone want to weaken the queen? If they wanted to get rid of her, why not kill her?"

"Maybe someone didn´t want to get their hands dirty?" Edlyn throws in and I shake my head. "With that amount of magic inside her, it must´ve been someone who´s constantly in the palace. Someone with enough time to poison her mind over and over." I let myself fall onto the chair already feeling defeated.

"How did it feel?" Kael suddenly asks and I look at him.

"How did what feel?" I ask.

"The magic coursing through her."

I look at the empty parchment laying in front of me, ink splattered everywhere as I try to remember this morning's feeling.

"It was cold and dark, I could barely see."

Goosebumps cover my skin when I think of the way the darkness held me back. How it clung to my feet, hindering me from taking another step.

"It felt empty. I knew I wasn't alone, I knew that something was residing in the darkness and yet it felt like the loneliest time of my life."

I focus my gaze back on both of them. "It felt like death."

Edlyn's gaze becomes thoughtful and Kael looks at me grimly. "We know someone whose powers would feel like death." He raises a brow, takes the feather and scribbles the name on the parchment. "Zayne?" Edlyn asks and he nods.

"No, it's not him," I say as I stare at the parchment.

"How are you so sure?"

"I asked him this morning."

"You asked him?" Kael stares at me incredulously and I shrug my shoulders.

"He said he wasn't the one who did it."

Edlyn furrows her brows, "And you believe him?"

I think back to the look in his eyes. "I do. It's not Zayne's style to act in the dark. He likes to gloat about his bullying."

"But maybe he wants you to think—" Kael gets interrupted by a knock at the door. We all freeze and I gesture for them to stay quiet. Maybe if we'll stay quiet whoever is behind the door will leave. Another knock sounds before a voice booms in the hallway.

"I rather don't want to knock down the door, love, but I fear I have to if you don't open up." I instantly relax at the familiar tone and roll my eyes at him.

"Rather aggressive don't you think? Why don't you use that glinting golden thing in the middle of the door? It's called a handle maybe it will help you with your wishes." I call back and not a second later the door opens and in steps the prince in dazzling dark clothes.

Cassian's curls are windswept, his cheeks flushed as he assesses the situation.

"Do I need to be worried about this situation?" He arches a brow.

I tilt my head slightly, blinking innocently. "Do we look like killers?"

I can imagine the picture we three make up at the table, conspiring theories.

"Do you want to answer honestly, love?"

I flush at his words and clear my throat when I see Kael grinning from the corner of my eye.

"Is there something you needed?"

"Yes, why I hoped to have a quarter of your time if that is possible." I shoot Kael and Edlyn a look and even if it is more like a question they both instantly get up. "Wouldn't want to hold you up." My friend says with a smug smile as she presses a soft kiss against my cheek before retreating.

"I'll take this with me." Kael rolls up the parchment and departs with a nod at me and a brotherly pat on Cassian's shoulder.

Soon the prince and I are alone and left in my chambers.

"How is your mother?" I ask as I sit down in front of the wooden dresser and start to take out the various pins in my hair. Cassian trails the room and I watch him in the mirror in front of me.

"She's complaining about the food, scolding my father for not starting the preparations for tomorrow, I think her exact words were 'I don't care about the traitor poisoning me, I will gladly poison myself if the celebrations tomorrow will end in a disaster'." My lips tilt into a smile as I grab the brush and weave it through my hair.

"I gather she's doing quite all right."

"She is. Thanks to you." He stops at the chair behind me, his eyes meeting mine in the mirror. I halt and smile at his reflection. "I barely did anything."

"Don't play it down, I've been there and I know what you did. What a toll it put on you." I put the brush down and turn on the chair to look up at him.

"It was the least I could do. I just hope it is permanent this time."

"It will be. You could see it leaving her body. *Him* leaving her body."

I cringe, knowing what will follow.

"Thirty days is not a lot of time."

"It is enough to figure something out." He lets out a distressed sigh.

"Carina, Adales said—"

"Please," I say a little desperately, "Let's not talk about this now."

"If not now, when?" His knuckles whiten on the grip of the rest.

"Soon." He deflates but accepts my wish with a nod. His hand covers mine on the rest of the chair and a small electrifying sensation travels through my fingers. "Thank you."

"It's fine."

"Carina." He warns and tugs at my hand making me stand up. I shiver as I slip my hand into his and let him pull me closer. "Accept the damn gratitude."

I chuckle lightly at his aggravated expression. "I do."

He shakes his head, "Always so fucking stubborn," He mumbles as he ducks his head a little.

Something closes in my throat, doubt spiraling inside me. He watches me curiously through his lashes, his cheeks flushed lightly. A stray curl dances over his forehead. My face dances toward his, anticipation building in my body like an oncoming storm. I shiver when his breath travels over my skin dauntingly. He angles his head further still not touching but he is so close that I can feel the heat emanating from his skin. His eyes meet mine with such force I cannot help but sigh when my heart flutters in my chest. It beats the syllables of his name and chants me on to move closer. *Cassian, Cassian, Cassian.*

Whatever he sees in my face as his gaze touches my skin it makes him bold. Cassian finally dips his head but I quickly turn mine, making his lips graze my cheek. I shiver at the contact, my nails digging into the ends of his shirt, tugging him closer.

"I don't think I'm ready yet."

He looks at me through his lashes, smiling gently. "That's all right, I can wait."

Something unscrews inside of me, my body floating into the sphere of him.

My hands are still in his shirt not knowing if to push him away or pull him closer.

He dips his head again, his lips trailing over my jaw.

"What about a kiss here?" He lets his lips hover at my jaw. I only manage a week nod as he presses his lips to my skin.

His lips travel higher to my cheek bones. "And here."

I shudder and feel his lips turn into a smug smile.

My hands travel towards his neck and I guide him to all the places I want him to feel, my heart fluttering in my chest like the wings of a hummingbird.

Cassian groans when he presses his lips to the center of my throat, his body shuddering against mine, his hands tangle in my hair.

I get on my tiptoes and press a kiss against his jaw, my fingertips wandering under the sleeves of his tunic, grazing the hair on his arms.

I feel the chair dig into my back as he advances on me, his cheeks flushed in scarlet. "You make me go mad, Carina." He mumbles before his lips hover over my skin again.

He stops when he reaches the top of my cheekbone and draws back to look at me. We're both flushed and if possible Cassian's curls look even more disheveled than usually.

The weight of the moment makes the air shift around us and I dare not think about what this means.

"I swear if I could taste just one thing for the rest of my life it would be the taste of your skin, Carina."

My eyes flicker to the side as I feel myself blush. "Don't stay stuff like that."

"It is the truth."

I look back up at him. "That doesn't make it any better."

His brows furrow creating the familiar creases on his tan forehead. I muster him for a second, trying to find the person I thought he was. The young boy who got on my nerves, the teenager teasing me in my castle, the boy betraying me, the man protecting me, sacrificing everything for me.

"What?" He asks softly, his hands wandering to my cheeks stroking the skin softly, absently. "I didn't say anything."

"But you're looking at me strangely."

I shrug my shoulders. "Maybe I like looking at you." It slips past my lips before I can hold it.

The crease on his forehead vanishes and the expression replaces itself with a boyish grin. "Look as long as you want."

That's my worry. I fear that once I look at him, really look at him I might not find a way back. That I will get lost in the maze of lines forming all different kinds of expressions. I detangle myself from him, inhaling to clear the fog from my head.

"Did you want anything from me besides telling me thanks?"

Locking my shoulders I try to close the walls I so carefully built around me. When I try I find that they are rusty, crumbling slightly at the edges.

I sit down on my bed and watch him stand in the room. His presence expands into every corner evading the space, uncertainty flickering in his gaze.

"I did. With everything happening, I completely forgot about tomorrow. I wasn´t in my kingdom for three years and already forgot about the traditions."

"You mean Speaking Death?" He looks at me startled before nodding.

"Edlyn already told me all about it."

Now leave. Leave me alone before I am tempted to kiss those lips.

"Oh, well, that´s great. I´ll have a dress prepared for you. Something airy and flowy." He shares a secretive smile with me and I feel like I´m liquefying into a puddle when the dimple forms in his left cheek.

He scratches the back of his neck, his tan skin flushing.

"That was it I guess."

I watch him turn and expect him to leave the room stiffly but he stops right in front of the door.

"Please…" he starts and turns his face so I can see his side profile. My body freezes at the longing reflecting in his gaze and my heart is back right in my throat.

"Please ask me to stay." He exhales, his eyes closing for a moment. I feel the pull instantly. See in his body that leaving is the last thing that he wants to do.

"Then stay."

~ 30 ~

I don't know what it is that wakes me. I can't grasp the feeling that crawls in my dreams. I just remember those red eyes lurking in the dark before I flinch and my eyes fly open. For a moment I wonder where I am, my eyes adjusting to the darkness until they land on the person lying next to me. Cassian's eyes are closed, his black lashes fluttering over the high points of his cheeks as soft breaths leave his slightly opened mouth.

I hesitate in my movement and for a moment I watch the prince lay peacefully beside me. The duvet slips off his tan shoulder, as he shifts a small frown etching his features.

I allowed him to stay last night but besides laying next to each other nothing happened. Falling asleep without facing each other we both seem to turn in our sleep, gravitating towards the other.

I shiver when a small gust of wind travels over my skin and I whirl around to see that the doors to the balcony are slightly ajar. The curtains are fluttering with the soft breeze traveling through the night.

I swear I closed them before I laid down a few hours ago. Another shiver travels over my spine and pinches at the back of my neck as I watch the clouds shift high in the night sky. My eyes scan the room, my breath forming small clouds of air in front of me. It seems like the temperature drops even more as I watch the shadows, watch anything that shifts in them. But nothing.

I am paranoid. I swing my legs over my bed and tiptoe over to the balcony doors, the hinges squeaking in the wind. The marble is cold underneath my feet and I rush quickly to the doors to get back into bed. I grab the golden handles and shut both doors, locking them afterward. For a moment I watch the dark outside through the glass doors.

One would think that a forest full of dark pine trees should look peaceful at night. No humans are traveling through the needles scattered on the forest ground. Nature is undisturbed only at night but the narrow passages of trees make it look like things are creeping in the shadows. Unseen and dangerous.

I freeze when I see something shift in the darkness and I quickly press my hands against the cold glass and narrow my eyes. Is there someone out there? The shadow shifts again and I tense up just to let out a small chuckle. It was just the wind moving the tree. I mumble to myself when I turn around.

"I'm going mad."

I turn and freeze instantly. Fear prickles underneath my skin like a thousand needles as my heart starts into a sprint. Someone is standing in the shadows, right behind the door that leads into the chamber. My hands start to shake as my eyes rove over the person or more creature that lurks there without movement. I take a slow step towards the bed. My knives are stashed on the bedside table but they're too far away.

"Cas," I whisper, trying to get the prince's attention.

My eyes fly back to the door but the shadows haven't moved. "Cas," I repeat taking another step toward the bed. I immediately halt when the shadow moves his arm. The prince grumbles and turns his head away, hugging the pillow to his chest. I can't believe this idiot is actually sleeping through this. The shadow tilts its head at me as if it is waiting for me to make my next move. Why is it still standing there? If it wanted to attack why would it wait for me to notice it?

I don't dare to speak to it, it is enough that I can feel it. The air that buzzes around it is filled with the essence of magic. Whatever this is didn't come to play.

"Cassian, get your ass up right now or I swear I will haunt you as a ghost."

"What is your problem, princess?" He grumbles as he pushes himself up, the duvet slipping off his naked chest as he squints at me. I slowly show him with my eyes to look at the corner as I take another step toward him. The moment Cassian catches the shadow, it steps out of the dark and the prince appears beside me. "Who are you?" His voice is dark as he speaks up, shadows already swirling up his arms as his fingers grow talons, black tints the veins beneath his skin.

The shadow hesitates as the smell of blood fills the air around us and I tense even further as clouds of darkness creep over the marble, like fog, making their way toward us. "

Tell me who you are." Cassian repeats but doesn't receive an answer.

The room starts to rumble and a sound close to thunder echoes around us as the shadow attacks. It is lightning fast as shards of onyx attack the prince and me.

The latter quickly shoves me behind him, blocking the attack easily. The ground shakes as Cassian tries to contain the attacker but how do you fight shadow with shadow?

A wave forms as both their forces collide and I barely see Cassian's form as he disappears into the dark cloud that floods the room. I scramble over to my night table and pull two knives out of the drawer, turning around to somehow help the prince.

I feel my heartbeat pound in my ears as I try to assess the darkness spreading in the room, swallowing all sounds. I hear someone grunt and a flash of tan skin appears in the dark blight.

"Gods, I must be insane," I mumble before I raise my hands and start to advance on the thunder cloud but I don't get far as an iron grip clads over my throat.

I get yanked back by an arm so forceful that one knife clatters to the ground as my airways get blocked. A chocked sound leaves my lips as I try to turn and face my attacker but his arm is clad over my throat so tightly there is no way I will. I swing my left arm and graze some cloth with the knife, a hiss sounding behind me before it turns into a dark chuckle.

"Let go of me!" I choke and ram my head back, colliding with someone's forehead. "Oh, you shouldn't have done that."

I freeze when a shiver runs over my spine. *I know that voice, where do I know that voice from?* I struggle even more now that

I'm sure that it is just a human behind me, stomping with my bare foot onto his boots but that only earns me a hard jab into my back. My spine cries out, dizziness spreading through me, the dark cloud in front of me turning blurry.

I don't know if Cassian is still fighting that thing but I hope he at least gets out of here. I claw at the arm over my throat, digging my nails into skin, until blood oozes over my fingernails. Iron floods my nostrils and urges me to gag.

"That won't work, princess, claw all the way you want, you can't win this fight."

The familiarity of the voice scratches at the back of my mind.

My mind starts to spin with the lack of air, as blood splatters to the ground, the liquid feeling warm against the tip of my fingers.

My eyes flutter close as thunder rumbles around us but my ears drown it out. Drown out the cackle of the coward behind me and focus on the drop, drop, drop. The blood is still oozing out of the wounds where I pierced my nails into his skin. His blood is crusting under my nails. I can feel it. But not only can I feel it drying on my skin, I can feel *it*.

Something sizzles before it flares up inside and overtake me like armor. I stop trying to struggle against the grip and let my arms go limp. The blood splatters onto my arms and I fully wilt and let go.

A wave crashes through me, takes every cell inside me, and causes the room to explode. Light rushes so bright that I have to squeeze my eyes shut.

"What the hell!" The man behind me finally lets go as he tries to shield his eyes but it is too late. I topple onto my knees and let everything explode out of me, burning everything down until I can sense it. It is pulsing in the center of the room. I feel the shadows of Cassian glimmer in the darkness and let my light rush towards it, reach for it and embrace it like a long-lost lover. The moment the light meets the dark a guttural cry echoes around us.

The foreign shadows start to twist in pain as the light drowns them in its power. The creature howls again before it pushes past me and the balcony doors fly open as it rushes into the night. For a moment I watch my light and Cassian's shadows dance around each other before it rushes back over to me and collides with my chest. I splutter and a gush of black blood rushes right out of my throat.

"Carina!"

A hand catches my hair and pulls it out of my face as I vomit right onto the floor, a warm hand drawing circles on my back. I heave a few times before I can breathe again and if it weren't for Cassian cradling me in his lap I would've toppled right to the floor.

His hands find my cold cheeks as the iron taste resides on my lips. His eyes are wide and worried as they rove over my face.

"How did it hurt you? I was fighting it the whole time?" He sounds breathless and I can see cuts over his face, blood splattering his lips.

"He wasn't alone." I can barely speak up, my vocal cords burning as they collide. It feels like his hands are still around my throat. I raise a hand to the tender flesh, making Cassian look at it. His gaze darkens as he softly takes my hand when I wince. "Who was it? Could you see his face? I swear I will search the whole kingdom for that bastard and slowly torture him until he regrets ever laying a hand on you."

I shake my head slightly. "I don't know who it was, He came on to me from behind."

"Fuck." Cas curses and I slowly get off of him and wobble over to the bed.

"Hey. Slow down." He helps me sit down and wraps the duvet around my shoulders. I just now notice that my teeth are chattering.

He quickly gets up and closes the balcony doors, locking them.

"What was that?" I ask him after a moment of silence and he watches me, shaking his head. "I have no clue. I've never seen something like this before. Until now I didn't even know that anyone else besides the Moreau heir could summon the shadows of death."

Another shiver runs over my spine. He advances on me again and sits down beside me. I'm grateful when he presses his thigh against the side of mine, his warmth transcending onto me. "Do you think it's connected?" I turn my head to look at him, his green eyes are watchful as they meet mine.

"What do you mean?"

"Do you think that, whatever or whoever that was, attacked me because I healed your mother?" His features harden at my words, and his arm slips around my waist before he pulls me flush against his side.

"I don't know but it seems oddly convenient that after you somehow figure out how to use your powers you get attacked."

I furrow my brows understanding what he's saying.

"You mean it is him? Adales?" He shrugs. "He is the only one knowing of the existence of your powers."

I turn to him, my knee grazing his as I try to grasp this.

"But why did it wait? We were asleep, it could've attacked us then? But it didn't even attack as I noticed it. It just hovered as if it were waiting for something."

"Or someone." He says and I nod gazing off into the corner where the creature lurked. There is no evidence that it ever was here. The only thing remaining are drops of blood painting the ground where the man stood.

"You mean it waited for the man?" I ask him now and he shrugs again.

"You couldn't see anything?"

"No, but..." I trail off unsure but he edges me on. "But what?"

"Do you know that feeling when you dream something and you could swear you've dreamed this before?" He nods as his hand draws reassuring circles on my knee. "It was like that. I knew his voice but I can't remember from where."

"Sometimes we think something is familiar because the unknown is far more frightening than the known." I sigh at his words. Could it be that I just imagined the familiarity in it?

"Listen, whoever it was we will find him. First thing in the morning we'll talk to Flynn. He's been around much longer than I have, there is no creature he doesn't know about. But now you should get some sleep."

I try to shake the fright off but it is useless. It is still sitting in my bones, that cold strange feeling.

"I don't think I can sleep," I tell him honestly and he nods.

"That's all right, just lay down for a bit, you can stay awake."

I resign to his words and scoot backward on the bed my head meeting the soft pillows. Cassian pulls the comforter around me and tucks my hair behind my ears. He settles beside me in a sitting position, his body still tense, alert as if he is waiting for the next attack to happen.

"Get some rest, love." His knuckles graze my cheek before he softly strokes my hair. I seriously don't think I can fall asleep in this frozen state of fear but after a few minutes of him stroking my hair, his body temperature oozing around me like a safety blanket, I feel my eyes grow heavy. And after a few more minutes I let them close, let the world of dreams capture me.

~ 31 ~

I barely keep an eye shut during that night. My dreams are filled with dark shadows winding around me in a chokehold.
Subconsciously I am aware of Cassian's presence beside me throughout the whole night, he doesn't move an inch. It makes me relax further into the pillows surrounding me.
Even though the prince doesn't move during the night the moment we step into the dining room, Flynn stalks over, a determined look on his face. Somehow Cassian told him of the attack that took place during the night.
Once he's close enough he bows for a moment, a few red strands escaping his braid, and dancing over his skin.
"I've already checked the wards around the castle; it looks all intact. There is no way someone could invade the palace."
"Well, apparently there is, or else I wouldn't have had a knife to my throat."
The words slip past my lips before I can refrain from them. His turquoise eye focuses on me, his lips forming a small grimace.
"I am sorry, Carina. But there is nothing we can do if none of you've seen the actual attackers."
"Attackers? Who was attacked?" Kael's voice appears up from the dining table, his eyes meeting mine over the distance.
Azzura is seated beside him, a bored look on her beautiful features.
"The princess is making up drama again."
I ignore her and walk past Flynn and Cas who are already planning to enforce the field surrounding the Royal grounds.
The table is filled like usual but the chairs of Zayne and Edlyn remain empty. Silver bowls of honey are clattered beside freshly baked bread and golden eggs.
I drop into the chair on Kael's right side, turning my neck to make it pop.
"Why were you attacked? No—wrong question—who attacked you?" Kael leaves his eggs on his plate his green eyes big and

worried as they access me. His hand finds my shoulder squeezing lightly.

"It was nothing. I rather not talk about it now." I pile some oily bread and eggs onto my plate trying to ignore his narrowed gaze.

"If it was nothing, why does Cas look like he wants to take the whole castle apart."

"He's had that look since she came here." The lazy drawl of Azzura's voice notices.

I shoot her a look but she isn't even looking at us, rather focused on cutting the honey-drenched tomatoes on her plate.

Kael moves back into my peripheral and raises a blond brow.

"Where is Edlyn when we need her?" I ask.

"She is with the prince, they found the one responsible for the queen's poisoning," Flynn speaks up as he and Cas approach the table. I'm on my feet in a matter of seconds.

"And you're telling me this now? Let's go talk to them." I turn to leave but Cas' hands come down on my shoulders and push me back into my seat gently.

"You need to eat, love. After that, we can go see him." He whispers beside my ear while I try to see reason.

Who cares about eating when they just caught the one who is responsible for cursing the queen? Maybe that someone has a connection to whoever broke into the castle last night. This means that we could be a step closer to Adales and his plans.

"It is no use, anyway. Eryx is going to question him first, order of the king, before anyone can see him." Flynn says and I stay put, making sure to glare at both of them.

Cas settles in the seat beside me, his knee knocking against mine. Our gazes clash for a moment, heat flooding my cheeks.

"Who was he?" I question Flynn who's already focusing on the various letters and papers laying in front of him, where his plate should be located. Do Tengeri eat? Their source of survival is blood so it probably isn't necessary for them to eat. Kael eats plenty despite his needing blood to survive. I can hear him munching on whatever sparked his appetite, beside me.

"A servant, they found the ingredients cooking up in his chamber and he confessed quickly afterward." Flynn isn't even looking at me as he goes over the scribbled words on the papers.

"A servant," I repeat his words, trying them out on my tongue and making sense of them.

A servant tried to curse the queen? Maybe they were tired of their orders and easily manipulated by Adales requesting to do his bidding.

"I can see smoke coming from your ears, love." I turn my head to meet Cas' gaze, a soft smile dancing across his lips.

"Why are you so relaxed? They practically found the one who wanted to murder your mother."

"Exactly." He shrugs and I narrow my eyes at him.

"They found him, Carina, he is not going anywhere. If Zayne can do one thing it is handling traitors. So first I'll make sure you get some nutrients inside you and then we can go see him. I promise you can ask him everything you want. We will solve this."

I hold his gaze for a moment longer before I turn and shove some bread into my mouth. The faster I eat, the sooner we can go and see the servant. After last night I don't feel like this is a coincidence. Somehow this is all linked but we don't have enough of the puzzle pieces to connect them.

"For once, I wanted to enjoy breakfast. Now my appetite is gone." Kael murmurs beside me and I turn to arch a brow at him.

"As if anything could dim your appetite." Azzura bites from his side and I watch his cheeks turn red immediately.

"It's unhealthy to eat that much. Be thankful that you'd have to stop."

"Unhealthy?" Kael raises his shirt to reveal the hard muscles on his stomach, a soft line of light hair trailing from his navel into his breeches.

"I think I'm good." His lips spread into a grin while I watch Azzura's eyes dip toward his stomach before she looks back up.

She narrows her eyes before she stands straight as an arrow. Today she is dressed in a light green saree, the color reflecting in the jades that dangle at her ears and decorate the golden rings around her slim fingers.

"You lot are getting on my nerves." That is as much as a goodbye one gets from her before she turns and leaves the room.

"Way to go, lover." I pat Kael's shoulder who's staring after Azzura, a longing look in his eyes.

Before I can stop him he gets up, ignoring us all, and follows her out of the room.

"Poor boy," I murmur.

"Why?" I turn to look at Cas whose brows are both raised.

"Why? Can't you see he's clearly in love with her? And she's a master at torturing him."

A soft sigh leaves my lips.

"Well, she isn't the only one." He murmurs.

"I think I had enough reason to. The difference to you is that Kael is treating Azzura like she lays the world to his feet." I counter.

Cas holds his chest in mock horror. "Have I not done enough? I'll make sure to plan my redemption as soon as possible."

I roll my eyes at his mockery before my fingers find his hand, tracing carelessly over his knuckles.

We both stare at each other for a moment, his eyes shooting sparks that run through my whole body.

My heart rate quickens as the loaded silence between us unravels in the crystal green of his eyes. A grunt makes me flinch and both our heads turn to look at Flynn who's still sifting through the papers.

"If you go on with this I will gladly vomit on both of you."

A small chuckle passes off of Cas' lips. "Your time is going to come soon, brother, no need to be jealous."

"Jealous." Flynn scoffs before he freezes. Cassian goes on taunting him but I focus on Flynn, whose eyes are practically flying over the words.

"Cas, shut up for a moment," I shoot the prince a look who turns quiet before I question Flynn, "What is it?"

His turquoise eye meets mine for a moment.

"This is a letter from Polyxena from two days ago."

There is a long moment of silence, stretching out the room, filling every corner and angle. My grip on the chair hardens as I lean forward, to catch a glimpse of what got him this upset. His brows furrow further and further until they almost meet in the middle.

"Flynn?" Cassian presses, his jaw clenching as the tension floods both of our bodies, making us ready to jump up and fight whatever it is that needs to be defeated.

After a heaving sigh, Flynn looks up and usually, he is composed. I don't think I've ever seen the scarred warrior look this pale and concerned and a pit grows in my stomach when I realize that his gaze is avoiding me.

"Chamilot castle has been under attack, the king and your brother had to flee." His words barely make any sense to me. I stand up, trying to string along the words to put some meaning into them but the more I try the more I dissect them.

"Carina," I focus back on Flynn whose eyes are still focused on me,

"Your brother has been the target."

~ 32 ~

"They're alright." I barely listen to Cassian's words as we both descend the stairs, leading further into the mountain. I barely feel the temperature dropping to inhuman ways with Cassian's body heat beside me but right now that is my least worry.

"Kian and your mother are going to be able to get to them as fast as possible."

"She is not my mother." I bite back, trying not to shed a tear. They've sent my brother into a different kingdom, away from me, so he would be safe. And now the kingdom has been attacked, with Henri being the target. There is no denying who's responsible for this.

He said this would happen. He told me that he would go after the people I loved. So what am I doing here? Shouldn't I be leaving Demeter as fast as possible before anyone else gets hurt?

No matter how fast Kian and Shailagh are, it's too late. The damage has been done.

I round the corner, my vision blurring with unshed tears before Cas wraps a hand around my arm and holds me back.

I turn around ready to scream at him but I freeze when I see the pained look on his face.

"I know you are worried about your brother but we left him with Hector for a reason. It is almost impossible for someone to defeat a Custos, Henri is safe."

"You're wrong." I shake my head and he furrows his brows already wanting to object. Luckily I'm faster than him.

"Someone who created the Custos would be able to destroy them in one blink."

The prince takes a step back, brows raising. "You think Adales did this?"

"He told me he would threaten the people I loved. And now he did." I take a step back and try to breathe through my anger as I start to pace.

"This is my fault. If I would just leave this Kingdom and go to him Henri wouldn't be hurt. You can't deny that it is my fault, Cassian, not this time." I shake my head at him.

I watch Cassian struggle for words before he takes a dedicated step forward.

"This is not your fault. Adales is the one who hurt him, not you." His hands find their way to my shoulders brushing the hair from my face. "If you leave Demeter he will kill you and then we all will be fucked. Without you, our world will literally cease to exist."

"He is going to torture me as long as he can if I don't leave and I won't. . .won't let anyone get hurt anymore because of me." I hiss.

"Don't say that." His breath hitches lightly as his eyes meet mine. "Don't ever say that, Carina. Whatever he has planned he will not succeed, I'll make sure of it. I promise."

"Don't promise things you can't keep." His hands drop from my shoulders when I turn but his hand catches at my wrist, stopping me. I turn only partly.

"Promise me." His voice is desperate. I look up to see his gaze glow like emeralds.

"Promise me you won't do anything like offer yourself up. I will make sure no one else gets hurt and if I die for them, I will. I will do whatever it takes for you to stay here. So promise me."

I hesitantly nod, watching him swallow.

"Say it." His voice turns urgent.

"I promise."

"Good."

The air grows hot around us and luckily he lets go of my wrist. I turn and we descend the rest of the way without another word spoken.

The lit lanterns show us the way toward the cells and once we turn around the corner, a small room reveals itself with five cells facing each other.

Thick metal bars are drilled into the brick ground, the material glowing in soft lilac. Bloodstone.

The cells are empty except for one, where Edlyn and Eryx lurk in the shadows. The moment Cassian and I come into view Edlyn rushes over to us.

"He hasn't said a word until now. Pretty stubborn if you ask me." Before she pulls me into a quick hug.

I straighten my shoulders when she lets go of me, even though I would want nothing more than collapse in her arms.

"No one is stubborn enough if you want answers." My features harden and I try to walk past her but she stops me, "Whoa—what happened?" I halter for a moment and turn my head slightly in Cas's way, "Fill her in."

With that, she lets me go and I walk over to the bars Eryx is looming in front. The king's advisor greets me with a small bow and I eye the servant behind the bars.

For a moment my dedication falters when I realize how young he is.

His face is still round like a child's, his cheeks full and freckled, his eyes a deep brown. He is human.

"Open the door," I tell Eryx, who looks at me surprised.

"What?"

"Are you deaf? Open the door."

"I have to object, Carina, he is far too dangerous."

I turn slowly, narrowing my eyes at the old man. His eyes are of a deep green and maybe his stance would've intimidated me once but not now. He meets my gaze steadily but I can see the small tick in his jaw. "It's Your Highness, not Carina. And as far as I know, he is human, how dangerous can he be?"

"He tried to kill the queen—"

"With poison. That is a pretty cowardly way to kill someone." I arch a brow and his gaze flies to Cassian but I quickly block his path.

"Don't look at him. Why are you looking at him? I gave the order. Follow it." I raise my chin and try to make myself taller than him, despite the height difference.

I catch his fingers twitching slightly before he finally reaches for the keys.

The metal jingles when it comes into contact and after a small yawn the door is open. He pushes the keys into my hands a little bit too aggressively if you ask me.

I tip it open with my boot not keen on hurting myself with the bloodstone.

"I'd like to talk to him alone."

My eyes focus on the scared boy. A moment of hesitation before the prince speaks up. "Do you think that's a good idea? Due to your condition."

"My condition?" I turn my head to look at him. His features harden immediately when he meets my fiery gaze.

"The king's advisor is unable to get any answers so I'll get my try. Alone." I shrug a shoulder nonchalantly. A shadow crosses Cassian's face and I know I'm being unfair.

But I've been distracted long enough, by him, by training, and a thousand other unimportant things.

I need to focus. And I can do that best when I'm alone.

"Fine." Cassian relents after a short stare down and he nods at Edlyn and Eryx to go.

The former does reluctantly until I shoot her a small smile and head nod.

I listen for their footsteps, trying to track them until I can hear them leave the mountain part of the castle.

I take a deep breath, let the air fill my lungs and drown any doubt. It feels like the soft material of my cloak drapes over my shoulders and the assassin takes place as I step into the cell and meet the eyes of the frightened boy.

"Now to you."

~ 33 ~

"What's your name?"

My shoes scuff against the floor, the end of my dress tinted in dirt and dust. The boy takes a step back as I tilt my head at him. Assess him.

His reddish hair sits in waves on his forehead, the tips slightly darker, drenched in sweat.

He's dressed in the typical servant's attire, a dark tunic that falls over his stockings, a demolished leather belt wrapped around his middle, and brown boots that looked like his toe would break through at any moment. His skin is mostly covered in soot or some kind of dark powder that has made its way under his nails, buried so deep he's probably never going to get rid of it.

He can't be older than sixteen, the juvenile features still marking his face and neck.

They've put shackles on his wrists as if he could get violent at any second, I almost have to laugh at that thought.

Once my eyes assessed him they meet his again and I wait for him to answer.

His name escapes his chapped lips, quietly, "Mihai, Your Highness."

I nod before my eyes flit over to the single small ledge in the cell. It is made out of stone accompanied by no pillow or blanket.

"And what have you done to be here, Mihai?"

His eyes flit around the cell, unsure to settle anywhere.

"If I'm being honest I am still not sure, Your Highness."

I hesitate for a moment, trying to detect if he is lying.

"Have you heard of the queen's illness?"

"Of course I have! It was terrible, my mother was the maid tending to her in those dark times."

I nod while I start to pace the small cell, making him follow me with his eyes. The poor child looks frightened to death, my heart goes soft at his fright but I have to stay vigilant.

I came here with an intent and a suspicion.
Someone who uses poison to get rid of their enemy is a trickster.
They don't want to be seen, they want to be left in the dark. So why did Mihai leave the poisonous powder, enhanced with magic, in his chambers? And how does a human boy of sixteen years come upon magic?
I slip the small sack Flynn gave to me out of a pocket in my dress and open it in front of Mihai. His eyes watch me take out a batch of the orange-colored powder. It immediately stains the tips of my fingers and I feel my magic calling to it. Wanting it to connect and create an undetectable mess.
"Do you know what this is called?" I ask Mihai and look up at him as he nods, and swallows hard. "Ambrosia."
"Right. I didn't, when they showed it to me. A really pretty color isn't it? Almost as pretty as it is dangerous." I push the small pouch back into my dress pocket before I grab his wrist.
He panics immediately and tries to back off but my grip is too strong.
"No need to panic, Mihai. This powder does not have any effect on humans,"
I open his palm and spread the powder over his sweat-slicked hand.
He watches me draw two lines before I continue, "The powder is not dangerous at all, it is often ground with milk and hyacinth to create—"
"Honey." Mihai interrupts me and I let go of his wrist smiling lightly.
"Perfect, you know it."
"Of course I do, my mother made me mix it because they believe the anti-inflammatory ability would help the queen."
I nod again as his brown eyes meet mine with commitment.
"We never wanted to harm her."
"I believe you, Mihai."
"Y-you do?"

"Of course. You probably know what Ambrosia does in combination with magic. That it enhances someone's skills, sharps them into a weapon, and makes the magic untraceable. It gives someone the power to poison someone in silence without ever being found out."

Mihai immediately starts to shake his head and traces back until his back collides with the cold cell walls.

"I didn't—I would never harm the queen."

"That is pretty obvious," I sigh and watch the powder trickle to the grown dusting the remains off with my other hand.

"But not many others believe that you didn't do it."

His eyes widen further.

"Tell me, Mihai, did a foreign man ever approach you? Or maybe your mother?"

He quickly shakes his head, his red strands flying around.

"We are not allowed to speak to anyone besides the servants. Please, Your Highness, I wish no one harm, I swear it on Adales."

How ironic.

I look back up at him and shoot him a hard stare, "Believe me when I say I will make sure that whoever was responsible for this will receive their punishment. Because you, Mihai, didn't do it."

"He didn't do it." I cross my arms in front of me as I step into the throne room. Servants are rushing around the vast space, decorating the dark place with paint that glows in the dark, garlands of dried flowers, and small green flames conjured by the healers.

Cassian and Eryx halt their conversation and turn toward me while Flynn walks over from the back of the room.

"Whatever do you mean?" Eryx furrows his brows at me.

"I mean that Mihai didn't do it. That poor boy is scared to death."

"That is exactly what someone guilty would play at."

The king's advisor counters and I raise my brows. "Then tell me, Eryx, how would a human use Ambrosia to enhance magic if he has none?"

"Maybe he has an accomplice."

"Why would someone who has magic need a human?" I take a step closer, narrowing my eyes at the man. Something falters in his face and I take another step closer.

"Why do you want him to be guilty so badly? Why not consider someone else doing this?"

"Is that an accusation?" He almost growls and my lips spread into a soft smile.

"You tell me."

Eryx sputters and looks at Cassian who has been quiet this whole time. His features are drawn in, his eyes placed on me as if he is pondering my words.

"I'm with Carina on this, Mihai didn't do it." To my surprise it is Flynn who speaks up, his arms crossed over his broad chest.

"What would a little servant get from poisoning the queen? There is no motive."

"Of course there is! We just haven't found out what it is yet," Eryx protests and looks at me, "not so much luck in getting answers to your questions then, have you, princess?"

"You don't always need to ask questions to get answers," I tell him and narrow my eyes even further. This man is getting on my nerves a little too much today.

"Just because you found the powder doesn't immediately mean he is guilty."

"I didn't find it," Eryx says and his lips twitch for a moment.

"Who was it?" I ask and Cassian finally speaks up, "My brother did."

"Zayne?" His name escapes my lips in a breath. Surprise prickles at my skin and quickly switches places with confusion.

"Where is he?"

"I sent him to help my father to continue the research on the Fatum's whereabouts. They found a diary that's been tracing their appearances over the decades."

The prince tells me and I nod. Then my eyes flicker towards Flynn whose lips are already turning into a knowing smile and he bows before retreating.

Whatever Edlyn has against him she has to admit that he never lets something remain unsolved. He turns and I know he's going to talk to Zayne without me needing to say something.

I focus back on Eryx and Cassian, the latter observing me.

"Where is Edlyn?" I could use her sharp mind right now.

"She needed to take a trip to the capital before the celebration tonight."

Right, Speaking Death.

As if we don't have enough problems, now I have to smile and act like everything is fine for the rest of the evening.

I stay quiet while Erx whispers something to Cassian, bows, and retreats from the throne room. My eyes focus back on the prince whose eyes didn't leave my form for one second, during that process.

"I know a lot has happened in the last hours," The prince starts taking a step forward. "But I was wondering if we could talk about last night. When we—"

Before the prince can finish his sentence the ground beneath our feet starts to shake. The castle vibrates as we both throw out our arms, trying to keep balance as our eyes meet.

A feeling of deja vu floods my veins when I think back to the Sebestyen castle as it started to crumble when our blood was combined.

But this time it is not something that we've caused. A high-pitched scream ricochets around the space and it is one of the servants working at the open archway of the room that leads to the forest outside.

The girl looks horrified as she turns and looks at us.

"They are coming! They're here!"

And that is when I hear it. A hard flapping of wings as if stone was colliding with stone as it sends another wave of vibration through the castle.

~ 34 ~

My breath falters as I watch it happen before me. Three beings shoot through the archway, their wings flapping graciously as they ascend to the onyx ground of the throne room.
A small shudder rushes through me as their feet hit the ground.
Two of them have smaller wings, glowing in a soft yellow, the color shimmers as if barely there. If you didn't know they had wings you'd not be able to see them.
Kian and Shailaigh make their way over to us, their wings still in full bloom but it is not them my eyes stay glued on. It is on the man behind them standing tall with a smaller boy beside him.
It takes me a moment to recognize the features, to swap out the once honey-colored skin with this new one. It looks grayish, permeated with glowing veins, the color spreads from his fingertips, making his arms look like they're carved out of stone.
His eyes are glowing in a dangerous orange, reminding me of the color of scorching lava.
But it is not his skin that makes my heart stutter or the veins that corrupt his skin like a curse, it is his wings stretching out behind him vastly.
There seems no end to them like they could envelop his whole body.
They're an anthracite gray, and look like they're out of solid stone.
I take a step forward, past Kian and Shailagh, making the narrowed gaze of the beast focus on me.
His wings twitch as if ready to defend himself but when our eyes meet a second time I watch his gaze soften.
"Hector?"
The sheer force of a Custos is immense, it trickles a wave of respect around the room.
As if triggered by his name, the wings fold in on his back and retreat, the veins and grayish color slowly leaving his skin, he

shrinks before he looks back at me. Honey eyes that twinkle lightly in the light.

"Your Highness, it is very good to see you." He bows and I do the same while I feel Cassian stepping up beside me.

"Well, good that you all are happy to see each other. But I'm still here—hi—the one who got almost killed?"

My eyes flicker to the boy beside him and my heart almost drops out of my ribcage.

I barely move, don't feel the wind dance through my hair before I envelop my brother in a hug.

Laughter vibrates through him as his arms envelop me and push me against his chest.

"Glad to see that I'm still likable."

I look up, not letting go of him as I arch a brow.

"Have you grown?" He furrows his brows when I take his chin in my hand and turns his face from side to side.

"Is that stubble? Gods, you're fifteen!"

"Nah, It's dust from the flight." I turn to look at Kian who grins at my brother.

"It's not dust." Henri gets his chin out of my grip, his cheeks flushing as he narrows his eyes at the Faye.

My eyes rave over his features, taking in the soft waves of his hair and the glow on his cheekbones. Before I can stop myself I pull him back into a bone-crushing hug. "I'm so grateful that you are unharmed." I choke past some tears.

"If you squeeze me like that I will not stay unharmed for long."

"Sorry." I quickly let go of him before I turn to Hector. "Thank you for bringing him here, safely. You have to tell me what happened, every little detail."

"Of course, I will. Is Nayaran here? I would like him to be present during this, there is much to talk about."

I turn to look at Cas.

The prince focuses his eyes on the small gap between the king and me, his hands pushed lazily into the pockets of his breeches.

"I'll call for him."

But instead of turning he stays rooted in his spot, a visible tension oozing from him.

I turn confused to look at Hector and my brother, Kian, and Shailagh's presence looming in the background. I feel my mother's eyes on me but don't acknowledge it while Kian breaks through the tangible silence.

"After this flight, I could do with some food, or else I'm unable to endure this."

A few minutes later we all assemble in the dining chamber, the table filled with various delights, which makes Kian groan in pleasure at the sight.

Shailagh excuses herself with more important duties and Cassian leaves us alone for a moment, to get to Flynn. Both of them reappear rather quickly before we all sit down at the table.

I don't touch the food I'm too engrossed in the details Hector has been spewing.

"It has been an ambush, led by Orkiathan."

I freeze at the name, a shiver crawling over my spine as I remember the Tengeri.

"Did anyone get hurt?"

Hector turns in his seat beside me, to look at me.

"A few guards but nothing too serious, most of the group of the Tengeri fled, and a few were killed."

"And Orkiathan?" Flynn asks opposite us, for a moment my eyes flicker to Cassian sitting beside him, his body unnaturally still. He hasn't said a word until now. I try to catch his gaze but it seems like he is avoiding it on purpose.

"We've managed to capture him but we don't know what to do with him. He's not saying a word."

"Have you been in contact with Aalton?" Flynn leans forward while he watches Hector nod. "I've been in contact with the new king of Oceanus over time. We'll get Orkiathan ready to travel to Oceanus in a few days so the king can question him before the wedding takes place."

"Aalton is getting married?" I ask, surprised. I've not yet met Flynn's cousin but it seems like he's doing just fine with his new duties. Flynn nods, his braid slipping over his shoulder in the process.

"Darya has been at my cousin's side for a long time and the official coronation will be entwined with the event. The whole family has been waiting for them to marry and now that he is king…"

"She would be safer as his wife," I conclude and he nods with a small grimace. I avert my gaze and stare at the empty plate in front of me for a moment. I thought that Henri got attacked because of me but now that Orkiathan comes into play I'm not so sure anymore. Is this Adales' work? Why would he choose someone so insignificant as the Tengeri to do his dirty work?

The constant chewing of Kian accompanies my thinking and I throw a look at the Faye who raises a brow. Flynn and Hector dive into their conversation of trials while I lean to the Faye to my right. "What do you think?" He stops chewing and looks at me, "About?"

"About if this was a planned move from a high god or just revenge from a persistent bastard?"

Kian puts his cutlery down, swallows, and props his chin onto his hands while his lips stretch into a smile.

"Why don't we ask the target?" He turns his head to his right to where Henri sits. "Don't call me that, I have a name." He glares at the Faye, whose grin stretches even wider.

"I find target great, or maybe little target? Has a certain ring to it, don't you think?"

"Stop teasing him." I shove his shoulder lightly, trying to hide my grin before I focus on my brother.

"Did Orkiathan say anything to you as he attacked you?"

"Well, I was weirdly distracted by trying to survive so I don't remember exactly." My brother puts on his mock-thinking face.

"Henri."

"You're no fun anymore. I am being honest, he didn't talk much. The thing is, he looked surprised when I woke up." Both Kian and I share a confused look.

"Why did he seem surprised?"

The Faye asks and my brother shrugs.

"He said I wasn't supposed to be awake. As if he planned to find me asleep."

I lean back against the rest of my chair, turning over his words. What was that supposed to mean? That he planned for Henri to be asleep so he could kill him? Or rather kidnap him?

"What if you weren't the target?"

The table turns silent as five pairs of eyes focus on me.

"How do you mean?" Hector asks.

"Maybe this didn't have anything to do with Adales. Orkiathan is a bastard, he doesn't need to work with a god to be cruel."

Flynn follows my thought process, "So you're suggesting Orkiathan had an ulterior motive that is not connected to our problem?"

I shrug a shoulder. "It is just a guess. Henri says Orkiathan was surprised to find him awake. So what if it was not a person he was after but a thing?"

Hector shifts in his chair. "That does not sound good."

"No," Flynn agrees, "It sounds like another problem on the long list we have conjured."

We all fall silent again, hanging after our thoughts. Even Kian doesn't pick up his fork again, his honey-drenched tomatoes sitting abandoned on his plate.

I look up, feeling eyes on me, and meet the blazing green of Cassian's eyes as he sits in front of me, quiet and brooding.

I arch a brow, asking him what is wrong. Instead, he averts his gaze and I watch his shoulders raise as he takes a deep breath before they fall as he exhales.

~ 35 ~

"Your arm."

I hold up one arm and let her slip the golden bangle over my skin until it sticks to my bicep.

"The other one."

I sigh and raise my other arm watching her repeat the process.

My body is clad in an airy black gown that has a million diamonds sewn into the fabric, glittering with every movement. It looks like the seamstress has captured starlight onto the fabric.

The black dress is accompanied by see-through silk that flows just over my arms and down my silhouette while leaving my arms bare.

"You look breathtaking." Edlyn turns me, her hands resting on my shoulders so we both look into the mirror and at my reflection.

I don't know why there's so much devotion tinting her breathy voice. I look like always. Dressed in the color of death, she said that everyone would appear in black tonight, to step into the shadows so death can make its appearance and glow in colors for one day.

"Like a sea full of stars," she says dreamily before a small frown paints her face.

"This has to go though, it doesn't fit." She goes for the gold coin around my neck and I protest.

"Gisella told me it was a good luck charm. I rather not test fate and put it off."

She raises a brow. "How much luck has it given you so far?"

I don't back off and she sighs. "All right, but at least take it off and wind it around your wrist?"

I stare at the coin grasping it between my fingers. It is cold to the touch, a reassuring feeling floods me once it comes into contact with my skin.

"All right."

Edlyn nods happily before she takes the necklace off, carefully winding it around my wrist a few times, the coin dangling against my palm.

"You're as tense as Kael when he doesn't get something to eat."

I turn to look at my friend. "Is that so surprising?"

Edlyn casts her eyes downward for a moment, making the paint on her eyes glitter iridescently. "I suppose not."

They've put Henri into a chamber in the castle with guards posed in front of it but what good are they when a god is after him? Provided that it is Adales but after the news of Orkiathan that remains a mystery.

"I just feel helpless and stuck. Aerwyn told me to find the Fatum but she never said how and now we're spiraling. Searching for a mirage that we´re not supposed to find."

"But Zayne is close, I can feel it. It's all coming down soon and then all of this will be over."

She grips my hands in hers but I can't even try to pretend.

"Is it? After all this is over, what do I do then? Go back to Aerwyna to kick Andréas off the regime and rule a kingdom that is not mine? The humans will never accept the Faye, you know it just as I do."

She shakes her head, her hair slipping behind her bronze shoulders. "There is a way to convince them. There's been so much hatred and war between the different creatures that they've all forgotten that we come from the same source. But I believe that we can change people's views. It will take time. And patience. But it will happen."

"Supposed we don't die on the way doing it."

She squeezes my hands. "We won't. You won't."

The look in her eyes is far from reassuring. I know what she's implying with her words. Even if there is collateral damage I will not be one of them. Because I am the image of life and that nonsense. And I might have healed the queen but I don't exactly feel like I can make up life out of nothing. I am getting better at the protection spells, lately I've been able to project a shield of water, but what is that worth? It is just a crumb of power that will not help me in ruling.

People expect me to be the creator of life, or something close to it anyway, but that is just not who I am or what I am capable of doing.

"That facial expression never means any good." Edlyn shoots me a crooked grin as I saunter off toward the opened balcony doors.

"It just doesn't feel right."

"What does?"

"To celebrate, hover, while there is a threat looming somewhere outside the palace walls." My eyes focus on the forest of pine trees, the last sun rays kissing the green tips. Edlyn steps up beside me, following my gaze.

"Maybe it is. But what else are we supposed to do other than wait? We might not have the upper hand but we can be prepared, can expect it. Adales will not catch us off guard."

The water of the lake ripples as if it is answering her urgent words. I suppose she is right. What else is there to do but wait? This day is holy for this kingdom and I should try to respect and celebrate that. Resolve flushes my conscience and I straighten my shoulders and turn to her.

"What exactly happens today?"

Edlyn goes to fix my hair as she tells me about the holy day.

"Speaking Death is essential to remember King Ronan's power, the responsibility he carries."

 "You mean ruling Gehenna?"

"Right," she pulls me back into the room, "it is no easy task to damn souls into endless punishment that is for sure. But we also use this day to commentate the dead, to remember those lost souls that were once wandering our world. When the clock strikes midnight you will see what I mean, it's one of my favorite celebrations."

Her eyes practically glow with anticipation and I lean against the wall beside the bed to study her.

Her facial structures are so restrained once we are alone. However the souls are visible, with the look in her eyes I can only imagine how beautiful of an image it will be.

"What?" She tilts her head to the side, a small smirk dancing over her full lips. "Nothing," I grab her hand in mine, squeeze it, "I'm just grateful you're here. With me."

She chuckles as she squeezes my hand, "No need to get all sappy, Your Highness. I will be here for a long time."

A shadow moves over my heart with her words. *But maybe I won't be.*

Before she can interpret the sudden change in the mood there's a knock that interrupts our conversation.

"Come in."

Hector strides through the door once my voice echoes in the chamber and he bows to both of us before we have the chance to curtsey. A king who bows. I catch myself thinking about what my father would say to that.

Hector apologizes for his intrusion but Edlyn is already on her way to the door. Shortly before she closes it she shoots me a look I can't decipher.

Is there worry shining in the hazel color, or rather curiosity?

She quickly slips out of the chamber before Hector moves into my peripheral. I clear my throat and turn to smile at him.

"Hello, Hector, how can I help you?"

"I fear you cannot."

He crosses his arms behind his back and I furrow my brows while I watch him start to pace.

"I wish I could stay, but I have to leave now."

"Now?" I take a surprised step forward. It is good to see Hector. It feels like some part of myself is back here, a part I thought I lost when I left Aerwyna. Hector stops his pacing and nods, facing me.

"I was hoping to spend some time with you and negotiate future relations of our kingdoms but I fear it has to wait. I will leave in a few hours to travel to Oceanus. Aalton is already awaiting me and I doubt that I will be able to shut an eye until I've talked to Orkiathan."

"Hector, you don't have to do this," I put my hand on his arm trying to make him understand.

"I do. Your brother got in danger because I was too careless."

"He got in danger because of Adales. This is no one else's fault. I appreciate your commitment but you have enough to deal with in Polyxena."

A freshly crowned king without a wife or any help besides his mother. His subjects must be waiting for him to change things, to revolutionize the kingdom and yet he is here, sacrificing his time for me.

"Polyxena will not be able to live in peace as long as Adales attacks our people."

I let go of his arm and settle on intertwining my hands in front of me. He is right, this is not just something that concerns me. I may be the trigger to all of this but when I think of Edlyn's troubles as a blood witch, the kingdoms being at silent war, I realize that this has been going on for a much longer time.

Things need to change and may it be Adales death that it has to start with.

"I guess this is goodbye then." I muster up a small smile as I look up at him. The seriousness instantly leaves his face, making a place for that look that only Hector can conjure. It instantly makes you feel at ease, somehow protected.

"I guess it is."

The two of us don't move when a sudden urgency shines in his eyes.

"Idon't want to seem like I am prying, I couldn't forgive myself if I would, but I was wondering about something."

"What is on your mind, Hector, you can tell me."

"You and the Prince..."

I avert my gaze.

"I have just heard that you annulled the engagement and...I guess, I wanted to ask if you were all right?" His voice goes higher at the end of his sentence. I look up at him. He, who seems to be the sun impersonated, right when it is ready to sink, tinting a horizon in a golden hour.

"That is not what you wanted to ask me, Hector."

He chuckles. "No, it is not. Would it make a difference, if I asked outright? If I declared my feelings and offered everything you would want? Because I have not forgotten you despite our sayings to be friends. I would be honored to have you as my queen especially having my friend as my queen. . ." He trails off.

Here he is. A king standing right in front of me, devoted and honest. Every girl would dream of a man this honest and uncomplicated. I grab for his hand and that seems to already be an answer as his smile turns slightly downward.

"Sadly, it would not change a thing. It has been him for a while. If I think about it, it was always him and it will never be someone else beside him."

He ducks his head, his cheeks flushing. "Yes, that is what I thought."

"You are an amazing man and I think great things will happen to you. You will find the piece of your heart that you deserve, Hector, and nothing less." I squeeze his hand

For a moment we're both unsure how to proceed but then we chuckle and embrace each other.

The soft tinge of honey and wood floods my senses as he envelops me in a hug.

For a moment I allow myself to squeeze my eyes shut to revel in this feeling before the doors to my chamber burst open.

Caught off guard, the king and I jump away from each other just to see Cassian halting in his steps. His eyes wander between Hector and me and I see it play out before him like a scene.

I shake my head and step forward but Cassian bows and speaks up, "Apologies for my disturbance," he straightens again, his eyes hard as emeralds when they meet mine, "I thought the princess was alone."

~ 36 ~

Hector left the kingdom. I barely could grasp Cassian's words before he turned and left my chambers with tense shoulders.

I didn't want to bother with questioning his appearance or his behavior. I did it anyway until Kael came to my chambers to pick me up for the festivities.

The sun has gone down and the castle is bustling with various guests, tracing the floors and servants running around, trays of onyx in their hands.

They carry pitchers and goblets full of liquid, plates stacked with sweet honey delights, and salty crackers.

Everyone is dressed in the most extravagant gowns, tinted in the color of night. A few have embroidered golden or silver elements onto their sleeves, and others have painted their faces with colorful streaks to contrast their clothing.

The halls are twinkling with small lights and I catch myself wandering off from Kael's side to realize that it is not a flame but a small buzzing energy and my magic instantly calls out to it. It is someone's magic. I reach one finger out towards the light, the tip already starting to tickle the closer I get and with fascination I watch the light fly closer when my hand starts to glow lilac.

"I wouldn't do that." I flinch and turn to look at Kael.

He's standing behind me in his black robes, stitched with silver embroidery on his arms. His curls are tamed today, someone put a bit of oil on the tips to make them look wet. He looks pretty handsome and tame if you don't know him.

"Why?" He steps ups beside me to watch the light that is still hovering close to me.

"If you touch it with your magic I fear all of them will go out."
I furrow my brows at him.

"Your magic would give them a zap and unbalance them and I don't think the creators would like that."

"Who conjured them?" I question, it's pretty obvious that this is crafted by magic. I didn't even know magic could be contained like this.

"The Magda, that's why Edlyn went to the capital, she brought them here."

"She is not using her magic is she?" I ask. I have wondered about this a lot and speculate every time, but I do not have the guts to ask her.

"No, she does not." Kael offers no further explanation and I can understand why.

"How many Magda's reside in Demeter?"

Edlyn said there were a few scattered here in there but she couldn't come up with an exact number.

Kael shrugs his shoulders, "Maybe a handful? Demeter is probably the kingdom with the most known blood witches, the others might be hiding because no one claims them as their own."

"But Cassian did?"

Kael nods, his eyes trained on the floating light.

"But they keep to themselves, most covens are in hiding, it is just the lonely witches who gravitate to the safety of the Moreau crown." I sigh and look back at the light. "It's tragic."

"It is but many things are,"

I feel his eyes on me for a moment,

"They call it noshtna svetlina."

I turn to him.

"Translates to night light."

"Noshtna svetlina," I mumble as I look back at the light. Before I can dwell on the guilt spreading in my chest Kael grabs my hand and drags me through the banquet hall.

"There is enough time to grieve tonight, first I need to talk to you alone."

"Is that not what we've been doing—hey!" I protest, a short breath escaping my lips as he pulls me past the crowds. We receive strange looks from snobby-looking ladies and curious glances from lords before we escape the inner chambers and resurface outside on the balcony.

The balcony runs around the whole castle, if I am not mistaken, and it gives you a perfectly clear view of the pine forest.

The stars twinkle in the night sky and it almost looks creepy how quiet everything lays, undisturbed and untouched.

"Spill." I turn my head surprised when I notice Kael's jade eyes turning to slits. My eyes wander around us for a moment to notice a woman in her midlife flirting with a lord a few feet away from us, a lonely girl leaning against the railing to our right.

"What are you talking about?" I'm unsure, never having seen him serious.

"I'm talking about the fact that you've been coughing blood, barely touching your food, and hiding it from everyone."

I feel the blood rush to my cheeks at his accusation. I wouldn't think Kael to be the observing type.

"I'm fine."

"You're not. You're dying."

My gaze flees from his and I suppose I rather focus on the giggling woman in the back, the younger girl who watches the pair lazily.

To hear the words come so clearly from his lips is entirely different from the feeling that's been spreading from my chest for weeks.

"I'm just exhausted. The last weeks have been defeat after defeat. I need a good night's sleep and I'll feel better."

"Carina." His fingers catch my chin and gently tilt it towards him.

"I know you're used to hiding emotions. But this is me you're talking to."

I don't know if it is his words or his gentle touch but I can feel it coming.

I can feel my chin start to wobble and I immediately turn my back to him, inhaling deeply.

The air rushes into my lungs, I clear my throat and turn back to face him.

Worry lines mar his flawless skin.

"I don't know what it is. Maybe it is my magic taking a toll on me. Kian said there is always a price for the magic we use, maybe because I don't consume blood like Upyr do, I have to pay with my own life? But it's fine."

"It's not fine." He protests but instead of fighting back I smile and take a step closer. "It is fine, Kael. What's important is that we get that bastard Adales so you all can live in peace,"

He starts to shake his head but I continue, "You all lived without me here for a long time and I think it was intended that way. Who knows, maybe I will be reborn in Oceanus next time, or maybe this will all finally be over."

"He will not survive it, Carina." Kael shakes his head again but I know what he's saying. That they all won't survive it. Something blooms in my chest so powerful it feels like it is going to burst.

"He has to." I grab his hand and squeeze it.

"Please, Kael, you can't tell anyone about this."

"They will notice it sooner or later."

I shake my head lightly. People see what they want to see. I'm surprised that Kael even noticed, I was trying very hard to stay upright, to appear fine. I hope the others won't.

"Promise me, Kael."

"I hate you." He murmurs and I smile up at him. "You wish you could."

He pulls me flush against him and my eyes widen surprised for a moment.

"We will find something. I promise we will." His voice is muffled due to my hair in his face but nonetheless, I squeeze him for his hope.

Hope is something dangerous, it can build up an empire and destroy it in a blink of an eye. But I allow him to have it, damn I've been clinging to it for the past weeks myself.

A deep voice interrupts our moment. "Unbelievable."

~ 37 ~

Kael and I turn surprised and I freeze in my movement when I lay my eyes on Cassian.

His eyes are narrowed on his anger-ridden face, his shoulders tense but it is not his obvious rage that oozes off of him and makes the shadows dance over his shoulders that makes me halter.

He is dressed in black robes, similar to Kael's, pretty simply cut with silver embroidery on his cuffs and a few silver bands adorning his elegant fingers.

His eyelids look like they were kissed by starlight, silver paint dragged over them with streaks, the same streaks that dance through his midnight curls and tinge the tips playfully.

I feel the draw that pulls me towards him, begs me to drive my hands through his hair, and my heart flutters when my eyes travel over the silver crown amid his head.

It is crafted beautifully, woven into each other like the stems of roses, emeralds encased in the safety of the metal, and it looks like the silver is melting off of it.

He looks like a prince sent from the sky to hold his wrath on us.

A moment stops in time, passes before he stomps over to us.

"I've told you to keep your hands off." His voice vibrates and for a moment I'm confused by his behavior.

Kael steps behind my back gripping my shoulders in fright.

"Do something, Carina, or he will murder me!" He cries and I roll my eyes as I look at Cassian. His face dances with shadows as he approaches.

"Is there a reason to murder you?" He asks cautiously.

"There isn't. It's fine really. Can we all calm down for a moment?" I ask but they both ignore me completely.

"I didn't do anything I wasn't allowed to!" Kael says and I'm considering if he's actually scared right now. What are they even talking about?

"I knew you were interested from the beginning. I swear I'm going to rip you apart, brother, if you touched Carina—"

"Touched me?" I ask at the same time Kael asks, "Touched Carina?"

Cassian growls and stops right in front of me, his chest pressing against mine but his eyes are placed on Kael behind me. My heart thrums at the touch of him, even though he is behaving like an imbecile.

"Why would I touch Carina? What are you talking about? I'm in love with Az!"

"I know I—what?" Cas asks, caught off guard and I puff out a breath. This is just a big misunderstanding these fucking infants.

"What is wrong with you!" I hit his chest making him stumble back, his eyes widening in surprise.

Anger surges through me at his stupidity.

"I am considering murdering you, Moreau! If your stupidity won't be the cause of your death first."

Cassian cringes and cowers slightly under my gaze.

"Why would you even think I'd be mad if you were interested in Azzura? I couldn't give one shit." He tells Kael, who finally steps around me. Both the blond and I share a look and I shake my head ever so slightly.

His jaw hardens for a moment but I can see that he is going to keep my secret.

"I think I'm too confused for this, you two surely have something to talk about."

Cassian eyes him warily as he slips past the prince but he doesn't go for him.

"You're unbelievable." I scoff and gain his attention.

"I am unbelievable?" I nod while I watch his cheeks flush in anger.

"Sorry, love, but I'm at a loss here."

"Don't call me love." I hiss at him and shove him by his chest. He barely moves as he glowers down at me.

"Because Hector is the only one to call you that?"

I'm ready to fight him for his behavior before I realize what he said.

"What are you talking about?" I ask.

"Nothing." He starts to turn but this isn't over. I grab his arm and turn him back around to me.

"You're having this 'nothing' for a few days now, Cassian. Talk to me, we've agreed to be truthful to each other now hold up your end of the deal."

"You want me to be honest?" His eyes search my face and I nod, half of the anger still surging through me, pumping me on.

"I'm sick! Sick of dancing around all the time, fearing that one step I take might draw you away. You let yourself be touched so easily by Kael and Hector yet I have to overthink everything I do!"

"And who's fault is that?" I question him and he rears back. I know it's a low blow. He doesn't understand that I'm so hesitant with him because he means so much more to me. Because he holds so much power over me. I fear I don't think right when I'm with him. That is why I draw back when it gets real with him.

"You're being petty, Carina."

I focus back on him and exhale, trying to lift off the weight bearing on my shoulders. "Kael is in love with Azzura for god's sake. You have to stop seeing everyone as a competition. I'm not the one who's going to stroke your ego every gods damn time."

"My ego is pretty fine, thank you."

I glare at his arrogance and his features harden.

"I want Hector gone. He is not welcome at my court."

"If that's your only concern, no need to stress. He already left." I brush past him, deciding that I don't want to have this conversation anymore. I notice that the few people outside have already scattered and a small crowd has formed in the banquet hall, their eyes turned to the sky waiting for something.

I don't feel like being stared at so I wander down the length of the balcony around the castle.

"Carina!" Cassian calls after me but I don't dare turn around.

I can feel the tears pricking at my eyes as I pick up my steps. Soon I see the balcony entrance leading into my chambers but I don't make it far.

A hand closes around my wrist and turns me around.

I'm not surprised when I look up into Cassian's face. He hates it when he doesn't have the last word. A flaw amid his unworldly presence.

His hold on me is gentle. I could escape from it if I wanted to.

Cassian crouches down and I let him touch his forehead to mine. His sweet breath travels over my face and caresses the highs of my cheeks.

His nose bumps mine, softly and he angles his face to the side as if to show me, tell me that he is sorry.

I feel my breath slowly sync itself to his and I turn my hand, letting the tips of my fingers wander over his knuckles before I intertwine our fingers.

"I hate it when you're jealous," I whisper, scared to destroy this bubble we're wrapped in. "That makes two of us."

"There is no need for you to be jealous, Cassian."

How can he even think I'd be able to focus on anyone else if he is there?

"Even if there were, I'll accept it. Even if you do choose, Hector. Because you can. Nothing holds you here, Carina, you're not a prisoner."

I know that I'm not. Why can't he see that I want to be here? Even if I don't know how long I will have, if Kael will find something to help me I will still want to be here.

"If you want to be friends that's fine," his eyes close as he presses his cheek to mine.

"So you think that what we did is something that friends do?" I ask him. He opens his eyes, emeralds shining back at me. Fingertips graze my cheek and sent tiny sparks of electricity through my body.

I sigh at the contact, "I'll take any piece you let me have of you. I will swear to protect it. As anything you want us to be."

"So then take it," I whisper back and he draws back, and looks at me.

"Take what?"

"My heart. It has only ever belonged to you anyway."

The words scare me but they feel sweet on my lips. They feel like the truth.

Cassian closes his eyes for a moment and I watch him. I watch him revel and release a small breath.

"I could kiss you right now."

"Then come here. I've been waiting long enough." I pull him closer with our intertwined hands and let his lips crash against mine.

The moment our lips meet my tummy flips and a sweet groan escapes his lips.

He tastes like the honey delights carried on the trays by servers and I find myself chasing his taste, trailing over the sweetness of his tongue.

His hands encircle my waist and pull me against him, my hands find their way into his soft hair. The silver paint spreads over my fingers as does the paint on my lips.

"Sweet gods." Cassian murmurs in between kisses and the soft timbre of his voice shoots goosebumps over my skin. My heart swells and sweeps with every tilt of his lips, with every move of his tongue and I fear I will turn into a puddle if we keep on continuing this dance.

His lips trail over my jaw, smearing the silver paint from my lips along my skin, over my collarbones and shoulders.

A soft breath escapes me when he pushes me against the railing of the balcony, shoving his thigh between my legs.

"If I could taste one thing for the rest of my life I'd be happy to resign to your taste, love."

"It'll bore you over time." My voice is breathless and he stops and looks up at me, his eyes glowing a faint green.

"Nothing could ever bore me about you."

With that, his lips are back on mine and his hands travel over my arms, the cold metal of his rings on my skin making me shiver delicately.

"You have been calling me that often lately." Cassian looks at me confused, his lips slightly bruised from our kissing.

"What?"

"Love," I state.

"You told me not to call you princess again," he brushes a strand from my face, "So I'll scavenge every endearment there is until I settle on the one you desire but please don't take that pleasure from me. I fear my heart would not be able to stand it."

My fingers subconsciously fist the front of his shirt and when he finishes with a soft breath, I find myself pulling him in again. Our lips meet so delicately like we're both afraid the other will break.

Cassian stops and my eyes flutter open confused. "What?"

"Carina, you're glowing." I roll my eyes and want to wave him off but my hand freezes mid-wave. My hands are glowing lilac. My cheeks redden as I try to get rid of the magic singing in my veins when a loud sound travels through the castle.

"IT IS STARTING!"

~ 38 ~

My glowing hands seem like a small puddle of water compared to the lights that explode around us.

A bell rings in the capital and the echoes of the sound reach the walls of the palace, ricocheting like small explosions.

But the sound quickly drowns out and turns into a gurgling as if underwater. I wind my way out of Cassian's arms and grab the railing.

I'm glad it's there or else I might leap off, trying to capture the view in front of me.

There is no source to the dozen of colors that rise from beneath the earth, floating and dancing around each other. They have no particular form, airy and light, they flutter in the sky and remind me of the shadows that dance around Cassian every time he calls them.

The only difference is the color. Blue, red, yellow and green, orange, and sweet lilac rise into the air and make their way to the sky intertwining with the stars.

"These are the souls?" I whisper when I feel Cassian step up beside me, his hand placing itself right beside mine on the railing.

"Yes, souls that have been wandering our world for the past year. Some might have unfinished business, some weren't let go by their close ones."

I look at him for a moment, watching how the color of the souls reflect in the abyss of his eyes.

"And where are they going?"

He turns his head to look at me, starlight glimmering in his crown. "Where do you think they go?"

Gehenna and Empyrean. I turn my head to watch the light and slowly sound bleeds into my system. On the other side of the castle the people are cheering, and music sounds from the capital behind the vast landscape. I lean slightly forward entranced by the view.

"Can you feel them?"

"Every single one of them."

I look at Cassian, "how exactly does that work? How do you have these powers if King Ronan is still the ruler of Gehenna?"

"My father is getting old. Passing the 500 mark and now that my mother is fine soon he'll give me all of his power."

"How?"

He turns to me and a smile spreads on his lips, the dimple on his left cheek surfaces. He knows what he's going to say will bother me. "A ritual. For the gods."

I roll my eyes and turn back to the sky.

"You and your damn rituals." I hear him chuckle lightly while we both stare at the sky and watch the Speaking Death unfold. I feel his pinky brush mine and we both cross our fingers, sending an electric shock through me.

"We try to remember the importance of Demetrus's task. That it is not always black and white to decide who revels in Empyrean and who suffers in Gehenna. The souls show us that we're all connected in the end, that fate has its hands in everything,"

I look at him and watch him watch the sky. His voice is almost gentle as he speaks up.

"They show us that death is more but pain. That death can be peaceful."

We both turn to each other at the same moment. Our hands knock together.

A desperate cry leaves my lips as the bracelet Edlyn so carefully wound around my wrist slips off my skin.

"No!" I lunge forward at the same time Cassian does but we are both too slow. Now I will have to watch Gisella's last gift to me bounce off the ground and slip right through the railing of the balcony.

Except it doesn't.

The coin collides with the ground and instead of bouncing off, the metal shatters into pieces like it's made out of glass. Blinding light breaks through the cracks, enveloping the prince and me in hellfire.

"What is happening?" Cassian's voice hardens as he turns and the light grows before us. Soon we both can't see but I feel Cassian's shadows form a protective shield around us and I quickly grasp my magic, the tips of my fingers glowing and tingling.

I crouch into stance, raising my hands to get ready for whatever is about to happen. Once the blinding pain subsides I can see three forms stepping out of the light and it is one voice that I recognize with my whole heart that speaks up a second later,

"No need to call your shadows, little prince, I've heard you've been searching for us."

I can feel Cassian still trembling with power beside me but I quickly dismiss his reaction when the pulsing light settles into a soft glow. The souls are still flying in the sky around us, hovering as if they too are mesmerized by the view in front of us.

Three women, equally beautiful, almost looking like carbon copies yet so different settle in the air in front of us.

Their bodies are airy and solid at the same time, standing still with elegance, curving beautifully under their shimmering translucent gowns.

A soft breeze picks up and it dances around them, molding itself around their bodies as if it yearns to touch their skin, to—at least—get one touch on something so glorious before it is gone.

My eyes travel over the identical gowns, the material looking like it is woven out of spiderwebs, glinting in lilac, and green and pink with every movement, returning to white once the breeze settles.

I find myself enamored by the symmetrical faces of all three, their midnight hair, long golden streaks running through, the high arch of their brows, and the deducting curve of their lips but it is not their beauty that makes me stare.

It is the woman standing in the front, eyes so familiar, a soft smile stretching along her lips.

I'm reluctant when I take a step forward and I immediately feel Cassian curling his arm around my waist. His head bows down, his lips grazing my ear when he speaks, "I don't think it's the right time for being courageous, love."

I hesitate, my eyes still on the woman who is now tilting her head at us watching our interaction.

"I'm glad you two finally found each other. It was exhausting to see the push and pull between you." She speaks up and it is the same voice as it was when I parted with Gisella in Aerwyna. Is this real?

Is she really one of the Fatum?

A woman behind her rolls her eyes while the other snickers. My attention gets dragged to the latter and my brows draw in. "Hey—I know you!"

Her smile widens and for a moment her beautiful, youthful face replaces itself with leathery skin permeated with wrinkles. Her back hunches over and she looks just like the old hag I met on the market when we traveled through the capital. She sold a wind chime to me.

"It's lovely to see you again, Your Majesty." She snickers again and turns back into her former form.

"It seems that my sisters can't stop meddling in matters they shouldn't," Gisella speaks up and something stutters in my chest when she scans me with a scolding look.

"Do I not even get a hug? Has it been that long?"

As if on instinct I want to take a step forward but Cassian stops me again.

Gisella raises a brow at him, "I'm not going to harm her you besotted idiot. She was my family first."

Something blooms in my chest and I shoot Cas a reassuring smile before I step into Gisella's offered hug.

The moment I wind my arms around her curves my eyes fall shut and I manage to inhale her familiar scent.

"You gave me that coin…" I trail off because I still can't believe that she is here.

"To protect you. And it did."

Tears spring to my eyes and I can feel them trickle down my cheeks.

"How is this possible? How can you be a Fatum?" I whisper in her hair.

"There is a lot you still have to learn, Carina, but from what I've seen you're handling this pretty well." She gently pushes me back by my shoulders to look me in the face.

I sniffle lightly, a smile breaking through the despair I felt when I recognized her. "You've watched over me, didn't you? Since the moment you came to the castle."

"Indeed I did. How could I not?" She brushes a strand of hair from my face.

"I mean with that bastard following you all along, she kinda needed to save your ass." We both turn to look at the woman who was rolling her eyes before.

Her features are more sharp, etched into a hard grimace.

"Don't listen to anything Andromeda says."

"Why, because I am—for once—telling the truth?" Gisella shoots the woman a hard glare before the three of them focus back on me.

"You should've told me about the coin. I searched for you, for a long time."

"The Fatum are not searched, silly thing. We come when you are ready."The woman to the right says.

I take a few steps back again, colliding with Cassian's chest. For a moment I inhale, trying to keep track of things.

"And I am ready now? For whatever I need to be ready for?" I question all three of them but my gaze falls lastly onto Gisella. A woman who has been more family to me than the people I believed to be my blood relatives.

"Certainly. We have seen that your powers would evolve and you did save the queen." The woman on the right says again.

"Estella is right. You are ready to know the truth." Gisella says and I blink confused for a moment.

"The truth? What is that supposed to mean?" Cassian asks behind me, the deep rumble of his voice vibrating in his chest behind me.

"It means that we'll tell her what she has to do in order to stay alive," Andromeda says lazily, her eyes focused rather on admiring her nails than us.

"To stay alive?"

I cringe at his question, knowing damn well what she is talking about.

"You haven't told him?" Gisella questions me and I glare at her because she knows damn well that I haven't told him.

"Maybe you are not as close as I thought."

"He is devoted to her. He would die for her." Estella swoons lightly and Cassian waves her words away before he looks at me with narrowed eyes. "What is she talking about?"

"You would die for me?" I arch a brow, trying to deflect but the prince doesn't budge. I sigh exasperated, "Lately I've been feeling a bit unwell."

"Elaborate. Now." His body tenses slightly and I'm hyper-aware of the audience listening to us.

"I didn't know it was this serious," I shoot a look over to the three sisters, take in Gisella's impassive face, Estella's empath-ridden features, and the smug look on Andromedas.

"I was coughing up blood, I feel a bit drained and I can't eat anymore."

"And you think that is not something you should've told anyone?" Cassian says and I shrug half-heartedly.

"Kael knows." The words slip past my lips before I realize the damage they could cause.

"For gods sake, fucking Kael." Cassian curses and walks a few steps away.

"No matter how much I'm entertained by this, we have a rather tight schedule," Andromeda mentions and I turn back to them while I let Cassian brood in his anger.

"You're a Fatum and you say you've watched over me my whole life, why didn't you say anything? Do anything against my father?"

"The Fatum don't interfere with someone's life. That is not our responsibility." Estella's soft voice mentions before Gisella goes on,

"Besides, your father is not who you think he is. It is not easy to grasp the powers of the highest god, I understand, but don't you see the difference?"

I furrow my brows confused by her innuendo.

"After your—Shailagh supposedly died, didn't Daragon change in his characteristics?"

He did. But I always thought it was due to the great loss that he became so cold. The three sisters stare at me as if the answer was always right in front of me.

"You're not about to tell me that Adales can shape-shift and pretend to be Daragon and raised me?"

Gisella shares a satisfied smile with her sisters, "I told you she is fast."

I wave her words away, anger burning up. "And you didn't tell me?"

"They can't." Cassian scoffs. I turn to look at him. "I'm not wrong, am I?"

"For once you're not wrong, Prince of Hell." Andromeda teases him and I narrow my eyes at her.

"Why can't you tell me?" Even though I ask the sister I look at Cassian who gives me the answer.

"The Fatum are an oracle, they are higher on the ladder than gods, seeing every string of fate conjure in front of their eyes but they cannot interfere. It is not allowed for them to change the course of fate."

"The handsome boy is right, we cannot interfere," Estella says as she steps forward, "but we do like to meddle sometimes. What else are we supposed to do, in this life of eternity?" She sighs, making Gisella wrap an arm around her shoulder.

"If you can't interfere, and are not allowed to tell me things, why did Aerwyn tell me to search for you?" I say.

I'm sick of all these twisted words and interwoven lies. I have to suppress a shiver if I think about how close Adales was to me most of my life.

"We are here because we answered your prayers, stupid girl." Andromeda hisses and Cassian takes a step toward her making her grin.

"You think you can take me? I can take you out in a blink of an eye."

"Don't forget that maybe your life is immortal but sooner or later you will end up in my kingdom."

The shadows dance at the prince's fingertips and I quickly catch his hand in mine, intertwining our fingers. His fiery gaze meets mine and for a moment I'm enticed to see how far he would go. Something inside me almost vibrates at the prospect but we don't need a fight right now. What we need to do is focus.

I turn back to Gisella, she seems to be the most neutral of the three.

"Aerwyn told you to come to us because, yes we cannot interfere, but we can share your prophecy if that is something that you want."

"My prophecy?" I ask unsure, isn't it bad luck to know what happens in the future? This time Estella steps forward, her lips stretched into a youthful smile.

"Every single creature on Adalon has a prophecy, it is mostly intangible because the lives change so frantically but you as a half-god have a more certain prophecy. Gods lives move slower which is why your prophecy is easier to grasp."

"But that doesn't mean that it is 100% reliable," Gisella adds, "it still could be the answer to all your problems."

I ponder their words for a moment. How could a prophecy help me to outrace my inevitable death? Or do they mean that it could help me with my task of fighting Adales?

A soft squeeze of Cassian's hand makes me look up at him. A grimace paints doubt upon his features.

"Prophecies are never a good thing, Carina, they end up driving most people mad. I promise we can find another way to fix this, without having to test your fate."

"Do you? Since a few moments ago you didn't even know she was dying?" Andromeda's question makes the prince flinch.

"It is up to you, Carina." Gisella rolls over her sister's words as she watches me. Something glints in her eyes so familiar that it makes my lips twitch. Gisella may not be able to tell me things with her words but I know her and her mannerisms too well not to understand.

"I want to know it."

Gisella's lips stretch into a proud smile.

"So it be."

~ 39 ~

The three sisters share a look of excitement as they step backward. The blinding light resurfaces from their bodies as they are lifted upon the night sky.

Cas and I shield our eyes from the light, barely able to make anything out as their bodies hover in place and their eyes flicker open.

White nothing meets me as their voices turn up in chorus multiplied in their volume.

"Balance is the true nature of magic. Where one can live the other must die,"

Their bodies start to convulse, arms outstretched as they keep on going,

"where one will kill, the other will resurrect."

Light wraps around them like spider webs.

Anxiety spikes up inside me as I watch one of my oldest friends perched up high in the sky and a shiver of goosebumps dusts against my skin.

"You can't deny that only one's true blood will have the effect that the true evil will be wrecked."

The final note of the words ring in my ears, making them bleed in agony as I step forward to get ahold of Gisella but she is unconscious, still perched high up in the air with her sister as if they are some kind of vessel.

"What is that supposed to mean?§" I question the three of them as the earth starts to shudder with its full force but they do not answer me. They cannot obey or interfere.

There is no trace of familiarity on their faces as their soulless eyes place themselves upon me.

"May a new age dawn with the rightful heir of our world."

Before I can grasp their words, turn them over, and scrutinize them, the three bodies erupt back in their light and I know what's coming.

"No!" I rush forward trying to leap as the light envelops their bodies and casts them away into nothingness.

"Carina!" Cassian makes sure to envelop my body in his arms holding me back from leaping over the balcony.

A shattering breath escapes my lungs as I stare at the point the sisters were ascending to seconds ago.

"I couldn't even say goodbye."

I start to trash in the arms holding me back, agony surging through me as I barely notice what happened. "Hey!"

Cassian turns me in his arms, his hands gripping my cheeks.

"Carina, you need to calm down!" His eyes search mine and for a moment I try to understand.

Try to see what I haven't been seeing but before I can grab the thought it already dusts into nothing, dancing into the sky with the midnight breeze.

"Hey," Cassian says, now much more gentle and his face comes back into focus. I focus on the high points of his cheeks, the tip of his nose, and the slightly parted lips.

"Sorry." I mumble and he shakes his head, "You've nothing to be sorry for."

Something breaks in me and I don't know what it is. The only thing I know is that Cassian is pulling me in for a much-needed embrace, not mending but collecting the broken pieces. I melt into his body, willing myself to take in his calming scent, burying my nose into his neck.

"It will be fine, I promise."

His lips touch my temple as he speaks, "We will find a solution, and if it's the last thing I do."

He's right, we will. But maybe that solution is not what we are hoping for right now.

"And Gisella was one of them?"

"Yes." I swing my arm letting my sword collide with the opponent's one.

"I always found her suspicious. You said there were three of them?"

"*Yes*," I grunt, escaping Henri's blade as he follows me around in the arena.

"What is it again what they said? Tell me everything in detail."

My eyes flit over to Edlyn who's laying on one of the resting benches, her lethal body stretched in a black tight-fitted uniform, I don't know where she got from. Her hair is in a braid today, her eyes turned to the ceiling as if she is going over my words.

I sigh and parry Henri's next hit with great force and he shoots me a superior smirk.

"Balance is the true nature of magic. Where one can live the other must die," I repeat the words through gritted teeth, sweat pooling at my temples as I duck, the words are etched into my brain since two nights ago.

"Well, that's pretty easy. That explains why you've been feeling so shitty. One has to die."

I glance at her surprised, narrowing my eyes. "I swear Kael can't keep a secret."

Edlyn has the audacity to glare at me. "You don't keep things like that a secret from your family, Carina."

I prepare to disagree but find myself in front of Henri's blade, the tip hovering at my throat.

"Fuck." I breathe as a smug look spreads over his face.

He lowers the blade and I let mine clutter to the ground.

"Okay, first, when did you get so good at sparring?"

Henri's cheeks flush a deep maroon, "I might've been training with Kian."

"Kian?" I take a step forward suspiciously and Henri seems to shrink into his neck. "What is that supposed to mean?"

"Nothing." He breathes in one word and before I can press further Edlyn interrupts us.

"Gods, let him be Carina, he's a teenager and he desperately needs friends."

"Not friends who are magical creatures and potentially dangerous."

"Technically I am half Faye," Henri pipes in but we both ignore him.

Edlyn leans against the railing of the stand, rolling her amber eyes.

"Kian is not dangerous."

I try to conjure the image of Kian's sneaky smiles every time I see him around Henri, the arrogant arch of his brow.

Nope. Not a chance.

"Kian is older than Henri—"

"By one and a half years!" Edlyn explains exasperated and before I can come up with new arguments my best friend chuckles.

"He's not listening anyway." She points to the far end of the room to show me that Henri is already leaving.

"Hey! Where are you going?" I call after him, suspecting that we weren't finished with our sparring round.

"Somewhere you aren't. You have enough problems, sister, don't concern yourself with mine."

I furrow my brows at his words. "You're unbearable!"

"Love you too!" Henri slips out of the arena and I wonder if he's going to search for Kian's company. I don't know if I like this turn of events. Kian might be loyal, he has proven himself to help me, concerning my powers and I'm very thankful for that but Henri is turning sixteen.

"Now repeat the words, Carina."

I flinch surprised as I watch Edlyn duck into the podium, picking up Henri's sword. She swings the blade lazily in her hand a few times, arching a brow.

I try to recall the last words, shaking the worrying picture of Kian and my brother out of my head.

She ducks into a predatory stance and we settle into our sparring routine.

"Right. Where one will kill, the other will resurrect." I repeat the Fatum's next words as our blades collide with a shattering sound.

"That's the part I don't understand, let's skip that first," Edlyn says as she twirls her body and gains a kick to my stomach.

I grunt, glaring at her before I continue.

"You can't deny that only one's true blood will have the effect that the true evil will be wrecked."

I faint a right hit with my foot and hit Edlyn against her left thigh. She stumbles grinning before she parries my next hits.

"So does that mean your blood is poisonous? That your blood will kill Adales?§

"I don't think so," I grunt at the next impact, my arms aching, my side burning from the kick I got from her.

"Why would my blood be only poisonous to Adales? And if it was, what does that mean? That I have to shove it down his throat?" I shiver at the thought and Edlyn fake gags.

I use her distraction as my opening to swipe her legs under her body and her back collides with the ground before my blade is at her throat.

She stares up at me surprised, her chest heaving brutally as if her lungs want to break out of her body.

I throw my blade to the ground and help her up.

"So what we gathered is that one of you has to die," she starts as we leave the podium, "which makes sense. Until now the magic in your blood was never triggered. With Cas making you drink is blood it unravels inside you."

I nod before I continue her thought, "and potentially my blood has something to do with defeating him."

I watch the sweat trickle down her delicate throat and slip into her thigh-fitted suit.

We grab the bottles filled with water, gifting our dry throats with liquid.

"There was something else they said," I murmur after a few moments of chugging the water.

Curiosity sparks in Edlyn's eyes as she dries her brown skin with the near-laid towel. "What?"

"May a new age dawn with the rightful heir of our world." I echo the words, trying to not look around because it feels like they're here. Watching me from every corner of the enormous room.

Edlyn scans my face as if she is trying to search for something.

"What do you think they mean by that?"

I shrug.

"I'm the only one who is known to have the same powers as Adales. However that happened, maybe because of Kaycen or through Aerwyn's, my mother's, blood."

"That is why just one of you can survive," she nods, "the balance of nature, it would be an anomaly if there were two forces who could conjure something as delicate as life."

I ponder over her thoughts as I let myself fall on the bench. But what makes them think that I am the rightful heir?

"So that is why Adales wants to kill me." I consider and Edlyn nods.

"He's probably withering like a plum just as you are."

I throw a glare at her and she smirks as she sits down beside me, throwing an arm around my shoulders.

"No worries, I won't let anything happen to you."

She squeezes me into a short hug. That is what everyone keeps telling me. That they will find a solution, that they will protect me. How can you protect someone from something you don't know?

"If we both, Adales and I, wouldn't act on it. Would we both die?"

Edlyn shrugs again and I let out a frustrated sigh. "It's just aggravating!"

"The waiting?" She guesses and I nod.

"And the not knowing. How am I supposed to fight against him and overpower him without leaving Demeter."

"I don't know," she says, "but Demeter has its current king and its heir as a ward. I'd guess it is pretty hard to get to you here, with so many protections."

I guess she's right. But does that mean that as long as I stay here I am safe from Adales?

But still, in the end, I may be doomed by nature, withering away like a plum, as Edlyn worded it so perfectly.

Squashed to the ground, dried out from its life.

~ 40 ~

After my sparring session with Henri and Edlyn, the day seems to drag on. I try not to think of what occurred on the night of Speaking Death, but it is as if the sister's voices are clinging to my steps, trailing me like my shadow through the castle as I spend the afternoon in the library. Kael and I try to search for blood-induced enchantments, scurrying through every book possible.

I barely get to see Cassian, he seems to be busy with some kind of uprising in the capital and leaves dinner early but he promises to visit my chamber in the evening.

I excuse myself from dinner early and land perched in the chair in front of my desk.

I've opened the balcony doors to let a soft breeze dance through the room and my wet strands.

I tried to relax with an earlier bath induced with Edlyn's rose potion but it did not help in escaping my thoughts.

I've written down the sentences of the prophecy wondering if I could maybe grasp them better but now that I have them visible they seem to disentangle, lost in a world of words and magic, forming new things over and over. They make even less sense.

A shift in the chamber occurs and a small smile spreads on my lips before the soft touch of fingertips trace my bare shoulders.

I turn my head slightly not looking at him, "I thought you had tons of things to do."

"There is always some time I can make for you. What are you up to, love?"

His hands envelop my shoulders as he leans over me, I imagine him furrowing his brows at the familiar words.

His curls tickle my throat and for a moment I feel like I can relax.

"Still thinking?" He mutters and I nod softly.

"Hm," his lips trail over my skin as he brushes the wet strands from my face.

"Maybe I can get your mind off of things?"

My lips pull into a small smile when he drops a kiss on my throat but I push him away.

I look at him with a cocked brow.

"If you're bored with your duties go get something else to occupy yourself with."

I make a shooing gesture and he raises his hands with a smile.

"Well, that's a first."

2First time a woman rejects you?"

A wide grin splits his lips, "You rejecting me."

I roll my eyes and turn back to the paper. After a few moments he starts to rummage through my drawer but I try to tune him out, memorizing the words over and over.

After a few minutes of loud noises, Cassian returns behind me and I look at him through the mirror to see him holding up my hairbrush.

"May I?"

My heart skips at his request and I slowly relax my fingers and let go of the parchment as Cassian steps forward.

He gathers my hair and lets it fall onto my shoulders, his knuckles brushing my skin. I can't prevent the goosebumps from traveling over my body and I feel myself slowly sink further into the chair.

Cassian starts at the bottom, carefully brushing out any knots or disturbances as he speaks up.

"Prophecies are never something that is set in stone. You can wonder over the lovely poem the three morbid sisters conjured. But keep in mind that they do like to trick people."

"Gisella wouldn't trick me."

I watch his concentrated face in the mirror, his brows drawn into a v as he focuses on a tricky part of my hair.

"I know that she is important to you but she is a Fatum. Their prophecies are as flimsy as Kaels crush on Azzura."

I raise a brow at his utter blindness. I don't think that Kael's supposed crush is something that will haunt him for weeks and then suddenly disappear.

"You don't agree?" I meet his eyes in the mirror and smile lightly.

"I think I have a rather different view on Kael's affections but that is beside the point right now,"

I have to stop for a moment as he gently drives the brush over my scalp and I hum lightly,

"Even if you say that most of the prophecy is flimsy, can't there be a part of the truth? They said it would help me in my ambitions."

My neck starts to tingle at the soft caress but before I can enjoy it further he puts the brush down, refocuses his gaze on my hair as if he is calculating something, and parts it into three parts.

I start to turn, "What are you doing?"

"What does it look like?" He tilts his head and asks me with his eyes. I slowly turn back to the mirror and let him braid my hair.

"I'm starting to think you have a feminine side."

"I'm not going to start to braid my hair with Kael that's for sure," he scoffs lightly, "but I've imagined myself doing this forever."

I grimace in confusion. I remember the last time he did this at the Sebestyen court, braiding my hair, even though he was hurt. It seems so far away now.

"What is that supposed to mean?"

His knuckles brush against my back, goosebumps following his touch in seconds, covering my skin.

He finishes the braid and I turn to meet his eyes.

"I remember your father telling you to tie back your hair every time we went for dinner when we were children, the way you always pushed your hair out of your face when you were shooting arrows or sparring with the guards, it's got me obsessed with it. I wanted to be the one to take care of it."

I get up with a soft smile as I remember how it always bothered me. It still does and now it doesn't have the sentiment of my mother having the same hair but I'm just so used to the length.

"I always knew you were strange, the moment you started beheading my dolls is the moment I knew you were a lost cause."

"I still got your attention, didn't I?" He arches a brows

"You're a freak," I shake as I wrap my arms around his neck.

He grins boyishly as he pulls me flush against him by my hips. His eyes search mine as if to ask if this is fine. It's more than all right.

"I'm yours," he brushes his lips over mine before he continues, "I was only ever yours."

I exert pressure at the back of his neck so our lips finally meet. A sigh passes his lips and presses it onto mine as I tilt my head.

Comfort flutters in my stomach and spreads like a warm crackling fire, easing my mind off the things swirling inside like a dark cloud.

Once his lips leave mine I try to stay close to him, my hands in a stoic grip around his neck.

His lips tilt into a smug smile before he kisses the corner of my lip for a moment. "There's something I wanted to talk to you about."

I get back onto the balls of my feet, tilting my head to the side. His eyes watch me for a moment, carefully, before he conjures a small envelope from inside his shirt.

I eye it curiously, wondering who could've written something that included me.

Cassian hands me the envelope with gold-tinted edges and I don't hesitate to pull out the thicker parchment.

It's just a small rectangular, a few swirls and dots gilded into two names that are written underneath each other.

"An invite?" I ask.

I look back up at him to see him nodding, "We don't have to go. But I think you need a break and Aalton could be a possible ally after all. They will intertwine his official coronation as the King of Oceanus with his wedding."

I eye the invitation again and turn it over to see a handwritten message.

It is my greatest pleasure to finally meet you, Carina. Darya and I will be giddily awaiting your visit.
Aalton.

> It is my greatest pleasure to finally meet you Carina
>
> Danya and I will be giddily awaiting your visit
>
> Aalton

"How does he know me?"

Cassian arches a brow at my question. "Everyone knows your story, Carina."

"Right. Everyone but me."

I let the envelope drop on the dresser turning my back on it. We have more important things to focus on than going to a wedding of a man I don't know.

Aalton could probably excuse me for passing after everything that's going on.

"Uh-oh,"

I stop my stroll toward the inviting-looking bed to look back at Cassian.

"What?"

"I can see the stubborn lines forming on your head."

I roll my eyes before I slip under the covers, shivering lightly at the cool feeling on my skin. Cassian lazily strolls over before he sits down on the mattress, making it dip with his weight.

"You need a break, love, this," he motions over to the scrap of paper that holds the words of the Fatum, "is not going anywhere."

I shake my head as stubborn as he claims me to be.

"How can I go and celebrate if I know what is going to happen inevitably?"

"Adales will not suddenly pop out of the cave he's been hiding in, we still have time. We will come up with a plan and travel to Aerwyna but not now." He leans forward, taking my cold cheeks in his warm hands. My eyes flutter close for a moment at the sensation.

"You're tired." He whispers, bitterness laced in his words, "And I don't like seeing you like this. This is not something you need to do alone. I'm here."

That's the problem. In the end, I will be the one facing Adales, not him and I'm happy about that. I don't want anyone getting hurt again because of me.

I open my eyes again, searching his forest green eyes for the answer I'm trying so desperately to receive.

"I'm dying—"

"Don't say that. You're not dying." He insists, his grip on my face becoming harder. I put my hand over his, lacing our fingers together.

"But I am. The sooner I solve this the sooner this is going to be over."

Either Adales will die or I will. It's as easy as that. Cassian's face contorts in agony and I try to muster up a smile, even though he can see right through it.

He blows out a deep sigh, thinking for a few seconds.

"Let's go to Oceanus. We can still think about the prophecy there, maybe Aalton can even help us, he's one of the elder Tengeri in the kingdom."

"If your father doesn't even know what this means, how is anyone else supposed to?"

"I don't know. But we won't leave anything up to coincidence. We will solve this. But you need a change of scenery or else I will lose you," his thumbs dance lightly over the dark skin under my eyes, "and I don't think I would survive that."

For a moment his eyes are distant as if he's imagining the instance. I pull out of his grasp to pull him down beside me. His lithe body stretches beside mine as I grip his hard cheekbones and let our lips collide in a heated frenzy.

I try to make him understand, with urgency, the hardness of my lips.

I pour my soul into every slight movement and I can feel our magic fizzling as they combine, creating something new in a whirl of fireworks.

We're both breathless when we part our lips.

"You will not lose me. Not now. Not ever."

Oceanus

~ 41 ~

I did let Cassian convince me to travel to Oceanus. But it wasn't without any help. Flynn decided to support the prince's decision, I don't know if it was because he thought Cassian was right or because they considered themselves brothers.

I thought it over and in the end, I was convinced enough to go to Aaltons coronation and wedding.

Maybe they were right and we will find something about this whole prophecy.

The harder you concentrate the more you fall into a rabbit hole and you end up walking in circles. Maybe this will somehow break the cycle and tell me what I have to do.

Kael and Azzura both decide to stay back and handle the Demeter court in our absence, Kael happily obliging with a wink in my direction.

I wish him good luck with a small smile, wanting to ruffle his golden hair but for that, I'd have to climb onto a chair due to his height.

Henri and Kian, inseparable as ever, insist on joining us and I oblige happily rather than having the two of them out of my sight.

Oceanus is just a day's ride away but instead of taking the carriage—I can imagine what a hell ride it would be with Edlyn and Flynn's bickering—we choose to mount the horses.

It feels good to be back on Nighttail, the cool wind touching my cheeks and cooling overheated skin.

We barely travel through any small villages and mostly stay in the forests and mountains, keeping us in the shadows of the kingdom.

Edlyn and Flynn are both awfully quiet, either grumbling under their breath or suffering in silence. I feel rather lethargic, my body and mind are tired. Even though Cassian stayed with me the last few nights I could barely close an eye.

I turn my head to look at him riding beside me, his face as criminally beautiful as the day I met him.

The wind is stroking his soft curls as his aristocratic fingers envelop the reign of his horse.

He meets my eyes almost instantly and shoots me a reassuring smile.

He rides a bit closer to my side, making his fingers graze my knuckles for a moment. His way of telling me that everything is going to be fine. I desperately hope he is right.

Early on in Oceanus, we end up in the vast swamp lands, the Odeur wafting around us.

Flynn upfront slows down his horse turning to look at us. "We have to be careful here in order not to wake certain creatures."

"Creatures?" I question and meet his narrowed eyes.

"I think that's a story for another time. Just make sure not to make any rash movements and we should be fine."

His voice sends a shiver down my spine and instantly makes Nighttail slow down. She neighs, unsure, and I pat her face for a moment.

"It's going to be all right, if something happens we'll sacrifice Cas."

"For you, I'd go willingly." Cas flutters his lashes and Henri groans, "I'm still here you know? Flirt with my sister when you're alone."

"Oh, I'm doing more than flirting when I'm alone with her." Cassian grins at Henri who gags.

"No worries, little prince, once you fall in love you will look at this differently." Edlyn teases him and I watch my brother's eyes flit around before he blushes.

Kyan stiffens when he notices my gaze and quickly rides forward to switch his position, now riding beside Flynn.

Henri keeps his mouth shut for the rest of the ride but Cassian joins him slowly, Edlyn switching to the place beside me.

"It will take forever to get this god's awful scent of wet wood out of my hair." She complains, making me snicker. Of course she would be concerned about her hair.

"I don't know what you mean, this is the first time you don't reek." Flynn pipes up from the front, making her narrow her eyes at him.

I furrow my brows confused, "Edlyn doesn't reek."

Kian turns his head from the front to look at me. "To you, she doesn't."

"What's that supposed to mean?"

"The creatures who are bound to life by their usage of blood have a very sensitive sense of smell regarding blood. The blood witches conjure their magic from their blood, it is practically in their veins which smells...in a way."

I blink surprised as I look at Edlyn who shrugs her shoulders as if it is completely normal. Well, it is for her.

"But Cassian doesn't have a problem with it?" I ask.

"Because I'm not a baby like Flynn. You smell fine, Lynn."

She bows her head, "I smell spectacular."

"I'm not a baby, she reeks," Flynn grunts again while I watch Edlyn's sinful lips turn into a smug smile.

"What?"

Instead of answering me, Kian goes on, "Tengeri and Magda are natural enemies, which makes them cautious and defensive. It's pretty normal. That's why the combination of the magic combined with their blood bothers them so much." Something clicks inside my mind at his words and I now understand the smug look on Edlyn's face.

"They don't reek at all to them, do they?"

Edlyn grins, "Nope. We smell like a sweet temptation to them. It's the perfect trap."

"It is not a trap. It's revolting in every way."

"Tell yourself that, Nayaran, we both know who has the upper hand here."

His body locks up at her words but he doesn't turn to answer her. Tension crackles in the air but we all decide to ignore it, focusing on the journey ahead of us.

~ 42 ~

I didn't have an actual picture in mind when I thought of the Guithier court—I knew that the castle was located on a cliff, adjacent to the South Ocean—and I'm glad I didn't.
Whatever I would've imagined could have not lived up to this moment.
My skin is damp with sweat once we break out of the suffocating swamp land, my hair sticking to the skin on my neck.
The others don't look any better, Edlyn's cheeks are flushed and the curls in Cassian's neck soaked. The air is stuffy but clear as it carries over the salty scent of the ocean. Something about it makes me miss the northern wind of Aerwyna. I barely give myself time to miss my home but somehow now I feel the longing for a home more than ever.
"Finally, I think my butt fell asleep." Henri breathes but falters when his eyes upon the castle. He gapes and I'm sure I look mostly the same.
The cliffs enhancing the enormous castle barely keep the waves from crashing against the first floor, damping the ground and land in front of the palace.
White foam coats the tips of the waves that are moving roughly like a storm is brewing in the deep ends.
The castle walls are nothing unusual, a color of Gray steel, with narrow windows, and towers that stack up high, ending in prickly tips. The castle seems rather average but it is the part connected to it that has me enraptured. Small tips of towers protrude from the water, glittering in the afternoon light.
I urge Nighttail forward, now that we're out on the beach she is much more calm.
The scent of salt wafts around us and tickles my skin, soothing the humid air that envelops us.
"You didn't tell me," I whisper and turn to look at Flynn who looks at me surprised.   "What do you mean?"

"That half of the castle is underwater." I swallow as I try to glimpse more but the water is too dark for me to see anything.

"Huh," he breathes, "I've grown up here my whole life it didn't seem like something worth mentioning."

He eyes the depths of the abyss hiding in the waves for a moment as if he's seeing the palace for the first time.

"Let's go. I'm aching for a bath." Edlyn gets off her horse and walks up the steep hill to get to the iron gates located around the castle.

I quickly get off as well, staying beside Flynn. His red hair flies in the wind, not in a braid today.

"Are we able to get to the underwater part from above?"

"Yes, there's a stairwell leading downwards. There are underwater entries for us," he motions to himself as Tengeri, "but we're taking the air entrance."

I nod, suddenly excited to see the castle rather than the underwater part.

It amazes me still how little I have seen of this continent and how much time I would need to explore everything I wanted to see. *If* I have the time.

"Cas told me about it," Flynn starts and I look up surprised, watching the crashing waves reflect in his turquoise and white eye.

"We will handle this, Carina, I promise you."

Something about his words makes my stomach churn.

"How can you be so sure?"

"I have walked through worse things than hell, and have fought more demons that are nothing compared to a single god. Adales will not win this. I would give my soul to ensure Adalon's safety. *Your* safety."

I stop for a moment, my hand gripping his upper arm.

"I don't want anyone sacrificing anything for me."

"I think it's a little late for that." His eyes flicker over to Cassian.

I shake my head, "No new sacrifices, Flynn. I'm being serious."

He stares at me for a moment and I start to grow uneasy, the long scar making him look so much more menacing.
I rarely get scared but something about Flynn is different. The way his gaze turns ancient once he believes no one watches him just assures me of his words.
Flynn has seen a lot of things in his life and I bet my right hand that most of it was horrific.
"As you wish," he finally concedes and motions over to the castle.
It only takes us a few minutes until we strut through the iron gates, the guards eyeing Edlyn with narrowed eyes but still letting her pass.
I wonder what we all must look like, our clothes stuck to our skin, our hair wet with sweat as we give up our horses and wander into the entrance hall.
Inside it is much cooler and I let out a relieved sigh as I eye the hexagonal chamber. The walls are made out of rose quartz, glittering in the candlelight, crystals hanging down from the ceiling with their sharp edges.
"That doesn't seem safe," Henri mumbles as he follows my gaze and I have to agree. Just a rumble of the earth and the edges could detach, hitting anyone standing beneath.
"No worries, princess, these are as steady as the gods' mood swings." I turn. surprised at the unfamiliar voice, the others following my movement, to watch a man appear at the entrance.
His steps are slow and deliberate, his body lithe and clothed in expensive-looking breeches, a turquoise shirt clings to his broad shoulders. He's almost as tall as Flynn, with a wide back that would've made him look intimidating if he wouldn't have his hands pocketed lazily.
I watch the golden chains move around his neck with every step he takes, clinking against each other, a stark contrast to his silvery skin.
Once I'm not too distracted by the earring adorning one ear, or the dangly bracelets on his left wrist I muster his face that is focused

solemnly on me. His plump lips are stretched into a wide smile revealing a healthy set of white teeth, his nose is narrow and lifted at the tip.

He raises a hand and brushes his shoulder-length, blond hair out of his face as he stops in front of me.

His turquoise eyes glitter humorously as he holds out his hand, palm up.

I stare at it for a moment, too baffled by this man's beauty. He chuckles before taking my hand and pressing a light kiss to my knuckles, his eyes not leaving mine during the action.

The moment is so short he straightens the second I feel blazing heat in my back.

Usually, I would find Cassian's behavior childish but this time I take a step back to feel him in my back.

His hand places itself immediately at my hip as the unearthly man watches us.

"It is my pleasure to finally meet you, Carina, you can't imagine the amount of curiosity I had about you! As famous as you are in Adalon it feels like meeting an idol." He tilts his head smiling and I straighten my shoulders.

"I appreciate your invitation, Aalton."

He nods in welcome before Flynn steps up beside his cousin. Familiarity flares up as I see them side by side, comparing the narrow form of their nose, and the silky look of their hair.

"Good to see you, Nayaran. Your father has already arrived and is waiting in the throne room."

Flynn stiffens again but nods, greeting his cousin with a pat on his shoulder before disappearing. I watch the strange interaction before I get swept up by Aaltons gaze again.

"I am sure you are all exhausted. I have some chambers prepared and the maidens will draw a bath for everyone before you're welcome to join my fiancée and me for tonight's dinner."

"That is very considerate of you, thank you." He grins for a moment, his eyes flashing crazily.

"Of course. Serena?" He calls for a moment and a woman appears from the hall, stalking over to us. Her strides are long and elegant, her curvy body clad in a glittering gown.

Her red hair is twisted in her neck enhancing her delicate features, the soft frown of red lips and green siren eyes staring at us.

"Yes?"

Once she stops beside him, meeting his height perfectly, his smile turns warmer.

"This is Serena, one of my oldest friends and my royal advisor, she will show you to your chambers."

"Follow me." She turns and Kian and Henri immediately strut after her, Edlyn eyeing her interestedly.

Cassian doesn't move an inch behind me, he still hasn't said a word.

"If you don't mind, Moreau, could I steal your woman for a moment?"

"Carina can decide for herself if she wants to talk to you or not." His voice is dull and I turn to look at him for a moment. His jaw is locked, his gaze meeting mine intensely.

"I'll be with you in a moment," I tell him and he squeezes my hip lightly before nodding.

I watch him catch up to our group effortlessly but not without throwing a last glance back at me and Aalton.

I turn back around to the king, wary but still curious about this person.

As beautiful as this mask is, I don't know what's hiding underneath.

"Follow me, Your Majesty." I frown at his title usage but follow him through a dark hall.

We pass a few doors in silence, take the stairs to the upper floor, and end up outside on a balcony.

A soft sigh escapes me as I look out into the vast ocean. The salt scent appears again and clears my head for a moment. I watch the crashing waves until Aalton speaks up in a deep voice again, all pleasantry gone.

"You are in great danger, Carina."

~ 43 ~

The chamber is empty when I step inside but I can hear the splashing of water in the bathing chamber that is connected to the living space.
"Carina?"Cassian calls from inside, his voice sounding alarmed.
"Yes, it's me," I call back and for a moment I stand in the middle of the chamber unmoving.
I ignore the enormous bed, and the blue canopy attached to it, fishnets with mussels and sea stars sewn upon the fabric, ignore the window that shows the swampland a few miles away, ignore the candles flickering in the afternoon light.
The water splashes again and I remove my clothes mechanically, leaving the material on the floor in a small lump before I join Cassian in the bathing chamber.
"Are you all right—", he chokes on his next words as he twists in the small pool that is built into the chamber.
A small series of steps lead into the pool, the water onyx-colored with a slight shimmer to it.
 "I'm fine," I say curtly, trying not to think of Aalton and I's conversation minutes ago. I'd rather shove it to the back of my mind and bury it deep.
I meet Cassian's glowing green eyes as I slowly take the steps into the hot water, fog traveling across the surface.
I swim over to Cas who's still looking at me with furrowed brows but he still envelops me close, pressing our bodies together when I reach him. I shudder at the skin to skin contact, so new and yet familiar.
"Why did Aalton want to talk to you?" He asks as I wrap my legs around his narrow hips.
I shake my head and press my lips against his, capturing them in a heated kiss.
Fog gathers around us as our tongues meet but before I can succeed with my plan, he pulls back.

"Something happened," he urges, "tell me."
I sigh and sink to my toes again and push him forward until his back meets the tiled wall of the bathing chamber. He grunts slightly but his eyes don't budge.
"He just thanked me again for coming. It seems like this whole wedding and coronation is pretty important to him."
"He already did that in front of everyone." Cassian frowns. My hands wander over his pectorals distracting him for a moment, he hesitates but pushes again, "Is that all that he wanted?"
My hands travel over his stomach feeling the muscles clench under the contact.
"That was all." I lean forward and kiss his jaw softly.
"Carina, I'm trying to talk to you."
My lips wander along his skin, my tongue darting out to taste him.
"Then talk," I tell him but don't stop kissing his skin.
I don't want to think right now, I want to do everything but think.
Cassian groans when my lips travel over his collarbones, biting the skin teasingly before letting go. His hands grasp my hips and in a slow rhythm, he starts to move me against his groin.
"I know what you're doing." He grunts and I smile before kissing his lips,
"What am I doing, Cassian?"
His eyes are dark as he stares down at me and I can see his canines growing out of his gums. "Trying to distract me."
"Trying?" I arch a brow as I still my hips and take hold of him. A short breath whooshes past his lips. His muscles tighten and I give him one lazy stroke.
"Carina." His voice says warningly. I give him another soft stroke feeling weird and unfamiliar.
"Please, Cas," I beg, "you brought me here to forget things. Then make me forget."
Any self-restraint left crumbles from him, he nods, as he lowers his head, his lips grazing over mine. "I will not only make you

forget, but I will also make you remember. Remember nothing but this. Us."

Cassians POV

She looks at me through the curtain of her lashes, sapphire glinting in the seducing light around us. Her hand pulls another stroke and I tip forward, caging her in against the tiles of the wall. She gasps as her skin comes into contact with the cold material but her hand does not stop her lazy rhythm.

"If you want me to make you forget, you need to stop moving your hand." I tell her and watch her lips pull into a smug smile. "Let me have control, Cas, for one time."

Thepace of her hand picks up and I grunt, "you are always in control, love."

She presses a kiss against my jaw. "Because you like it. Is this good?"

She fists my cock harder and I buck into the movement groaning. "Fuck yes."

I remove my hands from the tiles behind her head before driving them into her hair.

Her hair is going to be the fucking death of me.

"Faster," I choke out and she follows the direction, her other hand driving over my back, pushing her nails into my skin.

I attack her neck and pull at her air, eliciting a groan from those sweet lips. "If you make that sound again, I will not be able to hold on for long."

I gasp when her thumb moves over the tip of my cock, a drop of liquid following the movement. My hips buck again as I bury my face in her neck, not able to hold my canines from growing.

Carina shudders when the sharp edges of them graze her pulse.

"Faster, love." I beg and her hand moves faster, my hips pumping in sync with her as our lips meet.

She winds her tongue around mine in a slow dance, drawing everything I have in me. I nip at her full bottom lip and she punishes me with a hard stroke which almost makes me come. Our kisses grow harder and faster, maiming the rhythm of her hands and my hips, as my muscles coil harder.

"Almost there." I whisper against her neck and she moans as my thumb swipes over her breast. I repeat the movement as I move faster.

He pulls me flush against her and that does it to me. She strokes my cock before it grazes the skin of her stomach.

Instead of slowing down, Carina keeps the rhythm as I spill onto her stomach, the pull drawing from within me as I come.

For a moment my canines sink into the skin of Carina's neck before she shudders against me, the muscles in her stomach contract against the tip of my cock.

I whimper as she pulls a last time, my chest rising heavily as I lean against her.

"Did you. . ." I brace against the wall to look down at her, "did you just come from getting me off?"

Her lashes flutter before she looks up at me, her cheeks flushing beautifully. "No."

My lips tug into a small smile, "that is the hottest thing you might've ever done."

She starts to protest but I catch her lips in a searing kiss, drowning whatever words she wanted to say.

My thumb swipes over the puncture at her neck. Carina shudders again, the tips of her breast's grazing against my ribs. In a matter of seconds I'm hard again.

"How do you feel about round two?"

Instead of answering me she captures my lips with hers.

Her eyes are closed, her lashes brushing the highs of her cheeks as her lids keep on fluttering. She's dreaming. I watch her, fascinated by the soft breaths leaving her slightly parted lips, her body shifting lightly as if tracking what's happening behind her lips.
I wish I could know what she's dreaming.
Careful not to wake her I trace my fingers along Carina's cheek, feeling the soft skin underneath my fingertips.
Plum-colored veins are running beneath her eyes and I'm glad that she's finally catching up on some sleep. I can't stop but wonder what Aalton wanted from her. I know he didn't just thank her for coming, he wouldn't bother. So what did he say? And why does Carina feel the need to hide the truth from me?
I trace her soft jaw, my fingers dancing down her throat. A sigh leaves her lips and the fluttering behind her eyes stops as she falls into a deeper slumber.
My eyes wander to my breeches that I left behind on the floor, the small piece of parchment slipping out of the pocket.
I check one last time if Carina is fast asleep before I carefully pull my arm out underneath her neck and get up.
I retrieve my breeches, slipping them on and shrugging a shirt on before I unfold the piece of paper.

> Balance is the true nature of magic
> Where one can live the other must die.
> Where one will kill, the other will resurrect
> You can't deny that only one's true blood will have the effect,
> that the true evil will be wrecked
> may a new age dawn with the rightful heir of our world

No matter how many times I let my eyes wander over the words I still can't manage to figure them out. The prophecy indicates that just one of them can live and that somehow one of them will end up as the true heir of Adalon. But the heir of who? Until now everyone believed Adales to be the one worthy of ruling. He was the first god, who created our world and all the beings living upon it.

I risk a glance over at Carina's sleeping form before I crumble the paper and shove it back into my pocket. I force myself to leave before I fall into the habit of lingering, knowing that I'd rather stay secluded in this room with Carina encircled in my arms. But that is not going to help anyone and in the least, it is going to help her. I burst through the doors of the chamber, ignoring the suspicious looks of the guards posted outside. I keep my stride sure and even as I walk down the long hall, the scent of salt water wafting through the arc-shaped windows. I feel the shadows rippling beneath my skin, hissing and begging to let them go but I have more important things on my hands.

No one notices the small shift in the air, particles swinging disturbed before he appears at my side.

"What an awful kingdom. Everywhere it smells like fish and salt, it's making my skin all dry.", he complains as he dusts off his breeches of nonexistent dirt. I arch a brow at him, "Your skin is fine and it is not as if we're staying for a long time."

"Long enough for me to end up like a dry fish on land," Zayne says as he follows me around the corner. The torches are sporadically lit in this part of the castle and I know that soon we will have to descend to reach my destination.

I reach into my pocket and pull out the crumpled paper. With a movement human eyes wouldn't be able to see, Zayne catches the paper and unfolds it. I watch his eyes fly over the words over and over, considering things. I give him the time, even though my body burns every second Carina remains in danger.

I know my brother isn't fond of Carina—for whatever reason—but I know that if I need him I can count on him.

I would never enter what I still consider enemy territory without him.

"Huh." My brother breathes.

"Huh? That's the only thing that comes to your mind reading this?"

Zayne clasps his hand on my shoulder, "Typical for you to fall for a woman with a bag of problems."

I brush his hand off aggravated by his stance and continue the spiral downwards.

"Carina is the only woman I ever fell for."

"That's what I'm saying." My brother counters and I roll my eyes.

The torches have ceased to exist and we end up on steps built out of malachite that lead into black nothingness.

"Listen, that was not meant as a joke, I'm here to help you, am I not?"

"How am I supposed to know, Zayne? From the beginning, you've been against this, against her." I brush his hand off as he tries to grip my shoulder again.

"I am not against her, Cas, I am against anything that is hurting you."

"She isn't hurting me, she is the only thing holding me together, mending me." I breathe out a slow breath. I can't believe we're having this conversation again. "That's not true," he says, "If what on this paper is written is true one person will go out of this hurt or even worse; dead."

I freeze. For a moment I can barely hold the shadows back, not realizing that we're standing in front of the gilded doors.

"What?"

Zayne looks at me, a smug smile painting his lips. "You didn't know? *Where one will kill the other will resurrect*, Cas use your smart, little brain."

A brush of air leaves past my lips as acidic flavor spreads on my tongue.

"There's going to be a sacrifice."

I rip the paper back out of my brother's hands, staring at the words. How could I not have seen this before? Zayne leans in close, his voice bitter as he whispers into my ear. "And I bet you that she will go willingly."

My eyes fly up to his face taking in the cynical lines around his eyes, and the cold green of his irises. The gilded doors barely make a sound as they slide open, revealing what I've come here for in the first place.

~ 44 ~

"What a surprise! Prince Cassian, is there a problem?" The moment Aalton comes into view, Zayne vanishes beside me, his presence just a reminder now. I barely have time to push the parchment into my breeches, turning to look at the king with a lazy smile.
"Does there need to be a problem for me to talk to you?"
His features harden at my question but he steps to the side nonetheless, with a nod of his head, "Of course not, why don't you come inside?"
I bite my tongue until I can feel the blood pooling in my mouth. I shove my hands into the pockets of my breeches, crushing the paper in my grip as I walk inside the room.
The doors glide shut behind me on their own as I step into the turquoise-tinted room.
It seems to be some kind of study, it resembles the one Carina's father had in Aerwyna, with the elongated wooden table, scattered with papers and letters.
One wall is littered with shelves full of books and maps, the colors strangely matching the map attached to the whole wall on the left side.
I strut over to the wall, trying to drink in every piece that shows me who this man is. Aalton is far older than I am and regarding Flynn's information, he is a rather cunning man. For all we know he could've hired Orkiathan so he would kill Marrus and lastly take the throne.
In situations like this, you never know who is *the* enemy and who is *your* enemy. For all I care Aalton can have the throne as long as he doesn't start a war in Adalon.
Whirling light dances across the map picturing the lands of Oceanus and I turn my head to the source of light.
Floor-to-ceiling windows occupy one wall of the room, tinting the room in the blue depths. Of the ocean. I try not to grimace,

imagining what would happen if the glass broke and let all the water inside the room, drowning its occupants. I was never fond of the underwater part of the castle, even though I try to understand the reason behind it.

"Can I help you with something, my friend?" Aalton reminds me of his presence and I glance at him for a moment to see him eyeing me. I nod toward the map on the wall. "Wouldn't it be a bit presumptuous to hang a map just of Oceanus?"

Aalton takes a few steps to stand beside me.

"There is a much larger one in the throne room but I'm rather fond of this one in my office."

I nod, staring at a weird constellation not far from the palace.

"What is that supposed to be?" I put my finger on the map over the pentagram-shaped alignment. The map feels strangely wet, rather moldy. I shiver at the sensation.

"The tomb of St. Aegaeus and Oceanus, of course."

"Of course." I echo, eyeing the symbol for a last time. Tengeri are always extraordinary with their worshipping and gods. It is surprising that they would even have a tomb for Aegaeus, who was rumored to be the half-mortal brother of Oceanus. A bed night story more than ever. There are only four founding gods of our world.

"She is mesmerizing." I pry my eyes from the map to look at Aalton. His lips turn into an elongated smile that almost looks like a grimace.

"Who?"

"Carina," he puts his hands behind his back as he eyes me, "The people have waited a long time for someone like her."

"What is that supposed to mean?" I try to restrain myself, this is not my enemy. I repeat the words a few times just for good measure.

"She is strong-hearted and has a great sense for righteous decisions. I believe I have never met such an interesting character in all my long life." He says but he quickly backpedals when he notices the murderous look on my face.

"Now, now, Prince of Death, she is your perfect match."

My eyes flit over his face, utterly confused now. What is he trying to tell me with all of this?

"What did you talk to her about when we arrived?" I get straight to the point, to avoid whatever this conversation is turning into.

Aalton turns his body away, strolling over to the windows, staring into the nothingness of the ocean. "You are very much in love with her," he goes on as if he didn't even hear my question, "but how far are you willing to go for her?" He turns, arching a white brow.

"To the ends of the world and further," I answer without hesitation.

He nods as if he expected that answer, even though disappointment taints his translucent skin. The veins underneath pulse healthily, red with the blood of whoever he fed from.

"You didn't answer my question." I walk over to him, staring down at his face. He doesn't seem the slightest bit frightened by my proximity. I can feel the talons making their way out of my hands, feel the shadows travel up my arms but I don't let them go further.

"Princess Carina and I talked about future plans for Aerwyna and Oceanus. I swore her my loyalty and my willingness to support her in every decision."

I scoff because that cannot be the whole truth. His eyes narrow and his eyes flash white for a moment. I feel the temperature change immediately as he switches between his human and supernatural body.

"I told her that my promise would include Demeter as well, if she decided to stand by your side permanently. If she decides to part both your paths, for whatever reason, I would bother behaving better," He takes a step forward, his chest bumping into mine, "because right now, the only thing standing between Oceanus and Demeter is Princess Katarina."

I let the shadows retreat, shutting the mental door and locking it. Aalton changes his offensive demeanor back into his dazzling smile.

"I always liked you, Prince of Death, that is why I'm going to help you out a little."

I furrow my brows suspiciously, "What's the catch?"

"Well, what are you willing to pay for a secret?" He asks.

"Depends on what the secret is worth. Is it a secret concerning me?" I cross my arms in front of me, trying to sense where this is going. The way his soul changes constantly, makes it impossible to understand his intentions. It's like flickering light, colors morphing depending on the light that hits his soul, like an opal. His intentions are unclear, the color changing far too often.

His grin shifts again, turning triumphant as if he already knows that he's won.

"What if I told you there is a way to make Carina feel better temporarily, slow down the process of her nearing death?" I don't hesitate in my answer, cursing myself. How does he know of her death? Is that what CArina and him were talking about hours ago? No matter the answer I know what I would give in order to help Carina and the look on his face tells me that he does too. There is no sense in hiding it.

"I'm listening."

Carina's POV

I'm alone when I wake. The other side of the bed is cold when I put my hand on it but the prince's scent lingers. For a moment I turn and push my nose into Cassian's pillow, letting the scent of winter and pines calm me.

I know that I eventually have to get up if I want to join the others at dinner but my body is protesting. My limbs are aching so deeply it feels like the arrows of pain shoot straight into the marrow of my bone. I assume that the sun has already gone down because the chamber is left only in flickering candlelight. I can still hear the crashing of the waves, wafting through the windows as if the ocean is preparing for a storm to come its way.

Maybe I should just stay in bed, and gather my strength for the actual wedding tomorrow.

How am I supposed to defeat Adales like this? I barely can lift my arm on my own, there is no possible way I can fight against an ancient god.

Back in Demeter I need to prepare and push myself to the limits.

Before my spiraling thoughts can grab the upper hand my doors open without a warning. I sit up swiftly, hoping to see Cassian but a small woman rushes inside. "I'm very sorry to disturb you, Your Highness, but King Aalton wishes for you to get ready for dinner." The frail woman mumbles, her eyes cast downward. I suppress a groan and swing my legs carefully over the bed. Where is Cassian?

"Sure." I agree and the woman scrambles over to me.

I'm surprised when she pushes me into the bathing chamber.

"We need to run you a bath, your hair looks like one of Aegaeus' storms has swept through it."

I blink surprised and flush scarlet when I catch my reflection in the mirror that we pass. The blood creeps down my neck when I think of the reason that caused the state my hair is in. "Who is Aegaeus?"

The maid throws me a scandalized look. "Only one of the most important people in Oceanus. We worship him. He is the half brother of Oceanus and has come to great glory."

I turn surprised, making her glare at me for moving.

I mumble a small apology for the circumstances which the maid criticizes with a gentle smile. I did not know that the people in Adalon even dared to worship any other than the four siblings.

I let her bathe me carefully, already forgotten what it feels like to be taken care of.

I didn't say anything to Cassian but somehow he knew that I wanted to take care of my own, during my stay at the Moreau court.

My heart constricts when I think of Marianna combing through my wet hair just as the maid does. I don't dare to ask her for her name, feeling like it might deem her future just like I have with so many people.

I barely get through the motion of pinning my hair up, slipping the light blue gown over my body that shimmers lilac in the light.

The neckline is strapless, with long sleeves attached to the sides that sit almost too tightly around my arms, until they flutter outwards at my wrists.

I eye the purple shimmer for a moment when the maid clears her throat. My eyes widen when the servant picks out a last piece for the gown and I vigorously start to shake my head.

"Please, no." The woman hesitates, surprised. Her eyes flicker to the dark purple corset in her hands, littered with mother of pearls and small shells that shine iridescently.

"This was handmade for you, Your Highness." She says, still unsure.

"I appreciate that, but corsets and I are not great friends."

"The king will be really disappointed if you do not accept His Majesty's present."

Without another word, she winds the corset around my waist. I sigh exhausted as she starts to tug at the laces and I have to grip the bedpost to stay upright. For such a small woman she sure has a lot of strength.

"Huh." She mumbles making me turn. "What?"

"It seems like you lost a good deal of weight, I have to pull it a little tighter." I don't question how they even got my measurements. She pulls and pulls until my lungs feel like they're pressed against my heart. At least I'll have an excuse for not eating anything at dinner. "That's enough." I breathe out, barely audible. The servant listens to me and then parts with a small curtsey.

I hold my hand against my churning stomach as I walk over to the mirror perched in the corner of the room.

The gown is breathtaking.

It glitters in the soft blue and lilac like the shimmer of Kian's wings, even the frail texture of it reminds me of it. The corset is such a stark contrast against the light colors that it makes my waist appear awfully small and I grimace at the thought that it may be just that size. With barely eating anything this is the consequence. I promise myself to eat something tonight even if it tastes like burned ashes. I let my hands wander over the pearls and shells before I realize something.

Instead of using the turquoise colors that dominate Aalton's castle, he dressed me in the colors of my home. The color of Nightcrawlers. My heart swells at the thought before I'm distracted by arms winding around my waist.

"You look beautiful," Cassian grazes a soft kiss against my temple as he settles behind me.

I smile as I watch him through the mirror. Wherever he was, he got ready himself but instead of taking his kingdom into account, Aalton made sure to dress Cassian in various blue tones. I have to chuckle at the distasteful look on his face.

"You're not bad yourself. I never thought blue looked good on you." I turn around, winding my arms around his neck.

"Ha-ha." He grumbles not realizing that I'm telling the truth.

Even though I prefer Cassian in greens, blacks, and reds, this man is impossible to make anything look bad on him.

"Were you able to sleep for a bit?" He asks.

Worried lines form around his eyes as his thumb traces the dark circles under my eyes.

"A bit," I admit, "I think I woke shortly after you left. Where did you go?"

My hands play with the tips of the curls in his neck as his hand strokes my back lazily.

"I talked to Aalton." My brows raise, "What about?"

"Politics, war, weapons. You know, the boring stuff." He shrugs.

I eye him for a moment, wanting to account for his strange behavior but he quickly distracts me. His lips graze the highs of my cheeks, and plant soft kisses under my eyes, on the tip of my nose, and on my forehead. His lips linger as he draws me close and I push my face into his amazingly smelling shirt. I like to feel every ridge of his muscles against me, molding my soft curves against his hard edges.

It feels like we're two puzzles fitting together.

"If I'd ask you to be honest with me, would you?" I draw back. surprised at his pained voice. When I look at him there's nothing that indicates the pain he is in.

"Where is this coming from?"

"Answer the question, Carina." His jaw ticks and I feel the need to grab his face in my hands.

"Of course, I tell you the truth, I always do. We promised each other," He stares at me for a moment, searching for something in my eyes I thought I already gave him.

After a moment he eases up, his shoulders relaxing as he puts his forehead against mine.

"I know you're tired and in pain."

"I'm fine."

"No, you're not." He protests and I slacken in his secure embrace.

"I'm not."

He kisses my temple again.

"Do you trust me?"

"What?" I blink at him confused again as he draws back.

"Do you trust me?"

I search his eyes for the right answer. What is this supposed to mean? Despite my wavering, I give him the truth.

"Of course I trust you."

He nods as if confirming something in his head.

"Good. Then let me help make you feel better."

"Cas, I know you want to help—what are you doing?" I exclaim as I watch his canines appear in a flash before he rips them through his wrist.

~ 45 ~

"Drink it."

"Are you actually insane?" I grip his wrist tightly in my hand, trying to stop the blood from flowing. It's an irrational reaction because I know he will heal, nothing can hurt him besides the blade of a bloodstone but still the panic winds quickly around my heart.

"Drink it, love."

"Why would you—what?" My eyes flutter from the oozing wound to his face.

His canines are still drawn, now tinted in the red of his blood just like his lips. The picture makes something pull inside me strangely.

"Your magic is wavering because of what is said in the prophecy. You and Adales cannot exist at the same time. That is why the magic in your blood is going haywire, flickering like a candle shortly before going out," he grimaces, "Sorry, that is a terrible comparison. But there is no other way to put it. My veins are full of magic, if you drink my blood it'll make you feel better. Temporarily."

"I cannot drink your blood, Cas, that is disgusting." He mocks a hurt expression. "That's a first. I never got rejected before. I promise I don't taste bitter." He winks but I still shake my head.

I did let Cassian drink my blood but that is because he needs it to survive. I don't think I would enjoy the iron taste of it.

He tilts his head to the side, his eyes glowing. "Please."

The blood is already flowing slower, the wound beginning to heal with his powers. "Please, love." His face contracts as if in pain. He wants me to feel better because he believes his theory is right.

I hesitate. "How do you know that?"

His eyes glow. "Trust me."

My first reaction is to protest. After what happened it feels like a knee jerk reaction to say no but Cassian has proved himself.

He does want to help me and he can't stand to see me in pain, this I know for sure.

My grip softens around his wrist and I nod weakly. I never thought I would think this but his blood almost looks inviting. The red color is rich and glistening magically. I raise his skin closer to my mouth, trying to breathe through the smell. It works better than I thought.

Instead of irony, a sweet smell oozes from it, almost like sugar.

I start to shake, my body taught before I finally let my lips collide with his skin.

The blood is warm—almost sizzling hot—as it travels down my throat and warms the pit of my stomach. I wait for the disgust to break through and make me step back but it doesn't happen.

My body grows hot for the first time in weeks and when I hear Cassian groan in pleasure I flush. He grabs my waist and pulls me against his chest as we tumble through the room. His back collides with the wall and I barely feel him slide down, propping me in his lap.

His blood is all-consuming, a taste as sweet as honey and so alluring that it envelops me in a hot frenzy.

"Take as much as you want, love," I answer with a soft whimper. He starts to stroke my hair and I feel like I almost ascend from the ground.

"Good girl."

"You have a little. . ." Cassian trails off as his finger traces the corner of his mouth.

I hastily swipe at my lips, horror rising until I see the playful sparkle in his eyes. "You're an utter idiot." I hit his arm when he chuckles and quickly let my gaze wander around the dining table to see if anyone caught our interaction. Luckily everyone's attention is still on Aalton, who has been telling a supposed witty anecdote for the last half an hour.

My eyes flick from his imposing form at the head of the table to the woman beside him. Her hair is as blonde as his, streaked with turquoise strands and cut in a short bob. Every time she moves her head, the ends of her hair brush her soft chin. She looks soft and delicate beside him, the top of her head barely reaching his shoulders. Darya, Aaltons fiancée has been fairly quiet over dinner but her big watchful eyes, the color of the ocean, never once strayed from her lover. A soft smile settles on her lips as she listens to Aalton who notices her gaze for a moment. The king's arm moves subconsciously around her frame bringing her closer to him.

My gaze wanders to the rest of us, Edlyn perched beside Kian, mustering her nails as if she's contemplating changing the color: Kian's pose is tense and I can feel his eyes flicker towards me a few times as if he's worried by the distance to me. I try to send him a reassuring smile, which makes the lines on his forehead deepen further. Then his eyes fly to my brother who is whispering with Cas beside him about the gods know what.

Flynn is seated on my left side, his face stoic as always but he listens tentatively to Serena who is seated on his left side.

I'm surprised that she is sitting with us, my father never acquired his advisor at meals that often. But I can feel that Aalton is doing things differently, the first indicator being that his advisor is a woman. A very pretty one might I add.

Serena looks like a goddess ascended right out of the ocean, ready to put her wrath on every one of us.

When her siren eyes place themselves on me her lips stretch into almost a hungry-looking smile.

She leans forward in her seat, making her red hair swipe against Flynn's shoulder. "Are you enjoying dinner, Your Highness?"

"Please call me Carina." I insist and if possible her smile widens further. "Carina." My name rolls off her tongue like a berry glazed in honey and I can't help myself but flush. Is she being flirty?
"I am indeed enjoying the meal, thank you, Serena."
Her eyes narrow in doubt, "Aalton is talented in spinning a small acquaintance into a novel."
"Are you spewing lies about me again, Diavolii?" Altoon turns his head to throw a glance at Serena who meets his gaze with a soft smile. "Nothing but the truth, my king."
Aalton raises a fair brow and I catch Darya staring at Serena for a moment.
"What does Diavolii mean?" I lean forward in my seat but don't make it far with the restricting corset around my ribs.
Serena waves my question away but to my surprise, Flynn answers it. "It's a sort of demonic creature usually with red hair." I nod at his description.
"Funny thing, I always thought that you were a Diavolii." Edlyn perks up as she looks at Flynn. The latter clenches his jaw when Aaltons breaks out in rumbling laughter.
We all look at him surprised. "That is exactly why I love having a Magda to dinner, always so honest."
"Just in terms of this guy, Your Majesty." She nods her head lazily in Flynn's direction.
Our party settles in silence for a moment but the king still looks amused.
"What a cliché." Serena fixes her eyes on my best friend and I can see that she is now zeroing her charm in on her.
"What exactly?" Edlyn tilts her head.
"A Magda hating Tengeri. Shouldn't we overcome our differences already?"
"I can consider your offer with the right motivations." I watch Edlyn flip her hands, talons growing for a moment before they disappear back into her skin. I shiver subconsciously. I barely wrapped my head around the changing parts of my friends.

Serena and Edlyn continue their sparring but I get distracted by Cassian winding his arm around my waist.

"Are you feeling any better?" He whispers against my neck so the others won't hear.

I nod lightly when I feel his hand trail from my side to the small of my back. "Then why do you look like you're suffocating?"

Surprised, I look at him, noticing the worry in his eyes. His eyes flicker to my lips for a moment. "You know how I feel about corsets, it feels like my lungs are crunched to mashed stew."

A small snort escapes his lips. I bite my lip in surprise and he shakes his head. "Well, we certainly cannot let that happen to your poor lungs."

"What do you mean?" I squeak when he pulls me closer, almost making me topple off the chair. I watch as his hand retreats and he shrugs off his waistcoat. He turns the coat for me to put my hands through and I follow his actions even though I do not know what he's planning.

"Oh are you cold, Carina? Should I conjure the fire?" Aalton notices over the table and my eyes flicker over to the fireplace and I quickly shake my head. "I'm fine, thank you."

I couldn't imagine this place being anything other than damp anyway.

Once the others slip back into conversation Cassian's hand sneaks under the coat and my gaze flies to him but he shakes his head.

"Look at the others." He orders quietly and I wonder if they cannot pick up on his words.

His fingers trail up the corset until they meet the skin on top and a shiver runs down my spine when I feel his talons against my skin.

"Carina?"

"Hmm?" I mumble distracted, hearing Cassian chuckle in my ear, "You need to breathe." A breath rushes right past my lips.

"Sorry."

"Don't apologize. It's going to be better in a moment," He presses a kiss to my temple, "I'm going to make it better."

With one swift motion, his talons slice through the back of the corset loosening it immediately. I raise my hands on instinct to catch the corset but his slash is so precise that it still clings to my body enough for me to breathe normally.

The waistcoat hides the rip he just made.

I meet his eyes instantly, watching his lips stretch into a bright smile. "Better?"

My hand wanders to the back of his neck instantaneously and I pull him in for a short kiss. Or lips crash together in heated pleasure and for a moment it feels like I can taste my blood on his tongue.

A high-pitched whistle travels through the dining chamber and we quickly part to see Aalton crack a grin at us.

"Sweet, young love, I can't wait to visit Demeter for your wedding." He presses a short kiss to Darya's temple and I feel myself flush at his suggestion.

Once marriage was in the near future for me but wasn't I exactly so fond of Cassian because he made it possible for me not to bind myself and still rule?

"Do you have a date in mind?" Aalton prods further and Cassian thankfully answers him because my lips seem to be temporarily sewn shut.

"Whenever Carina is ready."

I meet his eyes almost instantly, surprised by his words. He raises a brow smiling gently at me.

~ 46 ~

My servant was livid when she saw what Cas did to my corset, she complained the whole day about how she was not able to order a new one at the harbor in time for the wedding this evening and that is how I ended up in a loaned dress from Serena. The dress is in a beautiful midnight blue, glimmering like starlight and most importantly there is no corset. The dress is a bit tight at my hips but luckily Serena and I both prefer high necklines for the cleavage. The fabric dips low in the back, so low I worry that someone will be scandalized but Serena assured me with a devilish smile that it will enchant everyone at the celebrations. Overall the people in the castle seem less uptight than in Aerwyna, which I prefer.

Serena also handed me some white gloves reaching up to my elbow enhancing the way the dress is sleeveless. Sapphire´s dangle from my ears and for a moment I hesitate. My thumb traces over the empty space of my ring finger and I shiver. The words Aalton said last night at dinner haunt me even the next day. I do see myself marrying the person I love someday but now? I don´t even know if I will be alive in the next week. What would it matter anyway?

I shake off those thoughts as I pass the guards standing in front of Aalton´s chamber. I want to talk to the king before the ceremony and make sure that if I am not able to fulfill the prophecy someone will know of my plans.

I raise a gloved hand, the guards nodding their heads at me as I drop a heavy knock against the gilded doors.

They open instantly, a voice reaching me from inside.

"Come in, come in."

I step inside Aaltons chamber expecting to find him ready to go but he is standing in front of a gigantic mirror, iron vines winding around the edges.

I hesitate in the middle of the room, trying not to glance at the vast space the bed takes in the room or the various drawers thrown open. Fabric spills out from them as if someone has ravaged the whole room.

"I apologize for the mess, Carina, I changed my mind at the last second." He watches me through the mirror as he fixes his waistcoat and I have to smile. He is dressed in the colors of the ocean, turquoise details running along the stitching of his black clothing, silver intermingled with the color like starlight. His hair is drawn back into a braid, revealing the sharp juncture of his jaw and cheekbones, his pointy nose. His eyes sparkle happily as he closes the silver button on his left wrist.

"You look dashingly handsome, Aalton." I smile and he chuckles. "Thank you, you outshine yourself as well, gorgeous. I must say I do prefer you in my kingdom's colors."

I can't help but grin as I step closer to him. Once he turns, he tilts his head at me. "I'm sure you didn't come here to complement my good looks?"

"No. I wanted to talk to you about something because I didn't know how long these festivities last."

He takes a few steps taking my hands in his and steadying their shaking. "You're worrying me, my friend."

I relax slightly when I look into his kind face. Whatever it was with Hector that made me feel at ease is the same with Aalton. Maybe somehow the descendants of the siblings still feel connected.

"There is nothing to worry about. I told you about the prophecy didn't I?"

He nods.

"I fear I don't have that much longer and I don't want to burden any of my friends, they always get so protective and want to help me but with this, they can't. Don't get me wrong I love them for their protectiveness, they mean the world to me."

"They are your family." He states and I release a breath, nodding. They are my family. Edlyn and Henri were always my family but now, I have even more. Kael with his light demeanor, pretending that everything bounces off of him, Kian and his morality preaches, Flynn who pretends he doesn't care about anyone, and even Azzura and Zayne.

I refocus on Aalton. "That is why I have to talk to you. In case I don't. . . I don't get to return to the throne. I had this plan, it would enforce the relationships of every magical creature and the humans, and it would make us all alliances rather than enemies."

I slip one hand out of his and reach for the note that I slipped into the top of my glove.

"I want you to have this, just in case." I press the folded parchment into his hand and it feels like I'm passing over a weight lasting on my shoulders.

"I appreciate your trust in me, Carina, very much. But I wonder if it wouldn't be better to give this to Cassian, his goals have never been different from yours."

I shake my head quickly. "If I tell Cassian that I need to leave tonight he will not leave my side."

"I wish you wouldn't have to leave." That makes two of us. I smile before he pulls me into a crushing hug.

"If I don't leave now I never will and as much as I want to be selfish and stay, that is not who I am. Even if that means I will see them all for the last time."

"You *will* come back Katarina Sebestyen and you will survive anything that comes your way." He whispers it against my ear with so much conviction that I almost believe him. *Almost.*

Once we part I quickly swipe at the corners of my eyes and muster up a small smile. "Okay, let's get you married and that golden crown on your head," I say.

He watches me for a moment before he quickly nods, his eyes sparkling when he thinks of Darya.

"I´ll sneak you into the ballroom." He offers me his elbow and I laugh, quickly winding my arm around his. He pulls at a candleholder and with a soft vibration a door opens in the wall.
I have to think back to my bookshelf in Aerwyna and as Aalton leads me through the tunnels of his castle I promise myself to try everything to see it again.

Aalton sneaks me into the enormous ballroom, taking his place in the front. Flynn is standing with him dressed in a long tunic in white, edged with golden symbols. I sneak over to one of the first rows where people are perched on stone benches, decorated with shells, pink starfishes, and corals glowing in various colors, small glittering particles rising into the air.
I quickly spot Cassian beside Edlyn who is talking to Serena.
"Where do you come from?" Cassian greets me with a soft kiss on my temple as I sit down beside him.
"I wanted to wish Aalton good luck. Where are my brother and Kian?"
He shrugs his shoulders. "I told them to meet me here but they still haven´t showed up."
Suspicion spreads in my tummy at that revelation. I eye the room, people talking with each other happily, I make out a lot of red-headed people, with turquoise eyes but a few humans as well, and once in a while I meet the widened gaze of someone.
A warm hand teases the exposed skin of my back.

"You look gorgeous, it's driving me mad." Cassian whispers. When I turn my head to look at him he's staring at the front where the groom waits for his bride. "I suspected Aaltons intention."
"To drive me mad?" His fingers graze my skin again and in answer, I clench my thighs together. His eyes follow my legs and he groans. "He's succeeding."
"Should I distract you?" I whisper a small smile on my face.
"Yes please."
"Tell me why Flynn is holding the ceremony." He shifts a bit but answers my question with a rough voice. "The Tengeri always let a family member hold the ceremony; it is a tradition. Usually, an elder would do it but. . ."
"But?"
Cassian sighs. "Aalton's father is dead and Flynn's father isn't that welcome at the court."
Oh.
"They don't get along?" I watch Cassian clench his jaw. "You could say that."
I would like to prod more but if Cassian even reacts like this to the mention of his father I can imagine what kind of man he is. My gaze wavers to Flynn in his robes, looking as ancient as he is. His turquoise eye meets mine and he raises a brow in question. I grin and hold up a thumb for him. He rolls his eyes right when the candles blow out in the room.
I look around unsure if it was planned or not.
"No worries." Cassian strokes my back and I relax, my eyes sharpening in on the little light that the glowing corals give us.
The doors to the room creak open as soft tranquil music bathes us in its sounds. I can see a form in white striding along the rows like a ghost but I can't see Darya.
"Shift." Cassian murmurs quietly as the sound of a violin accompanies the piano play. "What do you mean shift?"
"Into your true form,"

My eyes flicker towards him to see them glow green. Edlyn winks at me with her red glowing eyes and I try to concentrate. It takes me a moment until I feel the soft tingling of my magic inside me but once I have its grasp, I let it flow over me like water and the next time I open my eyes I can see the room clearly.

"Very good." Cassian murmurs satisfied and I roll my eyes at him.

"I'm not a five year old, I don't need to be praised."

"You surely liked my praise when you were sucking on my blood, love." The blood rushes so fast in my cheeks that I clamp my mouth shut and focus on the pair in the front. I ignore him when I feel his lips press shortly against my shoulder.

Darya and Aalton both kneel in front of Flynn. The music fades softly and Flynn starts to speak in a language I don't know.

Serena leans over from the right and translates the vows of both of them, telling us that this ritual will bind them as mates until one of them dies.

"*Crestere*." Flynn's voice booms, making both of them stand up.

"To prove their undying love they will share their blood now." Serena whispers and a shiver runs down my back.

Cassian's hand starts to rub my back lightly as we watch Flynn hand a silver dagger over. Darya takes it hesitantly but when Aalton offers her his wrist trustingly she manages to cut him. He does the same with her wrist and as if timed they both cross their arms and drink from each other's wounds.

The crowd erupts in cheers so loud I would flinch if I weren't so distracted by the sharing ritual.

Once they let go of their wrists Aalton pulls her in for a kiss that should only exist in the bedroom. I avert my gaze, catching the soft smile on Flynn's lips as he watches his cousin.

He walks over to a small box made out of glass that I haven't noticed before. Inside sits the most beautiful crown, silver and gold woven with each other. A sapphire sits in the middle, catching the reflection of light once and then. Aalton gets to his knees in front of his cousin who takes the crown and carefully places it onto his blond head. Everyone holds their breath as he gets up again, pulling Darya close and sharing another kiss.

Once the lovers part, Aalton cheers and raises a fist into the air. "Let's celebrate!"

~ 47 ~

Cassian's POV

I barely keep attention as the crowd is moved to the throne room. The room is decorated most in the same way, with fluorescent corals littering the tables that are strewn around carelessly. A long line of a buffet is located at the right side of the room, various delicacies of the Oceanus market plated on silverware, and I release a small sigh when I see the amount of fish carried in between the dishes. Loose scraps of material hang from the ceiling, billowing and dancing as if a breeze is traveling around the room. The music fiddles a sweet melody as Aalton carries Darya into the middle of the ballroom, swaying her lightly to the rhythm. His hand is settled at the small of her back just like mine is at Carina's. I haven't left her side since we started the real celebration. I listened to various people introducing themselves to the beautiful brunette at my side. I never thought I would like her in any other color than green or red but the dark blue looks like the deep ends of the ocean complementing the color of her eyes. Every time she moves the fabric glitters like she captured the stars in it.
More likely they would voluntarily descend to earth to caress her skin and make her glow.
A certain Lord and Lady of Salje are currently occupying her attention while I try to look interested, standing beside her. I would want nothing more than to sweep her off her feet and carry her to the dance floor.
 "Are you going to stay glued to my side the whole night?" Carina tilts her face to my side as she speaks up. I notice that the Lord and Lady have parted from us.
 "As long as you want me to." I duck slightly, my fingers traveling over the open back of her dress. She looks up at me through the curtain of her long lashes, making my heart skip a beat.

"Why don't you mingle a bit? Flynn looks like he could use some company." I don't need to look in the direction of my friend to know that the usual crowd of eligible ladies has surrounded him in a corner of the room.

"He can manage. I don't want to ruin his chances of getting laid tonight."

My eyes rove over the highs of her cheek, the slight flush. It developed after her second glass of wine.

"It doesn't look like he's interested in any kind of activity." She insists.

I sigh and turn my head to see Flynn in a designated corner. Like I predicted a small crowd billows around him, a sea of red and blonde hair blurring into a crowd of colors. Flynn nods politely at something the woman says beside him but his eyes are placed somewhere else. I follow them for a moment to see Edlyn and Serena perched on the dance floor, their limbs entangled delicately.

"That's an interesting development." I watch Carina follow my line of sight and a small smile jumps at the corners of her plump lips.

"I'm glad she's enjoying the moment."

Her eyes sparkle and I quickly get ahold of her glass.

"What are you doing?" She watches me place the glass onto the table we occupied for the last hours.

"Taking you to the dance floor." She slips her hand in mine with a hesitant smile before I pull her with me.

A moment later I encircle her body with my arms, slowly swaying both our bodies. The soft scent of roses makes me pull her so close that no space of air is left between us. That damn rose scent drove me crazy at the Sebestyen court and now I find myself yearning for it every time she is not with me.

A small surprised gasp leaves Carina's lips. "Cas."

"Mhh?" I make a non-committed sound as my hands wander over the naked skin of her back. My tips graze every vertebra of her spine, her skin covers in goosebumps. My lips attach themselves to the soft skin at her collarbone. It is as if she has put a spell on me, invading my body and mind.

"People are watching."

"Let them watch," I say before nipping softly at the flesh of her skin.

"Hey!" She pushes at my chest to glare at me. I can't help but laugh lightly when her skin flushes even more. "Delightful," I murmur while she keeps her distance. I twirl her for a moment before she collides back with my chest. Goosebumps cover my skin when she winds her arms around my neck. Her fingers start to play with the curls in my neck.

"What?" She asks with narrowed eyes.

"Nothing."

"You're grinning like a lovesick idiot." She sighs.

"Because I am a lovesick idiot." Her face grows soft at my words. Her hand travels over my cheek, her skin cold. Too cold.

I know that under that soft smile on her lips lays pain. She tries to mask it and most of the time she's doing a good job. But physical things don't lie. If possible I pull her even closer and bury my face in her neck.

I enjoy the soft breath that leaves her lips.

"You're the only thing holding me at this boring celebration." A soft laugh escapes her at my mumbled words.

"Maybe you should've guzzled some of that wine." She says.

I shake my head before I press a soft kiss against the side of her neck. I feel her pulse quicken under the contact.

For what I have to do I need to be completely sober, risking my plans tonight with wine would be stupid.

Carina's eyes narrow again.

"Cassian is there—"

"Excuse me for interrupting but I would love it if you would spare me a dance with your beautiful companion, Carina."

We both turn our heads to see Aalton and Darya beside us. I reluctantly let go of Carina as she nods at the bride.

"Of course. Be careful though, Cassian has two left feet." Carina jokes and I narrow my eyes at her as she winks.

Aalton bellows a laugh as he takes Carina's hand in his. "My bride can manage the worst dancer. She has to, now that she's dancing the rest of her life with me." His turquoise eyes shine as he leaves with Carina in his arms. I watch them go before I encircle Darya in a much more distant grip and carry her over the dance floor.

I lost Carina in the dancing crowd for a few hours. Edlyn and Serena have left the celebration early just when Henri and Kian finally surfaced. The young prince meets my gaze with flushed cheeks as I access the disarray of his curls and the swollen lips of the Faye warrior.

The celebrations are still going in full when I decide I have enough. I finally spot Carina at the banquet talking to a woman. I can't make out her face from the angle I am standing at. Blonde curls are hiding her face and she is dressed in a blood-red gown. Apparently, someone didn't get the memo of the dress code.

Not able to wait any longer I dart through the crowd of swaying bodies. Carina dips in and out of my sight as I dodge drunken men and women.

A girl stumbles into me and I quickly catch her by the elbows.

"I am so sorry, sir." She hiccups and starts to dab at the fabric of my shirt. I just notice that she has spilled her wine all over my shirt. The red color spreads as if blood is oozing out of a stabbed wound.

"It's alright, sweetheart, why don't you sit down?" I help her over to the few stone benches perched at the tables. She stumbles a few times which is why I keep my grip on her. I throw a glance over where Carina was standing seconds ago but the place is empty.

My stomach ties in a knot as the girl starts to laugh in front of me. Conflicted, I dart over to a table to grab a carafe of water and a glass. I quickly fill it with the liquid and dart back to the girl.

"Here. Make sure you drink all of this." It takes her a few times to get a grip on the glass. When she does, she nods and starts drinking like she almost died of thirst.

Checking that she is finishing her glass I turn and make my way through the rest of the crowd.

A path clears and I see Carina at the same place again. The woman has wound her wrist in her hands making anger flare inside me.

The hold makes the woman's knuckles turn white and I can see Carina flinching.

"Carina!" I call and dodge another pair. When I finally reach the banquet the woman is gone.

"Who was that?" I ask the moment I reach her. She looks at me perplexed when I wind my hand around her wrist. Blue fingerprints encircle her delicate skin.

I feel the familiar notion of dread spread through me and search the crowd for the dead woman. I can feel the dead soul like cursed lava burning through my blood but she felt different, she felt strange.

"Who are you talking about?" She asks me.

"The woman grabbing your wrist. Just moments ago." I search her eyes for the answer. She looks at me like I am mad.

"I didn't talk to anyone, Cas." She laughs lightly.

"I saw her, love, don't lie to me."

"I am not lying. Now would you let go of my wrist?" She waits patiently until I drop her wrist. "If there wasn't a woman what happened to your wrist?" I ask her suspiciously. She is not fooling me, I know what I saw. "I tripped while dancing and Aalton got a hold of my wrist, to stop my fall. Seems like I am the bad dancer, not you." She laughs again and I can't help from relaxing slightly.

Maybe she didn't talk to anyone. I could've confused her with someone else.

"Are you sure?" I ask again and she smiles.

Her hands wander to my cheeks before she presses a hot open-mouthed kiss on my lips.

My body thrills when my tongue meets hers. I pull Carina closer by her lips as the worry billows away with her taste on my tongue.

I moan lightly when her body shivers in my arms.

She gets back on her feet when our lips part. Her pupils dilate, a new shine in the sapphire of her irises.

"Why don't we get out of here?"

Her hand wanders over my chest. She gets on her tip toes and I quickly steady her with my hand on her back.

"You know this dress is special because there is no way to fit any undergarment beneath it." Her lips graze my ear and I harden in a matter of seconds. "Fuck."

~ 48 ~

Carina's POV

I find myself chuckling as Cas and I sneak out of the blaring ballroom, the guards outside eyeing us suspiciously as we break out into a run.

Our hands clasped together, our feet hitting the floor, in sync, we run.

A feeling of something so intense settles inside my chest right under my breastbone, distracting me that I don't see Cassian's next move coming.

His hand pulls at mine and we both tumble into an abandoned alcove. He whirls me against his chest before his lips catch mine in a hungry kiss.

My hands fist the material of his fancy shirt and I allow myself to catch his lips with mine, slide my tongue over his lasciviously.

His hands wind around my waist tugging me in, making our pelvises brush.

With a hard tug, I release his lips to stare up into his vicious eyes. "We're guests here, Cas." My voice is breathy as his lips happily attack the spot where my shoulder meets my neck and a soft sigh slips past my lips.

"Aalton wants his guests enjoying themselves." He murmurs as his tongue tastes my skin and my body goes completely boneless.

His hold on me hardens as he releases a dark chuckle, "Easy there, love."

I pull his face back up to catch his lips for a moment.

"We can continue this in our chambers," I say.

His eyes glint mischievously, "I'd rather finish this now. Let them watch, Carina, you know they want to."

I feel the heat flood my cheeks and I can see that Cassian catches the sight with delightful glee. His thumb trails along my cheekbone, "Tempting me with every breath you take."

My heart stutters in my chest but I decide to pull myself together. I catch his hand on my cheek intertwining our fingers before I tuck him further down the hall.

Toward our chambers.

He grins as I shoot him a bashful smile. "Patience, Prince of Demeter."

I break out into another run, drawing him with me and despite the few times he wraps me up in a languid kiss we make it into the right chambers.

We stumble right through the doors, barely keeping our hands off each other.

My hands start to fumble with the buttons on his shirt as his nimble fingers untie the laces on my dress.

"Fuck this," I grumble after a moment and rip his shirt open. Cassian cocks a brow at me as I stare at his tan skin and the fine muscles adorning his abdomen. I follow the lines adorning his skin, ending in the swirls of his tattoo on his narrow waist.

My fingers itch to touch him everywhere, drink him in and never let him go again. Our eyes meet as we move at the same time.

The next time our lips touch my body fills with a feeling so inexplicable and immense that I can't grasp its edges for the sake of me.

He catches my lips again as his fingers gently tuck the sleeves of my dress over my shoulders.

The dress falls around my body and pools around my feet.

Cassian pulls back and a soft breath escapes his lips.

His arm winds around me and he drags me against his chest, his lips pressed against my ear.

"You didn't lie."

His words are close to a groan as he pushes my naked chest against his. I can't help the small smile that forms on my lips, "Why would I, Your Highness?"

I trail my fingertips over his chest and down his midriff, eyeing the dark happy trail that disappears into his trousers.

When my fingers hook on the top of them a shuddering breath leaves the prince's lips. His forehead falls onto my shoulder and he places a soft kiss against it.

"Go easy on me, love, I've waited for this for a damn long time."

I can't help but chuckle as I let go of his trouser and drive my hands through his thick curls, my nails scraping against his scalp.

"Cas," I whisper, my lips tracing against the shell of his ear. His grip on my hips tightens as he grumbles, "Mhh,"

"Do you remember the last time I asked you to fuck me?"

His cheek grazes mine as he finally looks at me, his eyes of a midnight shade. "Yes." His fingers dig into the soft flesh of my hips.

"Do you want me to ask you again?"

Our eyes never let go of each other when he speaks.

"Do it," he swallows, "ask me again."

My hands trail from his curls to his neck.

"Cassian, I want you to fuck me."

A soft chuckle breathes past his lips, "That is not a question, love."

"Right," I say, not elaborating.

"But, I am honored to fuck you." He breathes.

I don't know who moves first and I guess it doesn't matter. He doesn't let me go after his promised words, clinging to my lips like a drowning man. Worshipping me with every whispered word, every trailed kiss along my skin, like he's standing in front of a goddess.

We make quick work of his trousers and undergarment and for a moment the air hisses through my teeth.

My eyes tell him what my lips can't, conjuring a smug smile on his lips.

He stalks forward and I have no choice but to trace backward until I feel the mattress dig into the back of my knees.

"No need to be scared, I'll be whatever you want me to be, do whatever you want me to do."

To my astonishment, he sinks, down to his knees.

A surge of desire floods my veins as his fingers hook into my undergarment and his eyes hold mine as he slowly drags the fabric over the valley of my thighs and down my calves until they land on the floor.

"You're the most beautiful being I've ever met in this world, Carina." He whispers before he drives me back onto the bed.

A breath of surprise escapes me as my back hits the mattress.

Cassian is over me in a matter of seconds as our lips meet hungrily and his hands dance over my skin.

I arch my back as his thumb grazes over the highs of my breasts, cupping and squeezing one for a moment.

I keen in delight as I feel him against my thigh, my heart pounding crazily inside me.

His fingers travel lower and lower, his thumb swirling one time over my navel and dipping inside before his hand finds his destination, "Gods." I moan when he finally hits the spot I've been aching at for the whole evening.

"Such an eager little thing." He murmurs as his lips trail over my neck.

His swirling movements turn frantic, matching the rhythm of my breath and I ram my nails into his back, trying to move with him as I chase my lips with his.

My body climbs higher and higher as I writhe under his hold.

"Faster, Cas." I breathe, once I let go of his lips and a dark chuckle leaves his lips, driving all over me, covering my skin in goosebumps.

His pace picks up and he tilts his fingers at a certain angle tipping me right over the edge.

Cas's lips catch mine and strangle the cry that erupts in my throat.

White flashes around me as he lets me ride my high on his hand, I can feel blood oozing out of his back where my nails claw at his skin.

Wave after wave it hits me, shaking my body, giving me the most beautiful kind of release.

Cas bites at my bottom lip, licking over the drops of blood that escape the torn skin while my heart slows down.

His fingers escape me and as he leans on one elbow I watch him lazily as his fingers raise to his mouth, glistening with my arousal.

His eyes roll back as his tongue meets the skin of his fingers and another wave shutters through me.

My cheeks flood with heat when he meets my eyes again. For a short sweet moment, his lips catch mine.

"I love you." He whispers, kissing my cheek. He shifts his body on mine, while he props another kiss on my jaw.

"I love you." He whispers again before I feel him between my thighs.

In a moment of fear, my body freezes, my arms grasping his biceps.

He looks me in the eyes, smiling gently. My heart melts at the sight of this beautiful man on top of me.

This. Him. Is what I want for the rest of my life.

My hands wander from the tense muscles in his shoulder blades down to the two dimples driven into his lower back. A hard push of my fingers and he drives forward taking my body upwards with his force.

"Fuck." I hiss at the burning sensation at the same time Cas groans.

His arms are trembling with the sheer force to hold himself back.

"Are you all right?" He asks through clenched teeth as I try to accustom myself to the feel of him.

I swallow as I look into his dark eyes.

"It burns," I admit as tears sting my eyes. Horror flashes along his face and he moves to leave but I quickly wind my arms around his shoulders.

"Don't stop," I whisper, wanting to be close to him.

"I'm not in by half, love."

Oh, gods.

"Relax. Breathe." His voice tells me and I do as he says. One hand of his trails over my skin, so soft and gentle that goosebumps cover my skin.

His thumb swipes over the rosy bud of my breast and a flicker of pleasure dances through.

"Just like that." He moves further, his lips catching mine.

When his tongue laps over mine I feel him ease in further and further.

The burning is still present but with his taste on my tongue, I relax. His hand travels downwards to where we're joined and starts to draw circles.

"Oh, yes." I moan at the next wave of pleasure and then I feel him push in completely.

"Fuck." We both groan in unison.

I hook my ankles around his narrow waist as he probs his first thrust and I feel like I almost burst from the amount of feeling exploding in my body.

"You're such a good girl." He thrusts again, "handling this so well."

His lips trail along my skin.

My eyes close in ecstasy with his next thrust, making the headboard whine under the pressure.

My body moves upwards with his force, driving me higher and higher again.

His lips encircle the bud on my breast, suck it desperately and I almost burst.

A ripple of pleasure splashes through me and I lift my hips to meet his when he stops mid-thrust.

"Watch."

A shiver runs down my spine at his single demand. My eyes fly open on their own accord and follow his to see him watching his length half inside me.

"I dare you to close your eyes again."

Even though my mind tells me to close them just out of spite I keep them open and watch how his cock slides easily inside me.
"Fuck."
Our breath mingles together while he drives us both towards what we desperately need, what we crave.
I feel myself squeeze around him with the next thrust and we both come undone at the same time. I do with a soft sigh, catching his deep groan against my lips.
I didn't expect the prince to be this verbal but the sounds he makes sends shivers of pleasure through me.
While we both come down from our highs, Cassian's forehead drops to my sternum. I feel his lungs expand against my own body, aftershock waves still disrupting me as my heart swells even more.
Suddenly tears start to sting my eyes and the desperation that flares inside me is so unbearable that I have to speak up.
"Ask me again." Cassian looks up at me, his gaze half-lidded as he props himself up. I immediately miss the warmth of his body.
"Ask you what?" His voice is gruff as his eyes search mine for the sudden change in the mood.
He's still inside me and I can feel his liquid running down my thighs.
"Ask me if I want to marry you."
In a matter of seconds, he's pulling out, his eyes flaring green.
"What?" The word is barely a sound inside the room.
He's put some distance between us that makes me crawl over to him winding my arms around his neck.
"Ask me if I want to marry you, Cas."
He shakes his head, his eyes building an angry v on his forehead.
"So you can reject me again?"
"I'm not going to reject you, you stupid idiot."
His eyes narrow suspiciously but despite his suspicion his arm winds around my waist and he pulls me onto his lap.
He licks his lips for a moment staring at mine.
"Do you?" His eyes meet mine desperately. "Want to marry me?"

My lips turn into a soft smug smile. "I do."

His lips catch mine so intense and hard I feel like I'm going to lift off at any second.

We part and both grin at each other, happiness filling my chest like a glass of wine almost overflowing.

"What now?" I ask him as a wolf-ish grin forms on his lips.

"Now. I'm going to fuck you again."

~ 48 ~

The moment my eyes flutter open I know that something is wrong. The sun doesn't reach the palace buried so deep in the ocean so I create my own little light letting it float in the room as I turn my body to look at Cassian. The light glimmers in soft lilac, a craft I only managed recently when I saw the floating lights at Speaking Death.

The left side of the bed is empty and I can't stop myself from reaching over and feeling the cold side of the mattress. He's been gone for a long time. Something settles in my chest.

I wrap my naked body in the comforter as I rush past the discarded clothing on the floor.

"Cas?" I call towards the door that leads to the bathing chamber, knocking even though it feels unnecessary after last night. When I open the door I'm met with blaring nothingness.

Maybe he already went to have breakfast with Aalton and the others?

The spot of darkness spreads in my chest and speeds the pounding of my heart.

My eyes flit over to the nightstand beside the disheveled bed and for a moment I'm thrown back in time. The headboard has a crack through the middle from our second round and usually, I would bathe in the embarrassment flooding my cheeks.

But I rush right over to the nightstand where I see the lilac stone glaring back at me.

I pick up the ring Cassian gifted me at the Sebestyen court months ago. I slowly let the ring slide over my left ring finger, fitting perfectly. The bloodstone shimmers in the floating light I created before it flies over to the envelope underneath.

My name is scribbled in an unfamiliar writing on top of it and I fear the worst.

My hands shake as I grab the envelope and pull out the scarce piece of paper with only a few sentences.

How precious something can be until it is lost.
Find me and you will find your most precious item.

Rage burns through me faster than any wildfire I have encountered.

The doors to the chamber burst open with my rage, making the guards outside turn around alarmed.

"He's gone." My voice almost a growl, making them cower under my gaze. I feel my magic start to gather inside me, my hands starting to burn as I swear to myself that this will end now.

Him or me. It was always gonna be it.

~ 49 ~

The guards flinch as I throw open the doors to the hallway, strutting past them with purpose.

I slipped into my clothing from our journey here, not patient enough to sneak out some armor from the castle.

I slightly register the echoing sound when the doors collide with the stone walls and as if the gods have called him Flynn appears at the end of the hall.

His steps are hurried, and his gaze narrowed in on me. "Carina, what happened?"

"Nothing, I'm taking a stroll," I tell him lazily.

His eyes rove over my clothing as he comes to a stop in front of me.

"What are you doing here, Flynn?"

"I wanted to talk to Cas, is he in your rooms?" I can see the tick in his jaw. Is that a trick question? Does he want me to expose myself? My pulse is fluttering and I feel like I should run, sprint so as not to waste a second. Who knows how long Cassian has been gone and what Adales has done to him and is still doing to him?

"He told me he went for breakfast."

"He hasn't appeared in the banquet hall." Flynn crosses his arms over his broad chest. He's wearing his hair down today, a few strands falling over his shoulders.

"Maybe you missed him, I'm sure he's already stuffing his face with baked goods."

Too impatient to bother with a disguise I try to step past him but he immediately blocks my way.

"Something is up, Carina, and you're going to tell me what it is."

"Nothing is up. I want to take a walk, I need some fresh air."

"Did you fight?" He asks. "What? No."

I finally outstep him but he falls right into step beside me.

"Well, I guess I'll talk to him later. Mind if I join you?"

Yes, I do.

I stare up at him as we round the corner towards the entrance hall. "Of course not."

He continues to eye me from the side, I can feel it. There is no way he will let me leave without him.

Luckily we don't meet anyone as we pass the entrance hall and jog down the stairs.

A fresh breeze from the ocean carries over to us once we're outside.

Gravel crushes under our boots as we make our way to the beach and I throw a longing glance towards the adjacent forest. The pull is there, I know what it means what it always has meant, I was just too blind or maybe too scared to see it.

I need to go now.

I turn to see that Flynn has been eyeing me. Something in my face makes him shake his head.

"No, Carina—"

He can't get any further before he suddenly slumps into a small heap on the floor. "What...?" I look up surprised to see the culprit standing with a smug smile on his lips.

"You look like you needed some help." A smirk stretches his lips

"What the hell are you doing here, Zayne?"

"Saving your and my brother's ass?"

He's dressed in dark breeches, a sword strapped to his back, joined by knives around his leather belt.

"I mean what you're doing *here*, in Oceanus?"

"That's not important right now. We need to go."

Before I can protest he grabs my wrist and pulls.

I fall into step beside him and throw a last glance over my shoulder. The imposing castle hovers under fray clouds, the occupants inside probably still at breakfast enjoying their day.

"Is Flynn going to be fine?" I ask breathlessly as we jump over fallen bark and branches.

Once we're inside the forest the dark envelops us. It gets colder the deeper we dive inside.

"I just let him sleep for a while. He's going to wake once we're back."

He pulls again at my wrist but this time I keep my ground. We stutter to a halt and Zayne turns to look at me with burning rage in his eyes.

"We have to go *now*."

"How do you know where we have to go? And why are you here?"

"Gods damnit." He curses as he lets go of me. One hand drives through the thick curls of his hair.

"I'm here because my brother can't let anything happen to you. He asked me to come because he didn't trust Aalton. I shadowed your group and stayed in the forest watching over you."

I stare at him incoherently. "He didn't trust Aalton?"

"Of course not! What do you think? He doesn't trust anyone with you. Not even yourself. You throw away your life so easily, not caring about how he feels."

Rage burns in his words and I take a few steps back. Talons start to grow out of his hands as he continues talking.

"There was never someone else other than you. No one he wanted to play with as a child, no one he wanted to listen to. He sacrificed his whole life for you. And I lost my brother because of you."

I shake my head quickly. "You didn't lose your brother."

"What do you know?" He spits at me. "Why do you think we're here? Cas wanted to lure Adales out of his cave that is why we're here. It was my brother's plan all along."

Realization washes over me like a cold bucket of ice.

That is why Flynn agreed to come here as well. I was surprised how important a wedding seemed to both him and Cassian.

But that is not important now, I can understand why Cas did it, if I were in his position I'd try to protect him too.

"Are you that stupid not to see? See how much he adores you? How much he lets you get away with, even though he knows you're an asshole. You don't deserve his love, Zayne. You never did."

He takes a few steps forward laughing.

"Of course not. The older brother, so cruel and cold, never deserved anything. I didn't deserve the throne, I didn't deserve my brother and I didn't deserve the girl."

I furrow my brows at that. "What are you talking about?"

He hesitates for a moment, his eyes darkening.

"I didn't abdicate the throne because I wanted to. I had to. Because it was his fault written in the stars. Intertwined with yours."

He's still advancing on me and I have nowhere to go when my back hits the trunk of a tree.

"I am the monster and still, I am here." He whispers as he stops right in front of me. For a moment I can't move when he raises his hand and lets it travel over the side of my neck. The fluttering of my pulse makes his lips tilt upwards.

"I am here because I love my brother."

I swallow pulling at the magic inside me, getting ready to fight him if I have to.

"And what does that mean?"

He shrugs as he takes a step back. "That I will torture, fight, and if I have to, kill."

So he is going to exchange me for his brother's freedom.

My heart stutters as adrenaline pumps through my veins.

"That's good to know."

Heat gathers at my fingers and I know they're starting to glow. Zayne furrows his brows at the action.

"What are you doing?"

I laugh lightly. "You're not expecting me to just stand here and watch you?"

Confusion riddles his face in an instant. "Watch me—"

I don't know how he does it. I don't see him move or do anything special.

But before I can even think of letting the buzz of my magic go, there is sharp pain.

And nothing but darkness afterward.

The next time my eyes flutter open I register a groan. It takes me a moment to realize that the sound echoing in this crate is my own. I blink in the darkness, trying to make out where I am or what the hell happened. Wherever I am, it is cold and I quickly wrap my arms around me trying to create some heat. It feels like the temperature is embedded into the place, spreading like a curse, enveloping you like a spider in its webs.

There is a steady dripping as if a water leak is located down here with me.

It reeks of ashes and mold. My bones ache with the cold that creeps inside me when I try to point out what I remember happening at last.

I was fighting with Zayne—who happens to be in Oceanus—before everything went black. I freeze when the thought of what happened crossed my mind.

Zayne brought me here, whatever here is, probably to get rid of me. Hand me off to Adales so he doesn't have to bother with me. It couldn't be clearer. The way he taunted me my whole life, the jealousy he talked about, the way he had to give everything up because of me. Now that Adales kidnapped Cassian, Zayne is going to offer me on a silver platter to get his brother back.

My teeth start to chatter when another chilly breeze hits my skin. I try to make out where the slow draft originates from but the only thing I feel and see is dark stone.

I need to get up, slip out of here and put all of this to an end. I can't believe that Zayne would go as far as to tip Adales off. Even though we could never stand each other I felt a quiet truce settle between us. For Cassian's sake but it seems like the truce was just one-sided.

I sigh, preparing myself to get off the freezing floor when I register a deep groan. I startle at the sound, moving my feet. Chains rattle in the darkness and I can't help but feel panic rise like bile in my throat. My hands skate down my legs to feel chains wound around my ankles, the material burning against my skin. I hiss when my fingers come into contact with its material. I singe my fingers at the bloodstone that is wrapped around my legs.

Someone coughs in the darkness and I flinch.

"Hello?" I whisper, my eyes darting around. If it weren't for the shackles blocking my magic I could change and make out where I am. Something shifts.

"Who's there?" I try again.

There is no answer but I can feel it breathing. Something is down here with me.

In my haste, I try to reach for the soft warm buzz of my magic but it is no use. The bloodstone is blocking every ounce of magic cursing through my veins.

"Love."

My head whisks to the side from where the whisper came from. I almost cry out when I move my legs so fast they rub against the chains. The moment someone wraps me up in a hug I forget about the pain, clinging to the hard curve of his shoulders, the soft scent of pines. "Cas."

"Holy gods, I thought I was hallucinating again." His breath skirts over my cheek, his voice shaky. Is he hurt? How long has he been here?

"It's me. I swear." I press a desperate kiss against the side of his temple.

"Are you hurt? Can you move?"

He shifts awkwardly. "I'm fine."

"That's the worst lie ever. More importantly, can you stand? We need to get out of here, now."

He needs to get out of here. I need to stay and finally get this over with but he doesn't need to know this.

"It's no use. There's a bloodstone gate blocking our path out of here."

"Where exactly is *here*?"

I try to make out his face in the dark, my hands skating over his side. My fingers turn sticky when they reach his waist. He's bleeding.

"You're bleeding," I stress and he winces with his next breath. Panic winds its cold claw around my windpipe crushing it under its sheer force.

"It's a kind of underground temple, located under the memorial of Aegaeus."

He says and ignores my comment. I quickly reach down to the hem of my shirt and rip off a large patch. The sound of ripping clothing echoes in the space around us.

"Lean forward," I command and he scoffs. "I'm fine."

"There's no time for your pride, Prince. Lean forward."

He does so with a small grumble and I quickly wind the fabric around his waist. I don't need to guess to know that he was injured with a bloodstone blade decorated with poison. It is the smell. The mix of blood and something rotten mingle in the air. I carefully tie a knot over the wound, feeling him shake under me.

"I thought I could come here and make things better for you, love. I couldn't stand watching you wither away. But I was surprised and he is not alone. He has my—"

"Brother, I know."

I sit back on my calves, my mind conjuring plan after plan to get him out of here. Cas doesn't deserve to be dragged into my mess. But even if he could conjure up his talons I doubt they'd be able to slice through the bloodstone chains at my ankles. I can feel myself growing weaker with every second they pulse against my skin.

"He is not evil Carina." He tells me.

"I know he isn't," which makes the betrayal so much worse, "which is why we'll get him out of here, okay?"

He sits up suddenly, grabbing my hands in his. The touch is cold, death clinging to the tips.

"You would forgive him." He sounds astonished.

If I stay alive I will. I have to for his sake.

"Let's focus on getting out of here first, all right?"

"Right."

I squeeze his hands before I let go. We don't acquire the chance to come up with a plan when a door creaks open in the darkness. Light floods the cellar which I now realize is some kind of prison. Multiple cells are located beside each other but they are empty except for Cas's and mine. The light source doesn't seem to be natural, flickering along the cobbled walls like candlelight.

Heavy steps approach the small space and I shift in front of Cassian before I see someone step inside the room, the breath knocked out of me at the familiar face.

"You."

~ 50 ~

"Get moving, princess, it's judgment day."
His hand winds around my bicep as he hauls me to my feet roughly. For a moment balance is a stranger to me as I try to get a grip on my feet. Once up I glare at the haunting face of Eryx. Cassian growls behind us and we both turn to see him get to his feet. Just now I realize how badly he's injured.
Blue bruises splash across his tan cheeks, his lip is split open, and blood drips from his teeth. He's far more chained up than I am. Dark violet chains wind around his wrists, connected to a chain that travels down to both his ankles. A horrifying cry slips past my lips when I see his back.
"What did you do?" I growl at him and watch his lips turn into a smug smile. "We thought it made a beautiful painting."
Bile rises in my throat as quick as rage when I see the red angry slashes on Cassian's back, blood oozing from his skin.
 "That's just the beginning but luckily it's not your turn yet, prince," Eryx says with a small bow of his head. Cassian lunges forward but Eryx is faster, already slamming the iron bars shut in front of the cell.
"How could you! My father trusted you with his life, you will be hunted for the rest of your life." The prince hisses.
"Not under Adales protection."
 A smug smile stretches his lips and reveals his fangs.
"Now let's get moving." He pushes me forward in the direction of the flickering light.
 "Carina!" Cassian calls after me, his voice so powerful the ground beneath us shakes. If possible the space grows even colder. Eryx grows uneasy beside me and I fear that Cassian might be able to break through the bars. But that would be impossible, right? Bloodstone is his true weakness. He wouldn't be able to escape it.
Just to be sure I turn to look at him while walking.
"Everything will be fine, I promise."

With a last shove Eryx and I step into a tunnel, lit with torches. I will make sure he will get out of here alive, even if that is the last thing I will do. Adales can torture me, hurt me, kill me but he has to let Cassian go. His revenge is solely for me, not for anyone else. The traitor and I travel various tunnels quietly, his grip on my arm bruising and I can feel the graze of his talons against my skin. Cassian was right, this seems to be some kind of underground dungeon, created millions of years ago, by the look of the stones.

The closer we get to our destination the warmer the air grows. I try to mentally prepare myself for whatever is to come.

Maybe Adales will spare Cassian if I give myself to him willingly. My skin grows cold when I think of his face all bruised up and bloodied. To distract myself I turn myself, to look at Eryx.

"I knew I had a bad feeling about you."

He doesn't spare me a glance but answers me still.

"Didn't do you any good that feeling, did it?"

I huff continuing to walk quietly for another minute. "Was this your plan all along, were you even loyal to the king?"

Eryx hisses and slams my back against the wall. The back of my head hits the stoned wall. Seems like I hit a nerve.

"It is because of my loyalty to the king that I am doing this."

A dull throb appears at the back of my skull and I feel something warm trickle down my neck.

"Right, that makes sense. And what do you think he will do if he finds out his son has been shackled in a cell, beaten bloody?"

He closes in on me, carrying the scent of salt and foulness right to me.

"He will thank me for keeping his son alive. He might not know it now but all *you* bring is destruction and death. I won't let the kingdom go down because of some stuck-up girl who doesn't know when to stop dragging people into her mess."

I shut my mouth at his last words. The distinct burning behind my eyes crawls through me.

"Sometimes you have to hurt people for them to stay alive, I don't expect you to understand that."

Confusion riddles me at his words before the frown on my face flattens.

"It was you," I whisper, realization hitting me like a fist in the face, "you poisoned the queen and then blamed the servant boy."

The Upyr looks at me grimly, his shoulders straightening with his next breath.

"Why?" I am genuinely curious. What kind of advantage would he draw from that move?

"To make it seem like she was ill because of you. The day Cassian agreed to that foolish ritual and marked his skin to protect you is when I started. I dosed her food and drinks with ordinary poison first but that was obviously not enough," he starts to pace and I eye the sword sheathed at his hip.

"When Cassian left I started to poison her with darker magic and it worked," he stops pacing, his dark gaze flying to me. His jaw hardens as he approaches and stops right in front of me. "Until you came along."

I hold my body as still as I can as I tilt my head to the side. "Oh, I'm genuinely sorry for disrupting your plans, why don't I do it again?" I smirk as confusion flickers in the deep ends of his eyes.

I unlatch the sheath of the sword and grip the handle.

The Upyr steps back surprised when I swing the blade and let it race down on him. He raises his hand at the last second. Talons clash with the blade of his sword. He pushes the blade to the side hissing.

I recoil from his exposed fangs but let the blade swoosh over my head nonetheless. It comes rushing at him again and again. What I can't do with my chained ankles I do with my arms. Jabbing at him from the left, using my elbows to blow his ribs.

He groans and steps back before his talons get a slash at my waist. I cry out when a burning fire erupts from the slash.

Blind with rage I trust the blade out again but hit only air. Eryx stumbles back, the force so powerful that he jabs the back of his skull against the cobbled wall. I grin happily before I stalk as quickly as I can over to him.

He's already back on his feet balanced but the moment he moves I hold the blade up to his chin.

His body freezes as the cold tip touches his chin. I can see his teeth grinding as he eyes me with black eyes, the color of Gehenna.

"Now why don't you get out the keys to that cell, Eryx." I smile slightly, despite the tautness of my body. One wrong move and I'll fall back to the role of prisoner and not executioner.

The Upyr narrows his eyes, his talons twitching at his side. When he doesn't move for the keys he pocketed moments ago I apply some pressure to the blade at his throat.

"Bitch." He growls before moving his hand towards his breeches.

"I know you are one but what am I?" I taunt him.

Hope sparks when I hear the keys dangle without me noticing the shadow growing behind me.

"*Enough.*"

Eryx's movement halts as his eyes flicker to the person behind me. I watch the wolffish grin take place on his busted lips. At least I got a hit on him before I will go down as well.

"Why don't you drop the blade, sweetheart." The voice of one's creepiest nightmares appears again. The sound crawls over me like a thousand small spiders are withering over me, trying to escape death.

Even though I don't want to, I drop the blade. I don't dare turn around when a hand lays itself on my shoulder. He applies some pressure on it and gently pulls me to his side, my insides shriveling. Every little ounce of life I felt inside me withers away, rotting desperately.

"I told you to bring her to me unharmed, Eryx." The voice says again as I watch the Upyr start to tremble.

"She was asking questions, Your Godness, I was just—" He shut up the moment he raises a hand in the air. Waves away his comment lazily.

"You didn't follow my orders," a deep sigh makes the dungeons shake around us.   "You know what happens when you don't follow my orders."

Eryx's eyes widen horribly. "Please, no—"

The traitor doesn't get further. His whole body is paralyzed from one moment to the next. My eyes travel slowly down his throat, completely intact, the fine clothed upper body. The white blouse is gaping open in the middle, a whole right where his heart was seconds ago.

I gasp when I see the hand with long fingers, elegant and almost too beautiful to be defiled with the color of blood. It lets the heart fall to the floor carelessly, a squelching sound appearing as it paints the floor crimson.

Bile rises in my throat and if it weren't for the hand on my shoulder I would probably bend over and empty my stomach.

I dry heave for a moment before the man tuts me.

"Don't feel bad for him. People like Eryx don't get far."

I put my hand to my stomach as the voice appears again.

"Now, now turn around and let me look at how you've grown up."

Even though everything in me tells me to stay where I am, memorize the slumped form of Eryx, his heart discarded on the floor beside him, I move.

Slowly I turn, my hands clutching my nervous stomach, to meet the looming figure over me.

Acid spreads along my tongue as I stop, the heat of the hand on my shoulder almost unbearable. I straighten up as well as I can.

"Hello, Father."

~ 51 ~

Some say that death is the most beautiful creature in our world. With its darkness, sharp angles, and tempting lips it is what everyone desires. A taste can make you addicted, claws digging through your chest and dragging you down under.
It is true.
Death is beautiful.
I have met his son and fallen in love with him, but not once have I heard someone talk about his brother, his creator, *Life*.
Life is supposed to be light, a soft breeze carrying over you, enveloping you in comfortable and hopeful bliss.
But the man in front of me is anything but.
He might be one of the most beautiful creatures I have ever seen. With broad shoulders and a lithe body, hair so dark it looks like the night sky of Aerwyna. It cascades down his shoulders, revealing a slender neck, a strong jawline, and lips lovely and inviting. The heart-shaped cupid's bow disappears as an awful grin stretches Life's lips. The darkness inside the god defaces his beautiful features.
His skin seems pale and rough, his eyes dull but sapphire colored. Lashes as deep as night curl so high they almost touch his brows.
A shiver runs over me when I see the resemblance to my own reflection.
"Hello, Father." My voice is strong and confident when I speak much in contrast to the crumple I feel I am. I watch delight dance in the mirror of his eyes.
"So you did figure it out." Adales's smile turns deeper as he watches me with a tilted head.
"Not without a little help." My mind flashes back to the moment with Aalton. He was the one who planted the seed in my head and from then on the theory spread through me. I knew it was true but I didn't have confirmation until now. The words of the Fatum make sense now. *May a new age dawn with the rightful heir of our*

world. Adales was the maker of our continent and with me being his daughter I am his heir.

"So I am your daughter, not Aerwyn's," I state, trying not to shake at the revelation. Whatever her motives were for keeping the ugly truth from me, I am grateful she did. Booming laughter escapes the god in front of me.

"Of course, honey, someone with a power so great as yours, couldn't be coming from anyone else than me."

So he is an arrogant ass as well, put it to the never-ending list of having psychotic parents.

I eye him again, the tilt of his smile that is so familiar, the spark of his eyes, the shiny hair. But underneath all of it, I see the truth. He is rotting, living dead, just like I am. That is why I so easily believed Aalton as he revealed his concerns. Adales has to be my father or else my being alive wouldn't threaten him.

I carry the same source of power inside me and that is why one of us has to die. Just like the Fatum have said.

"How is this going to go now?" I dare ask, all fight leaving my body. I can fight once Cassian is out of here. I fear that is exactly why Adales took him, to get some leverage on me.

"You look exhausted child, why don't you join me for dinner?"

"Cut the theatrics. We know why I'm here, I don't care for politeness."

"So eager to see your life come to an end? Well, if you wish so, I won't stop you from getting anything you want."

I narrow my eyes at him.

"Then why don't get rid of these awful shackles?" I move my legs, the chains clinking around the tunnel.

"You must know I cannot let you wander around with your magic at bay. Now follow me, I have a surprise."

Different from Eryx he walks first and I follow him around the corner. The air grows warmer once we enter a heptagon-shaped room. The room is flooded with light. The roof is open like an enormously shaped well.

I don't care about the furnished things scattered carelessly around when I notice the stone table in the middle of the room.

Strapped to it is an unconscious Cassian, looking worse than minutes ago.

Despair rushes through me as I take a step towards him but Adales winds his arm around my waist and holds me back.

"Don't even dare to go near him or he will die immediately."

"Let go of me!" I pry his hands off of me and stumble a few steps back.

"What did you do to him? He is not the one you want, I am!" My voice is far from controlled, my vocal folds feel swollen as they vibrate against each other.

"Wrong. It is not you, I want, daughter, it is your power." His eyes glow hungrily, lilac flickering in the depths of sapphire. My gaze flickers toward Cas's unconscious form. Great plan Zayne had for keeping his brother safe. Where is that bastard anyway?

"All right," I hear myself say without actually having made the conscious decision to speak. My eyes are still on the bruised face of the prince.

"Take my power, my soul, whatever you want," I turn to look at my father.

"I hoped you would say that. Personally, I thought you'd fight me but this is delightful news."

I would've fought him, but I don't want anyone to die anymore. If I can compensate for my death and not anyone else's I will do it.

I take a step towards the imposing man, rotting but still glowing with power.

"If I give you what you want, would you do me a favor? If...if our relations mean anything to you, would you?"

"I am intrigued, go on." He watches me like a hawk, crossing his arms in front of his imposing chest.

"Would you spare him? Spare this continent from your wrath once I am dead?" A satisfied look spreads over his face.

"I never felt the need to put this world upon my wrath. I created Adalon, my one and only love, I wish no bad upon it."

I eye him for a moment, trying to make out if he is being truthful. But I guess he is. He is a power-hungry bastard who wants to be glorified by the people living on the continent.

"Then I will give you what you want. As long as everyone else stays alive."

"Are you not the slightest bit curious about your heritage?" He says.

With slow deliberate steps, he stalks over to me.

"I don't want to know how you created me like your other children. I have enough broken bonds with my family." I counter.

"Oh, but that is the fun in it. Aerwyn, Demetrus, Oceanus, and Polyxenus, my beloved children. Sadly they're not perfect. And they're not your real siblings."

I know it is a ruse. Some evil way to torture me more.

"You are a love child, Katarina, you were never created from my power."

I frown at his words when something flickers inside me. I catch a movement in the shadows, a flash of dark curls and green eyes. Zayne. I focus my gaze back on the god in front of me desperate to keep him going. "Who was she?"

He doesn't need me to clarify.

"Enya was one of the most beautiful creatures I came across. The mother of Faye. It was just a liaison, I didn't genuinely care about her, what is love when there is beauty?"

I watch Zayne's eyes flicker toward the stone table. If he makes a run for his brother he will never get out. The stone table is right in the line of sight of the God of Life.

"Once I found out she was pregnant it was clear what I would do. I was not going to let a child steal my power, she needed to die,"

Rage shines in his eyes as the ground beneath us shakes lightly. I stumble a bit to the side so Adales has to turn his back to the stone table to keep looking at me.

"She escaped, my foolish children turned against me and once you were born, hid you from me. Of course, I slaughtered Enya afterward."

He says it so nonchalantly that I have to wind my arms around me. Is this why I so carelessly killed all these men without feeling an ounce of guilt? Children carry the genes of their parents, so what makes me think I am any better than him?

My thoughts dissolve as I watch Zayne at the table getting rid of Cassian's binds. The prince stirs lightly and I quickly focus on my father again.

"I'm sorry you had to go this far, I never wanted to take your powers." It takes all of me to say those words without actually gagging at the sound of them.

A pleased smile moves over his lips.

He grips my chin in his enormous hand tilting my face up to him. "*Lánya*, I am the one to apologize," his thumb swipes over my cheek.

A soft caress so contrasting to the grip he has on me. Just with one squeeze, he could squish my skull.

"But I did watch over you, your whole life. I made sure to slip into your life in between, see you grow up. Shape-shifting is just one of the great things our powers allow us to do, the power you yield has so much more to offer than you can even imagine. Sadly you will never experience it." Goosebumps cover my skin at the revelation.

"I watched you grow into an intelligent young woman, so why do you try to fool me?" His grip on my face hardens. I freeze.

"The Moreau men have meddled enough in my business, I dare you to move."

My eyes flicker toward the brothers, Cassian having an arm slung over Zayne's shoulder. One second they tried to escape, the next Adalon makes them crash against the wall. I watch in horror as they both groan at the impact unable to move from the hold Adales has on them.

"Don't hurt them, please!" I cry out but he ignores me.

I try to reach for the power inside me again. When I feel a soft tingle I almost weep. It's there, it's somewhere buried deep inside. *These damn shackles.*

"I have watched you both fall in love with my daughter foolishly and now you're going to die at her hands."

Horror strikes me at his words and makes the desperation spread like poison inside me. Instead of meeting Cassians's eyes, I look at the older Moreau brother. His gaze looks exhausted and I can't believe the affection that's mirrored inside them.

Adales glances back at me with a cruel smile.

"She didn't know? I couldn't tell you which brother loved you more but that's not relevant as you will both die tonight."

Shadows burst from around Cas, taking the form of spears as they shoot at the god. "Your little tricks won't help you now." My father says as he swipes the darkness away. What he doesn't see is them shifting towards me and as welcoming as I can I let them flood my veins.

Once the power of Cas reaches my magic slumbering in my body, I feel it.

The chains on my ankles evaporate in dust and my hands start to burn immediately as I feel it rushing through me. My magic greets me eagerly and edges me on and on and on.

Adales throws a glance at me. "Remarkable." He whispers. A flicker of his hand makes Zayne rush over to us. "How your magic corresponds to his, like two sides of a coin. Night and day."

He has a thoughtful look on his face as if he didn't expect this outcome. "No wonders. . ." He mumbles before refocusing.

The older brother squirms devastatingly as he's brought right in front of me.

"Do me the honor, *Lánya,* and bring an end to his life. He might've loved you but apparently, he loved his brother more, if he wanted to exchange you for him."

My gaze flickers toward Zayne. He would do anything for Cassian and I can't even be mad at him.

My magic hums at my decision.

"I will not kill him."

Adales frowns at my words before his face morphs into darkness. "You. Will. Kill. Him."

His voice vibrates around us and the ground starts to shake. Stones fall from above as he draws my hands to the bloodstone blade at the stone table.

"No!" I try to make my hands drop the weapon, to stop my legs from taking the steps towards the prince.

It is no use, Adales power has a secure grip on me. I am moved towards the Moreau brother like a marionette.

"Zayne." I shake my head multiple times as I whisper his name. His lips stretch into a smile.

"You will not kill me, Carina."

"Are you blind? I can't stop it."

Stones fall off the walls and stumble across us, a storm roars in the distance as thunder and lightning flash over the opening of the well.

I will kill him and then it will be over. He will make me kill Cassian too and I don't know if I will survive it.

The words of the three sisters flood my brain. *One will kill and the other will resurrect.*

It was his plan all along. He didn't want to spare the Moreau brothers, he wanted to use them. Make a true killer out of me so I wouldn't be worthy of my powers and die. I would be the one to kill and Adales will resurrect at his full power.

The tip of the blade pierces Zayne's sternum as I desperately try to move back.

Don't stab him, you can't stab him.

I watch the blade embed itself deeply in his chest, the only thing left to see is the grip, clutched between long tan fingers. *He killed himself.*

With a power I didn't know he'd possess he saved me. Zayne saved me.

Lighting crashes right beside Zayne as Cassian's desperate voice calls out so agonizingly hurt it pierces my skin.
"NO!"

~ 52 ~

Zayne's body goes limp as he crashes to the ground. It is only I who hears his last whisper pass his lips. "Take care of him."

Adales growls loudly when he realizes what has happened. I didn't do it. I didn't kill Zayne. It was the Moreau Prince himself who used the last ounce of his strength and gripped the dagger on his own, driving it through his heart.

The world explodes in shadows. A storm so cold and menacing rips at my heart and howls in my ears. Darkness envelops us, lightning crashing behind the shadows from the storm still going on on the other side.

My hair flies around whipping against my face with every powerful Bürste of air around us.

Adales is thrown back, howling as shadows attack his body over and over. I watch Cassian get up from where he was crouched seconds ago. His fingers growing black, and his talons growing from his nails.

His face is devoid of any emotions as he fixes his gaze on Adales. I shudder when I see him morph into something unworldly. Something so dark and cruel I've never seen before. Two slits pierce at his back and after a moment two leathery wings escape from within, shadows clinging to the edges, swirling around them.

Cassian looks like the reaper himself as his skin grows hard like marble.

"You will be punished for the rest of your life for this." His voice is not his own as he ends, the shadows swirling around us so fast it almost rips me off my feet. He looks like the Prince of Hell.

I realize almost too late what he is about to do when he raises his hands choking the God of Life.

"Stop!" I yell as loud as I can but he doesn't listen to me.

"Cassian you have to stop now! This is not how it's supposed to end!"

His jaw ticks while the choking sounds of Adales continue.

"I said stop!"

My voice echoes as my magic bursts from me, an elongation of myself as lilac strands race over to the prince.

They envelop his form gently like dust but the touch is real as I let it travel over the skin of his jaw tilting his head towards me.

His gaze meets mine reluctantly. The storm subsides just a little when he stares at me. My magic intertwines with his, death and life combined and I can feel his rage. Feel it in the pulse of my veins, the chattering of my teeth but I know what lies beneath. Agony.

"I know you're angry, but if you kill him now, you will kill me with him."

We need to do it right, like the prophecy predicted.

I watch something flicker in his eyes and I let my magic invade him deeper, let it caress his agony.

"It will kill me, Cas," I repeat trying to stand my ground as his shadows rip at me. "Do you trust me?"

Something flickers in his eyes and his skin grows softer, the marble receding as his shoulder sack.

"Like no one else." He breaks and I sigh. His shadows recede and Adales stops choking.

Cassian crashes to his knees and I would want nothing more than to run to him, take him in my arms and tell him that everything is going to be fine. But first I have to walk through hell if I want to get to him.

Adales grins at me, his teeth blood-soaked. "Damn right. You won't escape anything if you kill me."

He gets up on his feet groaning.

I didn't know the god of life could look so much like death.

The fact that a descendant like Cassian could injure him shows how much he's withering away. And I will put an end to him as long as he doesn't see through me.

"Kill me, kill my daughter, that's how love bites you in your ass Moreau scum." Cassian growls at his words but his eyes don't leave my form. I stalk over to my creator and let my hands glow, the lilac winds around my fingers, my magic growing uneasy inside me.

"Take what you want, I don't want this power anymore. It makes me sick."

"Carina." A low warning escapes Cassian and I shoot him a glare. "Shut your mouth," I hiss, "haven't you done enough?"

He recoils at my words but luckily he keeps his mouth shut. And before he can react Adales grabs for me, claws at my throat. I try not to heave for air, panic spreading over my tongue.

I silence the magic that recoils at me and tells me to fight back. But that is not how this is supposed to go.

If the god wasn't so desperate to return to his power he would act differently. But that is what greed does to you. It clouds your judgment.

"I will rip you apart and take everything that belongs to me." I taunt him

"You foolish child. Your bravery has become your death blow. I will finally be back at my power and once again rule." Adales rotten breath hits my cheek as his claws dive into my throat and I make sure to smile when I feel them rip through my aorta.

"Go to hell."

"Come on."

Am I on a boat? Nausea hits me as I feel shaken by the current.

"Don't give up on me, please. Please don't let me lose you too."

An angelic voice covers me in a warm embrace. Bile rises inside me when I get shaken again. No, not shaken. Something pushes down against my chest over and over.

I try to tell the angel to stop. To leave me be. I am fine right where I am. I don't want to go. The angel sobs as he pushes his lips against mine. I feel hot air billow in my mouth and expand my lungs.

"I cannot do this without you."

I want to tell the angel that it's okay. That he will indeed be able to do everything he wants without me. But the shaking doesn't stop and I'm getting annoyed.

With one swift rush of power my eyes open and I hiss at the angel over me.

"I'm getting sick of your pushing." I swipe his hands as he stares down at me.

I see the translucent faces of the four siblings hover over the angel. Once they see me open my eyes a relieved sigh leaves their lips, before they're swept away with the next breeze.

My gaze zeroes in on the angel.

"Carina? Holy gods." His body shakes as he pulls me into his arms. I cough lightly but wrap my arms around his torso when I feel the lingering presence of my heart in him.

"Cas?" I croak, my throat feeling dry.

He holds my cheeks between his hands, his green eyes raving over my skin.

"I knew you wouldn't die, I was so sure. The prophecy said you would resurrect but I was scared it wouldn't work."

"I'm here. Where is…" I turn my head to see the lifeless body of Adales lying beside me. His skin is pale, his eyes milky as he stares into nothing. His skin turns gray, flaking as if he is made only of dust. An ancient ruler is finally dethroned. I shudder and quickly look away hiding my face in Cassian's chest.

"I am so sorry Cas, Zayne—"

"Shh, it's all right." He rocks us back and forth as it finally hits. It is over. Adales is dead and Zayne died with him. I feel the magic pulse inside me so potent and sure I know it's all mine but even that can't stop the small sob from passing my lips.

"I didn't want him to die." Tears spill down my cheeks as Cassian presses a kiss to my forehead.

"He died an honorable death, Carina, he will pass the gates of Empyrean and live in peace."

"No. I can help him."

I push away from Cassian and quickly crawl over to Zayne's lifeless body.

"Carina." Cas speaks up but I ignore him. I pull from the source inside me, the feeling unfamiliar. There is so much power brimming inside me that it takes me seconds to grasp it.

My hands start to glow as I let them hover over Zaynés chest. I feel the power leaving my body and encircling his. Lilac sparks encase his body and I pull harder, try to search for a glimmer of life in his body. His back arches and I can hear the wound of the dagger heal.

I break out in a sweat but hope sparks inside me when I wove the fibers of his muscles back together. The wound is sealed.

He is still not moving.

"No," I whisper. Tears start to roll down my cheeks and I try to give more. He saved me. He needs to live.

Light explodes around us.

I crawl backwards on my hands as it appears out of Zaynés chest forming three familiar forms in the air above me.

The Fatum.

This time they're not only encased by light they are the Light. Their eyes are creepily white as their mouths open.

"His time has come, there is no way to save him." It is Gisella that speaks up first, though I am not sure she really notices me.

"His fate has come to an end and now he will thrive in the ways of Empyrean." Estella joins her.

I shake my head, "I can save him. I have enough power now! Please!"

Their bodies rise higher as their voices join a crescendo that hurts my eyes.

"Zayne Moreau is dead."

The light explodes and deafening silence remains.

No.

I quickly turn to look at cas I can clearly see it pains him to say that and try to move away when he advances on me.

"I can't believe you want to see me, I am responsible for his death."

He shakes his head his arms encircling me

I try to get out of his hold but he quickly grabs my waist pulling me onto his lap. "You're not going anywhere, love. As long as you will have me I will be at your side."

I look up at him, and let my gaze travel over the softness of his lips, the hard shadows of his cheekbones.

"My brother. . .is dead and I will owe him for that forever because of him you remain alive."

Something about him changed, giving him darkness I didn't know he'd possess. Darkness my light urges toward. His gaze softens as he swipes a strand of my hair from my face.

"Will you have me, Katarina Sebestyen?" His words are a mumbled whisper.

Though the hurt is fresh there is only one right answer to his question.

"For this life and every other."

I let our lips collide as everything falls off my shoulders. The war is over. His lips softly part mine and his tongue meets mine. Cassian groans as I taste him and I feel myself shudder.

This is where I want to be for the rest of my life.

~ 53 ~

We organized a proper burial for Zayne in the royal tomb of Demeter. I don't grow tired of telling every person how he sacrificed himself for me. Because that is what he did. If it weren't for Zayne, Adales would've been the one to receive the powers of life.

A great mass of people attend the burial, Cassian doesn't get it over him to say some words, his hands clutching mine as we watch his brother descend into the ground. I was sure I would see Zayne again.

Once I figure out my true powers I will make sure to visit him and thank him.

It turns out that on the night of Adales's attempt to take reign, King Moreau let his powers fade into his bloodline which made Cassian able to shift, inheriting Gehenna within it.

We celebrate his new duty as we mourn his brother's loss.

It is Ronan who raises his glass that evening, his eyes meeting mine over the table. Everyone is there, Aalton and Darya, Edlyn perched on Serena's lap, Flynn and Hector engrossed in a conversation, Kian and my brother who try desperately to keep their affection for each other in secret, and Cassian. Cassian raises his glass looking at me. "To the Rising Queen of Adalon, may she bring us a life full of fortune and happiness."

Everyone clinks their glasses as I blush. Cassian presses a kiss to my cheek, mumbling in my ear. "Tonight I will worship you like a Queen."

And he did. He worships me every moment he can and if I weren't so in love with him I might've found it unbearable, but I can't.

There is just one last thing I have to do.

It was Cassian's idea to hold the speech in the ballroom of Demeter. It would've been too far away to make them all come to Aerwyna and I have talked to my cousin Andréas who happily obliged to keep everything straight for me in my kingdom.

And now I'm standing in front of the elongated table with Cassian beside me as I clutch his hand. He likes to call himself my handsome accessory, and even though I offered him a place in the council he refused. Instead, he made a far more intriguing suggestion.

"I am very grateful you all made it here today," I say, my voice still rough. I clear my throat as I let my gaze wander toward Aalton. A soft smile stretches over his lips and encourages me to go on.

"I have announced this meeting to address some changes that will occur in Adalon."

Hector is seated beside Aalton, his amber gaze trusting and warm. Edlyn has come too, taken a seat beside Azzura, my mother— Shailagh— beside them.

Flynn is perched in a corner, I wanted him to be present at this moment even though he didn't want to participate as the head of the Tengeri.

"The four kingdoms will stay in glory but I fear it is not enough to keep everyone in peace. That is why I made up the *Council of Sors*, so we can have a member of every species to make sure something like discrimination among species, outcasting, and killing never happens again."

My eyes meet Edlyn's at the table, this is the first time I see tears welling in the deep ends of hazel.

"There is no place for hatred inside these lands anymore, I want us to work together. Magda, Tengeri, Upyr, Faye, human, and Custo, we are all the same. That is why I'm open to any suggestion for improvement in the inter-species relationship. I already addressed every single one of you and asked if you would like to be an ambassador for your species. You can leave the council any time you want if you feel not dedicated enough. But during your member time, I want to see everyone passionate and with one goal in mind. Peace."

The last word slips past my lips in a whisper. Cassian squeezes my hand as the room remains quiet. Aalton raises his glass of wine, with a charming smile on his face.

"To peace." Everyone follows suit and we raise our glasses.

"To peace," I mumble as I watch everyone break out in conversation. The room bubbles potently with fresh ideas and motivation.

Cassian's lips are at my ear a moment later, "You did it, love. Look at them, conversing as if they're the best of friends."

"As long as it stays that way I am happy."

My eyes flicker over to my mother who bows her head at me subtly. I don't know what kind of relationship will occur from our differences. But I am willing to try. I've been angry for too long. I want to look forward and bathe in every moment I am gifted with, that is what life is.

Breathing every breath, taking every step you have the gift of taking. I turn my head to look at Cassian who smiles at me, dimples appear, gaze softening.

I tend to do all that with him at my side.

Epilogue

They often say the world is black or white. I believed in that sentence for a long time, putting everything I did or thought into categories. How else would I cope with it? But it is easy to categorize everything as good or bad. It is easy to judge others for what they did and what they do, without looking in the mirror.

Who would think a 6'4 curly-haired man that can slice open throats and rip out hearts of people's bodies is the one who changes my mind? I certainly didn't expect him. But maybe that is the beauty of it.

My handsome, warm fiancé. My heartmate and best friend is sometimes gray.

But he is also green and dark brown, he is specks of yellow and dances of purple. His soul shines in many colors and it is my fault that I didn't see it from the beginning. No one is black or white and if someone seems duller in color than some other you need to ask yourself; what happened to this soul to change its colors? What circumstances wind their way around their mind and form a new soul, so different from the one that was there before?

"I can hear your thoughts," Cas grumbles deeply and my lips twitch when I turn around in the massive pillows to look at him. He's lying on his stomach, his face pushed deep into the velvet pillows.

I ogle the muscles that ripple through his back, moving every time he shifts. His skin is back to its normal bronze color caused by the many hours he spends outside.

"Stop thinking so much and get back to sleep." Cassiangrumbles again and I smile before I snuggle close to his body heat. His strong arm winds around me and he turns, pulling our fronts flush against each other. We are both still naked from last night, making me feel every hard muscle of his against every soft curve of my flesh.

"I bet someone is going to burst into our chambers in five minutes. With some unnecessary reason like the change of some curtain's colors." I say, while my hand runs through his dark locks and he lets out a deep purr.

"Well, then we have to make the best out of these five minutes."

"What do you—*Oh.*"

He slides his thigh right between mine and props his body up, his lips crashing against mine. I moan when his hands dig into my hips and his canines graze against my lips.

I open my mouth willingly and shudder at the hot stroke of his tongue, my body on fire in seconds. His lips wander down my throat, nip, bite, and lick my skin while wetness pools between my thighs.

"Stop teasing me and fuck me." I hiss and dig my nails into his back, making him groan.

"Your wish is my command, Your Majesty." I shudder at his words and open my eyes to see the black of his irises.

He nudges his cock right through my wet folds and I raise my hips to meet him halfway but he moves back.

"What are you doing?" I whine and chase him with my hips.

"Building tension." A deep chuckle rumbles through the chamber and I narrow my eyes at him.

"There is enough fucking tension push your cock inside me, Cas."

"Such a dirty mouth." He shakes his head, still hovering over me with a cocky smile. I dig my nails harder into his back, making him groan deeply.

"You didn't complain when this dirty mouth sucked you off?" I bat my lashes and he growls before he sinks right into me with one hard thrust.

"*Fuck.*" We both moan in unison when his whole length is inside me, my walls clenching beautifully around his cock.

"Oh fuck, I love it when you do that." He grunts and I tilt my head to the side, looking into his handsome face.

"What do you mean?"—I clench my core muscles again and he moans—"This?"
His grip on my hips tightens and his features harden.

"You should stop teasing me, My Queen." I want to bite back but he suddenly moves his hips and I moan when he rams back inside me. The headboard squeaks under his pressure and I arch my back.

"Fuck, I could stare at you forever." My heart burns at his words and he slowly starts a rhythm while his lips travel down my throat, between my breasts and he takes one rosy bud into his hot mouth.

"Fuck, yes." I breathe out and tug at his strands meeting his hips with mine. The air becomes stuffy around us, tension flying in sparks in the chamber. The steady squeak of the headboard mixes with the sound of our skin colliding.

I wrap my legs around his narrow waist and he groans when he sinks in deeper, his cock hitting just the right spot inside me. My core clenches and my breasts tighten while his rhythm becomes faster.

"Harder, Cas." I urge him on and he pounds harder, faster, and deeper.

We both groan and he looks down at me, his high cheekbones flushed with heat. It's the most beautiful look in the world.

"I hate you," I whisper and he growls before his cock retracts just until the tip is inside me.

I smirk lightly, moving my hips to tease him.

"You don't. You love me." He whispers and starts to trail kisses along my throat.

"You love me so much you couldn't live without me." He murmurs and I sigh with every soft kiss. Still, I yearn for his hard thrusts and dig my heels into his back. He enters me just a bit and I whine when Cas doesn't move.

My core clenches and my body begs me to finish.

"Say it." He demands, making me arch my back.

"I hate you."

"Carina." He growls and I smile, loving to tease him. I move my hands from his back and put them on his chest before I push hard. His eyes widen and we roll over, me on top of him. His eyes narrow while the desire swirls inside them.

"I love you," I whisper before I sink onto him and we both groan when I start to move my hips. Cas grips my hips to support the movement, fast and hard.

"Say it again." He pants and I arch my back while I increase my rhythm, grabbing the headboard for support.

"I love you, Cas."

"Fuck yes, you do." He growls and just when I think it can't feel any better he leans up and pulls me flush against him while he pushes in from underneath me.

"*Oh, yes.*" I moan and clutch his shoulders as he plunges deeper and deeper and hits just the right spot.

My world explodes in white and my core clenches so hard that I hear Cas groan in ecstasy, his skin slapping against mine in delight.

My body tingles all over and I screw my eyes shut at the earth-shattering explosion that runs through me, barely noticing Cas' sloppy thrust and the hot warm liquid that fills me inside.

"Fuck." Cas breathes out and the fog in my mind clears lightly when I come down.

My hands find their way into his dark curls while his forehead drops against my shoulder. His arms tighten around me and he lazily thrusts up a last time, sending another shocking wave through my body.

"I love you." He murmurs and places a soft kiss against my collarbone. I chuckle lightly, my lips grazing his ear.

"Are you saying that because you came inside of me or because you really do?"

"Fifty-Fifty." He teases and I slap his shoulder lightly. He lifts his head and grins at me, making my heart melt when I see the dimples edged into his cheeks.

He slips out of me and we lay down beside each other, content and satisfied. My hand lands on his chest right over his beating heart while he stretches his body, his eyes hooded.

He grabs my hand in his and places a kiss against one knuckle.

"You know I love you." His lips wander to the next knuckle.

"Today."—Another kiss—"Tomorrow."—I shiver at the next kiss and he looks up his green eyes glowing—"In this life and every other."

He pulls me close and presses a sweet kiss against my lips. I wind my hand around his neck and bathe in his sweet taste. He parts our lips for a moment and I grin.

"You can be romantic if you want to."

"Don't tell anyone about it." He presses a light kiss against my cheek before nuzzling my neck. My eyes fly outside the window to see that the sun reached its zenith.

"I think we made it more than five minutes," I mumble and he chuckles in my neck.

"Small victories—" he gets interrupted when a knock appears on our doors. He raises his face to look at me and I shoot him a sheepish smile.

"Let's pretend that we didn't hear it," I whisper and snuggle closer, making him grin. He shifts his hips and I feel his erection against my belly.

"We could go for round two that would certainly scare them—" he gets interrupted again by a knock. We both sigh and I speak up.

"Come in." I wrap the blanket around my upper body and pull it over Cas' hips, who doesn't make an attempt to cover himself.

He arches a brow at me when the door bursts open and a maid steps in.

Her eyes are wide and her shoulders tense.

"This better be something important." Cassian grumbles and I push him on his back so I can look at the maid.

"Is something wrong?"

"Your Majesty—it-t is the king." I furrow my brows alarmed. Cas sits up his arm winds around my waist.

"Is my father all right?"

Something drops deep in my belly. My instincts kick in and I know something is wrong. The air thickens and my power grumbles telling me that someone is in danger. And it doesn't take her whispered words or the horrified look on the maiden's face to tell me that this is earth-shattering.

Still, her words struck through me in one wave, horrifying the happy peace I had with Cas minutes ago.

"No, it's not your father. It's King Aalton. . .he is dying."

THE END

Coming soon....

The Scarred Warrior

By Mia Thorne

And take a look into Edlyn's story. . .

Hi!

If you feel like talking about books in general or are interested in more of my work my Instagram is mthornewrites! I hope you enjoyed Carina´s story and would love your opinions this book, so if you feel like it and have the time please leave a review it would mean the world to me <3
Stay safe and enjoy many more books!
Mia xx